ADVANCE PRAISE FOR THE AM

"THE AMENDMENT KILLER is tense, timely, and terrific!"

–Lee Child, #1 New York Times Bestselling author of the Jack Reacher novels

"From the vantage point of one who has spent many years in Washington, D.C., I recently had the pleasure of reading an advance copy of Ronald S. Barak's latest political and legal thriller, *THE AMENDMENT KILLER*, a terrific, timely and remarkably accurate portrayal of modern day political dysfunction centered in our capital. Blurring contemporary reality with his own brand of fiction, Barak cleverly intertwines the kidnapping of the 11-year-old diabetic granddaughter of a Supreme Court justice to control the outcome of Congress' attempt to persuade the Court to invalidate a constitutional amendment criminalizing political abuse and corruption. I have read many of John Grisham's bestselling novels. Barak matches Grisham step for step. He had me turning the pages of *THE AMENDMENT KILLER* from the first page to the last. I thoroughly enjoyed the ride."

—Dennis DeConcini, United States Senator, Ret

"Ron Barak's *THE AMENDMENT KILLER* might well serve as a primer for the commercial legal thriller. The concept is high, the pacing supersonic, the characters well-drawn and sympathetic. The novel should come with a warning: addictive reading ahead. It's as good a legal thriller as I've read this year."

–John Lescroart, author of a dozen New York Times bestselling novels

"With an unparalleled sense of terror forewarned on the opening page, Ron Barak's *THE AMENDMENT KILLER* is a high-speed, tense political thriller about one of today's most fundamental issues, the integrity of our Supreme Court."

–Andrew Gross, #1 New York Times bestselling author of *The One Man*

"Blurring moral and legal lines while gripping every parent by the throat who journeys into *THE AMENDMENT KILLER*, Ron Barak delivers a captivating, chilling and clever read."

–**Sandra Brannan,** award-winning author of the Liv Bergen Mystery Series

"Set among the hallowed chambers of the Supreme Court of the United States, Ron Barak's *THE AMENDMENT KILLER* is a high stakes legal thriller easily the best we've read this year. Beautifully staged, Attorney Barak expertly tells the story from alternating points of view. Fresh, fast and furious. And highly recommended."

–**Best Thrillers Magazine**

"Ron Barak's *THE AMENDMENT KILLER* is a contemporary political thriller benefitting from heavy research, a chilling villain, and a timely message. The text message that starts this book off is a fantastic hook, and the narrative rapidly rotates between a large cast of characters, resulting in a page-flipping thriller. *THE AMENDMENT KILLER* combines a legal thriller with a tense drama where the stability of the government hangs in the balance . It's timely, tense, and a perfect read in these uncertain times."

–**John M. Murray** (Foreword Reviews)

"From its electrifying opening line to its powerful conclusion, *THE AMENDMENT KILLER* is a ripped-from-tomorrow's headlines story of law and politics set against the backdrop of the Supreme Court. But more so, it's a story about the lengths we will go for the ones we love. Timely, fast-paced, and heartfelt, you'll mourn the turning of the last page. Ron Barak is a writer to watch."

–**Anthony Franze,** author of *The Outsider*

"Ron Barak's finely honed legal skills bring a refreshing authenticity to *THE AMENDMENT KILLER* a fast-moving, tense, power-charged thriller where the life of a young girl with diabetes and the foundations of American democracy are both at stake. Combining contemporary, timely themes with a classic moral dilemma, this novel entertains and educates."

–**K.J. Howe,** author of *The Freedom Broker*

"*THE AMENDMENT KILLER* is a high concept, hybrid blend of a political, psychological and action thriller all rolled into a smooth, savory, and suspenseful mix. Ron Barak manages to channel the best of John Grisham, David Baldacci and even Steve Berry in this amazingly timely tale cast with a Supreme Court backdrop. As prescient as it is thought-provoking and as much fun as it is factual, this is reading entertainment of the highest order. I'd be shocked if this book doesn't become a bestseller."

–Jon Land, USA Today bestselling author of *Strong Light of Day*

"Ron Barak has the mind of a legal scholar, the fight of a bareknuckle litigator, and the determination of the former Olympic athlete that he is. Add to those distinctions now, in *THE AMENDMENT KILLER*, the imagination of a natural born storyteller."

–David Corbett, award-winning author of *The Art of Character* and T*he Mercy of The Night*

"*THE AMENDMENT KILLER* by Ron Barak is a provocative and savvy, bold and exciting, political-legal thriller that instantly hooks, thoroughly captives, and resonates wildly, long after the final page has been devoured. Ron's keen eye, expert knowledge, and dramatic flair conspire to render this explosively timely tale the next big read."

–Benee Knauer, Editor/Book Doctor

"In *THE AMENDMENT KILLER*, Ron Barak has crafted an entertaining and engaging novel that captures and reflects the current American political landscape."

–Ron Galperin, Los Angeles City Controller

"*THE AMENDMENT KILLER* is a brilliant and timely novel about a Supreme Court challenge to a constitutional amendment enacted by 'we the people' to end corruption on the part of their political representatives, and demonstrate that their government is meant to serve rather than be served. More than just a page turning political and legal thriller, Barak demonstrates an impressive and thought provoking command of real world politics, constitutional law reduced to its basics, and the ins and outs of lawyering at its best."

–Donald Earl Childress III, Professor of Law, Pepperdine University School of Law

THE
AMENDMENT
KILLER

THE AMENDMENT KILLER

A BROOKS/LOTELLO THRILLER

RONALD S. BARAK

The Amendment Killer is a work of fiction. Names, characters, places, and incidents either are the product of the author's imagination or are used fictitiously. Except as otherwise noted in the Author's Note, any resemblance to actual events or people, living or dead, is entirely coincidental.

Printed and published in the United States of America by:

GANDER HOUSE
PUBLISHERS
Los Angeles, California
www.ganderhouse.com

ISBN
Paperback: 978-0-9827590-9-7
Hardcover: 978-0-9827590-5-9
eBook: 978-0-9827590-7-3

First Edition

Publisher's Cataloging-In-Publication Data
(Prepared by The Donohue Group, Inc.)

Names: Barak, Ronald S.
Title: The amendment killer / Ronald S. Barak.
Description: First edition. | Los Angeles, California : Gander House Publishers, [2017] | Series: A Brooks/Lotello thriller
Identifiers: ISBN 978-0-9827590-5-9 (hardcover) | ISBN 978-0-9827590-9-7 (paperback) | ISBN 978-0-9827590-7-3 (ebook)
Subjects: LCSH: Constitutional amendments--United States--Fiction. | Judges--United States--Fiction. | Detectives--United States--Fiction. | Abuse of administrative power--United States--Fiction. | United States. Supreme Court--Fiction. | Kidnapping--Fiction.
Classification: LCC PS3602.A73 A45 2017 (print) | LCC PS3602.A73 (ebook) | DDC 813/.6--dc23

*To my Goosers, who helps me to manage
in all ways, and then some.*

We hold these truths to be self-evident, that all men are created equal, that they are endowed . . .

With certain unalienable Rights . . .

That . . . Governments . . . derive[e] their just powers from the consent of the governed. That whenever any Form of Government becomes destructive of [its] ends, it is the right of the people to alter or abolish it, and to instruct new Government, laying its foundations on such principles and organizing its Powers in such form, as to them shall seem most likely to effect their Safety and Happiness.

—Thomas Jefferson in *The U.S. Declaration of Independence,*
Paragraph 2, 1776

Justice Douglas, you must remember one thing. At the constitutional level where we work, ninety percent of any decision is emotional. The rational part of us supplies the reasons for supporting our predilections.

—U. S. Supreme Court Chief Justice Charles Evan Hughes
quoted by U. S. Supreme Court Associate Justice William
O. Douglas in his 1980 autobiography *The Court Years,
1939-1975*

Lawyers, I suppose, were children once.

—Charles Lamb in his 1823 essay
"The Old Benchers of the Inner Temple"

TABLE OF CONTENTS

PART ONE

The Run-up

CHAPTER 1
Tuesday, May 6, 6:30 am

WE HAVE YOUR GRANDDAUGHTER. Here's what you need to do.

Thomas T. Thomas III reviewed the language. Again. He closed the phone without hitting send. Yet.

He stared through high-powered binoculars from atop the wooded knoll. As always, the girl hit one perfect shot after another.

Cassie Webber. Age 11. He'd been tailing her for three months. It seemed longer.

She was chaperoned everywhere she went. Two-a-day practices before and after school. Her dad drove her in the morning. He watched her empty bucket after bucket and then dropped her off at school. Her mom picked her up after school, ferried her back to the practice range, and brought her home after daughter and coach finished. Mom and daughter sometimes ran errands on the way, but always together. Even on the occasional weekend outing to the mall or the movies, the girl was constantly in the company of family or friends. *Having someone hovering over me all day would have driven me batshit.*

His childhood had been different. When Thomas was her age, he walked to school on his own. And he lived a lot farther away than the girl. His daddy had never let his driver chauffeur him around. Wasn't about to spoil him. *Spare the rod, spoil the child. Didn't spoil me that way either.*

He kept telling himself patience was the key. But his confidence was waning. And then, suddenly, he'd caught a break. The girl's routine had changed.

She started walking the few blocks between school and practice on her own. Dad dropped her off at morning practice and Mom met her at afternoon practice instead of school. Only a ten minute walk each way, but that was all the opening he needed.

Everything was finally in place. He would be able to make amends. He would not let them down.

This time.

She completed her morning regimen, unaware of Thomas's eyes trained on her from his tree-lined vantage point. No doubt about it, he thought to himself. She was incredibly good. Driven. Determined.

And pretty.

Very pretty.

He relieved himself, thinking about her. A long time . . . coming. *Haha!* As the girl disappeared into the locker room, he trekked back down the hill, and climbed into the passenger side of the van. He returned the binoculars to their case. He removed the cell from his pocket, and checked the pending text one more time.

Moments later, the girl emerged from the locker room, golf bag exchanged for the backpack over her shoulders. She ambled down the winding pathway, waved to the uniformed watchman standing next to the guardhouse, and crossed through the buzzing security gate. She headed off to school.

Without taking his eyes off her, Thomas barked at the man sitting next to him. "Go."

CHAPTER 2
Tuesday, May 6, 7:00 am

ELOISE BROOKS STARED at Cyrus and shook her head. After more than 50 years of marriage, she understood everything about him there was to understand. Still: "I take the time to make you a nice breakfast. The least you could do is eat it while it's hot."

She held the warm cup of tea in both hands. "And can't you talk to me, Cyrus? Why do you treat me like I'm not here? Like I'm some kind of a potted plant."

Cyrus moved the eggs around on his plate. Speared a bite of fruit, swallowed it, but showed no visible pleasure in it. "I'm eating. What do you want to talk about? You think the couple cut from *Dancing With The Stars* last night deserved to be sent packing?"

"Should have got the hook weeks ago. You dance better than he does. Even with your two left feet."

He didn't answer. She knew why. "What're you thinking about? Esposito? Whether 50,000 is enough? Your two left feet?"

"All of the above."

She gazed at him but said nothing. Notwithstanding his apparent disinterest in the plate of food in front of him, his appetite—and his imagination—were never-ending. He loved upbeat music and dancing. And sports. He couldn't carry a tune or dance a lick. Except for an occasional round of golf, his sports these days were mostly played out in front of the television.

But that didn't stop him from daydreaming. He danced like Fred Astaire. He sang and played guitar and harmonica like Bob Dylan. He moved around a tennis court like Roger Federer.

However, Eloise knew his real passion in life was the law. He had enjoyed a distinguished legal career, first as a trial lawyer and then as a D.C. Superior Court judge. Now retired from the bench, writing and teaching, and occasionally trying a case that got his hackles up, when it came to the law, those who knew Cyrus Brooks knew he was second to none. Amazing how sometimes he exuded that—with confidence bordering on arrogance—but at other times did not. More so since Frank Lotello had been shot, and barely survived.

Brooks sat there fidgeting restlessly with the newspaper. Eloise reached over and put her hand on his. "You'll be great, Cyrus. I need to walk Ryder and get dressed, so we can drive into Court together. Please make sure Maccabee's dishes have enough water and dry cat snacks."

Arguments in the case were scheduled to commence in barely two hours. The chance to appear before the United States Supreme Court was rare, even for Brooks, but to do it in a landmark case that could permanently change the U.S. political landscape was unparalleled.

When they were first married, Eloise often attended Cyrus's court appearances, both to show her support and because the judicial process was new to her. Now long accustomed to Cyrus's legal adventures, Eloise was a less frequent visitor to the courtroom. Given the importance of this case, she told Cyrus the night before that she planned to attend.

He looked up absently with a gentle, distant smile, still fixed in some far-off place, no doubt grateful for her efforts to distract him, and bolster his confidence. "Macc's snacks? Sure."

CHAPTER 3
Tuesday, May 6, 7:20 am

CASSIE LEFT THE PRACTICE RANGE, looking momentarily at the clock on her phone. School began at eight. She had plenty of time.

She strolled along the familiar middle-class neighborhood route to school, sticking to the tree-hugged, concrete sidewalk. Well-kept houses on modest-sized manicured lots, one after another, adorned both sides of the paved street that divided the opposing sidewalks.

Mouthing the words to the song streaming through her earbuds, she made a mental note of a few questions from her morning practice to ask Coach Bob that afternoon.

Using her ever present designer sunglasses—a gift from her grandparents—to block the sun's glare, Cassie texted her best friend Madison:

Hey, BFF, meet u in cafeteria in 10. Out after 1st period to watch ur mom & my poppy in S Ct—how dope is that? 2 excited 4 words!

As she hit "Send," she was startled by the sound of screeching tires. She looked up from her phone and saw a van skid to the curb a few houses ahead of her. A man in a hoodie jumped out and charged straight at her.

She froze for an instant, but then spun and raced back in the direction of the clubhouse. "Help! Help!! Someone help me!!!"

As she ran, she looked all around. No one. She saw no one. The guard kiosk was in sight, but still over a block away. *Does he want to hurt me? Why? Why me?*

Hearing the man gaining on her, she tried to speed up. *If I can just get close enough to the gatehouse for someone to help me.* She glanced back, shrieking at the top of her lungs, just as the man lunged. He knocked her to the ground, shattering her glasses in the process. "What do you want?! Leave me alone! Get off me!!!"

She saw him grappling with a large syringe. "No!" She screamed even louder, clawing and kicking him savagely—until she felt the sharp stab in the back of her neck. Then nothing.

CHAPTER 4
Tuesday, May 6, 7:30 am

STEVE KESSLER, CEO of The National Organization For Political Integrity, NoPoli for short, was sharing breakfast with the two of them: Anne Nishimura, host of the prime time nightly news at NBN-TV, and Christopher Elliott, head of the litigation department in one of D.C.'s most politically connected and prestigious law firms. Kessler would have preferred to be somewhere else. Almost anywhere else. But the NoPoli Board had prevailed.

And so here he was, in Nishimura's well-appointed mobile dressing room parked opposite the U.S. Supreme Court. NBN had landed the exclusive rights to broadcast the first-ever Supreme Court case to be televised live, beginning later that morning.

They were there together so she could introduce the two men and explain how their role was to maintain a balanced perspective and to prop her up throughout the broadcast. To make her look smarter than she already seemed to be.

Elliott's law firm generally represented Washington's deepest pockets, including NBN. Which no doubt explained his presence. Elliott had appeared with Nishimura before. In his rigid three-piece suit, his allegiance in the case would no doubt rest with Congress. Which he often lobbied for many of his firm's clients.

Nishimura quickly became familiar with Kessler. She knew how to be charming. The occasional flick of her hair, the lingering glances, and the brief touches on his wrist and arm were not lost on Kessler. She had his bio, knew he was married. *Maybe just her way of getting me to relax.*

Speaking to Elliott, she said: "I first met Steve when I covered the constitutional convention NoPoli convened to adopt the 28th Amendment to our Constitution nine months ago. NoPoli put on quite the show, filled every seat in the New Orleans Superdome. No coincidence that NoPoli held its convention on the 4th of July weekend."

Elliott interrupted Nishimura's speech. "It's actually now officially the Mercedes-Benz Superdome. Our firm represents Mercedes-Benz in the U.S. We assisted it in acquiring the naming rights to the stadium."

"How interesting, Nishimura responded. "In any event, the idea of an amendment was Steve's baby. When we landed the rights to televise *Congress v. NoPoli*, I called Steve and convinced him to help us with the broadcast."

Kessler didn't care for the attention. "Thanks for the credit, but it would never have made it to the convention floor without the leadership of NoPoli's Board, particularly Cyrus Brooks and Leah Klein. Leah did the actual writing."

"I'm sure you're just being modest, Steve. To keep the playing field level, I also asked Chris to join us. He graciously agreed."

Elliott nodded, mostly to himself, smiling slightly, saying nothing. Kessler responded in kind. He looked at his watch, bored with the small talk. In a few minutes, they would move to the television platform inside and high above the courtroom. Where they would record background info to air just ahead of the live broadcast. He wondered how the three of them would get along once things started heating up.

CHAPTER 5
Tuesday, May 6, 7:40 am

THOMAS GLANCED AROUND to make sure there were no witnesses. He yanked the girl's limp body and attached backpack into his arms. He stumbled to keep his balance. Her backpack opened and spilled its contents to the ground, a bunch of books and papers. *Shit! Not so fucking easy.* He hauled her to the back of the van. As if on cue, his accomplice, Joseph Haddad, opened the rear doors. Thomas managed to lift the girl up to Haddad, who pulled her into the cargo area. Thomas ran back and gathered up the books and papers from the sidewalk. He returned to the van and stuffed them in the backpack. He made sure its latch was now secure.

His breathing had become labored, but Thomas was more interested in the girl's vitals than his own. He climbed into the van and checked her pulse. It was a little weak, but she seemed stable. He'd done his homework and opted for more of the drug than less. He wanted her out of sight as quickly as possible.

Thomas preferred to keep her alive. For now. Might help him control the grandfather. *But if she ODs, so be it. Just a matter of time anyway.*

He took stock of his wounds, acknowledged to himself how tough the brat was. He taped her mouth shut, placed a hood over her head, and hand-cuffed her to the inside of the van.

He downloaded the contents of her phone to his, verified the transfer completed, and then used the butt of his revolver to demolish her phone. He stored the remains in a plastic bag partially filled with rocks.

"Damn, Thomas," Haddad shouted from the driver's seat. "The hell you doing? We need to get the fuck outta here."

Thomas ignored Haddad. He climbed outside the van with the plastic bag in hand and looked around again to make sure no one was watching. He hurried back to where he'd knocked the girl to the ground. He scooped up the scattered remains of her sunglasses, added them to the plastic bag, and returned to the van.

Satisfied that he had removed all evidence and that there were no onlookers he needed to eliminate, he scrambled into the passenger seat and stored his gun and leg holster in the glove compartment.

"Take the route I gave you," Thomas said to Haddad. "Make sure you stay under the speed limit."

Five minutes later, they crossed the Potomac. Thomas directed Haddad to pull over and stop. He rolled down his window, tossed the weighted plastic bag into the river, and watched it sink below the surface. *Let's see what anyone does with her damn Find Phone app now.*

He looked over his shoulder and observed the girl. Nothing.

"Okay, let's head to the cabin. Mind the speed limit."

"When this is all over, you oughta think about renting yourself out as an echo."

Thomas scowled at Haddad, but said nothing further.

CHAPTER 6
Tuesday, May 6, 8:00 am

NISHIMURA LOOKED INTO THE CAMERA. "Good morning, America. I'm Anne Nishimura of NBN-TV, joined by our two experts, Steve Kessler and Chris Elliott. We're perched on our broadcast platform high above the floor of the United States Supreme Court. In less than just one hour, the Court will begin hearing oral argument in the landmark case of *Congress v. NoPoli*. The first case ever to be televised live in the U.S. Supreme Court.

Because of the case's importance, the Court has also scheduled two full days of argument instead of the customary one hour. NBN will bring it all to you—live, without commercial interruption—the arguments today and Thursday, and the Court-promised accelerated decision in less than one week. Next Monday.

The Court's going to be *very* busy between the close of argument Thursday afternoon and the reading of its decision on Monday morning. A process that normally takes at least six months."

Nishimura mentally ran through Elliott's resume and then directed her first scripted question to him. "Chris, can you summarize for our viewers what this case is really about?"

* * *

Thomas had anonymously rented the cabin in the Maryland woods. By car, it was located about forty minutes outside D.C. Paying cash for one year in advance avoided the need for any references. In spite of Haddad's impatience, they arrived at the remote destination right on Thomas's schedule. "I'll take care of the girl," Thomas said. "Stay in the front room. Keep a watch out the windows."

He pulled her from the van and carried her cautiously down into the basement. It would hardly do to twist an ankle or a knee, or fall down the flight of stairs altogether. He walked across the room, crouched, and dropped her on the bed.

She was still barely breathing, again bringing into question the amount of the drug he had used on her. If she woke now, she wouldn't be able to make any trouble. The locks he'd installed were state of the art. He'd soundproofed the room. She could scream her pretty little head off. No one would hear a thing.

* * *

Elliott fidgeted with his tie, belying his carefully crafted calm exterior. "Happy to summarize the case, Anne. Congress filed suit against a grassroots organization known as NoPoli. The National Organization for Political Integrity. NoPoli was responsible for the unprecedented convention that claims to have lawfully enacted the 28th Amendment to the U.S. Constitution. To curb a variety of abuses on the part of many, if not most, public officials. Congress wants—"

Nishimura cut in. "Chris, I thought all amendments to the Constitution have to go through Congress. Have I got that wrong?"

"That's precisely why we're here, Anne. Congress brought this lawsuit because it believes NoPoli preempted the constitutionally mandated amendment process. It's asking the Supreme Court to rule on that very question."

Nishimura continued with Elliott. "What's so important about this case that would cause the Court to break from a number of its long-standing traditions?"

"*Congress v. NoPoli* stands to change the political fabric of our country. It also contains a controversial threat to cut certain welfare entitlements. For those reasons, Congress requested an expedited hearing and decision. The Court agreed, in my opinion largely because the 28th Amendment makes the violation of any of its provisions a criminal felony. And given that the case may actually impact the lives of everyone living in the United States, the Court also increased the allotted argument time. And, in a groundbreaking first, ordered the case to be televised. Live, no less."

Nishimura turned her attention to Kessler.

* * *

Thomas removed the hood, tape, and handcuffs, and the girl's backpack.

She'd be dead in a week no matter how the Court ruled, but she'd be less of a nuisance in the interim if she didn't know the fate that awaited her. Nicer digs would give her false hope. Besides, he'd had some time to kill—so to speak—before he grabbed her. And putting his design and construction skills to work while he waited beat working on crossword puzzles and was . . . oddly therapeutic: a stocked mini-refrigerator beneath a small open cabinet with two shelves and a microwave sitting on top of the cabinet. The air-conditioning system he'd installed was working fine. He'd also rigged a portable bathroom in the corner, fully equipped with toilet, sink, shower, and even a second, larger cabinet with a few changes of clothes and toiletries. *Always like my ladies to smell nice.*

Written instructions for her if she woke up were on the table next to the bed. He really did hope she was just sleeping it off. The grandfather might insist on some form of evidence that she was alive. And well. He took out his phone, snapped a few pictures of her. Live video would, of course, be a lot more convincing. But she wasn't moving. The pictures would have to do if necessary.

* * *

"Also here to help with our coverage of the case is Steve Kessler, CEO of NoPoli. Steve, what can you tell us about the constitutional crisis created by NoPoli's 28th Amendment?"

The cameras zoomed in on Kessler. He smiled politely at his host. "Well, Anne, not being a lawyer, I would prefer to leave the technical side of the case to NoPoli's counsel."

"That sidestep sounded very much like a lawyer to me." Nishimura grinned, obviously enjoying the repartee at Kessler's expense.

Kessler stiffened slightly. "Just being careful, Anne, not evasive. Chris is correct about what NoPoli is trying to do. And why. NoPoli—and the tens of millions of Americans who support us—believe that special interests have taken

15

our government hostage, and rendered it dysfunctional. Too many members of Congress spending too much of their time and energy—and too much of *our* money—procuring too many special perks for themselves. Instead of responsibly running our government. NoPoli organized a constitutional convention to break the logjam and do a little repair work. Cut down on all the perks."

"Amending our Constitution is a little repair work? I'll say. Can you please tell our audience some of the details of how the convention was created and how it played out? Have we ever had a constitutional convention before?"

* * *

As Thomas shot the still pictures of the girl, he noticed a small device protruding from her pant pocket. He froze, scared he might have missed a second GPS monitor in addition to the one destroyed with her phone. He had an involuntary urge to turn and look behind him. *At what?*

Cautiously, he pulled whatever the object was away from her body, spotting an almost invisible, clear, miniature plastic line coming off one end of the gadget and disappearing under her T-shirt. Now more curious than cautious, he peeled back the girl's top and saw the other end of the thin line—disappearing into her belly, no less.

His mind was racing. One question after another. *What the hell is that? Steroids? Is this why she plays golf so well? Does she have health issues? Does she play golf like she does despite a medical problem? Is this thing sending messages somewhere?* He wondered what would happen if he removed it.

He had to decide. If he left it in place, the girl was in control. If he removed it, *he* was in control. He grabbed the line where it entered her stomach, and pulled. It popped right out. Nothing. Just a couple drops of blood. Quiet. No alarm bells. At least none that he could hear.

Not happy. He hated loose ends. *Literally.*

He'd had no time to examine the contents of the girl's backpack when it opened and spilled out on the street. He emptied it out on the bed next to her and sifted through the contents. He found a bunch of school items, including those he had previously spilled and retrieved when he'd seized her. And a zippered canvas bag. He unzipped the bag and peered inside.

CHAPTER 7
Tuesday, May 6, 8:15 am

"WE'VE ACTUALLY HAD two prior constitutional conventions, Anne. The first in 1781, when the thirteen states adopted and ratified our first Constitution, the Articles of Confederation. The second in 1787, when the Articles of Confederation were repealed and replaced by our second Constitution. The one we still have today. The NoPoli convention last July 4th was actually the country's third constitutional convention."

"And the details of the convention?"

"A great deal of planning and work went into structuring our convention, but its conduct was fairly straightforward—and democratic. You reported it. Delegates participated from all fifty states—50,000 in number, plus another 20,000 alternates. Selected by the respective NoPoli chapters in every state, they assembled in the New Orleans Superdome and enacted the amendment by a two-thirds super-majority vote of each state delegation."

Elliott made a living as a wordsmith, but Nishimura observed that Kessler was the stronger speaker. "Gentlemen, this would probably be a good time to take a moment to show our viewers exactly what this amendment looks like. Chris, would you please walk us through its provisions displayed on the giant electronic screen on the wall behind us?"

* * *

Thomas laughed out loud. Mystery solved. Not some kind of GPS.

The unzipped bag contained a partially used vial of insulin, a couple of syringes, and some other paraphernalia. What he'd just yanked out of the girl's stomach was an insulin pump. He'd read about those somewhere. *Geez, she's a diabetic.* Maybe she can reinsert the pump, he thought. If not, she'll have to use those backup syringes. That's obviously what they're for. He wondered how long this insulin supply would last.

He returned everything to the backpack, including the pump he'd removed from the girl's body—and perhaps irretrievably damaged. He dropped the backpack on the floor near the table with his note. He was on a tight schedule. No more time to admire his handiwork.

He locked the basement door, double-checked that it was secure, and ascended the stairs. He expected to find Haddad in the front room where he'd told him to wait and keep a lookout.

But Haddad was gone.

* * *

On cue, Elliott stood and approached the large screen monitor mounted on the wall behind them. The television cameras followed him. "For such a profound document, it's amazing just how short and simple the 28th Amendment is. It's divided into three distinct parts."

He scrolled through and described each of the three parts, highlighting them with his finger as he proceeded, exactly the same as he would have done on his own handheld touchscreen computer tablet. "There are three introductory preambles, followed by five substantive paragraphs, and then, finally, three more procedural paragraphs. The three lettered preambles, Paragraphs A, B, and C, recite who is enacting the 28th Amendment, and why."

Scrolling down a little further, Elliott highlighted the five numbered paragraphs, Paragraphs 1 through 5. "These set forth the substance of the document. How our Constitution will be changed to reduce many of the perks to which our representatives have become so accustomed. That they take for granted. That will be taken away from them if the 28th Amendment is upheld by the Court."

Elliott scrolled down once more, this time highlighting the last three numbered paragraphs of the document, Paragraphs 6, 7, and 8. "These are the procedural ground rules designed to assure that the five substantive paragraphs of the instrument will not be circumvented or ignored. The last of these three procedural paragraphs provides that the failure of any of member of Congress to abide by any of the substantive provisions constitutes a criminal felony."

Nishimura pretended to be rapt as Elliott droned on, glancing at her notes on what she still wanted to cover before the actual Court sessions would soon begin. "Chris, please scroll back up to Paragraph 5 for a moment. While the first four substantive paragraphs focus on our office holders, this one focuses on our country's welfare recipients.

"In order to remain eligible to vote, they must continuously seek gainful employment. Many people around the country have found this anti-welfare provision particularly divisive. Doesn't this hit our downtrodden below the belt, Steve?"

* * *

Thomas looked outside and saw Haddad leaning against a tree, smoking a cigarette, in full view of any hikers who might happen by.

Thomas was livid. He went out the front door and locked it behind him, again double-checking that it was secure.

"Thought I told you to stay put. Indoors. Out of sight."

No response.

"Did you not hear me?"

Haddad glowered. "Needed some fresh air. And a smoke. What's the fucking big deal? No one around here anyways. Just like we planned it."

Thomas shook his head. "Like *I* planned it. Let's go."

Haddad turned and stepped toward the van. With lightning speed, Thomas reached across Haddad's left side with his own left arm and latched onto Haddad's right shoulder. He pulled hard on the right shoulder as he simultaneously grabbed and jerked down on a fistful of Haddad's long hair just above the right ear. The loud snap of the man's neck told Thomas his accomplice was now his *former* accomplice—even before the released body slumped to the ground.

* * *

Kessler didn't skip a beat. "Not so, Anne. The anti-welfare provisions of Paragraph 5 of the amendment work no prejudice on the *truly* downtrodden.

It merely provides that if you want to preserve your right to vote, you cannot be a freeloader looking for a handout from those with whom you might seek to trade votes for entitlements or benefits. All those who genuinely make a reasonable effort to do what they can to be self-sufficient preserve their right to vote."

Nishimura raised her hands in feigned surrender. She would not underestimate Kessler again. "It will certainly be fascinating to see what the Court has to say about the amendment, particularly the anti-welfare voting limitation and the criminal felony provision."

"Thank you, gentlemen. For those who want to read the actual 28th Amendment that you've been viewing on your television screens at home, we've posted it on a special NBN website at www.28th.info. Where you can also print or download the document to your own computer device.

"We're going to take a quick break to update our viewers on what's happening around the world. When we return, we'll ask Steve if NoPoli really thinks their constitutional convention and the 28th Amendment are constitutionally valid without having included Congress in the process. Stay with us, we're coming right back."

CHAPTER 8
Tuesday, May 6, 8:20 am

THOMAS LOOKED DOWN at Haddad's body lying motionless on the ground. "Cigarettes are hazardous to your health, fool. So was your long, ugly mop of hair. You woulda done better with a buzz cut."

Thomas knew that discarding Haddad had only been a matter of time, but it frustrated him that the timing turned out not to be of his own choosing. Especially when some of the work in the days ahead would have been easier spread over two backs.

The last time Thomas had dropped his guard—just a little—it had almost cost him his life. It was during the *Norman* case, in Brooks's court. When Brooks was still on the bench. Brooks was the impetus behind Lotello going after Thomas. Even though neither one of them then realized it was Thomas. If they do even today. There was a shootout. Thomas escaped, just barely. He was lucky. Lotello wasn't. He caught a bullet.

Although Thomas managed to get away, it cost him everything he'd been working for. This was now Thomas's last chance. He could not fail this time. *No more mistakes. No more misjudgments. Haddad was unreliable. Insubordinate. A fool. Should have known better than to select him. Had to reassert myself. Had to get rid of him. No choice.*

Thomas threw Haddad's corpse in the back of the van, and drove off. He stopped along a quiet stretch of the Potomac, miles away from where he had dumped the bag with the remains of the girl's phone and sunglasses. He

21

stuffed each of Haddad's pant and jacket pockets with rocks collected from the riverbed, dumped the body into the water, and watched it sink.

He chemically wiped down the inside of the van, and then burned the cleaning materials along with the latex gloves he'd been wearing all day. He sprinkled the ashes into the water and watched them float away. He would also soon dismantle and destroy the van. And everything else. In the meanwhile, he was confident no one could connect the van with him, the girl, or his ex-associate.

He hurried off to Court, again sticking to the speed limits. It was going to be close. He really wanted to monitor the girl's grandfather—and the results of all his planning and efforts—in person. If necessary, he had another cell phone ready to go and would watch the proceedings by television from a nearby bar he had already selected. Just in case. Control was everything.

CHAPTER 9
Tuesday, May 6, 8:30 am

KESSLER HEARD the words faintly resonating out of Nishimura's earpiece. "And . . . we're back live, Anne."

Nishimura wasted no time. "Steve, doesn't Congress have to be included in any attempt to amend the Constitution?"

This was precisely why Kessler had agreed to participate in the television coverage; to protect NoPoli's flank. "Congress could hardly be expected to cooperate in any exercise designed to cut them off at the knees. But NoPoli's lawyers researched this issue and concluded that Congress's participation is not required."

Kessler held his breath. He hoped Nishimura would leave it at that. He wasn't about to prematurely debate the meaning of Article V with her in front of the world. And tip NoPoli's hand to Congress's lawyers. Brooks would handle this as they planned it—and at exactly the right moment.

But Nishimura was not finished. "Well, I'm no expert on the Constitution, Steve, but it sure seems to me that Congress *is* entitled to participate in such a process. How does NoPoli expect to avoid the language of Article V?"

Kessler's mind drifted back to the events leading up to the convention. The first one to whom he'd brought his idea was NoPoli's house counsel, Leah Klein. Together, they wrote a first draft of the amendment and then showed it to NoPoli board member and retired judge Cyrus Brooks.

Brooks had liked the idea. As a single purpose amendment—reining in political corruption—he thought it might have a chance. A slight one. But if it became a free for all referendum on constitutional reform, he knew it would be dead in the water.

The three of them revised the amendment's language several times. They developed a framework for holding the first constitutional convention in more than 200 years, when the country was much smaller.

Brooks pushed and pushed on the delegates. They had to reflect a fair sample of the country. How many should they number? How should they be selected? On what would they vote? And in what sequence? What kind of vote should be required: a national popular vote, a state-by-state vote, majority vote, super-majority vote?

Kessler was not about to allow Nishimura to draw him into any of this. "Sorry, Anne. What you're asking me is beyond my comfort zone. You'll have to wait for counsel to explain all this stuff. To the Court."

Nishimura didn't press the point further. At least not for the moment. Kessler wondered how long it would be until she tried him again. Turning to Elliott, she changed the topic of conversation. "Speaking of counsel, Chris, can you tell our audience a little bit about the lawyers who will be arguing the case?"

* * *

Groggy, head pounding, eyelids so heavy, Cassie fought to break free of the cobwebs that were not yet ready to let go. No sense of time or place, muddled, she sought to gain some solid footing.

The day—if it were still the same day—had started like any other. Up at five every morning, the cost of wanting to be the best woman golfer in the world—not the best *diabetic* golfer, but the best golfer, period. And not *one* of the best, but *the* best. Her steady run of victories on the juniors' circuit demonstrated this was no fantasy.

She tested her blood sugar that morning, programmed a supplemental bolus through her insulin pump to cover her slightly elevated glucose level, threaded her orthodontic braces, organized her curls just so, put on her favorite earrings, and finished getting dressed. She fed Whitney, the family pup, next.

When she said, "C'mon, Whit, let's go potty outside," he looked at her curiously and hesitated. Hair too frizzy. Face full of freckles. Too skinny, the tallest in her class, even taller than the boys. Now, because of the ginormous lisp caused by her new braces, even her dog didn't know who she was anymore. In spite of her tough self-assessment, Whitney followed her out the door.

She remembered her dad driving her to morning practice. He answered emails and watched her hit until he left for work. Her parents still wouldn't let her walk to and from school on her own, but they'd finally caved in and allowed her to walk the few blocks back and forth between practice and school.

Cassie continued to retrace the morning. She'd finished hitting, was on the way to school, listening to music on her latest playlist, thinking about how practice had gone. She had also texted Madison that she would meet her in the cafeteria in a few and was looking forward to their trip to the Supreme Court.

Suddenly, it all came rushing back to her.

* * *

Nishimura waited to hear how Elliott would answer her question about the various lawyers.

He scanned the courtroom floor below them and pointed to the table on the left. The cameras followed suit. "Raul Esposito is Congress's first chair. He's brilliant. Has won more Supreme Court cases than anyone practicing today. Look at the state-of-the-art electronic equipment and all the associate lawyers hovering around him. Even the papers in front of him are lined up just so."

"Not to mention," Nishimura interjected, "the several leaders of both Houses of Congress sitting in the first row of the gallery right behind him." Like royalty, she thought.

Elliott nodded, and moved on. "At the table to the right are NoPoli's two lawyers, Cyrus Brooks and Leah Klein."

Nishimura remembered Brooks. He was the judge who had presided over the murder trial a few years back involving D.C. businessman Cliff Norman. Nishimura had covered the case. Norman's business had collapsed in 2008. He was charged with being the vigilante serial killer bumping off high-profile politicians he thought caused the crash. Leah Klein had defended Norman.

Klein subsequently married veteran Metropolitan D.C. Homicide Detective, Frank Lotello, who was sitting in the courtroom behind Klein. Lotello had worked the *Norman* case. He was shot and almost killed late in the trial. To this day no one knows who shot Lotello or why. Speculation has it that Brooks blamed himself for what happened to Lotello. Shortly after the case concluded, Brooks retired from the bench.

Nishimura asked: "What's Brooks doing these days, Chris—besides representing NoPoli in this case?"

"A little teaching, writing, spending time on the lecture circuit," Elliott said. "He's in high demand. This is his first return to the courtroom since retiring. On the other side of the bench no less. We'll have to see if he's still got it."

* * *

Just as Cassie had sent the text to Madison, that dirty old van had screeched up alongside her. Guy in a hoodie jumped out and ran toward her. She tried to make it back to the golf course. He was too fast. Knocked her to the ground. She had tried to fight. Saw the large syringe in his hand sailing toward her. Something sharp stabbed her in the neck. That was it. Until now.

She began shaking, crying. Her knees were scraped and throbbing. Her neck was sore. She was trembling from head to toe, but she wanted to be brave. *He's a real perv, a big bully. He should pick on someone his own size. See how he'd like it then.*

Trying to be brave wasn't working. And then it dawned on her what was happening.

* * *

Kessler frowned. *We'll have to see if he's still got it, my ass.* He had wanted to respond to Elliott's crack, but chose to remain silent. Until he saw exactly where the present exchange between Nishimura and Elliott was headed.

Nishimura continued: "Klein also represented NoPoli in the lower courts in this case, right?"

"Yes," Elliott said. "She obtained a verdict upholding the 28th Amendment. She and NoPoli recently persuaded Brooks to join in the appeal."

"That's curious," Nishimura said. "From what I understood, Klein was doing perfectly well on her own." Turning to Kessler, she asked, "What was the reason for bringing in Brooks, Steve?"

If Kessler were caught off guard by the question, he didn't show it. "Brooks has been supportive of NoPoli from its inception. He helped draft the amendment and the ground rules for the NoPoli convention. Klein's done a great job. We simply took advantage of the opportunity to add one of the best legal minds in the country to our team for this final round in the Supreme Court."

Kessler watched Nishimura yield and turn her attention back on Esposito, Congress's lead counsel. "Esposito looks rather formidable, Chris, a young Clint Eastwood smugly sitting there in his fancy alligator cowboy boots and all. Must be at least six and a half feet tall — Goliath personified."

"For sure, Anne," Elliott replied. "I've worked with Esposito on several matters. I was very impressed. Brooks ran his court with an iron fist, and very well. But that was then, when he was the boss, and this is now, when he's not. He's going to have his hands full. It will be interesting watching him on his return to the courtroom."

* * *

Oh my God. I've been kidnapped!

Cassie began shuddering uncontrollably.

Not good. Why me? What did I do?

Tears again spilled out of her eyes and swamped her cheeks and T-shirt.

Her mind raced in all directions. *Mom and Dad. Nanny and Poppy. Whitney. Will I ever see any of them again? What about my golf? Michelle Wie tweeted she wanted to play with me. I so want to. And Madison—Madison—she's going to be so ticked at me for not showing.*

And then—as if things couldn't get any worse—they did.

CHAPTER 10
Tuesday, May 6, 8:45 am

KESSLER HAD HAD ENOUGH of Elliott's self-importance. The innuendo that Brooks was perhaps not quite up to the task of playing in the big leagues with the likes of Esposito—and, of course, Elliott. Kessler jumped in front of Nishimura as she was about to say something further.

"Excuse me. Brooks may be smaller in *physical* stature than Esposito. He may not have all of Esposito's trappings. But, you're certainly right, Chris, it's going to be interesting indeed to see how Brooks fares on the other side of the bench after more than 25 years on it. And on the other side of Esposito. I wouldn't be too surprised, however, if Goliath is about to meet his David."

Kessler wondered if he'd gone too far. He waited for any possible pushback. Elliott stretched his neck, but was silent. As if Kessler's remarks weren't directed at him. Nishimura seemed to be concentrating on her earpiece. She looked into the cameras and smiled.

"Well, there you have it, folks. The nine U.S. Supreme Court Justices are now entering the courtroom to watch Brooks and Esposito do battle, and to then deliberate and decide the extraordinary case of *Congress of the United States v. The National Organization for Political Integrity.* We'll be right here with you through the final decision next Monday."

CHAPTER 11
Tuesday, May 6, 9:30 am

CASSIE COULDN'T BREATHE. *My pump! Where's my pump?*

PART TWO

The United States Supreme Court
Day One Argument
And More

CHAPTER 12
Tuesday, May 6, 9:30 am

THE UNIFORMED SUPREME COURT security officer shouted over the clamor of echoing voices and shuffling feet beneath the high-vaulted ceiling of the courthouse lobby: "Empty your pockets and bags, place the contents in one of the free bins, and put the bin on the conveyor belt. Cameras, cell phones, and other electronic devices are not permitted in the courtroom and must be checked before entering. You'll be given a claim check and can retrieve your items when you leave."

"Nothing in my pockets, Officer," Thomas said. "Just my billfold, a note-pad, and a couple of pens in my shoulder bag."

"Step ahead, stand on the marks, raise your hands above your head."

He did exactly as he was told.

"Come through," the security officer motioned.

Thomas entered the courtroom gallery, looked around, and limped over to the left aisle seat, one row forward from the rear. He stood there staring at the woman occupying the seat until she finally acknowledged his presence.

"Excuse me, ma'am. Any chance I could trouble you to find another seat? It's this darn stiff leg of mine. I sure could use an aisle seat near the exit."

She stared at him. He could almost see the wheels turning in her head. If she refused his entreaty, he had another couple seats nearby he'd try. If all three attempts fell flat, he'd have to revert to Plan B: Leave the courtroom, grab one of the other phones he'd hidden outside the courthouse, along with three extra SIM cards, each one barely the size of his thumbnail, and hurry to the bar down the street, where several wall-screen televisions would be carrying the coverage.

Finally, after what seemed like an eternity, the woman occupying his preferred spot nodded silently and moved over to one of the few remaining gallery seats. "Thank you kindly, ma'am," he called after her. Plan A it was, at least for this initial half-day session.

With an exaggerated effort, Thomas slumped down into the seat the woman had vacated, unlatched his shoulder bag, and placed it on the floor between his legs. He surveyed the courtroom in front of him with a mixture of admiration and amusement. The gallery was filling in quickly. Given the seminal importance of the case, Thomas knew the courtroom would soon be packed.

He leaned forward and coughed. He deftly removed one of the two phones and three of the six extra SIM cards he had two-way taped under each of the three-aisle gallery seats over the course of the prior week. He slipped the items into his bag.

So far, so good. It had been surprisingly easy for Thomas to get a night shift custodial position at the courthouse. Of course, it probably hadn't hurt his chances that two custodians—one was enough, the second was just for good measure—mysteriously went missing without notice only days earlier. Or that Thomas had been able to hack into the Court computer system and move his application to the head of the waiting list for custodial positions. *Not likely the incinerated bodies of those two janitors will ever turn up, or be tied to this case before the Court rules.*

Creating an employment history and references had required the fabrication of a handful of modest-sized custodial companies in several small easterly Virginia towns. Each with manufactured owners and phone numbers leading to additional prepaid cells Thomas had purchased. Of course, no one was there when calls came in to verify the references. But Thomas always promptly returned the voicemail messages left by the Court's human resources office. Using voice alteration software, he provided bona fides in sufficiently unique voices to accredit his fictitious applicant.

The interview had been a mere formality. Two weeks after he had sent in his application, Thomas's new job allowed him undisturbed access to the very courtroom where today's proceedings would take place. Over the course of several nights, he'd managed to sneak in six cell phones and extra SIM cards and taped them to the bottom of the three targeted seats. Including the one he now occupied.

Using three separate Craigslist ads, Thomas had surreptitiously hired three different people to stand in line this morning and get him a seat while he tended to more urgent priorities. He had paid each through a joint "Pay After Delivery" PayPal escrow account.

As for the phones, in addition to his personal smartphone for the possible rare occasion when he would need capability not included on burners, Thomas had purchased forty "burner" phones for cash over a period of several weeks. No identification was required. Each purchase was made at a different drugstore, electronics shop, or telecommunications carrier retailer. Fifty dollars bought a phone already loaded with one full month of prepaid service. The cost was a pittance.

It would have been easier, cheaper, and more efficient if he had purchased just a couple of phones and downloaded the latest burner apps to them that all the drug dealers, pimps, and hackers were using these days, but Thomas didn't trust the vulnerable security of that approach. He was far too cautious for anything that risky.

The extra effort expended was well worth it. So long as he meticulously followed his simple protocol, neither his identity nor his location could ever be traced: Employing a new SIM card for each text sent, removing the phone battery and old SIM card immediately after their use and breaking the old SIM card in half, and then reinserting the battery and a new SIM card at the time of the next use.

Each of the hidden burner phones, including the one now resting safely in the bag at his feet, contained the same unsent text message—the one he'd prepared before abducting the girl.

As the courtroom wall clock marched toward ten, Thomas basked in the grandeur of the chamber, its high ceilings, and its majestic finishes. He even admired the way everyone present had their respectively assigned places: Courtroom staff adjacent to the Justices, attorneys and their clients just beyond the staff, and, finally, the gallery of spectators. The buzz among the spectators was growing. They were there to see how the 28th Amendment would fare, but he wondered how specifically they would each be affected by the Court's decision. Perhaps he should say *his* decision.

Thomas's eyes settled on the three of them: Brooks, Klein, sitting next to Brooks, Lotello, seated behind Klein. He recalled bitterly his prior dealings with each. He knew that Lotello and Klein had married. Klein had also adopted Lotello's two kids, the brood sitting next to Lotello. *How I'd love to take the lot of them down right now. But no time for such whimsy now. First things first. Their time will come.*

As Thomas watched them, Lotello reached over and gave Klein an obvious last minute good luck squeeze on her shoulder. Klein turned and seemed to acknowledge the gesture with a preoccupied smile. Suddenly she glanced back, her line of sight intersecting Thomas's. Her smile transformed into a brief, puzzled expression. She returned her attention to the papers in front of her.

Thomas smiled. Sneered might be more precise. *Stare all you want, bitch. By the time you recognize me, it'll be too late. It already is. About 170 minutes to be exact. But who's counting?*

* * *

The nine Supreme Court Justices marched into the regal burgundy and gold hall right on time, exactly at 10 o'clock. Thomas respected that. He always sought to be on time too. Several cracks of the gavel, not unlike a staccato of gunfire, followed the Justices's entrance, reverberating throughout the courtroom. Momentarily startled out of his reverie, Thomas belatedly joined the remainder of the gallery in rising.

The Justices huddled and ceremoniously shook hands, demonstrating a lack of personal animosity despite whatever judicial differences they perhaps harbored. Thomas thought it played like a well-choreographed Broadway musical. As if on cue, they then took their places behind their assigned seats, the Chief Justice of the United States at the center and the eight Associate Justices alternating right and left of center in descending order of seniority, accompanied by the grand opening proclamation of the Court Marshal:

"The Honorable, the Chief Justice and the Associate Justices of the Supreme Court of the United States, Oyez! Oyez! Oyez! All persons having business before the Honorable, the Supreme Court of the United States, are admonished

to draw near and give their attention, for the Court is now sitting. God save the United States and this Honorable Court."

That was Thomas's cue. As everyone throughout the courtroom resumed their seats, he reached into his bag on the floor and discreetly removed the phone. Hunched over, as he had practiced countless times without having to look, Thomas quickly opened the app and hit "Send." And just as quickly and discreetly, he returned the phone to the bag.

Showtime.

CHAPTER 13
Tuesday, May 6, 10:07 am

ASSOCIATE JUSTICE ARNOLD HIRSCHFELD's cell phone started vibrating just as Chief Justice Sheldon Trotter began his opening remarks. Few people had Hirschfeld's number. He reached inside his robe, removed the phone, and opened the text.

We have your granddaughter.

His eyes widened. His knuckles turned pale. Remembering where he was, he tried to regain his composure. He took a deep breath, and continued reading.

We have your granddaughter. Here's what you need to do.

Chief Justice Trotter's opening remarks seemed to come from a far-off place. "As many of you watching today have learned from the media, this is the first time we . . ."

Hirschfeld pushed Trotter's words to the recesses of his mind as he hurriedly skimmed the balance of the text.

If you don't follow these instructions exactly, your granddaughter dies.

Trotter rambled on ". . . are televising the proceedings of this Court . . ."

Hirschfeld half-rose from his leather chair and all but gave way to his urge to rush from the courtroom. He caught himself. And go where? Do what? *Are they watching me? Am I telegraphing my anxiety? What'll they do?* He tried to swallow. He couldn't.

38

The kids had given Cassie a cell phone on her last birthday. It was always with her. As nonchalantly as possible, he managed to tap in and send a text.

hey baby girl r u having a good day? luv u

He closed his eyes. The few unfilled seconds stretched to infinity.

Gazing vacantly out into the courtroom and the whirring cameras that glared back at him, the next text he fired off was to his daughter, Jill.

chk if cassie @ school NOW

All the while, Trotter prattled on. "For the benefit of those looking on from your televisions . . ."

Hirschfeld's phone vibrated. *Cassie? No. Only Jill.*

What r u saying dad? ur scaring me!

He fired back: *no time chk NOW*

He felt certain everyone in the courtroom was staring at him. He remained painfully aware that someone was.

He strained to be unobtrusive, natural. As if he were concentrating on Trotter's remarks. His phone vibrated again.

dad shes not at school! FOR GODS SAKE WHATS GOING ON?

He could no longer process what Trotter was saying. He put his phone on the leather notepad in front of him, pretending to be making notes. He tapped out and sent still another text.

someones got cassie call school back say she just walked in not feeling well came home b4 reaching school DON'T SAY ANYTHING MORE get mark home. DO NOTHING MORE! NO POLICE! wait for me 2 call @ 12 they r watching me on tv and in crtrm 2 b sure I do as told I WILL GET HER BACK

No sooner had he sent the message then his phone vibrated for the third time.

u no by now this is no joke. we r ur worst nightmare. u r starting 2 draw attention. put ur damn phone away. NOW! do exactly as we say or no more sweet little girl. on u grandpa.

No doubt the bastards were watching him. Hirschfeld quickly scanned the courtroom. Nothing seemed out of the ordinary. Just a sea of faces. Among them his longtime friend and law school classmate, Cyrus Brooks. Sitting in the Court well with the other lawyers in the case. *Is Cyrus staring at me?*

Hirschfeld had to stop broadcasting his terror. Do as they instructed. Calm down. His left eye twitched uncontrollably. He willed it to stop. He tried to focus on Trotter. *How am I ever going to make it to the noon recess?*

* * *

Thomas stared at Hirschfeld. *Get it together, asshole. We have a lot riding on you. So does the girl.*

* * *

Cassie woke suddenly. At first, she couldn't find herself. As if she were in some long, dark, tunnel. She was confused. Her head hurt. Her knees ached. She struggled to remember what had happened. And then it came rushing back to her, along with the sheer terror she'd felt when the man attacked her, slammed her to the ground, thrust that scary needle at her. *But why me? Where am I? What time is it? And, where is my pump?*

Like tearing something sticky off her skin, she opened her eyes. *Ow! Burns.* She rubbed them and tried again. Lying on a bed. She struggled to sit up, look around. She was in a dingy room. Not much light. Just one hanging bulb. No windows. Stuffy. Cold. Walls dirty.

What kind of a room doesn't have windows?

A basement.

She spotted a door at the end of the room. She stood, but felt dizzy. She managed to cross the cellar. She grabbed at the doorknob. Locked. She listened for any sounds on the other side. "Hello? Is anyone there? Can you hear me? Please, can you help me?"

Silence. Now more afraid than ever, she returned to the bed. For the first time, she noticed a little table in the corner. She made her way over to it. She found the note addressed to her: *You have everything you need. You're going to be here for a while.*

CHAPTER 14
Tuesday, May 6, 10:14 am

HIRSCHFELD HAD BEEN KEEPING an eye on the clock, struggling to maintain his composure. Pandering to the television cameras, Trotter had already allowed the proceedings to fall fifteen minutes behind schedule; it was unclear how he would recoup the time. Hirschfeld had to call his daughter Jill and her husband Mark at noon. He needed every second of the break to work out how to free their baby girl from the clutches of these madmen. *Please, Lord, don't let Trotter delay or shorten the noon recess.*

Hirschfeld didn't have long to wait for his answer. At the conclusion of his opening remarks, Trotter casually announced that each side would receive fifty minutes rather than the sixty originally allocated to argue standing. Hirschfeld breathed a sigh of relief. Finally relinquishing the microphone, Trotter added, "We'll be in recess for five minutes and then hear from Ms. Klein."

* * *

Nishimura told the television audience that the remainder of the morning would be devoted to NoPoli's appeal of the lower court's ruling that Congress had "standing" to challenge the validity of the 28th Amendment.

"Chris, we're almost out of time. Can you quickly explain the concept of standing to our viewers?"

"Of course. Contrary to popular belief, and contrary to how it works in most state judicial systems, parties are not automatically entitled to their 'day' in court in the federal judicial system. They must first establish that they have a legal right to sue. That right to sue is called standing."

"Got it," Nishimura said. "With you so far. Standing is the right to sue. But what determines whether standing exists?"

"That depends on who wants to sue whom, and why. The party who wishes to sue must show that he's been injured in some way by the party he wishes to sue. And that there's some kind of useful benefit the court can award to compensate the injured party."

"Give us a couple examples of an injury," Nishimura asked Elliott.

"Sure. First example: You and I enter into a contract under which I am to paint your home for $100 using a high-grade paint and I use an inferior paint instead. Second example: I punch you in the mouth and break your jaw. Third example: I call you a crook.

"In the first case, you've suffered injury to your home. In the second case, you've been physically injured. In the third case, you've suffered injury to your reputation."

Nishimura grimaced. "Not sure I'm liking this, but I'd love to hire you to paint my home for $100. More to the point, what kind of benefit would the court have to award me for these injuries?"

"In the first case, the court could order me to pay you the amount of money it would cost to repaint your home. In the second case, the court could order me to pay your medical expenses, and perhaps a bonus for your pain and suffering. In the third case, the court could order me to stop calling you a crook, and to pay you some amount of money for the injury to your reputation."

"Assuming I have a reputation to be injured," Nishimura smiled. "But what kind of injury has Congress suffered in this case? And what kind of relief could a court grant to compensate it for that injury?"

"The law requires Congress to show a particular kind of injury—loss or reduction of the right to vote on some matter on which it normally does vote. The lower court ruled that the 28th Amendment eliminated Congress's right to vote on a number of such matters, including the salaries and other benefits of members of Congress. The relief Congress is seeking is a declaration that the 28th Amendment is unconstitutional and therefore invalid."

Clear as mud, Nishimura thought. "Perfect, Chris. We could talk about this all day, but I see that Klein's about to begin her argument to the Court."

* * *

Cassie gasped, fighting to catch her breath, her heart pounding. The note she'd just read was terrifying.

She noticed her backpack lying on the floor next to the table. She put it up on the table and opened it. She exhaled in relief, but the relief was short-lived.

Her diabetic supplies and equipment were there, but it included only one nearly empty vial of insulin. Barely enough to last her a single day. Maybe a bit longer if she stretched it.

And her pump. There it was. *Thank God. But why had someone removed it from my body? And placed it in my backpack?* She lifted her top and looked at the red welt on her stomach where the pump's mini subcutaneous infusion line had been torn away.

She cleaned the tiny opening in her stomach with an alcohol swab. It was not the small wound that was dangerous. But not knowing her situation, she had to minimize the chance of infection. Her doctors were always reminding her that infections could be very serious, especially for diabetics.

Cassie replaced the damaged infusion set with a fresh one—the last one she had—and reattached it to her body. Problem solved. *For now.*

CHAPTER 15
Tuesday, May 6, 10:38 am

BROOKS'S EYES followed Klein to the podium. She looked sure of herself. He hoped she genuinely understood the role she was about to play.

His mind drifted back to their prep session two weeks ago.

"Tell me, Ms. Klein"—she was Leah off the clock, but *never* on it—"why are we appealing the lower court's decision that Congress has standing?"

"Because if Congress doesn't have standing, the case is over. We win."

Brooks did not look pleased.

"Am I missing something, Your Honor?"

"Have you not been listening to me? Do you think I'm a potted plant, Ms. Klein, unworthy of your full attention? I'll ask you again. Please listen this time. Why are *we* appealing the standing decision when the overall ruling of the court below was in our favor?" He held her eyes with his.

She stood her ground. He gave her that. "Same answer, Judge. I don't get it. Sorry."

"You just told me why you are appealing standing. I didn't ask you about that. Do you not get it, Ms. Klein? You are the sacrificial lamb here."

She said nothing. Her eyes dropped.

He hated to be so tough.

He tried again. "Does Congress have standing here, Ms. Klein?"

There were two conflicting lines of applicable cases. "Doesn't it ultimately depend, Your Honor, on which line of the relevant cases a majority of the Justices choose to follow?"

"It does not, Ms. Klein. Indeed, a majority of the Justices will choose whichever line of cases suits their purpose." He had her attention now, but then he thought he'd had it before. He continued. "Whether Congress will be found to have standing will depend solely on whether five or more Justices want this to be the time and place when the Supreme Court of the United States will determine the meaning of Article V of the U. S. Constitution. You will be the vehicle, Ms. Klein, through which they will signal their desire. We will need to listen very carefully. But it will depend little on what you actually say to them."

Brooks wondered if Klein fully appreciated the gravity of what was about to hit her.

* * *

"B.C." Before . . . Cassie, Hirschfeld thought. He had just given new meaning to those letters. *What my mind has been reduced to, playing anagrams, talking to myself.* Cassie was both the reason he couldn't concentrate, and the reason why he had to.

Before Cassie, Hirschfeld had every intention of voting to uphold the amendment. "Checks and balances," one of the fundamental principles of the Constitution. Hirschfeld had no doubt the country's executive and legislative branches were impaired. If the governed feel the same, then the government must be "checked," meaning stopped. And "balanced," meaning corrected.

He refused to believe that the framers of the Constitution intended to give the government a veto over the right of the governed to direct their representatives. The only question is who speaks for the governed in a country whose numbers have swelled to more than 300 million?

If not 50,000 representative delegates spanning the country with no ax to grind other than improving the political system, then how many? 51,000? 151,000? 151 million? Certainly not all 300 million.

How could a constitutional convention of millions possibly be convened? The key had to be some form of fair and reasonable representation.

Hirschfeld felt that the members of Congress had to be constrained. Their job was to uphold the will of the people by proposing and enacting legislation to improve the country, not by filing lawsuits to serve their own personal interests.

But Cassie's circumstances complicated matters—although he refused to trivialize his own flesh and blood as a complication. On the one hand, how could he possibly place anything or anyone ahead of Cassie? On the other hand, how could he genuinely bring himself to abandon his true judicial beliefs to vote against the amendment for personal reasons—to save Cassie— as the kidnappers were insisting that he do?

He prayed for his baby girl, who had done nothing to deserve any of this. And for himself. And for the country. And for the noon recess.

* * *

Cassie recalled her mom often saying to her "Be careful what you wish for." Until now, Cassie hadn't been sure what that meant. Now she understood. She'd worked so hard to convince her parents to let her walk on her own between the driving range and school. And to become a great golfer. And to show the world—and herself—that her diabetes didn't mean she couldn't still be great. And normal. Now some creep had come along and spoiled it.

I'm gonna be grounded for the next ten years. If I ever get out of here.

As frightened as she was, she was also frustrated.

And angry.

Very angry.

Sometimes she played her best golf when she was . . . angry. *Whoever did this to me better watch out.*

CHAPTER 16
Tuesday, May 6, 10:20 am

BROOKS THOUGHT DEEPLY about these things. Even if others did not. At least not many others. His mind wandered back to his first discussion with Klein about Congress's suit against NoPoli.

"Ms. Klein, you understand, of course, that suing someone is not an automatic. It requires 'standing,' the *right* to sue because of damage suffered. But isn't standing generally pretty easy to establish? What makes you think, then, that the Supreme Court will conclude that Congress lacks standing to sue NoPoli?"

"You know the answer to that as well as I do, Your Honor. Congress's job is to make laws that serve our country, not to run around suing people. The law only permits Congress to sue someone that impairs or 'nullifies' its ability to do its job, to make some particular law."

Brooks had put Klein through her paces. She knew the blackletter written law, but would that be enough?

As Brooks had feared, however, any hope that Klein would be permitted to get through her presentation unscathed was quickly dashed. Associate Justice Jane Taser was the first to strike.

"If Smith physically breaks Jones's jaw, Jones is injured. If Smith burgles Jones's home and steals his art collection, Jones is injured. If Smith falsely and publicly accuses Jones of some reprehensible act, Jones's reputation is injured. In each of these instances, an award of money damages by a court of law will compensate Jones for his injury.

"But what injury, pray tell us, Ms. Klein, does the 28th Amendment visit upon Congress's responsibility to do its job? To pass laws that drive our nation?"

Brooks hoped his smile went unnoticed. Not one to tolerate any nonsense or bide her tongue, Taser was deadly serious. Her opinions were seldom in doubt. Or soft-spoken. Passionately anti-government, there was no question that Taser wanted to uphold the 28th Amendment.

Brooks imagined that Taser believed the easiest and safest route to achieving that end would be to deny Congress's standing to challenge the amendment. Exactly what NoPoli also wanted. Superficially appearing to challenge Klein, Taser was instead actually seeking to use NoPoli's anti-government platform to advance her own similar platform.

"My point precisely, Justice Taser," Klein replied. "The amendment only prevents corruption and abuse by individual members of Congress. In no way does it impair Congress's job to enact laws that serve the country. To the contrary, by reducing present-day political corruption and dysfunction, the amendment in point of fact helps Congress to do its job. Congress therefore lacks nullification standing to judicially challenge the amendment."

Justice Taser radiated a look of validation. Sitting next to her on the dais, Brooks could see that Associate Justice José Gaviota did not intend to let this softball exchange go unchallenged.

* * *

Looking at the clock on her insulin pump, Cassie realized it was a little over three hours since she had been drugged. Unless, of course, it was three hours plus a day. Or Two. She had no idea how long she had been unconscious. A little more clear-headed, Cassie began what her biology teacher would have referred to as a field survey of her environment.

First, her pump. While the home screen in the pump displayed only the time, Cassie had a vague recollection that some other screen somewhere else in the pump also displayed the date. The device was nothing more than a very small computer. Cassie scrolled through its home screen. She had to drill down two levels, but, sure enough, one of the sub-menu features on the Utilities screen was labeled "Time/Date."

She'd never had any reason to go to that screen before, but there it was. The date. It was still today. *The day I was kidnapped. So I haven't been detached from my pump all that long. No lengthy sugar highs. Yet.*

Encouraged that she had not been unconscious for days on end, Cassie now turned her scrutiny to the room that imprisoned her. A chest of drawers stood against the wall near the bed where she now sat. A makeshift bathroom with a toilet and shower had been built in the corner. Across the room, a table and some shelving rested atop a small refrigerator. A microwave and some food items filled the shelves.

She walked over and opened one of the chest drawers. And then the other two. In each she saw a bunch of clothes. She spread them on the bed. There was a packet of underwear, a few pairs of sweat socks, some T-shirts and sweat pants, and a hooded sweat jacket. She shuddered at the long-term implication of all this clothing and defiantly hurled them back in the drawers.

She was thirsty. Had to pee. Badly. Both signs that her blood sugar was climbing. Probably the result of being stressed out. She unzipped her test kit. Inserted a fresh pin prick needle into the plunger. Placed a test strip into the meter. Jabbed one of her fingers with the plunger needle. Placed a drop of blood on the test strip. And waited.

* * *

Brooks thought about Taser and Gaviota, both conservatives, but from opposite ends of the spectrum. Taser's anti-government views colored her against virtually every possible expansion of governmental power, in this instance claiming that the Constitution can't be amended without Congress's participation. In contrast, Gaviota's disposition caused him to support all traditional schools of thought, including the conventional wisdom that Article V sets forth the only two ways the Constitution can be amended.

Brooks was right. He didn't have long to wait for Justice Gaviota to spring into action on the heels of the Taser-Klein exchange. "Ms. Klein," asked Gaviota, "does not the adoption of the 28th Amendment without Congress's participation constitute nullification injury?"

Klein was quick to answer. "No Justice Gaviota, respectfully, it does not. Nullification injury requires impairment of Congress's exclusive responsibility to run the legislative branch of our federal government. But here Congress is claiming that the 28th Amendment conflicts with Article V. The enactment of Article V was the sole province and affair of our Constitutional framers. Not Congress.

"Even if, arguably, there is some inconsistency between the 28th Amendment and Article V, that occurs solely at the constitutional level. It does not in any way impede Congress in the performance of its lawmaking duties at the legislative level. There is no nullification injury triggered by the enactment of the 28th Amendment."

"An interesting thesis, Ms. Klein. But what about the fact that the 28th Amendment reduces the salary and benefits of the members of Congress previously enacted by Congress? Doesn't that constitute nullification injury?"

"Again, Justice Gaviota, I submit not. Under *Coleman v. Miller* and *Raines v. Bird*, two cases previously decided by this Supreme Court, the doctrine of nullification injury was established to prevent impairment of lawmaking undertaken to serve the country, not members of Congress. Reducing a Congressional benefit simply does not rise to the level of nullification injury."

"Perhaps so," Gaviota persisted, "but the 28th Amendment contains a provision that prohibits future lawmaking inconsistent with the amendment? Doesn't that limit what Congress might otherwise seek to enact somewhere down the road beyond the scope of salaries and benefits for members of Congress. And therefore constitute nullification injury for that reason? For example, what if Congress wishes to revisit what is being referred to as the anti-welfare provision of the amendment?"

"In both the *Coleman* and *Raines* nullification injury cases, the Supreme Court required *prior* legislative action to find nullification injury. Until some Congressional action is actually undertaken by Congress, there can be no claim of nullification injury.

"I would also point out that no welfare recipient who makes a good faith effort to find work consistent with his capabilities is denied any welfare coverage under the amendment. This provision is in substance directed solely at another Congressional perk, trading welfare entitlements for votes. My answer to your second question a moment ago applies to this question as well. Frankly, the entirety of the 28th Amendment is a rollback of Congressional perks that does not support nullification injury standing."

Gaviota seemed to be finished. Brooks was surprised that he let Klein off so easily. However, that did not mean he agreed with Klein. Or that other Justices would let her off as easily. Or as graciously.

* * *

Associate Justice Arnold Hirschfeld, Brooks' classmate and longtime friend, cleared his throat, as if he were nervous. Brooks wondered why an old pro like Hirschfeld would be nervous. No matter, Hirschfeld was always mild-mannered and in favor of government accountability. Brooks expected no trouble from him.

Hirschfeld seized the figurative baton from Gaviota. "Ms. Klein, are you intentionally ignoring the second part of Justice Gaviota's original question?"

Klein looked taken aback. Brooks couldn't blame her. It wasn't likely so much Hirschfeld's question, but rather his aggressive tone. Brooks sensed a stirring in the gallery behind him. The spectators obviously had not missed the hostility either.

"No sir," Klein said, "not intentionally. Justice Hirschfeld, would you please be kind enough to repeat the second part of Justice Gaviota's question for me?"

"In this Court, Ms. Klein, lawyers don't ask the questions. The right to ask questions here is generally reserved to the Justices. However, since I believe this is your first appearance in this Court, I will cut you some slack and restate Justice Gaviota's question for you. The effect of the 28th Amendment is to reverse or reduce certain Congressional benefits *previously* enacted by Congress itself. For example, compensation levels and benefits Congress *previously* granted to its members. With the ratification of our President, I might add. Doesn't the denial or reduction of those *Congressionally* enacted *prior* benefits constitute nullification injury? And if I may insert one question of my own, cannot this Court properly repair that injury by finding the 28th Amendment to violate Article V? Thus fortifying Congress's standing to sue?"

Brooks was no longer merely surprised. He was stunned. In all the years he had known Hirschfeld, he'd never seen him exhibit such rudeness.

Without skipping a beat, however, Klein politely responded. "My apologies, Justice Hirschfeld. I meant no disrespect. As you know, the principle of nullification injury is intended to preclude impairment of voting action. Not benefits. I believe that distinction offers us some guidance in addressing the first of your questions. You are correct that Congress's prior legislative grant of various perks to its members might seem to trigger nullification injury here. However, I respectfully submit that creating self-serving benefits merely for its members and not the country at large was never intended to—and does not—fall within the protective ambit of nullification injury. Moreover, I—"

"Excuse me, Ms. Klein. Do you have any case law to support that opinion?"

"No, Justice Hirschfeld, I don't. But I believe my logic is sound. Cases of first impression are frequently allowed to make new law. If that were not the case, our judicial system would be stagnant. As for your second question,—"

"I'm not surprised, Ms. Klein, that you're unable to cite any case for your unprecedented position."

Klein was plainly taking a beating. Everyone in the courtroom knew it. Even Esposito cringed. Klein was noticeably shaken, but Brooks appreciated that she was still trying her best to hold her ground.

"As for your second question," Klein began anew: "The fact that judicial relief from a reduction in Congress's perks and benefits might theoretically be possible, as you hypothesize, does not turn such a reduction in *benefits*, as opposed to an impairment of the right to enact rules and regulations, into an instance of nullification injury."

Although Brooks knew Klein couldn't see him sitting at counsel's table off to her side, he nevertheless gave her a quiet fist pump. *What's the burr here under Hirschfeld's saddle for God's sake?*

Hirschfeld was not backing off. "Ms. Klein, I'd like to examine your understanding of nullification injury a little further. If I negligently drive my car into yours on the way home from Court this evening, would you have the right to sue me for the resulting damages to your car?"

"I would, yes."

"Would you have any less right to sue me if you happened to be a member of Congress?"

"No, of course not, but I'm afraid I don't follow your point."

"Are you not familiar, Ms. Klein, with this Court's decision in the case of *Powell v. McCormack*? There, we found that Congressman Adam Clayton Powell was entitled to sue the U. S. House of Representatives for refusing to seat him following his election victory."

"I am familiar with the *Powell* case, Justice Hirschfeld. However, I believe it speaks to an entirely different point."

Brooks knew he and Leah had not reviewed *Powell*. He was momentarily encouraged by her response.

"In what way, Ms. Klein?"

"Because denying Congressman Powell the right to be seated and to vote on matters that would come before Congress during his elected term would, by definition, constitute the ultimate in nullification injury, denying him all of his rights to vote. But the 28th Amendment does not prevent any member of Congress from voting on any matters coming before Congress."

Brooks shook his head imperceptibly. What Klein said was true, but it was the wrong answer.

Hirschfeld knew that as well: "This Court recognized, Ms. Klein, that Congressman Powell had standing to sue because he was being denied the right to vote in any number of *future* votes. Not *prior* votes, as you claim is necessary. How is that any different than if Congress wants to consider and vote on any *future* revision to the current language of the 28th Amendment?"

"As I said a moment ago, Justice Hirschfeld—"

"Come, come, Ms. Klein, a little more candor, please. Are you really telling this Court that Congress has to go through the useless gesture of enacting a revision of the 28th Amendment in conflict with its anti-contest language—risking each of its members being charged with the commission of a 28th Amendment felony—before it can assert nullification injury?"

Brooks was aggravated by Hirschfeld's attempt to manipulate Leah. *Powell* was predicated on a denial of the Congressman's fundamental *property* right to receive his Congressional seat and credentials. The case had nothing whatsoever to do with any claim of nullification injury.

While perhaps clever, Hirschfeld's thesis was bad law. He had to know that. Brooks wondered why Hirschfeld would gamble his judicial integrity—and reputation—on Klein failing to assert the correct rebuttal to his question. It smacked of desperation.

Brooks blamed himself for Leah's gaff. He should have anticipated this possibility, remote as it was, and reviewed *Powell* with her when they prepped. For now, there was nothing he could do but hope the other justices would not put any more stock in Hirschfeld's argument than he did.

Brooks looked at Hirschfeld, who he could see caught the disappointed expression on Brooks's face. Hirschfeld turned away, rather sheepishly Brooks thought.

* * *

Three seconds later Cassie's meter confirmed her suspicions: 278. Her blood sugar was clearly too high. She dosed some additional insulin from her pump to bring it back down. She had to calm herself in order to reduce the amount of insulin she would need to use.

Otherwise, her insulin would be used up in less than the one plus days she had originally estimated when she reattached her pump. *I'll make things worse if I panic. Can't do that. Shhhh. Slow down. Focus. Calm down. Easy does it. Just like when I have to nail a five-foot putt to win a match. This situation's kinda like a match too.*

CHAPTER 17
Tuesday, May 6, 11:00 am

ESPOSITO'S TURN. He gathered his thoughts, including those he privately held about his clients. The esteemed members of Congress.

No doubt Congress had some honorable members, but most he knew were not. The Congressional leaders who engaged his services were more concerned about their own interests than those of their constituents. While confirming that he understood his fees would come solely from the taxpaying public, they emphasized to him that his loyalty and services were to inure to them, and them alone.

One Congressman had put it to Esposito this way in justifying the under the table kickbacks he requires from those for whom he arranges public works contracts: "You don't think I hold public office for just the salary and benefits that come with the job, do you? The real money is in what I make behind the scenes. The parties and the lobbyists who pay me are very pleased with my services and are quite willing to pay me for what I do. I'm just like any other broker who brings two parties together. They don't do that for free. Neither do I. The only difference is that I don't admit it."

Not quite, Congressman, Esposito told himself. Brokers and finders disclose what they receive, and based on their own good will, not that of their constituents. So many of these politicians were incredibly calloused and devious. In office to be served, not to serve, and often inept to boot.

Like them, I may be selfish and devious, but I'm not inept. As long as I'm paid, they get my services. Damn good services at that. But my loyalty? Really? Besides, what do they know about loyalty?

Unlike his clients, he owed no duty to their constituents. What he cared about, first and foremost, was reputation. *His* reputation. Thanks to his record, demand for his services was at an all-time high. A win here and he'd own D.C. Even a loss wouldn't damage him. He couldn't be blamed for the mess his clients had created for themselves. A win for them would be a coronation for sure, but he agreed to take this case on because it would be a winner for him no matter what the outcome.

He took a couple of deep breaths. In spite of all the resources and backup at his disposal, this was the time when it was on his shoulders alone. Just how he loved it. He was ready. He was always ready. Nevertheless, Hirschfeld's off-the-wall surprising remarks were a plus. He intended to put them to good use.

* * *

Brooks eyed Esposito strutting to the lectern in his expensive suit and fancy cowboy boots. Cocksure and full of himself.

He wasted no time. "With all due respect to my learned colleague at the bar, there can be no question but that nullification injury exists here and establishes Congress's standing to bring this lawsuit."

He commanded the lectern with a folksy keenness. A thinking man's backwoods lawyer, Brooks thought, a modern—and falsely humble—Honest Abe. But it had served him well.

"First of all, as Justice Hirschfeld so ably demonstrated in his use of *Powell* a few moments ago, our so called 28th Amendment denies Congress its fundamental Article V constitutional right to vote on any proposed future revision of the amendment. Yet, this is nullification injury. And it's exacerbated by the fact that this suit has been brought on behalf of all members of Congress. Not just a disgruntled few."

Esposito nodded appreciatively at Hirschfeld, then moved his gaze to the other Justices.

If Brooks were originally angered by Hirschfeld's abuse of Powell, he was now outraged. *But I can hardly fault Esposito for capitalizing on the opportunity. And nothing I can do about it right now. We'll see about later.*

Associate Justice Norman Veksler broke Esposito's stride. "Aren't you making a number of assumptions, Mr. Esposito? And do you think it helps your cause to mention that your suit is on behalf of all members of Congress? Is it not your position that nullification of a single legislator's vote, such as Congressman Powell, is sufficient to empower that legislator with standing to sue?"

"Fair enough, Justice Veksler." Esposito tugged on the lapels of his Armani suit. "You are correct that a single nullified legislator has standing to sue. However, do you really want 500 plus individual members of Congress spending the taxpayers' money on lawsuits every time one of them doesn't get his way? I wouldn't."

"Interesting style, Mr. Esposito," Veksler responded, "agreeing with me on something I didn't say. It was *your* position I addressed. I question whether such tactics serve your cause. Do you actually have anything instructive to share with us?"

Brooks noticed Veksler's scowl and chuckled to himself. All eyes in the Courtroom were now definitely trained on Esposito.

"I'm sorry if I misunderstood you, Justice Veksler, or if I sounded dismissive. That was certainly not my intention. I do have some further points to make."

Veksler replied, "Why am I not surprised?"

Soft laughter rippled through the audience. Brooks was careful not join in.

"The case before this Court today," Esposito said, "is a simple response to those who would seek to nullify Congress's Article V constitutional right to participate in amendment of the U.S. Constitution. And to use the threat of a criminal felony to raise the stakes. Courts have rarely countenanced such patently chilling practices."

"Counsel," Associate Justice Dennis Galanti interjected, "did you just say Article V requires the participation of Congress in constitutional amendments? While I recognize this will be the subject of our hearings this afternoon and on Thursday, and don't want to jump the gun, do you have any authority for that proposition? I didn't see that point briefed in your papers."

Almost unnoticeably, but not missed by Brooks, Esposito stiffened. "I'm sorry, Justice Galanti. As detailed in Congress's opposition brief, Article

V provides two means by which to amend the Constitution. Both require Congressional participation. I don't believe any additional authority is necessary."

Now Chief Justice Trotter entered the scrum. "Mr. Esposito, does Article V expressly provide that its two means to amend the Constitution are the only means by which the Constitution can be amended?"

"Uh, no, Chief Justice Trotter, Article V doesn't say that, but—"

"I didn't think so—"

"—I can't imagine any other reasonable interpretation—"

"Mr. Esposito!"

The booming voice belonged to Justice Taser, who then paused as if for effect, to be sure she had the undivided attention of everyone in the Courtroom. She did.

"Thank you so much for your unsupported view of what our Constitutional forefathers had in mind when they crafted Article V." She leaned forward and peered down at Esposito, her scorn evident. "Is there anything more you wish to say about the standing issue in this case? I note that your allotted time is about to expire."

"Two further points, Justice Taser. I'll be brief."

Brooks smiled. The mantra of every lawyer seeking more time from a court—feigned brevity.

"If NoPoli's National Convention can amend our Constitution, then we'll be opening the floodgates to every Tom, Dick, and Harry who may want to do so. As it is, we've had over eleven thousand attempts to date to amend the Constitution. Only twenty-seven—now possibly twenty-eight—have succeeded. Finally—"

"Well, Mr. Esposito," Veksler interjected once more, "Tom, Dick, and Harry have no pending amendments to the Constitution, at least none that have been judicially challenged. I'm afraid we'll just have to save that question for another day."

"Of course, Your Honor." Esposito offered a weak, deferential smile. "Finally, if Congress does not have standing to challenge the 28th Amendment, then who?"

"That's an interesting question," Veksler replied. "I'm grateful we don't have to answer it today. For now, it will be difficult enough for this Court to decide whether Congress has such standing. As always, Mr. Esposito, thank you for your inspiring vision."

"Thank *you*, Justice Veksler."

Esposito beat a hasty retreat from the lonely rostrum to his entourage, perhaps seeking safety in numbers. Brooks thought he looked a couple inches shorter than fifty minutes earlier.

"Thank you, counsel," Trotter said. "I see it's almost noon. We'll be adjourned until one o'clock this afternoon, when we'll consider the constitutional validity of the 28th Amendment."

* * *

Cassie stared at the toilet. It was right out there in the open. Who would expect her to live in a bathroom? She wondered if someone were watching her. *Eeew!* She had no choice—couldn't hold it in another second. She quickly did what she had to do.

Next, she opened the small refrigerator and looked inside. She noticed several bottles of water. She wasn't sure if they were safe, but she needed to hydrate herself. She would have to chance it. Besides, if they meant to harm her, they wouldn't need to be so sneaky about it. She opened one of the bottles and took a sip. It tasted okay. Her throat was dry. She gulped down the rest of the bottle. Elevated blood sugars always made her thirsty.

In addition to the water, she saw milk, juice, bananas, a jar of peanut butter, a jar of jelly, and a loaf of bread. On one of the shelves above the refrigerator sat a box of crackers, packages of instant soup, and small boxes of different dry cereals. It looked okay, but much of it was high carb, would require her to dose more insulin. Besides, she wasn't the least bit hungry.

But what would it matter? Within two days after her insulin ran out, she would go into a diabetic coma.

And die.

CHAPTER 18
Tuesday, May 6, 11:55 am

RELIEVED that Trotter didn't begin speaking to the television cameras again, Hirschfeld left the podium with the other Justices, walking hurriedly past them in fear that some might want to immediately discuss one or more of this morning's points.

He had thought about rallying to Esposito's aid, but the man had made such a complete ass of himself that Hirschfeld didn't want to be dragged down with him. He had much to accomplish. He had to pick his battles wisely.

More importantly, he was cautiously optimistic that at least four of his colleagues wanted to debate and decide the correct meaning of Article V and would join him in holding that Congress had standing so that discussion of Article V would not be preempted. Had that not been the case, surely one or more of them would have spoken out against his obviously strained use of *Powell*.

Hirschfeld reached for his phone. He was so wrought he needed to assure himself it was still there. He'd hated turning it off, but their text insisted that he do so. He couldn't chance ignoring the instruction. He hoped Mark and Jill understood. He had to get to his office now and call them.

* * *

"And . . . that's a wrap." The NBN-TV director's voice reverberated in Nishimura's headset. "Nice job, everyone. We're switching over to the 12 o'clock news. Get something to eat. Back in forty-five please, ready to start up again and introduce the afternoon session."

Nishimura turned to Elliott and Kessler. "Esposito didn't make any friends up there."

"I wouldn't be so sure," Elliott said. "Very tough to figure out exactly where each of the Justices really is, especially the three who haven't said anything so far. It won't matter what Esposito or Klein said if the Court wants to decide the 28th Amendment on the merits. If they do, they'll find standing no matter what the lawyers had to say about that."

Kessler shrugged his shoulders. But said nothing.

* * *

Brooks smiled at Klein as they packed up their briefcases. They had a private room reserved in a nearby hotel to review and update their afternoon strategies over lunch. Esposito and his vast team would be doing the same. As they rose to leave, Brooks leaned over to Klein.

Before he could speak, she said, "I know. I know. I can't imagine how I screwed up *Powell*. I'm sick about it. When I think of the thousands of NoPoli delegates I let down today, the hundreds I met with personally, who gave so much of themselves to help enact the 28th Amendment—"

"Ms. Klein," Brooks said, "stop berating yourself. Those things happen. Besides, I count at least five Justices who, for a variety of different reasons, will find in favor of standing no matter what."

He wasn't really that sure, but there was nothing to be gained by beating her up.

"What I wanted to ask you," he continued, "was to please invite your husband to join us for lunch. I have something I need to discuss with him."

"Your Honor, Frank has the kids with him. I think he was planning to take them to lunch so you and I could work without distraction."

"No worries. Bring them along too. Won't be a problem. I'm pretty much good to go for this afternoon." He offered a playful wink and grin. "Who knows, your kids might offer a useful tip or two."

CHAPTER 19
Tuesday, May 6, 12:05 pm

THE COURT WAS CLEARED for the lunch recess. Like most of the country, Thomas wasn't particularly interested in all that standing gibberish. He was certain the Court would find standing. Well, he was pretty sure. They had to if his efforts to defeat the 28th Amendment were to succeed. That was all he cared about. The rest was just details. He *had* to defeat the 28th Amendment. His very survival depended on it.

He went outside and retrieved one of the phones he had hidden outside the Courthouse. He opened the special video app he'd installed and checked up on the girl via the hidden camera in the basement room. He smiled. Nothing seemed amiss. She appeared to be sleeping.

He made his way into the afternoon session entrance line. The returning crowd was still on the thin side. People lingering over lunch, he supposed. Good. All the easier to reclaim his seat. He was enjoying Plan A.

* * *

A faint noise somewhere in the room woke Cassie. She couldn't believe how much she was sleeping.

The sound returned. It was real, not a dream. She looked around to see where it might be coming from. The walls and corners blurred. She blinked. Shook her head. Looked again. Her vision was now clearer.

Nothing.

Wait. Up there. A small red light on a tiny camera blinked in one of the ceiling corners. *That perv is watching me!*

Almost instantly, as though he'd noticed her looking back at him, the red light went out. The barely audible noise had stopped.

CHAPTER 20
Tuesday, May 6, 12:05 pm

HIRSCHFELD WHISKED PAST his secretary on the way to his office. "No calls. No visitors. No exceptions, please." He closed and locked the door behind him, his abruptness undoubtedly surprising her. He had no time for niceties right now. He felt bad about it, but would make it up to her another time. Assuming there'd be another time.

Each of the Justices was provided an encrypted telephone to facilitate confidential discussion of pending cases. Hirschfeld's son-in-law, Mark, was an executive at a publicly traded Fortune 100 company. The officers of the company also had encrypted cell phones to guard against insider trading breaches. Hirschfeld selected the video conferencing mode and punched in the speed dial for Mark's cell phone. He wasn't a fan of video calls, but current circumstances would dictate all the intimacy he could muster.

Mark picked up on the first ring. "Wait a second, Arnold, I'm casting my phone to the TV so Jill and I can see you better, and so you will be able to see the two of us through the TV camera."

After a momentary lapse, the improved images resumed on both ends. Hirschfeld saw his daughter seated on the family room sofa, crouched forward, fingers clenched tightly in her lap. Mark stood behind her, hands gently on her shoulders. Whitney, the family pup, was scrunched up on the sofa next to Jill. He was burrowed into her, his chin on her lap as if intuitively sensing that something was clearly wrong.

"Where's Cassie, Arnold? She's not answering her phone. There's no response on her Find My Friends app either." Mark's normally stoic disposition faltered. Cassie was their only child. "What the hell's going on?"

Jill finally glanced up. Her eyes and face were already red and swollen, but she completely lost it when she and her dad locked eyes across the television screen. Since she was a child, he'd always been able to make everything right for his daughter.

Hirschfeld wondered if that would be possible this time.

Either Jill hadn't heard Mark's question or chose to ignore it. "Dad! What's happening, where's Cassie, who—"

"Listen to me, please. Both of you. We don't have much time. This is what I know." Hirschfeld took a second to steady himself, get the quiver out of his voice. "Just as Court convened this morning, I received a text alert on my private cell. I always carry it with me. I opened it right there on the bench because only your mother, the two of you, and Cassie have that number. It began, 'We have your granddaughter. Here's what you need to do.'"

He hesitated to again collect himself. "They want me to cause the amendment to be defeated. Whoever they are, they say they will return Cassie unharmed so long as that happens. Otherwise—"

"She won't be returned," Jill finished her dad's sentence. "She'll be—"

"Arnold," Mark cut in, "how do you size up the vote?"

Hirschfeld didn't pull any punches. Or worry about the sanctity of the Court. "Right now it looks to me as if there are three definite votes to invalidate, four definite votes to uphold, including me, with two undecideds."

"Let me get this straight," Mark said. "Even if the three votes to invalidate hold firm, and you switch your vote, you still need to persuade one of the two undecideds to vote to invalidate."

"Or one of the three votes to uphold other than me to switch."

"Your vote alone can't control the outcome."

"Exactly. I'll have to turn one other Justice. I get that."

"We have to call the FBI," Mark said. "*Right now*. We are *so* in over our heads. Cassie's life is on the line. It was all we could do to wait until the noon recess to speak with you, Arnold. We can't wait another second."

"That's strictly up to you and Jill. I'll support whatever the two of you decide." Hirschfeld took a long, ragged breath. "But I really don't think that's the best option."

A wailing sound, coming from somewhere deep inside Jill, stopped Mark and Hirschfeld. "Daddy, I can't take this! Not for one more second. *What* options are you talking about? We don't have any options. You have to fix this. Right now! You have to get my baby back. Whatever it takes."

Hirschfeld watched his daughter through the video technology. He wasn't sure if she understood the significance of her words, all that might be required. Or the risks entailed in going to the FBI, a bureaucracy whose priorities and constraints might well differ from theirs. Her husband pushing her in one direction; her father resisting, possibly straining the relationship between husband and wife. Her only child's life was hanging in the balance. Jill was unraveling before his very eyes. The three of them had to be on the same page. Hirschfeld felt that was on him.

"Guys, I repeat, it's your call. But let me at least tell you what I think."

Jill put her head in her hands and shook it slowly. Mark stared straight ahead, his body coiled with fear.

"This is no ordinary kidnapping," Hirschfeld said. "There's been no demand for money. This isn't about money. This isn't about Cassie either. She's just an innocent pawn in all of this, a means to an end. This is about ideologies. These people, whoever they are, want to dictate how our country is run. If I can help deliver what they want, I believe they'll return Cassie."

"You're just guessing, Arnold. You don't actually know that."

"You're right, Mark, I don't. Admittedly, it's just my feeling. But I do think I have a way to find out."

Jill glanced up, momentarily seeming a little calmer. "How, Dad, what do you mean?"

"They're watching me. In the courtroom. Or on the television. Maybe both. They see me. I want to talk to them."

"Arnold, how do you know they're watching you? And how, exactly, do you intend to talk to them?" Hirschfeld could hear the skepticism in Mark's voice.

"This morning, when I was texting you guys, they sent me a second message, telling me to quit fiddling around with my phone. They had to be watching me.

"That's why I couldn't leave the bench to call you until the noon recess. It will mean the end of their plans if they're discovered. I can text them back from my cell phone, tell them I'm going to blow what they're doing wide open unless I can immediately speak with Cassie. I don't believe they've hurt her; they're smart enough to realize I'd insist on this."

"No," Jill murmured, shaking her head. "No. No, no, no."

"Arnold. How are you going to text them?"

"Easy. They sent me a text. All I have to do is hit reply."

"I don't think so. If that were true, then you could just hand your phone over to the FBI. They're communicating with you through one or more burner phones. As soon as they send you a text, they remove the phone's battery and destroy its SIM card to make sure they can't be traced. That also means you can't text them back."

"I don't think they've done that. They've already sent me two different messages."

"SIM cards are cheap, Arnold. They've probably got dozens of them."

"Trust me. If I can't reach them, I'll make them get in touch with me."

Jill suddenly stopped shaking her head. Mustering a tone of grim resolve, she said, "We do trust you, Dad."

Mark said nothing. The significance of that silence wasn't lost on Hirschfeld. Under the circumstances, their unmistakably differing levels of faith in him could seriously undermine their relationship. Hirschfeld couldn't let that happen.

"I want to mention something, sick as it may sound. These people aren't the only ones with any chips to play. We are, of course, desperate to get Cassie back. And they know that. However, I think they're desperate too. To go to this extreme just to defeat the amendment. I don't want to play chicken with Cassie's life, but if I manage this right, I think there's going to be an opportunity for *me* to pressure *them*. Create a dialogue. Before Cassie is in any serious jeopardy. I think time is on our side."

Mark looked aghast. "Arnold, are you prepared to do what they want? Can you actually bring yourself to trade your vote to get Cassie back?"

Jill looked savagely at Mark. She screamed, "What kind of a question is that, Mark? Dad will clearly do whatever it takes."

"I know, Jill, but your dad has responsibilities we can't begin to appreciate. This places him in a terrible position. I had to ask." He glanced back up into the screen. "And I haven't heard an answer."

"You're right to ask, Mark, but you don't have to worry. I'll do whatever it takes." *Switching my vote isn't the issue. It's how I persuade others to join me.*

"Dad," Jill interrupted. "You just said time was on our side. How long is all this going to take?

"I don't know yet, baby. I'm going as fast as I can."

"Are you saying it could take until the Court rules on Monday and these monsters confirm they've got the result they want?"

"It could. We just have to be patient."

"Dad, listen to me. Cassie does not have enough insulin with her to make it until next Monday. She'll run out by tomorrow and be dead by Monday—even if these freaks don't lay a hand on her."

"What are you talking about? Doesn't Cassie always carry enough insulin on her?"

Jill exploded. "When she left home this morning, she didn't know to pack for a week! What's the matter with you?"

"I—"

"Arnold, that's not the only problem," Mark said. "Assuming somehow we can arrange to get additional insulin to Cassie, and assuming you can persuade these people to keep her safe until you give them the result they want, what leverage do we have *then*? If she can possibly identify any of them, won't they just kill her at that point when they have what they want?"

Jill went white. "Mark! Don't even—"

"I'm sorry, I know. But we can't overlook this." Mark clutched her hand, then returned his eyes to the TV. "How do we get her back, Arnold?"

"I don't have an answer for you right now, but I'll figure it out. One step at a time." Right now, that was all he could think to say.

"You don't understand, Dad, Cassie will—"

"I *do* understand, Jill. I do now. Believe me. But I have to return to the bench in six minutes. Are we agreed for now? No police, no FBI, we all behave like nothing's wrong? At least until we talk again this evening?"

"Dad, I'm just—"

"Arnold, the whole afternoon—really? I gotta stand by my first instinct. The FBI—"

"No!" Hirschfeld shouted into the phone. He was no longer going to pretend to defer to his kids. "I'm convinced of this. The surest way to guarantee Cassie dies is to contact the FBI. There will be no way to keep matters under wraps once that happens. The kidnappers will no longer be able to quietly control the case. Cassie will no longer be an asset to them. They'll kill her and take off. Please. Try to keep it together. I'll meet the two of you at your place as soon Court adjourns for the day. I'll get there as fast as I can."

"All right," Mark said, his voice exhibiting less conviction than Hirschfeld had wished.

Jill simply whispered, "Okay."

"I could end up getting stuck going back and forth with Cassie's kidnappers for a while. And I have to stop by the house and pick up your mother. I haven't had time to speak with her about any of this. With her heart, I have to be the one to break this to her. And I have to do it in person."

"Dad, call us when you're on the way home," Jill said. "We'll meet you at your place. It'll save time. And that way Mom can stay put." Her voice started to crack again.

"I know, baby. Be strong. I have to go now." He punched off.

CHAPTER 21
Tuesday, May 6, 12:40 pm

BROOKS, Klein, Lotello, and his kids, Madison and Charlie, had just finished a hurried lunch. All Madison and Charlie talked about was checking out the DVR when they got home to see if the television cameras had captured either of them.

Brooks and Klein had briefly reviewed what he planned on arguing in Court that afternoon. Brooks hadn't yet said a word to Lotello. As they left the restaurant and headed back across the street to the courthouse, he motioned him to fall back a few steps behind the others. Klein must have noticed because she scooched Madison and Charlie back toward Court with her, leaving Brooks free to speak privately with Lotello.

"What's up, Judge?"

"Not exactly sure, Detective. How best to put this . . .?"

Brooks hesitated.

"One of the Justices, Arnold Hirschfeld, is an old law school classmate of mine. I've known him for years. He seemed preoccupied this morning, out of sorts, as if his mind were somewhere else. On top of that, the line of questioning he pursued with your wife was exactly the opposite of what I would have expected from him. Both in style and substance."

"Hmm. Small world, Your Honor. Hirschfeld's granddaughter, Cassie Webber, goes to school with Madison. They're best friends, inseparable. Cassie was supposed to come with us to Court this morning. They wanted to watch

Gramps and Mom in action. In fact, Cassie had arranged to introduce Madison to her grandfather after Court finished for the day. Cassie texted Madison early this morning, saying they should meet up in the school cafeteria before class. But Cassie never showed. Not at the cafeteria and then not later when we were all supposed to meet up and leave for the courthouse together."

Brooks stopped in his tracks. "*And?*" He made a rolling gesture with his hand. "Come on, Detective, we're not getting any younger here." He knew that Lotello would choose to ignore his taunt, but he enjoyed trying to tussle with him now and then anyway. *Keeps the man on his toes.*

"Madison wanted to run back to Cassie's class and find out why she didn't come meet us out front. I didn't let her. We would have been late to Court. Leah was up first. Hirschfeld was probably expecting to see Cassie in the courtroom and was a little off his game when she wasn't there."

Brooks shoved his hands deep into his pockets. "That might explain his inattention, but not his harshness with Ms. Klein. I think there must be something more."

"Why don't I do a little checking on Cassie's whereabouts this afternoon?"

"Great idea. Never would have thought of that myself. I'll let Ms. Klein know why you won't be with us in Court this afternoon." Brooks draped his arm around Lotello's shoulder, offering up a mischievous smile. "Besides, you can catch my brilliant performance on the DVR this evening. I heard your kids mention they were recording everything."

With that, Brooks turned and marched off briskly toward the courthouse, leaving Lotello behind, hopefully talking to himself.

* * *

Lotello knew Brooks was always two steps ahead of everyone else—in this case, literally as well as figuratively. He smiled at Brooks's backside, and went to retrieve his car.

As he drove off, Lotello reflected on the growing number of uncertainties surrounding Cassie. It was not in his nature to leave any loose ends hanging, especially when they might relate to the welfare of a youngster, his daughter's best friend no less. He felt the need to buy some time to check things out.

His Metro D.C. partner knew he was at the Supreme Court today. She expected him back tomorrow. He called and told her he was going to take a couple more days of personal leave to be with his wife through the Monday conclusion of her first ever case in the U.S. Supreme Court.

* * *

Madison had noticed her dad fall back with Brooks. Grown up stuff, she guessed, not for us kids. She hated it when her dad did that. But she liked the old guy, the one everyone called "Judge" Brooks even though he wasn't a judge anymore. She was fine hanging with Leah so that her dad could talk about whatever she wasn't allowed to be a part of.

Her mind drifted to Cassie. She was a little miffed that her best friend had stood her up for their cafeteria date this morning, but figured she'd just decided to hit another bucket of balls. So like that girl, she thought, to forget everything else when she had a golf club in her hands. But not showing up to watch the big show in Court? Not answering my text at lunch a few minutes ago? *Girl has some serious explaining to do.*

CHAPTER 22
Tuesday, May 6, 12:45 pm

CASSIE'S APPETITE HAD RETURNED. Using a plastic spoon, the only utensil anywhere in the room, she spread some peanut butter and jelly on a slice of bread. She removed the glucose test kit in her backpack and tested her sugar. She needed to monitor it more frequently than normal under stressful situations. It was 257, way too high given that she hadn't consumed any carbs since breakfast. It had to be the circumstances. Maybe also whatever that creep had used to drug her.

The sandwich would add carbs to her system and elevate her glucose level. But she had no choice; she had to eat to preserve her strength—even though it meant also having to dose more insulin to prevent her glucose levels from rising too high.

Looking at the clock on her pump, she waited about fifteen minutes, the amount of time it usually took for the insulin to kick in and lower her sugar. Only then did she eat the peanut butter and jelly sandwich.

It tasted okay, sort of, but her recovered appetite was dulled knowing how much insulin she had just used up to cover the meal. And watching the insulin reserve in her pump reservoir observation window sliding dangerously lower only made it worse.

And, to make matters still worse, her nausea was returning. Probably the combination of the peanut and jelly and the drug that man shot me up with me to knock me out. *Uhh, I'm going to be sick. Right now!*

* * *

Fifteen minutes before the top of the hour, when the Court proceedings would resume, the NBN-TV feed again went live.

Nishimura smiled at the television cameras. She knew just how to play her viewing audience; she didn't consistently get the ratings she did by accident. And her bosses hadn't given her this one of a kind assignment for nothing.

"Welcome back, everyone. Despite the somewhat abstract nature of the standing issues, the morning session certainly didn't lack for tension or drama. It seemed to me that both sides were pummeled by the Justices. Chris, what can we expect during the remaining three sessions?"

Elliott, his face already shiny with perspiration, coiled his neck and gave his necktie its obligatory tug.

"This afternoon will be devoted to Article V of the Constitution, specifically the question of how and by whom the Constitution can be amended. Thursday morning's session will examine the NoPoli Constitutional Convention. Thursday afternoon will be spent measuring the NoPoli Convention against the requirements of the Constitution. Given that all of these remaining issues were prompted by Congress's appeal of the decision reached by the lower court upholding the 28th Amendment, Esposito will go first in each remaining session. Brooks will then follow."

"Which will bring us back full circle to Article V," Nishimura said.

"And perhaps other relevant constitutional provisions," Elliott added.

Nishimura turned to Kessler. "What about Klein? Won't she appear in any of the remaining sessions, Steve?"

"This is her first appearance in the Supreme Court," Kessler said. "Brooks argued countless Supreme Court cases prior to being appointed to the D.C. Superior Court. It makes sense that Klein was tasked with arguing the easier standing part of the appeal while Brooks will handle the tougher constitutional challenge of the 28th Amendment."

The camera closed in on Nishimura. "If what we heard this morning were the easy part of the case, we'll certainly depend on the two of you to help us interpret and understand what's coming up next."

CHAPTER 23
Tuesday, May 6, 2015, 12:50 pm

LOTELLO KNEW where Cassie and her family lived; he'd dropped Madison off there many times. Even so, he looked around as if he'd never been there before. Nice house. Nice upper middle-class suburban neighborhood. Nothing out of the ordinary.

He walked up to the front door, rang the bell, and waited. Nothing. He tried again. Still nothing. He was just about to move around the side of the house when the door opened.

"Can I help you?" The man's appearance didn't fit the greeting. His tie was undone and hanging loose. His shirt was unbuttoned at the neck and rumpled. The words felt more like: *What do you want?*

Lotello realized he had never met Cassie's father before. Odd, he thought, given how close their daughters were. He wondered what kind of work the man did that he would be at home in the middle of a workday.

"Hi. Name's Frank Lotello. Cassie and my daughter, Madison, are classmates." Consistent with his training, force of habit no doubt, Lotello nonchalantly inched forward into the doorway. He also stuck out his hand. The man in the doorway stared at it blankly before finally responding in kind.

"Yes. Hello. I'm Cassie's father. Mark Webber."

"Nice to meet you, Mark." He released the man's hand, which felt clammy and lifeless. Reacting to the man's appearance and demeanor, Lotello inched forward a little more. "I was supposed to take the girls from school to the

Supreme Court hearing this morning to watch Cassie's grandfather. Cassie didn't show. Madison was worried and made me promise I'd stop by and make sure everything was okay."

Webber stared at Lotello as if he were a visitor from another planet. Finally, he said, "Cassie wasn't feeling well after her golf practice this morning. She decided to come home. She should have let your daughter know. I'll speak to her about that. Cassie, I mean. I'll speak to Cassie." His eyes remained glassy, remote. "Sorry for your troubles."

An agitated grandfather in the courtroom this morning. Now a twitchy father in disheveled work clothes at home on a weekday instead of at his office. Something was definitely wrong. *A family matter? Something else?*

"Actually, Madison gave me a message to pass along to Cassie. Can I say hello to her?"

Webber hesitated. "Uh, now's not really a good time. She's sleeping. I'll tell her to call Madison. Nice to meet you." He backed away and started to close the door.

Lotello thought about it. One part of him wanted to flash his badge and insist on seeing Cassie right then and there. The other part of him knew he had no right to do that and should butt out. Either way, whatever he decided to say now could prove incredibly awkward in the future on any number of levels.

"Mr. Webber. Are you *sure* everything's okay?

"I am," Webber said

Webber didn't sound convincing.

They stood there eyeballing one another. Lotello didn't have enough to go on. He would have to back off. See what more he might otherwise be able to come up with first.

If the problem were inside the family, it was unlikely to get much worse in the near term, especially since Webber now knew Lotello was sniffing around. But if it were something outside the family, time might be of the essence. For now, Lotello was stuck.

"Okay, then. Nice to meet you too." Lotello reluctantly stepped back from the doorway. "Please tell Cassie we hope she's feeling better soon."

"Will do. Thanks." Webber closed the door without so much as another word.

Lotello turned and walked back to his car. Not for a second did he believe Cassie was asleep in that house. He hoped his instincts were wrong and that she was in fact home and safe.

* * *

Webber hurried back to the kitchen, where Jill confronted him immediately, arms clutched across her chest.

"Who was it? What'd he want? Something to do with Cassie?"

He answered her questions as calmly as he could. She started pacing round the room.

"Hon, settle down. We have to hang in here. For Cassie's sake."

"Easy for you to say. It just doesn't work that way for me."

"Damn, Jill. You think this is easy for me?"

"I'm sorry. It's just . . . . My God, Madison's father is some kind of a detective. Do you think he suspects something? Could he mess things up? Maybe you just should have told him the truth."

"Jesus, Jill, that's enough! C'mon. *I'm* the one who wanted to go to the FBI. But, no, we had to do it your way. Your dad's way. I gave in. Now we have no choice but to give him a chance. That's why I didn't say anything to that guy. I couldn't run the risk of screwing up whatever your dad might be putting in play this afternoon. You can't keep waffling like this. At least until tonight, we have to stick with what we decided and see what happens."

"Don't you start lecturing me." She rubbed her eyes with clenched fists, as if that might somehow help. "It's . . . ." She left the rest unsaid. So did he.

CHAPTER 24
Tuesday, May 6, 2015, 12:55 pm

CASSIE'S NAUSEA tapered off after she tossed her peanut butter and jelly sandwich. But now she was beginning to shiver. Either something was really wrong with her or the room was just too cold.

She searched the walls for any kind of heater controls, but there weren't any. So, she did the next best thing she could think of; she heated up some instant soup in the microwave and began sipping it. Slowly. Because it was hot. And she was also worried that she might get nauseous again.

But she didn't really have any choice. The shakes weren't any fun either. The soup helped, a little, and at least it stayed down, but she was still cold. Grudgingly, she walked over to the cabinet, took out one of the sweatshirts, and put it on.

Her first compromise. She wondered if there would be more.

* * *

Just five minutes before Hirschfeld had to return to the courtroom. Mark had told him that he would not be able to text Cassie's assailants, that they were using untraceable burner phones. Whatever that meant.

Mark's generation certainly understood technology better than Hirschfeld's. But who was to say that the kidnappers were running things the way Mark said? Hirschfeld definitely needed to reach them. And he needed to do it soon, before Cassie's insulin ran out. He couldn't see the harm in trying.

Hirschfeld composed a short message in the cellphone box just below the last message he had received.

I have information you NEED. Imperative we talk NOW. Please call me.

It seemed straightforward. He hoped it would get their attention. Cassie's life depended on it. He hit Send. And waited. Nothing. No response. He tried two more times. Still nothing. He wondered if that meant Mark was right about all that burner phones and SIM cards business.

He looked at the time. He had to join the others in the courtroom. He had failed to reach them. *What do I do now?*

CHAPTER 25
Tuesday, May 6, 1:00 pm

QUEUEING up early after the noon recess, Thomas succeeded in obtaining the same seat he'd occupied during the morning session. When Esposito took the podium to begin his afternoon remarks, the wording of Article V of the Constitution suddenly appeared in large, bright letters on the multisided monitor suspended from the ceiling.

All eyes in the courtroom appeared to be glued on the display. For a moment, Thomas thought he had been transported to some NBA sports venue. As Esposito began his remarks, Thomas's attention was drawn to the highlighted words on the screen.

ARTICLE V OF THE CONSTITUTION OF
THE UNITED STATES

The Congress, whenever two thirds of both houses shall deem it necessary, shall propose amendments to this Constitution, or, on the application of the legislatures of two thirds of the several states, *shall call a convention for proposing amendments, which*, in either case, shall be valid to all intents and purposes, as part of this Constitution, *when ratified* by the legislatures of three fourths of the several states, or by conventions in three fourths thereof, *as the* one or the other *mode of ratification may be proposed by the Congress*. ... (Emphasis added. Inapplicable language omitted.)

"May it please the Court. Constitutional amendments must, one, be proposed either by Congress or at a convention called by Congress and, two, be ratified only in one of two specified modes selected by Congress. The participation of Congress is required both on the front and back ends of this process. Period. It's not that complicated. In fact, it's rather straightforward. NoPoli bypassed Congress from start to finish. Its 28th Amendment isn't worth the paper it's printed on."

Thomas was ecstatic. He couldn't have said it better himself. And he was intimately familiar with Article V. He'd memorized it. Word for word.

Hirschfeld was the first Justice to intrude. "So, Mr. Esposito, tell us, is it your position that Congress can just run around willy-nilly *extorting* we the people and taking us *hostage*? Have I got that right, sir?"

Thomas immediately sat bolt upright in his seat, laser-beam eyes staring right at Hirschfeld. *Huh? Bad choice of words? Extortion? Hostage? Just a coincidence?*

"I'm sorry, Justice Hirschfeld. I don't believe I said anything about extorting anyone or holding anyone hostage."

Associate Justice Larry Lukesh, tall, thin, and purposeful, entered the colloquy. "Hold on, counsel, I think you misunderstood Justice Hirschfeld. All he was asking you was whether you see anything in Article V, or anywhere else in the Constitution for that matter, that says Article V is the only way an amendment to the Constitution can be proposed and—"

Hirschfeld broke in. "With all due respect, Justice Lukesh, I meant exactly what I said. I want to know if someone out there has the temerity to think the freedom of this great country can be taken hostage and extorted."

Slouched over in his seat, as if he were not feeling well, or perhaps just concentrating intensely on the discussion, Thomas frantically inserted the battery and a fresh SIM card into his phone and sent a text to Hirschfeld.

Hell u think ur doing grampa? Playing with dynamite! Literally. Shut the fuck up! LAST warning.

Just as quickly, he removed the battery and SIM card, snapping it in half, and slid everything back into his bag. As Thomas returned his attention to Hirschfeld, he could hardly believe his eyes. In full view for all to see, Hirschfeld casually raised his left hand to his cheek, cupped his three middle fingers to the heel of his palm, and placed his thumb to his ear and his little finger under his chin. The universal sign for *CALL ME*.

A moment later, Thomas tapped one more text.

3:30.

He looked up from his bag just in time to catch the slight affirmative bob of Hirschfeld's head.

"Justice Hirschfeld," Esposito said, "I assure you no one is trying to hold anyone hostage. Or to extort anyone. Plain and simple, the framers of our Constitution couldn't have been clearer. They spelled out in Article V what is required to amend the Constitution. I'm just taking Article V as I find it."

Associate Justice Victor Stone, whose name, Thomas thought, ironically matched his sandy hair and fair complexion, interjected: "Mr. Esposito, I don't want to quibble over the wording. As a recognized Constitutional scholar, are you aware of any language in the Constitution, anything at all, that provides any other means by which the Constitution can be amended?"

"No, Justice Stone, thank you, I'm not. There's no way NoPoli's constitutional convention can be recognized for anything other than what it is: a pathetic, empty attempt to end run our Constitution. If there is any hostage taker here, it's NoPoli."

"Hold it right there, Mr. Esposito," instructed Chief Justice Trotter. "Let's not get ahead of the Court's announced agenda. We will be discussing the NoPoli convention on Thursday. You'll have a chance to speak to that at the proper time."

"Thank you, Chief Justice, I understand. I have nothing further to add at this time."

"Well, then, thank you, Mr. Esposito, Trotter responded. We'll hear next from Judge Brooks."

* * *

Brooks knew exactly what he was about to say. What he was less certain of was what Hirschfeld had just said. And then it suddenly dawned on him. *Extortion. Hostage.* Hirschfeld wasn't talking *to* Esposito when he used those words with him, twice no less. He was talking *past* him, to someone *else* in the courtroom, or watching on television.

And that's why Hirschfeld's granddaughter didn't show up this morning. Someone's kidnapped that little girl!

He had to get through the next hour and rendezvous with Lotello. He wondered if Lotello was having any luck on his own.

CHAPTER 26
Tuesday, May 6, 1:20 pm

LOTELLO FOUND the sequence of events troubling.

Cassie had texted Madison at close to eight to say that she was on the way and would meet her in a few minutes. If she then took ill in just a matter of minutes, wouldn't she have sent Madison a second text that she was going home instead? Especially when Cassie was supposed to meet Madison again in barely another hour to ride to Court. Whether she'd truly gotten sick, or something else had happened, how would the grandfather have learned of that so quickly, and been so completely off his game in Court?

Lotello parked in the lot at the driving range where Cassie practiced. He wasn't exactly sure what he was looking for. Given Cassie's text to Madison, Lotello proceeded on the assumption that Cassie had finished at the range but then never made it to school. He decided to walk the route Cassie likely would have taken.

It took him about twelve minutes. He saw nothing out of the ordinary along the way. He retraced his steps. More slowly, this time.

He would never have noticed it but for the flicker of sunlight that momentarily flashed across his face.

He knelt down. Sitting in a crack in the sidewalk staring back at him was part of an eyeglass stem. He took out a pair of latex gloves from his inside coat pocket and put them on. He picked up the cracked stem and examined it. It looked fresh, like it hadn't been there very long. He removed a plastic bag from the same pocket, placed the stem inside, and zipped it closed.

Lotello examined another fifty feet or so of sidewalk in either direction. It all looked the same, smudged, dirty, leaves here and there, even some doggie remains not too far away—except right around where he had found the stem. That area was nice and fresh, as if it had recently been swept clean.

He took out his phone and captured the entire scene in a dozen or so pictures from multiple angles. Some up close and some further back.

Satisfied there was nothing significant that he'd missed, Lotello hurried back to his car. He wanted to canvas the neighborhood for anyone who might have seen anything, but that would have to wait. He needed to get back to Court before it adjourned at three, and hook up with Brooks.

CHAPTER 27
Tuesday, May 6, 2:00 pm

BROOKS MARCHED RIGHT up and seized the lectern. "Thank you, Chief Justice Trotter. May it please the Court ... Oh..." Brooks pretended as though a thought had just occurred to him for the first time. "Excuse me, Chief Justice. NoPoli doesn't enjoy the unlimited resources at Congress's disposal. We're unable to bring to the table, quite literally, the high-tech equipment my esteemed colleague, Mr. Esposito, enjoys. I wonder if Mr. Esposito might be willing—for the benefit of the Court—to put that attractive visual of Article V back up on his screen. And allow my colleague, Ms. Klein, to use his keyboard for just a brief moment."

Esposito's IT consultant jumped to his feet and quickly wrapped his arms around his keyboard. The man scrutinized Brooks as if his computer equipment were under attack, about to be blown to smithereens. The technician silently entreated Esposito, who waved him off.

"Only too happy to oblige, Judge Brooks," Esposito responded.

Brooks knew that Esposito had no choice given his characterization of the request as a favor to the Court. Brooks also knew he wasn't fooling anyone, but he wasn't really trying to. That would come later. What mattered was that his ploy had worked.

He smiled and bowed to Esposito. "Thank you, Mr. Esposito. Ms. Klein, would you please be kind enough to do the honors?"

On cue, Klein instantly rose and walked over to Esposito's computer setup, putting to rest any lingering suggestion that this was any unplanned epiphany that had just occurred to Brooks. Klein took the keyboard from Esposito's reluctant operator. After a few keystrokes, the slightly altered version of Article V reappeared on the overhead monitor for all in the courtroom to see:

ARTICLE V OF THE CONSTITUTION OF THE UNITED STATES

The Congress, whenever two thirds of both houses shall deem it necessary, shall propose amendments to this Constitution, or, on the application of the legislatures of two thirds of the several states, *shall call a convention for proposing amendments, which*, in either case, shall be valid to all intents and purposes, as part of this Constitution, *when ratified* by the legislatures of three fourths of the several states, or by conventions in three fourths thereof, *as the* one or the other *mode of ratification may be proposed by the Congress*. . . . **EXCEPT AS SET FORTH IN THIS ARTICLE V, THE CONSTITUTION AS ORIGINALLY ENACTED SHALL REMAIN UNALTERED, AND UNAMENDED**. (Emphasis added. Inapplicable language omitted.)

Brooks was in no rush. He wanted to be sure he had the nine Justices's undivided attention. Finally, almost as an afterthought, he stated: "My colleague, Mr. Esposito, would have this Court interpret Article V as the exclusive means by which our Constitution can be amended. In every possible instance, requiring the intimate participation of Congress in the process. Justice Hirschfeld rightfully characterized that interpretation as enabling Congress to extort or hold hostage the governed with respect to any potential amendment of greater interest to the governed than the government.

"Had our constitutional forefathers intended such an extraordinary consequence in drafting Article V, surely they would have included the clear and simple sentence Ms. Klein has added to the above screen in uppercase highlighted letters. They would not have left such an extraordinary power to override the will of the governed to our imagination. They would have been oh so carefully explicit.

"My thanks again to Mr. Esposito for his gracious cooperation in making his technology available to Ms. Klein and me."

Brooks ignored Esposito's obvious ire and instead looked straight into Hirschfeld's eyes, nodding to him ever so slightly. Cassie's grandfather turned his head as if to avoid Brooks's seemingly random but piercing glance.

A defining moment indeed, Brooks thought. *I now know Hirschfeld knows I know.*

Associate Justice Fred Nettleman, generally recognized for his quiet introspection, in contrast to the sharp style of Justice Taser, broke the interlude. "Excuse me, Judge Brooks, I get your point. But not your logic."

"According to you, without the addition of your insert, Article V does not provide an exclusive means by which to amend the Constitution." Justice Nettleman paused for effect. "But if our constitutional framers had envisioned alternative ways in which to amend the Constitution that did not require express authorization in the Constitution, then why was there any need to single out and set forth the supposedly non-exclusive single means embodied in Article V for such specialized explicit treatment?"

Precisely the retort Brooks had expected. And wanted. "Because, sir, I respectfully submit to you that Article V is not a provision of exclusive *empowerment*. As Mr. Esposito contends. Or a non-exclusive provision of *empowerment*. As you would appear to ascribe to me. Rather, sir, I believe Article V is a provision of *containment*.

"The people created the Constitution with no one's blessing but their own. Certainly they can *change* on their own what they could *make* on their own.

"You will recall, of course, that this is our second Constitution. The people created the first one. On their own. They repealed it in its entirety. On their own. And they made a second one. Again on their own.

"The government serves at the pleasure of the governed. Not the other way around. The governed never need the permission of the government to set or revisit the rules that apply to the government. It's only the government, under Article V, that must involve the governed if the government wishes to propose any changes.

"I humbly advise that the intent and purpose of Article V was to set forth the conditions under which our *government* might *also* venture forward into the field of constitutional amendment. But in a highly limited and arduous manner to protect the governed from any mischief on the government's part."

Brooks was sure he had caught those opposed to the 28th Amendment off guard. His argument had not previously occurred to Klein and so it was obviously not raised in NoPoli's legal briefs in the lower court. Brooks had strategically chosen—for the classic tactical element of surprise—not to raise his interpretation of Article V in NoPoli's Supreme Court papers.

Beyond doubt, Esposito wanted to immediately answer back. Brooks could see it on his face. And in his body language. But, alas, his allotted time for this session was exhausted during his own presentation. For better or worse, Esposito got to go first. But he was not entitled to any right of rebuttal. He would find some way to slide in an attempt at rejoinder on Thursday. Two days down the road would hopefully be too little, too late.

For the moment, that left only Hirschfeld. As if on cue: "Judge Brooks," Hirschfeld said, "such speculation as to what the framers of our Constitution intended is just that, rank speculation. You should take great care when you presume to venture into matters beyond your purview."

Seeing the laser-like glint in Hirschfeld's eyes, which he assumed was meant only for him, Brooks did not back off. "You and I have no quarrel, Justice Hirschfeld. We understand one another perfectly. One only has to do the appropriate research, as I have, to move beyond mere speculation, and to know precisely what our forefathers—and *grandfathers*—intended."

Brooks watched Hirschfeld frown. And again look away. Brooks silently vowed the utmost discretion in attempting to help Hirschfeld and his granddaughter.

To Trotter, Brooks said, "Mr. Chief Justice, I've concluded my remarks to the Court this afternoon. I thank the Court for its indulgence, and attention."

Brooks promptly returned to and took his seat. The discernable drone in the courtroom was not lost on him. His unexpected interpretation of Article V had apparently taken most in the courtroom by surprise, including, he observed with no small satisfaction, his worthy opponent, Mr. Esposito.

"Very well, ladies and gentlemen," Trotter announced, "we will stand adjourned until this Thursday morning at 10 o'clock."

The nine Justices rose in unison and stoically exited the courtroom. Leaving the spectators—and the murmur—behind them.

CHAPTER 28
Tuesday, May 6, 3:00 pm

NISHIMURA HAD INFORMED her viewers that NBN-TV would be cutting away to the three o'clock news, but would present a one-hour special on the first day of *Congress v. NoPoli* that evening at eight o'clock. In her earpiece, she heard the words, "And . . . that's a wrap. Great work everyone. In the studio at five sharp please to record our special."

* * *

Cassie woke with a start. She remembered being unable to overcome her chills and deciding to lie down for a few minutes. According to the clock on her pump, a few minutes had turned into more than two hours. *It must be the drug he forced into me.*

She was feeling better, more clearheaded. Time to get up; figure out how to behave when the man returned. She rolled over onto her side. *Ouch!* What was that? She reached into the pocket of her jeans and found one of her golf tees poking her in the thigh. It made her laugh. First, losing her sandwich. Then getting the shakes. Now stabbing herself. *What next?*

To be sure, she was in big trouble. And she knew it. She was scared out of her mind. But it wasn't the first time. Well, yes, it was the first time she'd ever been kidnapped. But it wasn't the first time she'd even been in big trouble, and really scared.

When the doctors told her parents she had diabetes, she was in trouble. But she wasn't scared; she was too young to understand. When she was a little older, her parents described her illness to her, and how she was . . . different. They explained to her that it was serious, but could be managed if she behaved responsibly. She didn't know what managed meant, or how to do it. She was frightened. Big time. Her parents told her not to be, that they would help her. But she still was.

She stopped being afraid when she grew up. When she understood what "managed" meant, and how to do it. And that her fear served no purpose.

She thought back to when her golf was giving her trouble. She had lost a golf match. She was shellacked. It was horrible. She wanted to crawl into a hole and die.

Afterward, her coach had talked to her about what had happened. She said she felt terrible. He asked why. "Because I don't like losing," she answered. He asked if she had been afraid. She said yes. Again, he asked why. Unsure what to say, she said because people would think she was a loser.

"Cassie," her coach said, "sometimes fear can be a good thing, but most of the time it's not. It just gets in the way and stops you from performing as well as you can. And if you can't always control it, never, ever let your opponent smell it on you." It took Cassie a long time to fully grasp that, but when she finally did, she stopped losing matches. Well, she did lose one every now and then. But not many, and never to opponents who let her smell their fear. And she's never been shellacked again.

Besides the fact that fear is seldom a good thing, both diabetes and golf had taught Cassie something else too: it's sometimes okay—even nice—to let other people help you, but the very best help is the help you give yourself.

Cassie had no idea who this man was or what he wanted to do with her. And, yes, she was plenty frightened now, but it would not help her to let the man smell it on her. *Never, ever.*

* * *

Lotello used the pass Leah had given him the night before to get back into the courtroom. As he entered, the security officer told him they would be clearing the Court in a matter of moments. Lotello explained that he was there merely to collect his family and leave. He joined Brooks and Leah at their table.

"Nice job, Your Honor," Klein said to Brooks. "Your gamble sure paid off. The eyes of several of the Justices were up from half-mast to full alert."

Brooks nodded briefly to Klein as the two of them packed up their briefcases. When Lotello shot a glance at Brooks, Klein turned to the kids and said, "Time to go home, guys." To Lotello, she added, "Will you be able to make it in time for dinner?"

Brooks responded for Lotello. "Mrs. Brooks drove us to Court this morning, but had some errands to run here in town after Court. May I borrow your husband to hitch a ride home? Save me the cab fare. Perhaps you would also be kind enough to deal with the press. So the detective and I can duck out the back and continue our lunch time discussion."

Once they were alone in Lotello's car, Brooks wasted no time. "So?"

"I think you had it right, Judge." He pulled out his pocket-sized notepad, referring to it as he continued. "I first went to Cassie's home. Her dad was a wreck, though he tried not to show it. He completely stonewalled me. Said that Cassie came home ill and was sleeping. Wouldn't let me give her a message from Madison either."

"Didn't invite you in?"

"Not even close."

"Next?"

"I traced Cassie's route from the driving range to school." Lotello produced and showed the broken eyeglass stem to Brooks through the clear plastic bag. "Found this on the street a little less than half-way between the driving range and the school. Looks like it matches the sunglasses Cassie wears, at least whenever I see her with my daughter, Madison. The area around where I found this seemed to have recently been swept up. I think Cassie was grabbed there this morning right after she texted Madison."

Lotello flipped his notepad closed, and returned it and the plastic baggie to separate coat pockets. They climbed into his car and pulled out of the parking lot. They headed into the D.C. turnpike commuter traffic and rode in silence for a few minutes.

"Watch your DVR for a few minutes before you turn in tonight, Detective. Pay close attention to the grandfather's remarks to Esposito during Esposito's presentation. I believe Hirschfeld was talking to someone other than Esposito. Listen as well to his remarks to me near the end of mine. He was telling me not to get involved."

"Will do," Lotello said. "What's your take on what I've said?"

"No question the girl has been abducted. Given Hirschfeld's behavior in Court, we appear to be dealing with a group intent on sabotaging the 28th Amendment. They obviously have the poor man under their thumb. Our first concern, however, must be for the safety and welfare of the girl."

"What does that mean, Judge? Just what are we free to do? What are we obliged to do? Especially when the family has told us both to butt out?"

"Well put. We need to address your question both legally and ethically. Let's start with the law. Except for aiders and abettors, and certain professionals who work with children and must promptly report child abuse, broadly defined, to the authorities, the law does not require a third party to report any knowledge of a crime previously committed, in the process of being committed, or about to be committed.

Your Honor. You and I *are* professionals. Do we have to report our suspicions that Cassie is being abused? Also, there are at least two overlapping crimes here: the kidnapping of Cassie Webber and the apparent attempt to manipulate the outcome of a judicial proceeding, a felony obstruction of justice. You said our first concern is to save Cassie. What if that facilitates an obstruction of justice?

"The reporting exception is directed at school teachers, social workers, doctors, folks like that, who deal with children in their professional capacities. I doubt that it applies to other professionals, say an architect or an engineer, who just happen to stumble across an incidence of child abuse simply as a citizen. I think you and I fall into the latter category, but if not we've each reported our suspicions to one another. If the law would cast the net broadly enough to make you and I 'reporting professionals,' I would also argue that it should make you and I 'authorities.'

Let's turn to the other piece of the puzzle, shall we, our *moral* duties, before I respond to your question of possible conflict between the crimes of kidnapping, on the one hand, and obstructions of justice on the other hand.

"All ears, Judge."

"According to historical writings, our laws derive from 'sound moral principles.'

Thus, your and my legal responsibilities must be measured in terms of these sound moral principles. And good conscience as well."

"You observed that the crimes here overlap. I'm not sure I agree. As a matter of moral substance rather than legal form, I believe there is only one crime being committed here. I don't think we have to break that up, choose favorites, and prioritize.

"Bottom line, I'm morally unwilling to suffer the fool who suggests that we must apply any law in a way that might injure the very person it is designed to protect. Our young victim."

"Okay, Judge, that makes me a little more comfortable than I was. But what do we do now?"

"At the risk of further trying your patience, there are three possible avenues we can pursue based upon our newly decided freedom.

"One, we can do nothing, as the family apparently wishes. Leave all this entirely up to them. Part of me wants to do just that. But something about that troubles me."

"Me too. Don't we have some moral responsibility to Cassie independently of what her family wants? Even if she is a minor."

"And what if there are more lives at stake, Detective?"

"I don't follow."

"There are eight other Supreme Court Justices. They all have loved ones. Why should we assume that Hirschfeld is the only Justice under assault?"

"Hard to imagine, but you could be right. I didn't think about that."

"Second alternative. We bring this to Chief Justice Trotter and let him decide what to do. The problem with this is that any one-sided communication with a judge about a pending case is prohibited. We would have to be willing to include Esposito in the process. Unless Trotter decided not to enforce the rule. While academically I have an ethical duty as an officer of the court to immediately report this to Trotter, that will almost certainly lead to a stay of the proceedings. That might be tantamount to signing the young girl's death warrant. I'm not willing to take that chance."

"Not only that," Lotello said, "but this route would become even more complicated if there actually are other compromised Justices. Maybe even Trotter himself."

"So, this brings us to the third option. Going to the authorities. Present company excluded. Or perhaps not excluded.

"So, *Detective*. What do *you* suggest?"

Lotello knew it would come to this. "I've accumulated a few favors. One of the lab guys at Metro owes me. I can get him to run the eyeglass stem for prints to see if anything shows up in any of our databases. Prints of Cassie and her family won't likely pop up and hopefully won't obscure any other prints that might be there. If I can reach him before he finishes up for the day, we should know one way or the other by early in the morning."

"Good," Brooks said. "And?"

"I can also go back this evening, knock on every door between the driving range and the school and see what I might find. There aren't that many homes. I should be able to hit them all before it gets too late."

"I like that step," Brooks responded.

"I could also process footprint and tire track impressions in the area where I found the eye stem. But without more, someone who saw something, those results would probably be worthless."

"Agreed."

They drove on in silence for a few more minutes until Lotello pulled into the driveway of Brooks's Georgetown condominium. Brooks got out, then leaned back into the car.

"Thanks for the ride. As far as I'm concerned, this is on me, not you. *I've* made the right decision, at least for the present. Taking this to you. The *authorities*. You're investigating the matter.

"Call me on my cell whenever you have anything."

* * *

As he entered the front door, Brooks called out, "Hello, dear!"

Maccabee sauntered into the entry hall and rubbed against his leg. That was it. No other response. Neither from Eloise nor Ryder. Probably out walking, he thought.

He exchanged his business suit for his favorite threadbare sweats and drifted into his office. He wanted to think through one or two things before hearing back from Lotello. He opened his computer, not because anything *in* there would help him, but because looking at the screen and typing out a few thoughts he could stare *at* usually helped him to think more clearly.

He and Lotello had discussed three alternatives. He listed them on the new electronic file he opened on the screen.

It wasn't until he saw the list written out that it occurred to him there was a fourth option: He could also try calling Hirschfeld. He was pretty sure Hirschfeld's home telephone number would be in their law school directory. He added the fourth option to his list.

Contacting Hirschfeld during the course of the proceedings would constitute just as much a violation of the rules of professional conduct as would contacting Trotter. But what would he say to his friend and classmate that he hadn't already "said" in the Courtroom earlier this afternoon?

And hadn't Hirschfeld already responded in kind, telling him to stand down?

He continued to stare at the four items on the screen for several minutes. Finally, he added still a fifth possibility to the list, named and saved the file, and powered down the machine.

How long, Cyrus? And why? He waited for an answer. Nothing.

CHAPTER 29
Tuesday, May 6, 3:40 pm

HIRSCHFELD HAD BEEN GLUED to his cell phone from 3:15. Just sitting there staring at the silent apparatus. No texts, no calls, no emails.

He'd felt pretty good when the kidnappers signaled 3:30 in response to his demand to talk. By ten minutes past when they were supposed to call, he was again frantic. He had so wanted to solve this on his own, to safely extricate Cassie without all of this becoming public—and very likely ending his career.

He berated himself for focusing on how any of this might impact him personally. *Maybe Mark's right. Maybe I really am in way over my head. Maybe we do need to go straight to the FBI.*

* * *

Thomas looked at his watch. *Let the bastard wait awhile. Good for him to know just who the boss is.* After a few minutes, he inserted still another SIM card in one of his phones and dialed Hirschfeld's number.

Hirschfeld picked up on the first ring. "It's me. I'm here."

"What do you think you're doing, asshole? You know you're playing with the girl's life, don't you?"

"Listen. If—"

The line went dead.

"Hello? Hello? Good God, no! Please!"

Thomas imagined Hirschfeld glaring at the phone as though it might burst into flame. Having to sit there waiting. Waiting some more. Helpless. Not knowing what else to do.

After five minutes, Thomas figured he'd sweated Hirschfeld long enough. He called him back. "Shut the fuck up and listen to me, old man. Not a word unless I tell you to speak. You got that?"

"Yes."

"Okay. The fuck you think you were you doing in Court today? Playing all those word games. You some kind of a wise guy or something?"

"No—"

"Shut the fuck up! Did I tell you to speak?" *By now the poor schmuck must be realizing he has no idea what he's up against. How to deal with me. Perfect.*

"You asked me if I were a wise guy. I was just trying to answer you."

"That was a rhetorical question, asshole. I'll make it clear when I want you to speak. Understood?"

Thomas was enjoying the moment. *Now he has to be wondering if I just asked him another rhetorical question. Love it.*

"Yes," Hirschfeld answered.

Thomas could hear the desperation in the old man's voice. "Okay, Grandpa. Now, tell me, what the fuck were you trying to do in the Courtroom?"

"Can I answer?"

"Yes, dumb shit, answer me!"

"I needed to talk to you. I tried texting. You didn't answer me. I didn't know what else to do."

"You think I'm stupid? Leave you with a number you could give the FBI? Are you a moron? Do you think I am?"

"No. I don't think you're a moron. I don't know what to think about you. Or whether I can trust you. I just knew I needed to speak with you."

"You don't need to think anything, and you don't need to speak to me. You just need to do what you're told when you're told and everything will be fine. Got that?"

After several seconds, Hirschfeld said, "No."

Now it was Thomas who waited. Finally: "*No*? The hell you saying? You don't understand me or you don't agree?"

Another pause. "I understood you. But, no, I don't agree. If you want what you want, then you're going to have to give me something *I* want."

More silence. Thomas wondered if he were emboldening the old man. Then: "You have thirty seconds. Make it count. Or else."

"Right now, there are five or six votes to uphold the 28th Amendment, including mine. The only way you get what you want is if I flip *and* bring at least one other Justice with me. That's *not* going to happen unless I speak to my granddaughter in the next twenty minutes and confirm that she's okay, that she has enough insulin to manage her diabetes, that she's going to get through this, come out whole on the other end."

"Listen—"

"No! *You* listen. I don't believe you've gone through all this just to lose what you're after—and what I can deliver—just because you've got a fat ego. I'm your *only* ticket here.

"Anyone smart enough to pull off what you've accomplished so far is smart enough to know that. If you're the out-of-control egomaniac that you *pretend* to be, then I've already lost everything I care about here. And have nothing more to lose. You need to think about that.

"If you don't want to lose what *you're* after, then you're going to have to deal with me, and in a rational way. Starting right now, this has to become a partnership that works for both of us. If you can't demonstrate to me that you can function in a way that will get each of us what we want, then I have to painfully accept that there's nothing I can do to save my granddaughter. That she's already dead.

"If that's so, the last thing I'm going to do is give you what you want. Do you hear me? I am the *only* chance you have to get what you're after. If you don't convince me that I can get Cassie safely through this, then we're done. I lose. But so do you.

"Got that?"

Another prolonged silence. "Ten minutes. I'll call you back in ten minutes. Answer with your FaceTime app."

The line went dead.

Hirschfeld was dying inside, if not outside as well. He had no way of knowing where he stood. He wasn't nearly as cocky as he had tried to sound, but what he said was basically true. He didn't believe there was any other way to assure Cassie's safety.

Telling me to answer on FaceTime sounded encouraging. Thank God Cassie taught me how to do that.

Hirschfeld kept looking at his watch. Twelve minutes later, when there was still no call, he started hyperventilating. His back was killing him. His sciatica was burning down into his right foot. He stood, tried to slow his breathing, placed his hands on his desk, stretched out his back.

And then he waited. Some more.

* * *

The horn blasted Cassie out of her malaise. When Thomas had installed it, he made sure it couldn't be heard beyond the remote location of the cabin. Looking through his surveillance monitor, he smiled as she held her ears and grimaced. The noise stopped.

"Listen up, brat," he said into the microphone. "There's someone who wants to see you. To verify you're okay. Just sit up and behave yourself until you hear another blast of the horn." He positioned the two cell phones so they faced each other, the first also pointed at the video monitor to display the girl and the second one, the one he would use to FaceTime with Hirschfeld, facing the image on the first phone. *Won't win any cinematography awards, but it'll get the job done.*

Unsure of what was going on, Cassie did as she was told. She sat up on the edge of the bed and remained still. She was squeezing her hands so hard they started to hurt. Shaking them out, she started to stand, but then remembered he'd said to just sit there. She didn't want to cooperate, but it seemed best to do what he said. At least right now. She sat back down and stared at the wall opposite her. As if there were something there to see.

* * *

Fifteen minutes. Either he'd blown it or this head case was still trying to play games with him. He closed his eyes and willed himself to calm down.

Finally, the phone rang.

Using his FaceTime, he answered again on the first ring.

Oh my God. Oh my God.

It was Cassie, sitting on the edge of a bed. She looked okay. In a trance? Drugged?

"Cassie, Cassie. It's Poppy. Can you hear me?"

She just sat there, ignoring his entreaties.

"What have you done to her? Why isn't she answering me?"

"Cool it, Gramps. She can't hear or see you. This is only one way. You got what you wanted. You saw she's fine. *So far.* Behave yourself."

The line went dead.

"No! We have more to discuss. We have to talk about the endgame exchange and Cassie's insulin requirements."

But the man was gone.

Two times, without notice, the man had hung up on him before he could engage him on these points. When would he have another chance?

* * *

Ten minutes later the horn sounded again. *What's he doing?*

"Hello? Are you there? Why are you doing this to me?"

No answer. She started to tremble, but then gathered herself. *No! No more. Gotta stop this. Not giving in.*

CHAPTER 30
Tuesday, May 6, 4:50 pm

HIRSCHFELD RUSHED HOME FOLLOWING his telephone experience with Cassie and her captors. He called Mark, briefed him on what had transpired with the kidnappers, and told him when he thought he would safely reach the house. Commuter traffic was awful, as usual. He called Mark back, told him he'd call when he was close to home so they could arrive fifteen minutes after he did. He needed the fifteen minutes to explain things to his wife. To prepare her.

Once he arrived home that was exactly what he did. Sitting Linda down in their living room, he ran through everything that had happened since the first text he received in Court that morning.

She listened with an expression of barely contained panic, then rose from her chair, crossed the room, stared out the curtained window into their yard. When he spoke her name she shot out a hand, as though to say: *Let me think*.

Finally, she returned to her seat and said quietly, "When will Jill and Mark get here?"

He felt an oddly painful sense of relief, like something sharp and jagged had been pulled from his chest. She was always the tougher and calmer of the two of them.

* * *

Lotello dropped the eyeglass stem off with his lab pal, explaining only that it was urgent he get the results right away. When the man stared back at him with an expression of irritated disbelief, Lotello simply said, "You owe me, Lester."

His friend looked at the stem from several angles. "Honestly? I don't hold out much hope. But since you're such a swell guy, I'll run the tests myself and call you straight away if I get any hits. Probably won't be before tomorrow, but if I get lucky, who knows? Could be tonight."

"Great. Thanks. Call me on my cell. Not sure where I'll be. I don't want to wake up Leah or the kids."

Back in his car, Lotello phoned home. He'd promised to take the family out for dinner, but he begged off, saying he couldn't make it, something had popped up at work that couldn't wait. "That's okay," Leah said. "I wrapped up my part of the argument today; Brooks has to carry it from here. I'm pretty much just a spectator at this point. I can handle dinner solo."

Lotello could hear the disappointment in her voice. "I'll make it up to you."

"You bet you will." She clicked off.

Given all the back-and-forth between him and Brooks, he wondered if she sensed that something was up. If so, it was just like her to say nothing about it.

Lotello returned to the street between the driving range and the school. He approached the first house within proximity of where he thought Cassie had been abducted and rang the bell.

CHAPTER 31
Tuesday, May 6, 5:50 pm

THOMAS WAS DISTURBED by the old man's remark that the girl is diabetic. He didn't care one whit about her, but it really pissed him off that he'd missed this in all of his careful planning over the past several months. He didn't like surprises. And he didn't like mistakes. Especially his own. He'd have to think about this. Not only about the significance of her diabetes and how that might impact his control over the old man, but also about his own sloppiness.

The grandfather was also proving more obstinate than he had expected. This meant Thomas was going to have to kowtow to the girl more than he planned in case he had to parade her in front of the old man again. He would have to keep her in better condition than he originally planned, physically and emotionally. It also meant he would have to wear a mask when he was with her. If he didn't conceal his identity she would know she had no future, and Gramps might pick up on that.

He unlocked the front entrance to the house, carrying a large takeout pizza with everything on it. Exactly how he liked it. If the girl didn't, too bad for her. There was only so far he was going to go to try to keep her feeling optimistic.

He stopped to turn on his surveillance camera in the room. It could come in handy to show the old man he was treating her okay. Sharing the pizza with her.

He also put on the Halloween mask. The convenience store had a limited selection. Bambi and Frankenstein. He preferred just wearing a stocking over his head, but it made him sweat and it didn't really hide his facial characteristics very well. It was also harder to get on and off, not as practical as they looked on bad guys in the movies.

He descended the stairs, released the bolt on the basement door, turned the handle.

* * *

They sat down to eat. Brooks was distant, lost in thought.

Eloise looked at his plate. "How's your dinner?"

"Excellent."

"And you know that, how?"

He glanced up quizzically. "What do you mean?"

"You haven't taken a bite of anything."

"Your cooking is always excellent."

They returned to their shared silence.

"So, when were you planning on telling me?" He knew she wasn't talking about the food.

* * *

Cassie heard noise on the other side of the door. She watched the knob slowly turn, jumped to her feet, and backed away from the door.

She watched as the door slowly swung open.

A man entered, wearing a mask, and carrying what looked like a large box of pizza. He set the box down on the only table in the room.

"I come bearing gifts. Pizza. Help yourself."

She stood silently across the room.

"Don't you want any pizza?

She remained silent.

"Fine. More for me."

He pulled up and sat in one of the adjacent chairs, and opened the lid. "Perfect. Not a drop of cheese on the inside cover. Don't you just hate it when that happens?" He pulled away a slice and took a huge bite. "Really good. Sure you don't want any?"

Finishing off the first slice, he stood and removed his jacket. Turning and looking around the room for a moment, he neatly set the jacket down on the edge of the bed.

Cassie took a deep breath. "Now!" she said to herself.

* * *

Brooks tried to call her bluff. "Planning on telling you what?" Nothing to tell. Really. Just mulling over some details of the case."

He felt her gaze. No use. She'd get it out of him sooner or later. She always did.

He told her what he and Lotello had discussed. Everything he knew. Everything he didn't. But feared.

She listened quietly. He knew he wasn't going to get off easy. He seldom did. But it often helped.

* * *

Thomas never saw the swing coming. It was one helluva wallop. Caught him square in his chest. When he later examined the videotape, he was amazed. Even catching him off guard as she had, the blow shouldn't have done so much damage. Not with his size advantage over her. But he failed to account for two details.

First, this was someone whose tee shots consistently sent sluggish range balls flying past the 200-yard marker on the driving range.

Second, the golf tee she'd discretely removed from her pocket while he turned to set down his jacket, and solidly wedged between her first and second fingers just before she swung.

He supposed she'd say she'd "nailed" it. As he later learned at the urgent care facility, it was just his bad, dumb luck. The tee entered his chest between two ribs, slid through the intercostal soft tissue laced in between his ribs, and pierced his thus unprotected right lung.

He screamed instantly. The pain was excruciating. The sight of the blood pulsing out onto his tee shirt didn't help either. He heard the air hissing out around the tee still stuck in his chest. He grabbed the tee and yanked it out. He fell to his knees. In a daze. Fighting to remain conscious.

His primal scream apparently startled the girl. She momentarily froze, but then spun around and ran to the basement door. She pulled it open and sprinted up the stairs.

Thomas struggled to his feet almost as fast as he had hit the ground. *Bitch sucker-punched me!* The pain was agonizing. With each breath in, his chest pulsated and emitted an eerie sound. He knew he needed a doctor, but if the girl escaped, everything was lost. He would not survive another failure.

Holding his hand over the burning candle in the aftermath of Watergate, Gordon Liddy famously said you just need not to want to feel the pain badly enough. Thomas needed not to want to feel the pain in his chest badly enough.

He managed his way up the stairs. The front door was open. He hurried through the door. How much of a head start did she have? *She's gonna be worse than sorry! If I catch her.*

CHAPTER 32
Tuesday, May 6, 6:00 pm

"My God," Eloise whispered. "That poor child. And her family. Cyrus, you've got to call the authorities."

"Don't you think that's up to the girl's family? They've told me not to get involved. Besides, I have told the authorities. Detective Lotello. He's working on it right now."

"You're satisfied that's enough?"

He wasn't. Much as he put the best spin on it with Lotello, Brooks wasn't satisfied at all. He had no useful answer for her. He wasn't sure one existed. So he didn't give her one. And right now he couldn't taste her dinner. He didn't tell her that either.

CHAPTER 33
Tuesday, May 6, 6:15 pm

HIRSCHFELD OPENED the front door the minute he heard the car pull in the driveway. In seconds, mother and child were nestled in each other's arms. Linda might now be Nannie, but she was Mom first. No words were spoken. Or needed. They just held onto each other, while Hirschfeld and Mark stood by in strained silence. After a few moments, they moved into the family room and sat on the comfortable, oversized sofa and chairs around the large glass coffee table.

When Hirschfeld arrived home, he began by repeating for Jill what he'd previously told Mark and Linda from the car. He emphasized what he had convinced himself was most important to say: He had seen Cassie and she seemed okay.

"Dad, what do you mean you saw Cassie? How? When? Where? What did she say?"

"Hon, give your dad a chance," Mark said. He reached for her hand, perhaps a bit too late.

She pulled her hand away and scowled at him. "Don't tell me what to say! How could you not want me to know what's going on?"

Mark did not answer.

Hirschfeld then walked Jill through his edited version of what had transpired on his phone call with the kidnapper. "I think I now have them convinced they won't get what they want unless Cassie remains unharmed and well."

"Dad, I thought you weren't going to play chicken with Cassie's life on the line. And just how many of them are there?"

"You had to be there, Jill. There was no other way. Let's not dwell on it. It worked. And I've only spoken with one person. I don't know how many more there might be."

"What do you mean it worked, Dad? How do you know?"

"Like I said, you had to be there."

Mark met Hirschfeld's eyes. "But what's the endgame, Arnold? If you give them what they want before we get Cassie back, what's to assure that we *will* get her back? And how will you ever persuade them that if they let her go first, they'll get what they want?"

"I understand. I don't have an answer for you yet. At noon today, we didn't know whether Cassie was alive or dead. Now we know she's alive, and well, and will be until at least next Monday. That's a start. One step at a time."

"Monday?" Jill almost shot out of her seat. "No way! You're not right. She won't be fine until Monday, Dad. I already told you that!"

"Jill, honey, driving yourself crazy is not going to help anyone. I don't think they'll do anything to Cassie until—"

"You're missing the point, Dad. I told you this morning that Cassie doesn't have enough insulin to last until Monday."

"Right, I know you did, and I specifically mentioned the diabetes to them this afternoon. The only thing I was able to accomplish right now was their general agreement to keep Cassie safe, including her insulin requirements."

Hirschfeld recognized he was putting an awfully positive spin on this, but he didn't feel there was any alternative if he were going to keep things remotely calm.

"Jill, I've watched Cassie refill her pump several times. I've also watched her inject insulin using a syringe. I'm a little unclear right now how this all works. Can you please show me again now because I'll need to pursue this with her captors."

"Sure, I have everything Cassie could possibly need right here. I pulled it all together right after we spoke at noon." Jill grabbed a small leather bag out of her larger purse, emptied its contents onto the coffee table between them, and, in spite of her shaking hands, gave her father a quick course in diabetes management. Hirschfeld watched and listened carefully. When Jill finished, he repeated everything she had done—twice—and then put it all back into the leather bag himself. It was not difficult.

He then asked only one question: "How long will all these supplies here last?"

Jill emptied the bag out once more and surveyed each of the items before her, like a collection of precious jewelry about to be negotiated. "It depends on the item, and on what condition Cassie's in, but there should be enough there for at least three weeks.

"If her insulin pump acts up, which it sometimes does, she'll need to switch over to syringe injections. Cassie knows all about that. I've included syringes as well as pump reservoirs and infusion sets.

"There's also an extra blood sugar meter, finger stickers, glucose test strips, alcohol, cleaning swabs, and four vials of insulin. Everything Cassie could possibly need. I've actually included twice the number of insulin vials required for three weeks. Just in case."

"And Cassie can responsibly manage all of this on her own?"

Jill looked straight at him. "Dad, I thought you knew all this. Mark and I had to help Cassie with all this until she was about five. From then on, for almost seven years now, she's managed all of this on her own. Every single day.

"All I do is make sure that her endocrinologist sees and checks her out once every three months and renews all of her prescriptions. I fill the prescriptions. Cassie takes it from there. And she does it very well."

"Okay. I'll keep the case with me. Somehow, I'll get it to her, if not tomorrow, then by Thursday."

"Dad, it can't be any later than that."

"I know. I get it."

"Are you sure, Arnold?" These were the first words Linda, Hirschfeld's wife, had uttered. She said it softly, and without recrimination. "Cassie is counting on you. We all are."

* * *

With nothing more to be done that night, Jill and Mark returned home. To Mark, they seemed on different planets, not speaking to one another, not even glancing in each other's direction.

He did not share his wife's belief in her father. The old man hadn't even managed to find out what Cassie presently had with her in the way of diabetes equipment and supplies. This won't do, Mark thought. He decided he'd wait until Thursday afternoon—at the latest. If Hirschfeld didn't produce something more tangible and reassuring by then, he would take matters into his own hands.

CHAPTER 34
Tuesday, May 6, 6:20 pm

NISHIMURA WAS PLEASED with the taping of the one-hour special that would air later that evening. "Nice job guys," she said to Elliott and Kessler. "It could easily have taken us much longer."

"I have a question for the two of you," Elliott said. "I think there might have been something odd going on in the Courtroom today with Justice Hirschfeld. I didn't mention it before because I wasn't sure I was right, or that there was anything we could do with it during the broadcast. Several times today, Hirschfeld made remarks that struck me as contrary to opinions he's expressed over the years. I don't have anything any more solid than that, but I wanted to see if either of you had noticed this."

Nishimura's journalistic instincts were always at the ready. She turned to Kessler, who said simply, "Yeah. A few things he said struck me as perhaps a bit off-key as well."

Nishimura took that all in, then said, "Thanks for the tip, Chris. Too bad we can't just ask him. But let's definitely keep an eye out."

She rose to signal that they were done for the night. "I've got a little more work to do here. See you both bright and early Thursday morning."

* * *

Nishimura too had been intrigued by Hirschfeld's choice of words at times, which were gratuitously terse, but figured it was probably just her imagination and lack of familiarity with the subject matter. Now, Elliott had elevated her curiosity.

She pulled up the day's tapes in her office and fast-forwarded to each of Hirschfeld's remarks, watching them carefully one after the other. *Very interesting. Elliott might just be on to something.*

It was hard for her to know if Hirschfeld was being inconsistent with his prior views. The Justices didn't speak except in published case decisions and she hadn't followed his prior written decisions. But he sure did seem distracted today. And anxious. *Wonder why he made those several references to extortion and hostage?*

She went through the tapes a second time, this time more slowly, focusing on Hirschfeld's appearance as well as his words. *Wow. Look at that. Was he covertly motioning for someone to call him?* She thought to look at footage of the gallery and the lawyers seated in the well, but none of that was in time proximity to Hirschfeld's gesture and she saw nothing out of the ordinary.

She viewed the footage again, now concentrating on the exchanges between Hirschfeld and the various lawyers. And then she caught it. The exchange with Brooks. *Damned if they're not double-talking one another.* Elliott's instincts had been right on the money.

Nishimura made a few notes, turned off the equipment, and headed home. She was exhausted, but she wanted to think this over a little more. With some dinner. And a glass of wine.

CHAPTER 35
Tuesday, May 6, 6:25 pm

LOTELLO REVIEWED the completed lab report that Lester had sent to his phone. There were several prints on the eyeglass stem, but none clear enough to check against the various databases. A dead-end.

He'd now canvassed fourteen homeowners, seven on each side of the tree-lined suburban street of eclectic but mostly nicely maintained single family residences that ran between the driving range where Cassie practiced and the school that both Cassie and Madison attended. No one had seen a thing. Another dead-end. He was cold and he was hungry. He wasn't sure which was worse.

He could only imagine how poor Cassie must be feeling right now. And her family. *My God, what if this were Madison?* That thought was enough to make him cringe—and keep going.

There were just another four homes. If that produced nothing, he'd be right back to square one. Could he somehow be reading this incorrectly? Maybe it was time to pay another visit to Cassie's home, this time a little more aggressively.

He knocked on the front door of the next home, and waited. A couple of moments went by before the door slowly opened. An elderly woman in an oversized, gaudy flowered muumuu hanging down to her ankles peered out at him.

"Good evening, ma'am, I'm—"

114

"I know who you are, young man. You're with Animal Control."

"Uh . . . not really. But I am with the Metropolitan D.C. Police. Name's Frank Lotello, Detective Frank Lotello. What made you think I'm with Animal Control?"

The woman leaned out of her doorway to glance furtively up and down the block. "Reckoned you were finally out checking up on that awful business this morning."

Lotello was no longer cold. "Right. Please tell me what happened."

The woman folded her bulky arms. "I was at the door, about to go out and get the newspaper when I heard it."

"Heard what, ma'am?"

"A loud screech. I thought there must have been a car accident, but then I realized there was no thud following the screech. Usually when there's a collision, I hear a screech and then a thud. This time there was no thud. So, of course, I looked outside my window right away. I saw some man burst out of this van and take off running down the street."

"Really. Do you have any idea why?"

"I thought maybe he was chasing after his dog."

"Why'd you think that, ma'am? Did you see a dog?"

"No, not exactly, but he came back to his van carrying something pretty big, kind of the size of a German shepherd. I didn't get a good look through the window, but he put it in the back of the van and then started sweeping up the sidewalk. I assumed it was dog poop. He had a bag. Swept the poop into the bag, tossed the bag in his van and drove off."

Lotello dug in his pocket for his notepad. "Go on."

"He seemed very responsible and conscientious. I just hate it when the neighbors don't clean up after their dogs. I don't see the shit until it gets in my shoes and starts smelling. Pisses me off no end."

"Yeah, I know exactly what you mean. Pisses me off too. Do you think you would recognize the man if you saw him again?"

"No way. He had one of those sweatshirts up over his head like it was raining. Even though it wasn't."

"Tell me, ma'am, did you maybe get a look at what kind of van he was driving?" He waited. And hoped.

"Sure did. It was one of those Japanese models. A Nissan, I think. Old. Tired looking."

"Did you happen to notice the color?"

"I'm old, Mister, but I'm not blind. It was white."

"Any particular shade of white?"

"Yeah. Dirty. It was dirty as hell. Suppose I'd call it dirty white."

"Got it," Lotello said, thinking: Unwashed white, maybe beige. "You've been very helpful, ma'am. Don't imagine you got the license plate?" He held his breath.

"Course not. I wasn't witnessing a crime, or anything. Why would I have wanted the license plate?"

"That's a shame. I own a dog and try to clean up after him. I would love to track the guy down and thank him for doing his part."

"Well, I did happen to glance at the plate as he drove off. Remembered a part of it, anyway, 'DPS.' I thought it was kind of coincidental."

"How's that?"

"Yeah. Coincidental. Here was a guy sweeping up his dog's poop. And his license plate said DPS. For dog poop sweeper."

"Right. I get it. Ma'am, you are a wonder." He got her name and contact information. He handed her one of his cards and told her to give him a call anytime she needed any help.

She thanked him. "Never know when it might come in handy," she said. "Might need help with a traffic ticket some time."

* * *

Spotting Lotello's name in the dialog box, Brooks picked up on the first ring. "Tell me something useful, Detective."

"We caught a break, Judge."

"Detective! Are you trying to make the *Guinness Book of World Records* for the most drawn out call ever? What is it, for Pete's sake? Almost past my bedtime here."

Brooks thought he heard Lotello sighing indulgently. He didn't laugh out loud, but the sigh would do.

"We may have a witness." Lotello reported his conversation with the old lady virtually word for word.

"You really expect me to believe that story?"

"Up to you. If there's a white Nissan van out there with DPS in the license plate, I'll have it fifteen minutes after the DMV opens in the morning."

"Any chance of getting it sooner?"

"Are you kidding? We're not looking to share what we're doing. It's difficult for me to make this kind of inquiry when I can't explain why I need the information. This is the day and age of coddling the privacy rights of the guilty. Not protecting the innocent.

"I won't be able to turn a partial license plate into a full one with as little as we know without the help of a genuine DMV techie I have in mind who I think will do this strictly on the QT for me. Without needing to know why. Another guy who owes me big. But no way I can set this in motion before regular DMV hours in the morning."

"Don't keep me waiting, Detective."

* * *

Brooks hung up the phone and turned to Eloise, whose attention had shifted to him from the book she was reading the minute the phone rang. "Not out of the woods yet, but some progress." He then spent another fifteen minutes explaining to her what Lotello had found. "Do you still think we need to call in the cavalry?"

She was clearly ignoring him. Not that he had expected any concessions.

CHAPTER 36
Tuesday, May 6, 6:30 pm

ALL CASSIE KNEW WAS that the cabin from which she had escaped was in a forest. A great big one. According to the clock in her pump, she had been jogging non-stop for about thirty minutes, and there was still nothing to see but more forest. In every direction.

It all looked the same to her. Having cross-trained five Ks several times a week, she knew she could maintain her pace for a long time. But the problem wasn't stamina. It was all the trees and bushes. They slowed her down. Forced her to zig here and zag there.

She had no idea where she was. Or whether she was going in a straight line. And it was getting darker and colder by the minute. Her pump said 6:30. She wasn't dressed for this. And she couldn't run in the dark.

When she shot out of the house, she had seen the van parked on the road. The one that pulled alongside her when he grabbed her. Her first instincts were to take off down the road, but she heard the man screaming and racing after her. She figured he'd look for her on the road. She thought she could outrun and outlast him on foot if she had any kind of a head start. Especially since she hurt him with the tee and he wasn't breathing well. But she wouldn't stand a chance on the road where he could use the van. So she chose to stay off the road. Now she wasn't sure that had been so smart.

Everywhere she moved, branches tore and clawed at her. Cutting up her face. She tried to be as quick and quiet as she could. But it wasn't working.

The ground was covered with twigs and leaves that crunched every time she took a step.

She hoped she was moving away from the cabin. Away from him. And then she heard him. More than once. Nearby. His breathing sounded gross. Gasping and hissing.

His footsteps crackled even louder than hers. Whenever he seemed to be really close, she crouched down and hid in the bushes. One time, she peered out and actually saw his legs moving past her.

Less and less light streamed down through the trees. She was thirsty. Tired. Cold. She didn't seem to be getting any further away from him. She was *so* scared. *Maybe trying to escape hadn't been such a good idea.*

* * *

As he ran out of the house, he could barely see or breathe through the Frankenstein mask. He removed and tucked it through his belt.

He glanced around. Spotted the girl turning off the road into the forest. As best he could, he hobbled after her. His chest was on fire. He couldn't see much through the trees. He listened instead for rustling branches, twigs cracking underfoot.

They weren't that far from the highway. He couldn't keep up the chase much longer. If she made it to the road she'd be able to flag down a ride. He'd have failed again. *Beaten this time by a punk ass little girl.* He grimaced.

Out of nowhere, she practically ran smack into him. Hopefully, before she saw his face without the mask, he raised his left hand through a torrent of pain and slapped her across the side of her head with everything he had left.

She fell to the ground in a heap. She wasn't moving.

If he hadn't been so incapacitated, the blow probably would have killed her. He wanted to do precisely that, but revenge would have to wait. He needed her alive. For just a few more days.

With a searing bolt of fire in his chest, he hoisted her up over his left shoulder, opposite his wounded right lung. He headed back in the direction of the cabin.

She was heavier than she looked. And damn near as tall as he was. He was having difficulty maintaining his balance. He staggered past one tree after another. He was afraid he'd not be able to get the two of them upright again if he slipped and fell. Breathing was becoming more and more difficult. He needed to stop and rest, but he didn't dare.

After what seemed like forever, and in spite of it all, he finally managed to find his way back to the cabin. Carrying her down the steps to the basement was another matter. Each awkward step sent a jolt of savage pain into his chest.

One step at a time. Stop. Try to swallow some air. Bite back the pain. Let it fade. Then one more step. And another. Each one more agonizing than the one before.

He felt his knees weakening. A tremor ran through his thighs. His muscles were beginning to spasm. Looking down the narrow stairwell, he imagined giving in, pitching forward, tumbling the rest of the way. *No! Can't hardly see anymore. Feel forward for the next step. What would Gordon Liddy do? Keep moving!*

He didn't realize he'd reached the basement until his foot felt solid floor instead of another cumbersome, wobbly step. Stumbling across the floor, he leaned forward, dropped the girl from his shoulder onto the bed, lost his balance, and collapsed smack on top of her.

He just lay there. Not sure for how long. He couldn't move.

Finally, he managed to get back up on his feet. He stared at the girl. She still wasn't moving. He felt light headed. Like he was about to pass out. *What if she comes to before me?* He had to lock her in the room, somehow get back upstairs. Before he really did pass out.

PART THREE

The Next Day

CHAPTER 37
Wednesday, May 7, 6:00 am

WHITE HOUSE CHIEF OF STAFF MANNY REYES loved his job. Most of the time. He was good at it. And the clout—not to mention the perks—were more than he'd ever imagined. In less than two years, Wall Street would surely come calling for him. With boatloads of money. And very little expected of him in return: just make a few introductions and attend some power lunches and dinners.

So long as nothing blew up in his face during his remaining White House tenure.

The problem was his boss, President Roger Tuttle, POTUS, who insisted on micromanaging everything, including Reyes. Tommy Thomas was a good example of how Tuttle could mess things up. And had.

It had been five years since the Norman fiasco. It was not so much Norman and his explosive trial, as if that weren't bad enough, but rather the role Thomas had played in it. At Tuttle's insistence, Thomas had been assigned to keep certain legal theories out of the Norman case. Thomas failed to achieve Tuttle's goal, and two people ended up dead.

Unfortunately, Thomas was not one of those two. Fortunately, he had fled the country before he could be captured and interrogated. Had the truth come out, Reyes would have been expected to take the fall for Tuttle. It just went with the job. The *Watergate* scandal had been Nixon's doing. But H. R. Haldeman, Nixon's chief of staff, and other White House lieutenants, had taken the blame for Nixon and gone to jail. Of course, Nixon was still impeached.

Had the truth surfaced about Thomas, who was to Tuttle as Gordon Liddy was to Nixon, Reyes would certainly have ended up in jail, and Tuttle probably would have been impeached anyway. If Thomas were back, it could still happen.

Only Tuttle, Reyes and Thomas knew the truth. For five long years, Reyes had waited. And watched. Just when he had finally begun thinking all of this might actually be behind them, Thomas was back. Or so it seemed.

The voicemail message had been vague. No name had been left. But what Reyes had heard left little doubt. "This time I won't let you down," the voice had said. Reyes recognized the attitude, the voice as well. And who else would have anonymously said something like that?

Let him down? The only way Thomas could not let him down would be if he blew his brains out. Or let them know where he was so they could do it for him.

He didn't want to share this with Tuttle. But he had no choice.

* * *

Thomas rolled over on his right side and groaned. He was still sore as hell.

His mind drifted back to the night before. He had managed to get the girl back into the basement and onto the bed. She hadn't moved. But he had been in no condition to know whether she was really out, or just faking it. He had locked the door and dragged himself back upstairs.

He had laid down in one of the two main floor bedrooms. Tried to will the pain away. Tried to sleep.

Five minutes.

Ten.

Not happening.

He had used his phone to check on the girl through the basement ceiling camera. She still wasn't moving. He shut the camera off.

He had yelled in frustration. Thinking about what he wanted to do to her.

But that hadn't helped either. The pain continued, and was getting worse. He could hardly breathe.

He struggled outside, hobbled over to a nearby tree. Leaning into it, he scraped his palms back and forth across the rough bark. Hard. The skin on both of his hands tore open. Gordon Liddy had nothing on him. At least the pain in his hands somewhat masked the pain in his chest.

He switched on the garden hose sitting on the porch and washed off most of the blood on his hands. Getting this right was crucial.

* * *

Jill Webber had been sitting at the kitchen table in her bathrobe for the past two hours. Dazed, exhausted, distraught, sipping on a cup of tea in an unsuccessful attempt to settle her nerves. A line from Kelly Clarkson's track kept popping into her mind. It played over and over and over. She couldn't get rid of it. *What doesn't kill you makes you stronger.* They hadn't killed her. Yet. But Jill definitely wasn't feeling any stronger. What she did feel like was giving in to her hysteria, screaming as loud as she could.

The noise from behind had startled her. She spun around and actually did scream: "*Jesus*, don't sneak up on me like that!"

"Wow, sorry, babe," Mark Webber said. "I wasn't sneaking."

"Well, you were." She stared at him, shaved and dressed. "Are you going somewhere? Leaving me here by myself? In the middle of all this?"

"I'm not going anywhere."

"You're all cleaned up."

"I didn't feel like sitting around in my pajamas. We could get a call any minute, have to rush out. We need to be ready. You should get dressed too."

"We have things we have to do right here."

"Like?"

"We have to call the school. Call Cassie's coach. Make up an excuse for why Cassie won't be in school or at practice today. Before they start wondering."

"The two of us? Together? To say she's under the weather? That'll look real natural.

"You should make those calls yourself. But it's only six. Who're you going to reach at this hour? What you should do now is have something to eat. And shower. And put on some clothes."

"Eat? How do you expect me to eat in the middle of all this?"

"Jill, this might take days. Are you planning on not eating for days? Who'll that help? You need to be responsible."

He walked into his office off the kitchen. She watched him disappear. Just like him not to understand her. She didn't have something to eat. She didn't get dressed. She went into the family room and picked up the phone. But it wasn't to call the school or Cassie's coach.

CHAPTER 38
Wednesday, May 7, 6:10 am

CASSIE STIRRED. The side of her face ached. She knew where she was, locked back up in the basement, but she had no idea what time it was. She grabbed her pump and checked. It was the next day after she had been kidnapped. Almost 24 hours had gone by.

She had the feeling she was being watched. She looked around the room. She didn't see anyone. She looked at the camera up in the ceiling. The blinking red light from yesterday was dark. *Maybe he's gone. Maybe he's left me here. To die.*

She took a couple of breaths. Rubbed her cheek. Tried to gather her thoughts. And then it came back to her.

It had been almost pitch black. She had run right into him. He hit her in the face. And then it *was* pitch black.

She had come to, with that monster lying right there on top of her. He seemed like he was dead. Or at least asleep. *A complete freak. Right here on top of me!* It was all she had been able to do, not to scream. But she was too afraid. She held as still as she could, pretending to be unconscious. Hoping he would wake up, climb off her, leave her alone, go away.

And then he did. She could see he was in pain. *I did that to him?* She watched him stumble out of the room. Heard him lock the door and go up the stairs.

She got up, put some ice from the refrigerator into a towel, laid back down with the cold towel pressed against her throbbing cheek. The next thing she knew, she heard yelling coming from somewhere. He was walking around upstairs. And howling.

Then he started talking. At first she thought there were two people up there, but then she realized he was talking to himself. Out loud. What kind of head case does that? *Sure. Sometimes I talk to myself. But not out loud. Maybe hitting him with that tee was a mistake.* She was really scared.

* * *

"Morning, Manny. Pilates in five," the President said, in his sweats. "What's up?"

"Good morning, Mr. President. Only need a minute. You remember the former Director of Security at the Committee to Reelect?"

There was no misinterpreting the look on the President's face. He remembered. He didn't answer.

"Apparently, he's back, Mr. President. Not sure why, or—"

"Jesus Christ, Manny! You were supposed to handle this. You don't understand why he's back? The imbecile thinks I want the 28th Amendment defeated; that he's the one to get that done for me. I retire in two years. I'm all set. Why would I burn through any political capital fighting a popular grass roots amendment like this that doesn't hurt me? I told you to take care of this before. I'm telling you again now. Do not fuck this up!"

This time it was Reyes who didn't answer. Tuttle didn't give him any chance. He stormed out, leaving Reyes standing there.

* * *

Sitting at the desk in his home office, Mark had no confidence in Jill's dad. He might be a capable and respected judge, but he was no match for Mark in the real world. And now Jill was falling apart. Nor could Mark just ignore his responsibilities at the office. He somehow had to seize the initiative.

He opened the contacts on his laptop. The first call was to one of the members of his work team. He caught him on the way into the office. With everything on their team's plate at the moment, and in the middle of the school year, he could hardly say the family was heading off on a holiday.

He explained that he'd come down with a bad stomach bug and had been grounded by his doctor for a few days. He went over what needed to be done in his absence. He never took any sick leave. No one would begrudge him.

The next call was a little more unusual. And a lot more delicate.

"Security. Adams."

He worked with Adams on his company's recently escalated counter-ter-rorism program. Not so much that the board worried about a physical attack on any of their personnel or assets, but rather that hackers might access data on their computers, or shut down their operations altogether.

He wasn't ready to go to the FBI yet. But he didn't know who else to call. Mark had been on the two-man ad hoc committee that had hired Adams. Their families had become friendly. He didn't know if Adams could help, but at least he thought he could be trusted.

"Hey, Larry, Mark Webber."

"Mark, hey. Haven't heard from you in a while. Something I can do for you?"

"Actually, there is. I'm hoping you can help me with a problem, a bad one actually. Or that you might know someone who can. It requires some special know-how. And even more discretion."

Without hesitation, Adams said, "I getcha. Tell me what's going on."

Mark told Adams everything he knew. Exactly what was going on. Adams listened, occasionally asking a question or two.

"Let me make a few calls," Adams said finally. "While you wait to see what your father-in-law comes up with. And while you take care of Jill. I'll come back to you as soon as I can. May not be until sometime this afternoon. Should I use your cell?"

"Yeah. It's on vibrate. Any ring'll set Jill off. It'll be wherever I am. Thanks, Larry."

Nothing definitive, Mark thought, but at least it was something. And it helped that someone more than Jill's dad was working on it.

CHAPTER 39
Wednesday, May 7, 6:20 am

RETURNING TO HIS OFFICE, Reyes called the number picked up in the voicemail system. It wasn't a working number. All the more Thomas's style.

* * *

Recognizing the number on the caller ID, Jill picked up on the first ring. It was her mom calling her back. "Anything?"

"Nothing. Your dad had to go to the Courthouse to meet with the other Justices. To keep up appearances. He has his phone and will call the minute he hopefully hears from the kidnappers again."

"Mom—"

"I know, baby, I'm on the way over right now."

"No. You're not supposed to be driving on your heart medicine."

"I can drive fine."

Jill started to protest further, but her mom had hung up. She was still holding the phone when Mark walked in, looking at her inquisitively.

"Heard you talking. Any news?"

"No." She told him what her mother had said. "She's on her way over."

"I thought she's not supposed to drive."

"I know. I'm going to call the school now. By the way, I received a text a couple minutes ago from Cassie's friend, Madison. She's wondering why Cassie's not getting back to her."

"Her dad's the cop who was nosing around here yesterday?"

"Yes. I won't answer her now. Let's see if we get any news first."

"How long 'til your mom will be here?"

"Not long." She looked at him and shook her head. "You could be a little more subtle, you know. As soon as I make my calls, I'll shower and eat something."

They hugged. Tentatively. It was the first time they had touched in 24 hours.

CHAPTER 40
Wednesday, May 7, 8:03 am

ESPOSITO and his team had just started their meeting, reviewing what had transpired in Court the day before and, more importantly, planning and dividing up the work to get ready for the next day. The highest priority was trying to figure out how to reopen the question of the interpretation of Article V.

Esposito was in a foul mood. He didn't like being blindsided. Brooks had intentionally omitted from his papers his theory that Article V limited only amendments of the Constitution initiated by the government, not raising the point until after Esposito could no longer counter. He didn't know what upset him more, that Brooks had come up with such a damn clever interpretation of Article V or how effectively Brooks had outwitted him.

One way or another, he would slip a response on Article V into Thursday's agenda. Brooks could object, but he wouldn't be able to unring the bell. Hopefully, it wouldn't be too late; Brooks's theory would be percolating on the Justices' minds for a full day and a half before he could respond.

The meeting was about to end when one of the younger associates brought up something new. "Anyone notice yesterday that what Hirschfeld was saying was totally the opposite of what we'd have expected from him? We had him upholding the amendment. It sounds like he plans to vote against it."

Esposito had noticed. But he wasn't ready to speculate on what to make of it. And he had bigger problems than worrying about a vote *in* his favor.

"Let's not worry about hypotheticals. Back to work. Plenty to do. Anyone looking for more, let me know."

* * *

Lotello tried to connect by phone with his DMV contact but the call rolled over to voicemail. *So much for the early bird.* He left a message, emphasizing the urgency of his call, and waited for a return call.

Nothing.

He tried again fifteen minutes later.

"McGregor."

"Hey, Mac, Frank Lotello. Need a quick run on a partial."

"Not bad, Frank, thanks for asking. How's by you?"

"Sorry, Mac, this one's really on fire."

"Aren't they all? Whatcha got?"

"The license plate includes DPS. It's a van. Maybe a Nissan."

"That's it?"

Lotello answered with silence.

"Okay, give me an hour. I'll call you back."

"How about if I hold? Not kidding. This one's really hot."

"An Amber Alert or something?"

Loose lips. "Nothing that dramatic. Just incredibly time sensitive."

"Hold on."

McGregor took his sweet time. Fifteen minutes passed, then twenty. Lotello suddenly realized he hadn't yet filled Leah in on what he was doing. When he got home last night she was already asleep. By the time he woke up this morning she was already off taking the kids to school. *Maybe tonight.*

"Frank, you still there?"

"Right here, Mac."

"Got something to write with?"

"Shoot."

"Plate is DPS173. You were right. It checks out. A 2011 Nissan NV van. VIN is XLMCYZQB7GY009472. Registered to Herbert Johnston, 1748 North Sycamore Street, Arlington, Virginia."

"Got it. What about the prior owner?"

"Umm. Right here. Ramon Hernandez, 11873 Southeast Remington, Cambridge, Maryland."

"What's the date of transfer from Hernandez to Johnston?"

"Last year. April 1. Anything else?"

"No. That's it. Thanks, Mac."

"So, now we're even, right?"

"Not a chance. Take care."

CHAPTER 41
Wednesday, May 7, 8:20 am

His cover last night had worked well. When he arrived at the all-night urgent care facility, he told the receptionist he'd tripped and fallen while out jogging, banging up his hands and ribs. The young woman asked for his driver's license, insurance information, and credit card.

He produced a D.C. driver's license in the name of Robert Gerstner. When he said he had no credit cards or insurance, she frowned.

"I have cash," he said, fingering through bills in his wallet. "I can pay in full."

She eyed him warily, then sighed. "Fine. Whatever. Take a seat."

Forty minutes later, he heard his "name" called.

"Here! I'm Robert Gerstner." He rose from his chair tenderly, the pain in his chest growing worse by the moment.

The doctor approached and offered to help him to his feet.

"I'm Dr. Sangit. Let me assist you to—"

"Tripped and hurt my ribs this morning," Thomas said, the words hissing through his teeth as he waved the doctor's hands away. "Hands, too. They aren't so bad, just scrapes. My chest is worse."

Sangit led him back to an examining room. He took a quick look at both of Thomas's palms. "We'll clean these up, bandage them." He asked "Gerstner" to remove his shirt.

He leaned forward, adjusted his glasses. "That's pretty nasty. How did this happen?"

"Jogging along the Potomac in Rock Creek Park." He tried to take a breath, winced. "Stumbled, fell against a tree. Used my hands to break the fall, but . . ." Another breath, this one much shallower. "A branch was sticking out of the trunk. Jagged, sharp. Actually broke off and was sticking into my chest. Couldn't stand the sight of it. Pulled it out." A couple weaker, short breaths. "Didn't seem so bad. Went home. Cleaned up. But the pain, it's just . . ."

Sangit returned his attention to probing the wound and listening to Thomas's chest. "You punctured your right lung. I don't think it's fully collapsed, but we'll take a couple of X-rays to be sure. If it's not too bad, surgery won't be necessary. I can just use a needle to aspirate the air trapped between your lung and chest wall and reinflate the lung. With some pressure bandages, we should be able to prevent more air leaking into the wrong places."

"Okay," Thomas whispered. "Thanks."

"That will take care of most of your discomfort, but the wound to the intercostal soft tissue between your ribs will remain tender for a few days. I'll give you a shot now for the pain and some strong pain meds you can take for the next few days as needed. We'll also start you on a course of antibiotics to eliminate any possible infection."

Thomas worked up a smile. "Gee, doc, does this mean I'll be able to sing in the choir again?"

For the first time, Sangit grinned.

Two and a half hours later, Thomas was $600 poorer and back in the rented cabin. The girl was still asleep in the basement. He slept for a while himself, but not very well.

* * *

Cassie wondered what their next face-to-face would be like. If there would be another. And when it would happen. What would he do to get even with her for stabbing him? She'd only intended to distract him long enough to escape, not to hurt him. She couldn't believe it when she let go of the tee and saw it there, still sticking out of his chest. Well, he deserved it. She was actually glad she'd done it. Even if she hadn't meant to. And even if he decided to get even. Not like he had been treating her very well before.

The only question was, how much worse would he be now?

CHAPTER 42
Wednesday, May 7, 8:50 am

LOTELLO PULLED up in front of the Arlington address shown in the DMV records for the current owner of the suspicious van. There were also two Virginia drivers' licenses under the same name, Herbert Johnston, but neither of them tied to this street. He had a pretty good notion that the name would prove to be phony, and he wouldn't be terribly surprised to learn that this address was bogus too. This was precisely why he'd asked McGregor for the prior owner's information as well. *Momma didn't raise no dummy.*

Good news, the address actually was real. Bad news, it was a three-story apartment building.

He walked up to the building and wandered around until he found a cluster of mailboxes. Most of the apartment units listed one or two occupants. Herbert Johnston wasn't one of them. Hardly surprising. There were, however, a few units that didn't show any names. Presumably vacancies. But maybe not.

A round, balding man poked his head out of the nearest apartment. "Hello. Can I help you?"

"Name's Lotello. Detective Frank Lotello, Metropolitan D.C. Police." He handed the man one of his cards. "And you are?"

"Joe Turner. I'm the building super."

"Nice to meet you, Joe. I'm looking for a Mr. Herbert Johnston. He gave this address as his residence, but I don't see that name on any of the mailboxes."

"No one living here by that name long as I've been around. Three years. He might know one of the other residents, or be related, but you couldn't prove it by me."

"He drives a white Nissan van. Seen one around?"

"Nope, not that I can recall."

"Alright then. Thanks for your help. Please keep my card. Give me a call if you spot that van hanging around. Don't approach the driver, though. Okay?"

Turner just stared at the card. "I don't want any trouble."

"Me either. That's why I want you to steer clear. Don't play hero. Just call me."

* * *

Nishimura was at her desk bright and early. Chasing her curiosity, she Googled "Arnold Hirschfeld" and found plenty of hits, but nothing particularly useful. A bio on the Supreme Court site listed his academic and professional histories, as well as a number of professional and charitable affiliations. Digging deeper, she discovered that he and his wife had a married daughter and a young granddaughter. Beyond that the information was largely redundant.

Hirschfeld seemed to live a pretty dull life—no fascination with poker, no love of the ponies, no troubled ex-wife—pretty much what Nishimura expected for a Supreme Court Justice. Still, something was wrong. She intended to find out what it was. Given that there was no way she'd be able to arrange an interview with him, or his wife, that left the daughter.

CHAPTER 43
Wednesday, May 7, 9:15 am

THOMAS HAD BEEN up for almost an hour. With Court not in session today, he was restless. The bandages on his chest were tight. They itched. But at least they diverted his animus away from the 28th Amendment. And the girl. His mind drifted back to her, but he wasn't sure why. He wondered what she must be thinking, and whether the side of her face was hurting as much as his rib cage.

He stood up, slipped on his mask, and walked toward the basement steps.

* * *

Cassie heard someone unlocking the basement door. *The freak? Someone else?* She rose to her feet, not knowing what was coming next.

He came in wearing that same stupid thing on his face. They stood there staring at each other. No one spoke.

Was this going to be payback for what she had done to him the night before? Maybe so, but she just wasn't going to roll over. She wasn't going to allow him to smell her fear. Finally, she steeled up the courage to say, "Where am I? Why are you doing this to me? I want to go home. Now."

He didn't answer. Because of his mask, she couldn't see his facial expressions; it was hard for her to gauge what was on his mind. Maybe his mask wasn't so stupid after all, she thought.

"None of your business where you are, or why," he answered. "Say, brat, how's your jaw this morning?"

She wanted to assert herself. At least give it a try. After all, he hadn't killed her last night, and he hadn't come at her in a rage this morning. She also didn't want to give him the satisfaction of knowing how much her cheek was pounding. "None of *your* business." She even mimicked his tone, and mirrored his stance. And if he could call her a brat, she could call him a creep. Which was what he looked like in that mask. "Say, creep, how's your chest this morning?"

He suddenly drew and cocked his fist, but just as suddenly stopped, doubling over slightly and moving his raised hand to his ribs. "Watch your lip, girl," he all but groaned. "Unless you want some more of what you got last night."

Frightened as she was, his unfulfilled threat encouraged her to goad him even more. "And why your stupid mask? Probably better looking than the real you."

This time he didn't stop himself midstream. His exasperated backhand blow knocked her to the ground before she ever saw it coming "Quite the smart aleck, aren't you, kid? I warned you to knock it off."

She stubbornly fought back, at least with words, willing her tears away. "Smarter than you, Mister. *That's* for sure. And why don't you pick on some-one your own size? We'll see how brave you'd be then."

"You think you're smarter than me? Then how come you're the one locked in here and not me?"

It actually felt good acting tough, but she knew she couldn't out tough him like she could out-tough a golf opponent. *Sometimes I do better with grownups dumbing it down. Playing the kiddy card. Maybe that's worth a try.* "Well, if you're so smart, then what's the longest word in the dictionary? Bet you don't have a clue."

He didn't answer. He just seemed to gaze at her through the eyeholes in his mask.

Then, out of nowhere: "What in the world are you talking about, kid? Why would I possibly care about something like that?"

"Smiles," she said, completely ignoring his questions.

More silence. Then: "You're nuts. There's lots of words longer than 'smiles.'"

"Uh uh."

"If that's all you can say, then *you're* definitely the one who's not very smart, and not worth any more of my time."

"Yeah? Then name me a longer word if *you're* so smart."

He paused. "Washington."

"Not even close."

"Where did *you* go to school? I'm done wasting my time with you."

"At least *I* go to school."

"Okay, brat, you win. I'll play along. For one more minute. Tell me why—"

"Because there's a mile between the first letter and the last letter. Get it, creep?"

His breath came a little more quickly. He clenched and unclenched his hands. "That's your idea of smart?"

"You have a better one?"

"Yeah. The reason you're here. That's plenty smart."

Despite herself, Cassie felt her knees buckle. Her skin turned cold. She tried to regain her cool. "What's so smart about that?"

"Told you. None of your business."

"So how long are you going to keep me locked up?"

"Also none of your business."

"It is too. Whose business is it if not mine?"

"It's *my* business."

Once more, they traded quiet stares. Then, after a few seconds, the man turned and left the room, locking the door behind him.

Cassie could not figure out what was going on. She wondered why the man had come down here in the first place; why he almost smashed her in the face, again, but then stopped himself. And why, barely a minute later, he went ahead and knocked her to the floor anyway. *Who is this monster? What does he want with me?*

CHAPTER 44
Wednesday, May 7, 2015, 10:05 am

LOTELLO HEADED from Arlington to the address he had for Ramon Hernandez, the prior owner of the van. He was surprised that Maryland had only one driver's license for that name. The address on it was in Cambridge, but didn't match the Southeast Remington address from the van's registration. The license seemed more current. It brought him to this shabby two-story wood-frame house.

Just as he was about to get out of his car, his text alert sounded, catching him off guard. He received plenty of emails, but not many texts. It was from Madison:

No worries, but can U meet me in the school cafeteria 4 lunch? My lunch is 11:30-12:30.

He looked at the time on his phone and responded:

Be there about 11:30. Wait for me if I'm a few minutes late. Love, Dad.

He knew he didn't have to say who it was from, or to add "Love." She hadn't, but, hey.

He approached the front door and rang the bell.

A middle-aged woman in a bathrobe and slippers, her face a little short of pleasant, answered the door. "Not buying anything," she said. "Not interested in whatever it is you're selling."

"That's okay, I'm not selling anything. Looking for Ramon Hernandez."

"Figures. Over the garage in the back. Follow the driveway."

She stepped away from the door and shut it. Lotello wondered what it was about Hernandez that "figured."

He walked around back to the garage, climbed the stairs on the side of the structure, knocked on the door. No answer. He waited. Knocked again. This time the door opened to reveal a young barefoot Hispanic male probably in his twenties, wearing boxer shorts, a tee shirt, a sullen pair of bloodshot eyes, and a shaved head that hadn't seen a razor in several days.

"Yeah? What up? Who're you?"

"Detective Frank Lotello, Metropolitan D.C. Police. You Ramon Hernandez?

"Shit. I ain't done nothing, man. 'Sides, this ain't D.C. You lost or sumpin?"

Lotello said nothing. Then, without warning, he shot his left hand forward, grabbed Hernandez by his right ear and tugged him closer. "Listen, *man*, you ain't done nothing wrong *yet*. This morning, that is. Answer a few questions for me and you may be able to keep it that way. Okay?"

"C'mon, man, you're hurting me. Let go. Whatcha wanna know?"

Lotello loosened his grip. "Much better, Ramon. You own a white Nissan van?"

"No way, man. Telling you, you got the wrong guy."

"Ever owned one?"

"Why you asking?"

"Because you're the registered owner and it was involved in a hit and run."

"No way, man. Not me. Got rid of that old beat up piece a shit."

"When?"

"When the hit and run?"

"Doesn't work that way, Ramon." Lotello raised his left hand toward Hernandez's right ear. "You first."

"Cut it out, man! Sold the van late March. Remember 'cuz I gave the form to the DMV on April 1st. April Fool's Day."

"Who'd you sell it to?"

"Just some dude, all's I know."

"Try harder. Did he give you a check?"

"I look like a banker? Dude paid cash, man, fifteen big ones."

"And you don't have a name?"

"Just Franklin, fifteen of 'em."

"One more time, Ramon. If you don't give me a good name, I'll pull you in as an accessory after the fact and let you spend the day looking at mug shots."

"Aw, man, dude was kinda strange. Don't want no trouble."

"I'm already trouble. Name, Ramon. Last time."

Hernandez hesitated. Jerked his neck to the side. Lotello heard the vertebrae crack. "Johnston. Dude's name was Johnston. Kept calling him Johnson like in that commercial 'You can call me Johnson' and he didn't think that was funny. Dude didn't think nothing was funny."

"How do you know that was his real name?"

"You think I'm dumb, man? I knew I had to file that DMV form. I made him show me a driver's license to prove who he was. He had a D.C. license. Picture looked just like him."

"What'd he look like?"

"Little taller than me, maybe six feet one or two."

"White or black?"

"Yeah."

"Okay, genius, which?"

"What? That was funny, man. You don't think nothing's funny, either. Dude was white as blow."

"Hair? That's not a yes or no question, *man*."

"Light brown. No buzz cut. No ponytail, either."

"Eyes?"

"Light."

"Glasses?"

"Dude wore shades."

"Thought you said his eyes were light."

"Took the shades off to count out the Franklins."

"Any marks on him?"

"Nah. Don't remember any. Wore sweats. Running shoes."

"So, how'd you and Johnston hook up?"

"Ran an ad on Craigslist. He made the call."

"Happen to have a telephone number or email address for him?"

"Nope."

"Where'd you do business with him?"

"Right here."

"How'd he get here? Did he have a car? Someone bring him?"

"Just showed up on foot. Don't know how."

"Did he say what he wanted a van for?"

"We wasn't playing twenty questions, ya know? Money in hand, take the damn van."

"He ask you about any accidents, or repairs?"

"Nope. Just drove it around the block together."

"What kind of shape was it in?"

"It goes, man. Didn't make no promises. He didn't ask for none."

"Okay, Ramon. That wasn't so bad, was it? Barely twenty questions." Lotello handed Hernandez his card. "If you see or hear from Johnson, you get in touch with me right away. Got that?"

"You mean Johnston." Hernandez inspected the card. "Let you know if I hear from John*ston*."

"See? I do have a sense of humor, Ramon."

* * *

Hirschfeld looked at his colleagues gathered around the conference table. Inner sanctum personified. The process he loved, and realized he'd taken for granted. No more. It was exactly 24 hours ago that his life had changed forever. By those four simple words. *We have your granddaughter.* Never again would he be just one of their colleagues, enjoying the unencumbered luxury of pondering, debating, meting out right and wrong.

Then again, was he among them the only one with such dark secrets? Burdens to be carried upon their shoulders, compromising their perfect worlds and decisions?

Would they soon sit in judgment of him? Understand what he was going through, about to do? Forgive him his sins? Insist that he be expelled forever from their ranks? *Will I give them the chance?*

He had to stop these useless digressions, and concentrate. Right now, only two things mattered. He had to follow what they were saying, what their vote would likely be, and what he would have to do to assure the outcome that would bring Cassie back safe and sound. And, in the meantime, he had to figure out how he was somehow going to get her the insulin vials he had with him.

So far, he was making no progress on either front. Several attempts to text her captors that morning had yielded no response. He might have to wait until Court resumed in the morning, when they would no doubt again be watching him.

Until then he prayed that Cassie's onboard insulin would keep her okay.

As for the meeting, there was nothing helpful. It was clear they were going to find Congress had standing to sue. Some of them really believed it. Some just wanted to make sure the merits of the amendment would be heard. That would only be possible if they first found Congress had standing.

Beyond that, his colleagues were playing it close to the vest. Keeping their votes to themselves. The one noteworthy discussion so far concerned Brooks's unanticipated argument that Article V constrained only the government from initiating amendments. The Justices were impressed with how crafty Brooks had been in finessing his theory past Esposito. Cutting Esposito off from any immediate opportunity to parry.

No thanks to Brooks, the odds were increasing that Hirschfeld would not only have to flip his own vote, but also the votes of one and even possibly two others as well. Absentmindedly, he shook his head, and muttered apprehensively.

Sitting next to him, Trotter leaned over and said, "Say something, Arnold?"

"Hmm? Oh, sorry, Sheldon. Just thinking out loud, I guess."

CHAPTER 45
Wednesday, May 7, 11:00 am

AT THE SOUND of the door again unlocking, Cassie stood up. He entered, wearing that same ridiculous Frankenstein mask. He just stood there, back to the wall, gawking at her.

Finally, he said, "What's the smartest state in the country?"

She silently glared back at him, wondering what was going on. Like most of her friends, she'd known the answer to that silly riddle for years, since she was a little kid. "You came in here just to ask me that?"

"Didn't your parents teach you it was impolite to answer a question with another question?"

"You just answered *my* question with a question. Didn't *your* parents teach you not to do that?" Two could play this game, she thought. If it were a game. "Or to go around kidnapping people?"

"You're posturing. You don't know the answer."

"Okay, say I don't. So what? You win. Big deal."

He didn't answer. Just kept looking at her. The weirdness of it all was getting to her. *Frankenstein* was staring at her. But what was the man under the mask doing? Or thinking?

She said, "Well?"

"Well what?" he replied.

"There you go again," she said.

"Go again *what*?" he asked.

"Answering a question with a question," she clarified. "So, what's the answer, already?"

"Alabama," he said.

From the tone of his voice she thought he might be smirking. "Okay," she said. "*So?*"

"Aren't you going to ask me why?" he asked.

He seemed disappointed, she thought. Perfect. "I know why," she answered, matter-of-factly.

"No way," he declared.

He was disappointed, she observed. "Way," she toyed.

"You're stalling."

She was. For the first time since she'd tried to escape she felt like she might be gaining some kind of an edge. But how could that be? What was with this man? Grown-ups just didn't behave this way. Of course, grown-ups don't go around kidnapping kids either.

She milked the silence a little more, then said, "Because it has four As and a B."

She resisted the urge to laugh, sensing that he may actually have wanted to win, to get even with her.

"Now I have a question. Why did you take off my pump?"

"Is that what you call it?"

"Answer the question, Mister. Why did you remove it from me? Were you trying to hurt me?"

He shrugged. "Not your concern."

"How could you say something like that. It's *my* pump. It's important to me."

"Why? Is something wrong with you?"

Should she tell him? "Not *your* concern."

He turned around and opened the door, no longer looking at her. "Right now, *everything* about you is my concern."

She wasn't sure how much to tell him. "It's how I get my insulin."

He paused. Closed the door. Turned back around and faced her. "How long have you been diabetic?"

"What's it to you?"

He didn't answer.

"How long am I going to be here?"

"I told you before. It's none of your business."

"I don't have much insulin on me, Mister. Do you know what happens to me when my insulin runs out?"

"No idea. You get headaches? Don't feel so well?"

"In a day or so, I go into a coma. And then I die. Is that what you want?"

"Nice try, girl. You expect me to fall for that? You're putting me on. You don't seem sick."

"Not exactly something I kid about."

"In a day or so, you said? From when? Now? When your stash runs out?"

"From when my *stash* runs out."

"And how soon will that be?"

"In another day."

"Can't I just go to a drugstore and buy you some more?"

"You need the right kind of insulin. It takes a prescription from a doctor."

"What kind of insulin do you use?"

She knew. Of course she knew. But something told her not to tell him. Not yet, anyway. She also had a little more time than she was letting on. She was beginning to wonder who was in more trouble here. She was obviously in a tough spot, but he seemed to have some problems too.

How important was she to him? How important was her health to him?

"I don't know what kind. My mom takes care of that. I just know how to use it."

He crossed the room and sat down, not saying anything. The silence was eerie. Once again, she wondered what the man she couldn't see was thinking.

And then he got up without another word, turned away from her, and walked out, locking the door behind him.

* * *

Thomas was on the verge of exploding. How could he have messed this up so badly? Again! First the *Norman* case. Now this plan to make things right. Not discovering in advance that she was diabetic. Not taking into account everything that might require. He hated being behind the curve, rather than out in front of it. The old man had put her well-being front and center. Thomas had to keep her calm and healthy—until the Justices decided the case.

What now? He couldn't just walk into the nearest drugstore and ask for some insulin. Sure, he could break into a pharmacy tonight and steal some, but what kind? The girl *said* she didn't know. If she were playing games, he could get it out of her. But she was showing some real spunk. She was damned stubborn. If they got into a game of chicken, he wasn't sure who'd win. If he didn't hurt her to get his way.

Guess he needed to put another call into Grandpa.

CHAPTER 46
Wednesday, May 7, 11:35 am

LOTELLO FOUND Madison standing outside the entrance to the cafeteria.

"Not a lot of time until I have to be back in class," she said. "Let's get our lunch and sit outside. It'll be quieter, more private."

Listen to her. Growing up way too fast. She'd already turned away before he said, "Don't I even get a kiss?"

She turned back, smiled, reached up on her toes, and gave him a peck on the cheek, then took his hand and led him inside. They got in line, filled their trays.

Lotello said, "Your invite. Your treat."

"Very funny."

He paid. They took their trays outside and Madison led them beyond the quad to a quiet bench by some trees.

"Okay, Princess, not that I don't love your company, but you got me down here on the fly by telling me you had a problem. What's up? You okay?"

She glanced around, to make sure, he thought, that no one else was in earshot. "Okay. Cassie was a no-show yesterday, right? Trust me, that's a major deal. I mean, Supreme Court. Hello? We'd been planning it, talking about it, for weeks. Got school passes and everything. First, she doesn't meet me in the cafeteria after texting she'd be there in ten minutes. Then she doesn't show for the trip to the Courthouse."

He was becoming uncomfortable. Madison was growing up fast, but she was still only eleven. Still his little girl. "Maybe she just started feeling sick and went home."

"Without texting me? Uh-uh. Not a chance."

"Madison—"

"There's more. After lunch yesterday, I saw you and Judge Brooks whispering. All secret like. Then you didn't come back to Court like you were planning, to watch the case. You didn't come home last night until after I was already in bed. And you were gone this morning before I got up. I *know* all this stuff has something to do with Cassie. Are you seriously going to tell me I'm wrong?"

Nothing's gets past her. What happens when she's a couple years older? "Your imagination's running wild, honey. Nothing that unusual here. The judge just had a few things he wanted me to look into. Technical stuff. Amendment issues. Nothing worth sharing. Promise."

"C'mon, Dad. Cassie's not answering my texts or returning my calls. Not yesterday. Not today. She wasn't at school today, either. And her mom hasn't answered two texts I sent to her."

"Madison, I'm sure there's a good explanation for all of this."

That didn't sound convincing to him. It sure wasn't going to convince her.

"Not fair. Do you just expect me to do nothing? How am I supposed to feel about the way you're treating me? Cassie is my best friend. I'm worried about her. A lot. What's going on? And what are we going to do about it?"

We? "Whoa. Slow down, Princess. You're—"

"Dad, you can't shut me out. You have to let me help. I may know things you don't. I may be able to, I dunno, move in certain ways you can't."

He was not about to let her start playing Nancy Drew. But she had given him an idea.

"Maybe there *is* something you can help with."

* * *

Turning down a lunch invitation from two other Justices he really should have accepted, Hirschfeld sequestered himself in his office wondering what he could possibly do next. Suddenly, the text alert on his phone sounded. He froze. His heart started pounding. He couldn't catch his breath. It was all he could do to open it.

We have a situation, pops. Will call at 1. Make sure you're alone.

Fate had traded him one imponderable for two more. He no longer had to agonize over how to reach the kidnappers sooner than tomorrow. Now he just had to suffer—he looked at the clock—until one to find out what was wrong. And whether to immediately share this latest development with his family. Reluctantly, he ruled out doing that until he had something more specific to report. Good or bad.

CHAPTER 47
Wednesday, May 7, 12:15 pm

AFTER FIRMLY REJECTING Madison's insistence on joining him, Lotello pulled up in front of the Webber home and approached the front door. He had no idea what was going on inside, or who would be there. He wasn't about to let Madison walk in on that, not even in his presence. She might have earned the right to a voice, but not a vote, not yet, and not for a long time if he had anything to say about it.

Still, she'd given him some books and papers, and he had them in hand as he rang the bell. If he couldn't use that to wangle his way inside, he'd go the other route, head to the station and pound out his argument for probable cause and a search warrant.

A woman who bore a striking resemblance to Cassie's mother answered the door. Probably the grandmother.

"Hello, my name's Frank Lotello. My daughter, Madison, asked me to drop off Cassie's school assignments for yesterday and today, and to check up on Cassie, see how she's doing."

The woman just quietly stared at him. She didn't seem to know what to say.

"They're classmates," he prompted. "Good friends."

Still nothing. He held out his hand. "And who might you be?"

"Forgive me, please. Where are my manners? I'm Linda Hirschfeld, Cassie's grandmother."

"Right. Right. I see the resemblance."

"I haven't met Madison, but I certainly know her name. Cassie talks about her all the time. This was very thoughtful of you, and Madison. Please thank her for us."

She reached out to take the materials from Lotello, not inviting him in.

Lotello pressed: "Cassie was supposed to join us on a field trip to the Court yesterday, to observe her grandfather in action. Is she feeling any better today?"

The woman's eyes froze in what seemed a kind of subdued dread. Finally, she said, "That's so kind of you. Unfortunately, Cassie's still not feeling very well, I'm afraid. She may be contagious too. I'll give her the assignments. I'm sure she'll call Madison in a day or so."

She took a quick step back inside the threshold.

"Mrs. Hirschfeld. Please excuse me. I don't wish to be rude or make matters worse than perhaps they already are. But this is feeling stranger by the minute. I really must insist on seeing Cassie."

She tottered a little on her feet, quickly grabbing the door for balance. She had that same frightened stare, only worse now. "I'm sorry, what did you say?"

"Perhaps I'm the one who should apologize. As your daughter and son-in-law know, it's *Detective* Lotello." Under the circumstances, he decided against using his full title, *Homicide* Detective.

"Very well, Detective Lotello. Please wait here and let me get my son-in-law."

She gently closed the door. Lotello chose not to interfere.

A moment later, the door re-opened. Mark Webber stood there. Unlike yesterday, this time he looked angry rather than confused.

"Detective Lotello. Did you just threaten my mother-in-law?"

"Threaten? Not at all. Look—"

"Do you know who she is?"

"I do. Please understand. I have nothing but Cassie's best interests at heart."

"That's very kind of you, but Cassie doesn't need your help. She has her family to take care of her."

"Mr. Webber, there's no point in our belaboring this. If you don't step aside and let me speak with Cassie without any further delay, I'll have a search warrant brought here within the hour, two at the most. And I'll stay right here to make sure no one leaves or enters your home until the warrant arrives. If you then continue to interfere, I will cuff and place you under arrest. I don't want things to come to that. I can't imagine you do either. I just need to know what's going on. And that Cassie's okay. Right now." *Getting a warrant under these circumstances may not be quite as sure fire as I just made it out to be. But I'm guessing Webber doesn't know that.*

Webber's shoulders sagged. The resolve in his eyes faded. He tried to say something, but then just took a step back and motioned Lotello inside.

* * *

Cassie checked the time on her pump. It was 12:15. She wondered if the creep were aware that she knew the time. Probably not. He hadn't put a clock in the room. Did he think she'd be more frightened, more submissive, if she didn't know how long she'd been locked up?

She was trying as hard as she could to remain calm. Being frightened wasn't getting her anywhere. All it did was raise her blood sugars, which she needed to check again. She opened the kit, pricked her finger, put a drop of blood on the test strip, and waited the few seconds it took for the meter to register the results: 260. Definitely too high.

Consistent highs were bad, but she'd learned how to behave to keep her blood sugars from climbing too high. Her doctor said she could cheat every once in a while. An occasional date night, he called it. Even if she didn't date yet.

Being held in this room didn't help. The food the man put in here was all high carb. Carbs turned into sugar. She had to "cover" carbs with insulin and with exercise. Her online chat group called exercise a poor man's insulin. Her insulin supplies were running out. She would have to exercise more to lower the amount of insulin she needed to take.

She could do that. But not *too* much. Too much exercise backfired because it caused a form of stress. All stress raised blood sugars. She knew exercise and stress were tricky. Practicing golf was good exercise. It lowered her blood sugar. However, playing in a tournament was stressful and raised her blood sugar. So, she needed to force herself to be calm in tournaments.

She thought about the man. As much as possible, she couldn't let the man frighten her, stress her out. *Well, maybe a little. Like date nights. But not too much. I can't let him raise my blood sugars, make me sick.*

She'd learned to manage her diabetes, just like she managed her golf and her studies. And now she had to manage how this psycho-scumbag-loser was affecting her blood sugars. It would hopefully make her insulin last a little longer. Maybe.

* * *

Thomas sat in the van a few miles from the cabin. So long as he constantly changed out the SIM card and removed the phone battery, he really couldn't be traced, but he still hated the thought of making a call from the cabin. Or more than one call from any single place. Unless he absolutely had no choice.

It would soon be time to make the call, but he first used the surveillance camera to check up on the girl. As the image flickered into clarity, Thomas couldn't believe his eyes. The girl was darting back and forth across the room, pushing off from the wall every time it came time to turn around. Boredom? Exercise?

Despite his sore ribs, and all her insults, he was oddly drawn to her, fascinated by the sight of her charging back and forth, back and forth, arms pumping, hair bouncing. He watched a little while longer before finally switching off the camera app. *First things first.*

* * *

Lotello entered the living room. Mother and grandmother bunched closely together on a sofa. Expressions and demeanor constituted a poor attempt to suggest nothing more serious than a youngster with a bad case of the stomach flu.

Mark Webber went and stood behind them. All three glared at Lotello as if he were pointing a gun straight at them. He felt badly intruding; he wanted to say something to break the awkward silence, but his instincts told him to wait it out.

Finally, Mark said, "Well, you're the one who insisted. What is it you want?"

"The truth," Lotello said. "All I want is to help. I can't do that unless you level with me."

The three of them looked at each other. It was Cassie's mother who spoke, her voice barely above a whisper. "They've kidnapped Cassie. On her way to school yesterday morning."

* * *

Despite the lack of surprise and the awful nature of the news, Lotello was relieved to finally have it out in the open. "Who?"

"No idea," Webber said. "Not who, or how many."

Lotello sat down. "Tell me what you do know."

Webber closed his eyes, took a deep breath, let it out, and said: "Cassie's being held by people who claim they aren't after money. They say that all they want is for the Supreme Court to invalidate the 28th Amendment, that they will kill Cassie if that doesn't happen, but will let her go unharmed if it does. So long as nobody's the wiser about any of this. This is why we couldn't tell you what was going on."

"Who are they communicating with? And how?"

"Justice Hirschfeld. By cell phone. Both text and voice. But it's only one way. No way to trace it. Or even to contact them. We've tried."

Lotello hated to ask. "Do you know what shape Cassie's in?"

"Apparently okay so far," Mark said. "They let Hirschfeld see her live on his phone. The problem is that even if they honor their word, Cassie doesn't have enough insulin with her to keep her pump working until the Court rules on Monday. We have to make that known to the people who have her. But they may not get in touch again before Court resumes tomorrow. If we don't get Cassie more insulin, she'll be in a coma by Friday."

Lotello absorbed everything they were telling him, but sharing nothing he'd learned so far. The less they knew the less trouble they could get into. And the less they'd get in his way. "Okay," he said. "Please listen carefully. I'm not the enemy here. I'm just another member of *your* team. I only want what you want, to get Cassie home safely. Trust me. I won't get out in front of you or do anything unless you okay it first." He stood up. "I'll be back in touch with you today. Sit tight until you hear from me. I won't let you down." He wasn't nearly that confident, but didn't know what else to say.

Mark walked him to the front door. Lotello handed him his card. "Call me if you hear anything more, especially if Hirschfeld speaks with the kidnappers again."

Just as Mark was reaching to open the door, the doorbell rang.

CHAPTER 48
Wednesday, May 7, 1:10 pm

THOMAS DIDN'T CALL Hirschfeld until a good several minutes past the appointed time. Once again to remind Hirschfeld who was in control.

"Hey, Gramps, how're they hanging?"

Hirschfeld didn't answer. After a moment, Thomas hung up.

Another five minutes, another SIM card—Thomas dialed the number again.

Hirschfeld picked up before the first ring ended. "What's the situation you mentioned?"

"Not yet. When I hang up this time, walk outside and stand on the sidewalk until I call you back. Got that?"

"Yes."

The line went dead.

Thomas waited ten minutes this time before inserting another SIM card. Again, Hirschfeld picked up instantly. Thomas said, "Your granddaughter doesn't have enough insulin to last until you deliver the result we require."

"I know. Cassie's mother told me last night. She gave me more supplies. I have them with me now. How do I get them to you?"

* * *

Mark looked through the peephole. "Christ," he whispered. "It's that broadcaster Nishimura who's been televising the case. If she finds out what's going on, Cassie's through."

Lotello motioned for him to hold her at bay, then stepped back out of sight from the door. Mark waited a moment, closing his eyes to compose himself, then opened it.

The woman flashed a blinding smile, a cameraman standing behind her, lens trained on Mark's face.

"Hi. My name's Anne Nishimura, I'm with NBN-TV. Is Jill Webber home?"

Mark tried not to stare into the cavernous lens. "Yes. I've seen you on TV. I'm Mark Webber, Jill's husband. Do you have an appointment?"

"I don't, but we're doing a series of interviews with the families of the Supreme Court Justices. You know, in connection with the case we're covering, the 28th Amendment. This will only take a few minutes of her time."

"I'm sorry, Ms. Nishimura. This isn't a convenient time. If you'll give me your card, my wife'll get back to you if she's interested."

"I realize I don't have an appointment, and I apologize." That smile again. "But this assignment just came up. We have an incredibly tight time window, given the hearing schedule. Are you sure I can't talk to Mrs. Webber now? I'll just take a very few minutes?"

"This really isn't a good time."

"If your wife's not available, then could we ask you a few questions?"

With that, the cameraman stepped back slightly to reframe his shot.

Webber placed his hand in front of his face. "Ms. Nishimura," he said, raising his voice. "I'm trying not to be impolite, but you're not giving me much choice. There's no way we would agree to speak with you without first clearing it with Mrs. Webber's father. There may well be rules against this sort of thing."

"I assure you that's not so, Mr. Webber. All we want to cover is how proud you and Mrs. Webber are of her father. Family background, that sort of thing."

"I'm not going to repeat myself. If you don't leave, I'm going to call the authorities."

This prompted a quizzical smile, as though Nishimura were weighing the odds of calling his bluff. Instead she reached into her purse, took out a business card, and handed it to him. "Please have Mrs. Webber call me if she'd be willing to tell us a little bit about her father. Thanks very much."

Mark nodded, stepped back from the entrance, and closed the door before Nishimura could say anything further. He turned to Lotello inquisitively, who gave him a thumb's up, then both men waited until they heard the TV van pull away from the house.

Mark said, "Do you think she was telling the truth? Do you think she suspects anything?"

"Honestly? I find it pretty far-fetched that she'd be running around trying to interview the families of nine Supreme Court Justices. She's the main correspondent for the hearings, not some intern assigned to do society page puff pieces."

"What do we do?" Webber could not believe what he had just said to Lotello: "We"? He wondered if Lotello had noticed. From the look on Lotello's face, it seemed as if he had.

"You sit tight. I'm going to wait here a few minutes. They may park down the street to see if anyone comes or goes. We don't want to let her see me leaving."

* * *

Thomas listened as Hirschfeld frantically sought a way to get the girl's insulin to him. Very good, he thought.

"There are several trash receptacles," Thomas began, "just inside the National Botanic Gardens, northwest entrance, corner of Third Street and Maryland Avenue. One of them has a '28' scratched on its side. You know, to celebrate the trashing of the 28th Amendment."

"This is amusing to you?"

"Relax, old man. Life is short. Laugh a little. You know that song—'Smile when your heart is breaking'?"

Silence. Then: "Just tell me what you want me to do."

"Roger that. Put the supplies in a brown paper bag. In exactly thirty minutes, I want to see you walking down Maryland Avenue all by your lone-some—no trail cars, no disguised cops. Any of that, I'll know I can't trust you and the girl's insulin runs out."

"I'll be alone."

"When you get to the marked bin drop the bag inside and keep on going. If I see you hanging around anywhere close after you put the stuff in the trash, all bets are off. I'll just leave it where it is and you can spend the rest of your sorry life taking the blame for what happens next. Got that?"

"I'll do what you say. But how do I know I can trust you?"

"You don't. But if I weren't trying to keep my end of the bargain, why would I be talking to you?"

Hirschfeld didn't answer. Thomas could almost feel the hatred radiating through the phone line. That was okay. *In my line of work, you get used to being hated. Sometimes it's okay; sometimes it's not.* "There's more," Thomas said.

CHAPTER 49
Wednesday, May 7, 1:15 pm

As THEY DROVE AWAY from the house, Nishimura's instincts told her some-one had been behind the door, directing Webber's performance. *Let's see if we can't find out.*

At the second corner, she told her cameraman to make a U-turn, ease back up the street, and park within eyesight of the Webber home.

He did as she instructed, then asked, "What's going on?"

"Just a hunch," she responded. "We'll give it a few minutes."

Five minutes passed, then ten. She was about to call off their little sur-veillance when a man walked out of the house, looked around, and headed toward a dark sedan parked two doors away.

"That's not the guy who came to the door," the cameraman said.

"It certainly isn't," Nishimura responded, smiling.

"Any idea who . . .?"

"Name's Frank Lotello. Metropolitan D.C. Homicide Detective Frank Lotello. More to the point, he's the husband of Leah Klein, one of the lawyers representing NoPoli."

The cameraman pushed up his cap, scratched his brow. "No shit! Why would he be here?"

"Now that's a question I bet a great many of our viewers would like to ask."

"That couldn't be legit, could it?"

"I doubt it. I also doubt that it was just a social call. And even if it were, it seems highly questionable for the husband of a lawyer arguing a case before a judge to be visiting the judge's daughter at the very same moment. I'd sure like to know what's going on." Nishimura dug her phone out of her purse. "We need to get back to the studio."

CHAPTER 50
Wednesday, May 7, 2015, 1:20 pm

Thomas wasn't done playing with Hirschfeld yet. "I noticed the girl had a Find Phone app connecting her phone to yours."

"Yes. She told me it was so she could find my phone for me if I ever forgot it somewhere."

"Which means I can track every call you make, and every text you send. I can also trace every step you take. And that's exactly what I intend to do. And what you'd better not try to stop me from doing." Pure bunk, but Hirschfeld wouldn't likely know that. A little insurance to keep him honest was a good idea, a bluff worth taking. "Got that, Pops?" Thomas held his breath to see how Thomas would answer.

"Yes, I understand," Hirschfeld said.

Thomas laughed to himself. The poor sap thinks I'll be able to see him wherever he goes!

"Don't go inside any buildings along the way or use your phone to make any calls or send any texts until I call you back to confirm that I have the supplies. You do and the next text you get will be a photo you won't wanna see. Understand?"

Silence.

"I said—"

"I won't do anything like that. You have my word."

"Excellent. By the way, it might be good to say a prayer or two that I don't get in any car accidents. Could be hazardous to our health, mine and the girl's."

He clicked off.

* * *

Hirschfeld felt utterly isolated. He desperately wanted to call his family, tell them he'd made contact. Let them know what was going on. But he didn't know whether the man really *could* monitor his movements and communications the way he'd said. The risk was too great. Besides, he didn't have much time to make the drop.

CHAPTER 51
Wednesday, May 7, 1:30 pm

MARK'S PHONE VIBRATED. He looked at the number. It wasn't Hirschfeld. But it was Larry Adams.

"I was hoping it would be you. Anything?"

"You first. What about your father-in-law? Any word?"

"Nothing. I tried his phone a few minutes ago. He's not picking up. I don't get that."

He told Adams about the visits from Lotello and Nishimura. "Lotello backed us into a corner. We had to tell him everything. Almost everything. He doesn't know about you. Neither does my family. He seems to be on our side. I can only hope he's being straight with us. Nishimura definitely smells something, but I don't think she knows what."

"I've met Lotello a couple of times. He's a good guy. You can take him at his word. As for Nishimura, if she unravels what's up, you're in trouble. All she cares about is the almighty scoop. The good news is that if she had anything, you'd already know. The whole world would. Keep your fingers crossed. Don't talk to her under any circumstances. Make sure your family understands that too. Do not get roped into anything she says."

"Don't worry. We're all on the same page here." But for how long, he wondered.

"I've been able to connect with a couple resources," Adams told him. "One might be able to help, but it'll take him at least until tomorrow. Maybe

Friday. I know what you're gonna say. I completely understand. But for now it's the best I've got. I'll keep trying."

Mark didn't want to end the call. It was like letting go of Cassie. But there was no point in asking him for more than he had. At least Adams represented a glimmer of hope if his father-in-law and Lotello struck out. "Thanks so much, Larry. Please call as soon as you have anything more."

"Count on it, Mark. You do likewise. Good luck, pal."

CHAPTER 52
Wednesday, May 7, 1:45 pm

HIRSCHFELD MADE it with not one minute to spare. Cold as it was, he was sweating all over.

The hard part had been finding a brown paper bag without walking into a store. It made him wonder how carefully the man had thought through his instructions.

He got lucky. He'd recently admired the artwork of a street vendor and bought Linda and Jill hand-painted Mother's Day cards. The artist put the two cards in a brown paper bag. They were in his briefcase awaiting Mother's Day this Sunday. The brown paper bag was just large enough to hold the insulin supplies.

He dropped the supplies in the "28" trash container, fighting the impulse to look around, see if there was anyone lingering within eyesight. *What would I do if I saw someone looking at me?* Instead he hurried to the other end of the Botanic Gardens, where he sometimes ate his lunch when he felt like he could use some fresh air. He sat down on "his" bench to recover.

After a moment he allowed his eyes to close and let the sun warm his face. He really didn't want to be alone. He wanted to contact the kids. To get in his car and go straight to their home. But the man had been clear. No calls, no messages, no detours inside a building, *any* building. Until the man called him again.

No telling when that would be. What else was there to do but wait?

So helpless. He could only imagine how Cassie must be feeling.

CHAPTER 53
Wednesday, May 7, 2:05 pm

CIRCLING IN THE VAN, Thomas cautiously watched the drop spot for fifteen minutes after the old man left, checking for anything out of the ordinary. The problem was that if anyone were canvassing the area, waiting for him to show, they'd know their job. They wouldn't position themselves too closely to the drop. They wouldn't draw attention to themselves. But they wouldn't leave, either. So each time he circled he looked for familiar faces, loiterers, bench bums, chatting couples. Anyone lingering in the area.

Sooner or later he'd have to take a chance, snatch the supplies from the trash—before some homeless forager did. If the authorities grabbed him, so be it. One bite on the capsule and it really won't matter any longer. *I'll be gone. Knowing I failed. Again. That knowledge more painful than the capsule.*

His luck held. Sometimes you had to make your own luck. He found the brown paper bag right where he'd told the old man to leave it, grabbed it out of the trash, quickly carried it away, didn't stop to check the contents until he was back in the van. Only then did he take a look to be sure there were no tracking devices. That it contained only more of what the girl already had with her.

He headed back to the forest, wondering how long to leave Hirschfeld twisting in the wind. He'd get to the cabin, give the girl the supplies, take his bows. If no one came busting in on him within an hour, he'd go back out, place another call to the old man away from the cabin. Let him go home.

* * *

Brooks paced around his home office, exceeding his quota of exercise for the day. The resumption of oral argument in the morning wasn't the source of his distress. He couldn't get Hirschfeld's granddaughter out of his mind. Assuming his and Lotello's assumptions were correct, what must the family be feeling, not to mention the poor little girl herself?

Why hadn't he heard from Lotello by now? If he didn't hear soon, he'd have to call Hirschfeld, the rules against one-sided calls to judges in a pending case be damned.

Finally, his phone rang. He was so anxious he forgot to look at the incoming number. "Brooks."

"It's me, Judge. Sorry to be—"

"Not a problem, Detective. I was just sitting here working my crossword puzzle. You know how it becomes more challenging by the middle of the week. What, pray tell, have you been doing to while away *your* day?"

"I get it, I get it, but until a few minutes ago I had nothing worthwhile to tell you."

"Nothing worthwhile. How about you let me be . . . the judge . . . of that?"

"Haha," Lotello responded. Beyond that, he just filled Brooks in on his morning, beginning with the DMV, then his trip to the Webbers's home, the family reluctantly coming clean on the kidnapping, and the girl's insulin shortage.

"I promised I wouldn't do anything without their okay," Lotello added. "Right now, I'm totally stumped. I don't have anything to tell them. Or anything more to tell you."

"Not very encouraging," Brooks said. "Insulin's not available over the counter. Hirschfeld must intend to reach out to the kidnappers in Court tomorrow, force some kind of meeting with them in person. If that hasn't already happened. My guess is the family didn't fully level with you today about their plans."

"I agree."

"If possible, you need to stick on Hirschfeld when he leaves Court tomorrow. For now, call the family back, tell them you're continuing to honor their wishes. See if they'll agree to let you know if they hear anything more from the kidnappers."

"Okay, but how long can we continue to let them run the show?"

"I don't know. As an officer of the Court and a lawyer for NoPoli, I also don't know how long I can sit idly by and allow Hirschfeld to undermine the proceedings, and our case, as clearly he is attempting to do."

"I thought you said Cassie's safety was our first priority. Are you changing your mind?"

"There are no easy answers here. A young girl's life against one of the most important cases in the history of our country. And that's if the kidnappers will turn her loose under any circumstances. If you learn anything more from the family or come up with any bright ideas, please call me right away. No matter the hour. Otherwise, stay by your phone tomorrow."

"There is one more thing you may want to know, Judge."

"And you were planning to tell me that when?"

"Just as I was about to leave the Webbers's place, Anne Nishimura, the broadcaster who's televising the Court sessions, showed up unannounced, with a cameraman, wanting to interview Hirschfeld's daughter."

"She *what*? Good God, Detective, you let that slide until now?"

"She said she was doing a piece on the families of all of the Supreme Court Justices."

"Of course she is. And I'm queen of the faeries."

"Webber sent her packing."

"Not good. She obviously smells something. Probably the same Hirschfeld double-talk I picked up on yesterday. All the more reason to keep your phone close."

"You got it, Judge."

CHAPTER 54
Wednesday, May 7, 3:15 pm

STILL FEELING the wrath of President Tuttle, Reyes had spent an already busy day anxiously wondering what Thomas was up to. And hoping to hear something further from him. It didn't happen. Guardedly, he approached one of his contacts at the NSA. That was useless. In spite of all of NSA's infamous wire-tapping prowess, they told him there was nothing they could do if a caller kept his calls short and used multiple phones and SIM cards.

The more Reyes thought about it, the more his instincts told him it was no small coincidence that Thomas had surfaced again out of the blue just when one of the most important Supreme Court cases in the country's history was about to be heard and decided. Reyes could almost see the wheels turning in Thomas's head: The sense that the amendment was a threat to the government—*his* government. And that he was the only one who could save it.

Reyes arranged for several FBI agents to discreetly attend the Court hearing tomorrow, to keep their eyes and ears peeled. Knowing Thomas as he did, Reyes was not optimistic. If Thomas wanted to be in Court, he'd be there. And he'd surely make it his business to be invisible.

CHAPTER 55
Wednesday, May 7, 3:00 pm

ALERTED by the click of the lock, Cassie was up on her feet before the man entered the room. It made her feel more like his equal when she was almost able to stand eye to eye with him. This was one time she didn't mind being as tall as she was. They were nearly the same height.

"What's doing, brat?"

"Just chilling, monster man, wondering what you're hiding in there. You must really be ugly if you think that thing improves your looks."

"Your material's getting stale."

"I'll work on it. You need to give me a little notice the next time you plan on stopping by."

He tossed the brown paper bag down on the bed. She looked at it with a mix of fear and hope. "Brought you a little gift."

"The only gift I want from you is for you to let me go."

"Check out the bag."

She was dying to know what he was so proud of, but she wouldn't give him the satisfaction. "Not interested."

He marched over, tore open the bag and spewed its contents out on the bed, violently enough that some of it missed the bed altogether and landed on the floor. "Look at all the trouble I've gone to for you. The least you could do is show me a little appreciation."

She saw the vials of insulin and other supplies. The exact brand of insulin she used. Try as she did, she couldn't hide her relief.

"Where'd you get this?"

"Was that a thank you?"

"The stuff is probably fake."

But she knew it wasn't. Insulin was clear like water, but it had a slightly different look. Plus, the vials matched the ones she knew, and the sealed caps appeared unbroken.

"Oh, it's the real stuff, kid. Only the best for you."

"How'd you get it?"

"All you need to know is that you now have all you'll need. For a *long* time."

Her stomach twisted into a knot. Yeah, she now had plenty of insulin. But what did he mean by "a long time"? *Will I ever get out of here?*

"If you have to know, I got it from your grandfather."

"Poppy? Is he okay? Did you hurt him?"

He left the room, locking the door without answering her questions.

* * *

Once back upstairs, Thomas pulled out one of his phones. With all of her problems, the girl seemed to be more worried about her precious Poppy than she was about herself. Or all the trouble he'd gone to for her and all the risks he'd taken. With all of Hirschfeld's troubles, Thomas couldn't help but envy him. Ironic. He punched in the number.

"Yes?"

"She has her insulin. Go home, Grandpa."

* * *

Hirschfeld looked at the time on his phone, not believing his eyes. He must have dozed off right there on the park bench. No one passing by had bothered to see if he were okay. He thought for a moment what it was like to be homeless, truly destitute and alone on some cold park bench. But he heard what the man said. And he had to remember that he was not in this all by himself.

He speed dialed the number. He heard Jill's voice.

"Cassie has her insulin."

"How? What happened? Are you okay? Where are you?"

"Is your mother there with you?"

"We're all here, Dad. Mom's holding up better than we are."

"I'm on the way. I'll be there as quickly as I can. I'll explain everything I know."

CHAPTER 56
Wednesday, May 7, 5:00 pm

LOTELLO WAS SITTING with Leah in her home office, belatedly filling her in. "You don't seem surprised."

"I'm not," she said. "NoPoli's board had lunch today to go over where things stand on the case. You know Steve's acting as one of the TV consultants. He mentioned that the TV people were focusing in on Hirschfeld; that they thought he was behaving strangely. They're suspicious. According to you, Cyrus was more than suspicious. I guess I must have been unconscious."

"You don't need to go there," he said. "There's a lot going on. And this is your first time in the Supreme Court. Your hands are full."

Lotello knew she was not buying his long overdue attention, or letting him off that easily. "And driving the kids home from school this afternoon, Madison told Charlie and me what the two of you had been up to on her lunch break."

"We weren't 'up to' anything."

"Why didn't you bother to tell me?"

"I was just about to. It's not like my plate hasn't been pretty full too."

"Well, a little sooner would've been nice, Frank."

"Leah—"

"Go update your daughter."

* * *

"Okay," Lotello answered, exiting from Leah's home office. He had chosen not to tell her that he'd already updated Madison. She'd cornered him the minute he came through the front door.

PART FOUR

The United States Supreme Court Day Two Argument, And More

CHAPTER 57
Thursday, May 8, 6:00 am

IN THE EARLY MORNING DARKNESS, Brooks could barely make out Hirschfeld's features. He was, however, exactly where he said Brooks would find him, between the water and the northerly trail winding toward Georgetown Waterfront Park. As good a spot as any for two people not wanting to be seen together.

The man gripped the guardrail running along this stretch of the Potomac, gazing into the water below as if afraid he might fall in. Aside from the occasional jogger detouring off the Capital Crescent trail, still a rarity at this early hour, they were entirely alone. For the time being.

Brooks walked up and handed the man a steaming cup of coffee, a symbolic peace offering. The man hesitated at first, then reluctantly took it in both hands, as though to ward off the morning chill.

"Thanks for meeting me," Brooks said. "I can only imagine what you and your family have been going through."

"Cyrus, if you could imagine that, you wouldn't have called, let alone forced this meeting on me."

Hirschfeld took a sip of coffee, grimaced, then looked off across the water once more.

"You and I have no quarrel, Arnold. We both want exactly the same thing, to—"

"What's that, Cyrus? What is it we *both* want?"

"To bring your granddaughter safely home. And to let this case run its natural course, whatever that might be. Can we please sit?"

Brooks pointed to a nearby bench. Another small peace gesture. Hirschfeld didn't move.

"Cyrus. Have you told Esposito we'd be meeting? Invited him to join us? You know the rules as well as I."

"I've not told anyone about this meeting, and I won't," Brooks said. "You're certainly free to do so if you wish. Personally, as an officer of the court, I'm much more concerned about silently sitting by without reporting to Trotter what I now know. And that's without taking into consideration my duties to NoPoli as its legal counsel. To me, this little tête-a-tête pales by comparison. Can we now please turn to the subject of your granddaughter?"

Hirschfeld sighed, then moved to the bench and sat. "I'm listening."

Brooks sat down next to Hirschfeld. "Two days ago, your granddaughter—"

"Cassie. Her name's Cassie."

"My apologies, Arnold. I meant no disrespect."

Hirschfeld ignored Brooks's atonement. "Cassie's been kidnapped. I know that. You know that. The man you sent to my daughter's home, Lotello, the detective, he knows that. Fine. Everyone knows that. So what?"

"The kidnapping required at least two people. One grabbed her. The other drove the vehicle. A white Nissan van. An older model. We have the license plate."

Hirschfeld frowned at Brooks.

"How do you know all this? What have you done, Cyrus? Hopefully nothing that might put Cassie in greater peril than she already is."

Brooks recounted Lotello's efforts of the past few days, the retracing of Cassie's route from the driving range, the neighborhood canvass, the lone witness, the description of the vehicle, and its partial license plate.

"Are you telling me," Hirschfeld asked, "you know who owns the van?"

"No." Brooks found it hard to look his old friend squarely in the eye. "I wish we did. So far, a dead end on that front."

Hirschfeld lowered his face in his hands, rubbing his eyes with his fingertips.

"And now there's the woman broadcaster poking her nose in things as well. I assume Lotello told you she showed up at my daughter's home while he was there?"

"He did. Your son-in-law was smart to turn her away, but I don't know that'll do any good. You weren't that circumspect in Court on Tuesday. She's a reporter. She may have become suspicious of your particular choice of words. Just as I did. Let's hope she doesn't know Lotello was there when she paid her visit."

"Let me get this straight," Hirschfeld said. "You insisted on this meeting, risking exactly the kind of exposure you fear would occur if this woman discovered your detective was at my daughter's house, but you have nothing whatsoever new or concrete to tell me?"

"Lotello also told me Cassie doesn't have enough insulin to see her through this."

Hirschfeld glanced away. "That's been taken care of."

"How?"

"It truly is none of your concern, Cyrus."

"You've met with the kidnappers?"

"I didn't say that."

"Then what?"

Hirschfeld begrudgingly told Brooks about the drop outside the Botanical Garden.

"The man I dealt with was hideous. But Cassie now has enough insulin for the foreseeable future."

"Good. That's good. I'm glad to hear that. So we've bought some time." He used the word "we" intentionally. Time for his old friend to realize that whether he liked it or not, they were in this together. "But that just brings us to the next problem."

CHAPTER 58
Thursday, May 8, 6:15 am

NISHIMURA WAS FRUSTRATED. Something strange was going on with Hirschfeld and his family. Something Lotello's presence at the house yesterday confirmed. However, despite hours of online research keeping her at it until after two this morning, she'd been unable to turn up anything useful.

She had to be careful, and not ask the wrong questions or approach the wrong people. The story could be absolutely explosive. She didn't want anyone beating her to it.

Complicating matters was the fact she had to spend much of the day broadcasting the Supreme Court coverage as well. But that might offer a logistical opportunity. Lotello would be there watching Klein, his wife. Nishimura could choose to confront him. If she did and he tried to stonewall her, she could reveal that she had footage of him leaving the Webber home.

She and Joey, the field cameraman with her yesterday, had covered a lot of stories together. He was loyal to her, for good reason. She had him keeping watch on the Webber place. If anyone ventured forth today, he'd follow them.

Sooner or later, someone was going to make a mistake. And she'd be there, to have her story.

* * *

Cassie's normal routine was to get up every morning at five. She usually did that on her own, but always set the alarm on her phone for 5:10 just in case. On schedule, she'd been up for about an hour this morning.

As with many diabetics, Cassie experienced what was commonly referred to in diabetes circles as "dawn effect," early morning elevated blood sugars. No one knows for sure what causes this, but the fix was an early morning compensating dose of insulin or exercise. Cassie's solution was to increase slightly the amount of insulin she calculated to cover her breakfast. And, of course, there was also her morning golf practice.

Her blood sugars this morning were actually a little lower than yesterday, probably due to the lowered stress of knowing she now had plenty of insulin on hand. Thanks to her Poppy. And if Poppy were involved, that meant there could also be some kind of a plan in the works to rescue her.

I have to do my part to be ready when the time comes. Eat, sleep, exercise, drink lots of water. Try not to worry too much in the meanwhile. No golf to practice right now, but she did some running in place, some pushups, and some sit-ups before eating a light breakfast.

As she exercised, she thought about the man who was doing this to her. She still had the feeling that he was more stressed than she was. She needed to keep him off balance, uncomfortable, the way opponents often did to one another in match play golf tournaments. *Don't worry, Abigail, your golf stroke looks really good.* Meaning it didn't. One had to be careful though not to be too obvious with such tactics.

* * *

Adams hung up the phone. He owed his job to Webber. More than that, their families had become close. He knew Cassie. His wife and kids knew Cassie. He wanted to help them any way he could. But the White House? What was he getting into?

CHAPTER 59
Thursday, May 8, 6:30 am

BROOKS WAS CAUTIOUSLY OPTIMISTIC.

Hirschfeld nibbled at the bait. "What 'next problem' are you talking about, Cyrus?" Hirschfeld had softened just a little his initial outward hostility. Perhaps they were moving toward some form of détente after all.

"The endgame. What's your endgame, Arnold?"

Hirschfeld's gentler demeanor hardened almost immediately. He rose from the bench and returned to the guardrail, gripping it even harder than earlier.

"I didn't mean to upset you," Brooks said.

"You seem to think no one has been thinking about this other than you."

"Not at all. Please sit down."

"I don't want to sit. I can hear you fine from here. Just say what's on our mind."

Brooks didn't like talking to his old friend's back. He stood and quietly joined him at the railing. They stared together out across the Potomac.

"With her replenished insulin supplies, Cassie's now safe. For the moment. The kidnappers need your vote on the outcome of the case and, if necessary, your influence to corral another vote or two. They know you won't deliver if anything bad happens to Cassie before the Court's decision. So, for the time being, their interest in Cassie's well-being is identical to yours."

"Your command of the obvious continues to astonish."

"Yes, but what if there aren't four votes in addition to yours to invalidate the amendment? What if you can't enlist another vote or two beyond what you probably already have?

"For that matter, what happens to Cassie even if the amendment is overturned? Once the decision is announced, whatever it turns out to be, what continuing leverage will you have at that point? Do you really think you can count on the word of these rogues?"

"You sound like Mark, my son-in-law."

"I'll take that as a compliment."

"Do you honestly believe I haven't already been agonizing over precisely that? I know I have to somehow convince them to release Cassie first. Tell them that if they honor their word, then so will I. Emphasize that if they won't release her first, then I'll blow their cover, see to it that the amendment is upheld." Hirschfeld's voice faltered. He looked ashen.

"Sorry, Arnold. That just won't work. If they turn Cassie loose, they lose their only hold over you. And once that happens they will *assume* that your priorities will then return to your ethical roots. They know your reputation. Your character. Even if you convince yourself to honor your word to Cassie's assailants over your duties to the Court, you'll *never* convince *them*. They have no honor. They won't believe you'll have any either. No matter what you say. It's not what *you say*. It's what *they believe*."

"I know those who lack honor often have the upper hand. But what choice do I have?"

"Perhaps there's another way," Brooks said.

CHAPTER 60
Thursday, May 8, 6:45 am

WEBBER HURRIEDLY ANSWERED THE PHONE. He knew Adams wouldn't be calling to make idle chit-chat.

"Larry, hey. Anything?"

It was all Webber could muster. No *"How's the family?"* No other small talk.

"Maybe a nibble," Adams said. "I'll come to that, but first tell me if there's anything happening on your end."

Webber wanted to hear about that "nibble," but he forced himself to recount the insulin drop, and how it had almost undone Hirschfeld. He thought about mentioning Lotello's visit, Nishimura showing up, but he didn't see how it could help and he didn't have the patience.

"Larry, did you say you have something for me?" He was dying for Adams to get to it.

"Does the name Manny Reyes ring a bell?"

"White House Chief of Staff?"

"Yes. Do you know him?"

"Only the name. What I read in the papers now and again. Why?"

"Reyes put a call into the FBI last night. Arranged for a bunch of undercover FBI agents to show up at the Supreme Court proceedings later this morning. I wondered if you or Hirschfeld might have put him up to that somehow."

"No. Like I said, I don't know Reyes. There's no way I'd even know how to reach out to him."

"What about Hirschfeld?"

Mark thought about that. Would his father-in-law do exactly what he prevailed on everyone else in the family not to do?

"I guess it's possible. But, geez, I don't see him going off the reservation like that. I think he'd first discuss that with Jill and me."

"People do strange things under pressure."

"I get that. But no, I don't think he's called Reyes."

"Well something—or someone—prompted Reyes to make the call he did for agents to attend the Court proceedings today."

"How'd you find out about this, Larry? And what makes you think it has anything to do with Cassie?"

"One of my contacts, he's pretty tight-lipped, said Reyes made the request, but said he doesn't know why. Frankly, that doesn't make any sense to me."

"I don't follow," Webber said.

"That my contact would know *what* Reyes did but not *why*."

"Hmm, now that you put it that way, I agree."

"I think my contact's trying to help, but needs to cover his own ass at the same time."

"You're losing me again."

"I don't think my contact has a source *in* the FBI, Mark. I think he's electronically eavesdropping *on* the FBI."

"Jesus. Someone can actually do that? Meaning, *anyone* can?"

"Don't get me started. We don't have time. But that's the only explanation that occurs to me why he'd have just the limited information he relayed to me. No context, no background. Just a packet of data he electronically captured."

"Larry, you still haven't told me why you think this has anything to do with Cassie."

"I didn't say it does. I said it might. Think about it, Mark. If Reyes wants to know what's going on in the case, all he'd have to do is set his DVR. Or have someone in the White House do it for him. So, I think this tells us he's looking for someone in the Courtroom not likely to be picked up by the TV cameras."

"Sorry, Larry. Can you run that by me again?"

RONALD S. BARAK

"Sure. There are two possibilities. One, this has nothing at all to do with Cassie. Pure coincidence. But I'm not much of a believer in coincidences."

"Larry, are you telling me—"

"Two, Reyes somehow knows about the kidnapping. But if not from your father-in-law, Mark, then from whom?"

Webber had no answer. Nothing to contribute.

Adams continued. "My guess is that Reyes somehow knows about what's happened to Cassie, and is trying to identify, contact, or even apprehend, the kidnappers."

"You think they may be *in* the Courtroom?"

"To keep an eye on Hirschfeld, yeah. Maybe. But the bigger question to me is if Hirschfeld *didn't* reach out to Reyes, then why the hell's Reyes involved?"

"Larry, are you saying the White House might have something to do with this? With Cassie's kidnapping?"

"Well, the amendment is pretty unpopular in political circles. In any event, my contact says he'll follow up with me as soon as he knows something more. As soon as I know, you'll know."

Webber felt as though the ground beneath him was giving way. *What am I supposed to do now?*

CHAPTER 61
Thursday, May 8, 6:55 am

BROOKS THOUGHT BACK to the first time he had heard about it. Freshman year philosophy. "Occam's razor." A fundamental principle of argument often referred to as the law of parsimony, or efficiency. Among competing hypotheses that predict equally well, the one with the least number of assumptions, or variables, should be viewed as correct.

In Cassie's circumstance, each side had virtually the same single assumption: *Man is driven solely by self-interest.* The corresponding hypothesis: *Whoever goes first loses.*

Brooks knew a different hypothesis was needed, one that would equally favor both sides. He expounded on his clipped suggestion to Hirschfeld that there might be another way. "I do believe there's another way, Arnold. A way to break the logjam that might be acceptable to both sides."

"But you said they have no honor."

"I did. And they don't. But there might be a way around that. Let's dig a little deeper.

"I want to buy your house. And you're willing to sell it to me. We've agreed on the price. Do I pay you the purchase price first or do you record the title deed in my favor first?"

"I don't follow."

"The answer is neither. I deliver my money 'in escrow' to a mutually agreeable and trustworthy third party, referred to as an escrow agent. You deliver the deed to that same third party. He records the deed in my favor and simultaneously releases my payment to you. We both get what we want, but neither of us had to go first."

"I'll remember that, Cyrus, the next time I purchase a piece of property. For God's sake—"

"Stay with me, Arnold. If only one of us performs, depositing the money or the deed in the escrow account, the escrow agent returns the performing party's consideration and the deal is off. No downside for either party. People have been successfully breaking logjams and doing business this way for centuries. And often in strict confidence."

"You honestly expect to enlist a title company in a kidnap scheme?"

"Not a title company, no. Give me a little credit, Arnold. But a middleman, yes. Someone each side trusts implicitly to follow the simple—confidential— ground rules."

"We're back to trust again. But that's the problem, Cyrus. There's no trust here."

"That's really not so unusual, Arnold. It's actually quite common. Through an escrow arrangement, each side gets what it wants, but neither has to take the risk of going first. Having to trust the other side. They only have to trust the middleman."

"And where does one find the mutually agreed upon third party? On Craigslist? Under Reputable Scoundrels?"

"I've actually been giving that some thought, Arnold."

"You know it won't work here, Cyrus. In an escrow you have an exchange of a lawful sum of money for a lawful deed of title to property in a lawful escrow transaction. Here we are talking about an unlawful exchange of an unlawfully held child for an unlawful abuse of judicial authority."

"Now who's overcooking things, Arnold?"

"Do you really think some mutually agreeable third party exists who will do this? Someone, in particular, who would agree to return Cassie to her kidnappers if the 28th Amendment is upheld in spite of my voting to invalidate it?"

"I'm working on that, including the fact that just because the hijackers and you are doing something unlawful doesn't necessarily mean that the middleman escrow agent is."

"Cyrus, putting that aside for the moment, how would I deliver my vote into such a theoretical escrow in human traffic?"

"It's the same idea as the house sale escrow. The kidnappers would deposit Cassie with the middleman. If the Supreme Court invalidates the amendment, Cassie is released to you. If the Supreme Court upholds the amendment, Cassie is returned to her kidnappers. That latter prospect would, of course, be catastrophic. But please keep in mind we are only discussing how to circumvent the issue of trust and either side having to bear the risk of going first. This is not a plan on how to go in with guns blazing to shoot the kidnappers and free Cassie."

Hirschfeld glanced at his watch. "I'm sorry, Cyrus. I know you're trying, but this is just too much for me to process and I simply don't have any more time for this. Even if I did, do you actually have someone in mind, someone each side might trust, someone who'd be willing to—"

"And if I do?"

CHAPTER 62
Thursday, May 8, 7:30 am

WEBBER REALIZED there was nothing more he could accomplish at home. Jill would be here, and her mom said she would be too.

He had quickly showered, shaved, and dressed. He explained to Jill that he needed to do something, anything, take a walk, clear his head.

Secretly, he intended to go to the Courthouse and see if he could possibly detect anyone particularly interested in Hirschfeld. If not, then maybe he'd spot the FBI agents, see what or who they were focused on. It was a long shot, sure, but he just couldn't sit around anymore doing nothing in the face of what Adams had just told him.

He didn't tell Jill his real destination, or about his conversation with Adams, either. He didn't want any arguments, and he had little time to spare if he were going to get to the Courtroom and find a seat. He would be gone longer than a walk around the block would take. He'd have to deal with that later. Somehow.

* * *

As soon as Brooks and Hirschfeld had parted company, Brooks placed the call.

Lotello answered on the first ring. "How'd it go?"

"Not so bad. At least he didn't reject it out of hand. He listened. He's thinking."

"Of course he listened. He's desperate."

"He can't imagine someone out there who would actually agree to accept the youngster in escrow. Because each principal is engaged in unlawful activity, Hirschfeld assumes that the escrow agent would also be engaged in unlawful activity."

"Judge, certainly you've heard of the word 'accessory.'"

"Are all homicides criminal, Detective? Aren't there instances where the law recognizes a homicide as justifiable or excusable? Besides, it's one thing to aid in a kidnapping. It's quite another to aid in its possible unwinding."

"I don't know," Lotello said. "It seems to me like the ice is pretty thin out there where you're skating."

"Do you really think the escrow agent here would be doing a bad thing, something for which he should be branded a criminal and punished by the law?"

"In a word? Yes. And I doubt that I'm alone."

"You're reacting emotionally. Give me twelve jurors, and I'm sure I'd prove you wrong."

"You really want me to chase this down?"

"Exactly as we discussed last night. Go meet with him, see if he'll agree to do it."

They hung up. Brooks wasn't half as confident as he'd tried to sound. But he wasn't about to defeat the narrative before it was fully vetted. That's what lawyers do. *Speaking of which, I have a case to go win.*

* * *

Joey watched Mark Webber pull out of his driveway. He waited a moment, then started his engine and followed from a safe distance.

* * *

Thomas pulled into the parking lot adjacent to the Courthouse, feeling confident he'd be able to reclaim the same seat as before, and find his cell phones waiting for him, taped in place. If not, he'd have to fall back on Plan B, the nearby sports bar.

His mind wandered to Reyes. He wondered what Reyes thought about the voicemail message he had left. Thomas hadn't left his name, but would that matter? It had been a while since they'd last spoken, but Thomas wouldn't likely have forgotten Thomas's voice, all they had been through together. As loyal teammates.

Thomas would call Reyes again this evening. He wanted to make sure they knew they could still count on him.

CHAPTER 63
Thursday, May 8, 9:15 am

CASSIE WAS BORED. After breakfast, she'd spent some time looking through the school material in her backpack, but she didn't know what assignments the teachers would be giving. Deciding to err on the side of too much rather than too little, she pushed herself several chapters ahead of where they'd left off. It wasn't as if she didn't have the time!

She also decided to go through another hour of exercise, not just to help her blood sugars but also to maintain her conditioning.

* * *

With a few minutes left before Thomas had to queue up in the Courtroom admission line, he switched on his phone and launched the camera app.

Geez, the girl was at it again. All she did was exercise. What a waste. Not going to make a damn bit of difference in the end anyway.

* * *

She'd been jogging in place for about twenty minutes when she heard the ceiling camera start humming again. Maybe another chance to make him feel guilty. "Hey, can you hear me? Does that thing have a microphone? You know, it's really become kind of lonely around here. If it's not too much to ask, could you please maybe bring me some books or magazines to read? Maybe some puzzles. Anything like that."

No answer. After only a moment, the light on the camera went out.

So much for that bright idea. Time for a little cardio. She shadow-boxed for a few minutes, working in several types of kicks—ax, hook, butterfly, roundhouse—and then collapsed onto her bed. For variety, she liked working on the self-defense stuff. *Never know when it might come in handy.*

She was trying so hard to keep her spirits up, to stay positive, but it wasn't easy. She missed her family. And her friends. A lot. She even missed taking Whitney out for his morning walks.

And no matter how hard she tried to push it away, she was incredibly frightened. The man really scared her. He was just too weird. She tried not to think about it, but she couldn't help wondering how long she was going to be here, and what was going to happen to her. *If I get out of here, I'll never complain about my chores again.*

The workouts helped. They kept her mind off things, and she knew they lowered her blood sugars. But then, without warning, it all closed in on her. She couldn't catch her breath. She felt like she was suffocating. And then the dam just burst wide open, and the tears came flooding down her cheeks.

But then, slowly, she thought of the man again. And the fact that he could turn that camera on again anytime he wanted, and start spying on her again. She *hated* that. And she hated him. *Stop it! Concentrate. Deep breaths. In. Out. In. Out.* She wiped her face off on her sleeves and gradually pulled herself back. She couldn't let him see her like that.

As she drifted off to sleep, her mind returned to the insulin supplies the man had brought to her yesterday. And that he had mentioned her poppy rather than her mom or dad.

CHAPTER 64
Thursday, May 8, 9:30 am

IN SPITE of arranging for FBI agents to be in the Courtroom for the remainder of the case, Reyes had decided to spend the morning there himself. Maybe the afternoon as well. He'd provided a description of Thomas, but knew he'd personally have the best chance of recognizing him. Assuming Thomas was even in the Courtroom. He alerted the lead agent at the back of the Courtroom of his presence, scanned the gallery, then took a seat in the rear with a good vantage point.

* * *

Thomas closed his eyes. He thought about how the girl wanted him to get her some reading material and puzzles. Quite the little princess. Like Thomas was her manservant. Like he had nothing better to do. Her poppy might hang on her every wish, but certainly not Thomas. *Besides, how would I know what girls her age like to read? And why would I even care?*

He reopened his eyes. Off to his right, less than ten feet away, he saw none other than Manny Reyes speaking with some guy wearing an earpiece. As Thomas continued to watch out of the corner of his eye, the two men finished speaking and Reyes took a seat in the back of the gallery. Glancing around the Courtroom as inconspicuously as possible, Thomas spotted at least three more suits with the same earpieces.

These agents weren't in the Courtroom on Tuesday, but here they were today. He thought about what their sudden interest in the case might be, and whether it possibly had anything to do with him. He had left a voicemail message for Reyes after legal argument on Tuesday, but his message was perfectly harmless and he hadn't said anything about why he was in town.

Still, Reyes was nobody's fool. He could have reasoned that if Thomas had chosen to return to D.C. at this particular moment, it might well be due to some interest in the 28th Amendment Supreme Court goings on. But such interest on the part of a loyal soldier and teammate shouldn't be of any concern to Reyes.

If Reyes were now looking for Thomas, there could only be one possible explanation: Hirschfeld must have broken his compact with Thomas, talked to someone about the girl, perhaps even to Reyes himself. No matter how, it appeared that Reyes was now aware of what was going on, had probably connected it to Thomas due to his voicemail message, and was apparently upset with Thomas for not coordinating his plans with Tuttle and Reyes in advance.

Girl wants magazines and puzzles? Yeah, right. What for? Your precious grandpa just let you down, big time. You're not going to need any damn magazines and puzzles.

* * *

Nishimura, Elliott, and Kessler had just spent thirty minutes reminding the television audience what arguments they would be hearing this morning. Fortunately, this was pretty much per script and pro forma because Nishimura's mind was elsewhere. She was anxious to know if Joey were having any luck. *Why hasn't he called?*

* * *

When Webber first entered the Courtroom, he also managed to find a seat at the rear of the gallery. He noticed two conspicuous men standing together near the entrance.

The large one, resembling an NFL lineman, was wearing one of those Bluetooth earpieces. The other bore a distinct resemblance to the images he had poured over after speaking with Adams, and Googling "White House Chief of Staff Manuel Reyes."

Adams was right. Reyes was somehow involved. Mark felt his pulse quicken. It took everything in his power not to get up, rush over to them and shout: "*What have you done with my daughter?*"

CHAPTER 65
Thursday, May 8, 10 am

WITH LEAH KLEIN seated to his right, Brooks watched Hirschfeld and his eight colleagues take their seats. It was precisely ten o'clock. Standing at the lectern before the Court Marshall had even conducted his opening ritual, Esposito appeared to be wound really tight. Trotter greeted everyone, both those in the Courtroom and those watching on television. He invited Esposito to begin his remarks and reminded him that he had one hour. Meaning, Brooks noted, whatever portion of that one hour the Justices didn't appropriate for themselves.

Brooks knew as well what needed to be said on NoPoli's behalf in the second hour, but, of course, that would have to be refined on the fly depending on what transpired in the next sixty minutes.

"Good morning, Your Honors," Esposito began. "If it pleases the Court, Article V of the Constitution sets forth the two procedures by which the Constitution can be amended. First—"

"Excuse me, counsel." It was Chief Justice Trotter. "I know I'm losing track of these things in my advancing age, but isn't this Thursday morning?"

Brooks smiled at the attempt at levity, no doubt heightened by the presence of the TV cameras. This was at Esposito's expense, and on his clock. It was fine with Brooks.

"I'm sorry, Your Honor," Esposito responded. "I don't think I follow your point?"

"Our discussion of Article V was Tuesday afternoon. This morning is reserved for consideration of the NoPoli constitutional convention."

"Yes, Chief Justice, you are, of course, correct, but discussing NoPoli's so-called constitutional convention without some contextual background would, I respectfully submit, be difficult. Especially when circumstances prevented me from fully addressing Article V on Tuesday."

With a slight wag of his head, it was now Brooks's turn to feign confusion. And innocence.

"Very well, Mr. Esposito," Trotter said, "I suppose a little context would be fair. Forgive my intrusion."

"Not at all, Your Honor. As I was saying, Article V spells out how the Constitution may be amended. The NoPoli convention was not conducted in accordance with—"

Justice Taser was all but up on her feet. "That's not context, Mr. Esposito. That's argument. If all you have to say about the NoPoli convention is that it was conducted outside your take on the scope of Article V, I think we can all acknowledge your position and you can yield the floor to Judge Brooks. Do you or do you not wish to be heard further about the actual characteristics of the NoPoli convention?"

"I do, Justice Taser."

"Well please proceed then. I'm sure all of us would like to hear what you have to say about the actual convention before you run out of your allotted time to say it."

No doubt Brooks was enjoying Taser a lot more than Esposito. He couldn't be sure if it were just her style or her obvious support of the 28th Amendment, but either way Taser was doing all she could to prevent Esposito from finding his rhythm. And eating into his time as well. He'd get another shot at Article V this afternoon, but his attempt to do that now was getting him nowhere.

"Thank you, Justice Taser. Assuming for sake of argument, as NoPoli would have us believe, that Article V is a constraint only on constitutional amendments sponsored by the government, and not by the governed, the NoPoli assembly still did not satisfy the requirement that the governed must act—when they are permitted to do so—through a *majority* of them. Even NoPoli does not dispute this constitutional predicate."

This time it was the generally soft-spoken Justice Galanti who growled, "Mr. Esposito. We just don't seem to be coming together on the same page here. First you were trying to take us back to our *Tuesday* afternoon discussions about the meaning of Article V. Now you seem to be turning to what we are supposed to argue this afternoon. Once and for all, I'd like to know if you have anything you'd like to bring to the Court's attention this morning about the actual characteristics of the NoPoli convention, which is the sole topic on *this morning's* agenda? If not, perhaps you really should consider yielding your time."

"Very well, Justice Galanti."

"Very well what, Mr. Esposito," Justice Lukesh inquired. "Are you yielding?"

"Not at all, Justice Lukesh. I will point out the characteristics of the NoPoli convention that I then wish to argue further this afternoon."

"Well, then, Mr. Esposito, it would be helpful if you would please move to that," Justice Stone said.

Brooks knew that Stone was expected to vote to invalidate the amendment. He was obviously attempting to encourage Esposito to accomplish something toward that end this morning.

Esposito must have realized he wasn't getting anywhere trying to game the Court's agenda. He finally quit trying, resigning himself to itemizing the convention's characteristics, the deficiencies of which he would then argue this afternoon. He first ran through the procedures NoPoli employed to select and seat its 50,000 delegates and 20,000 alternate delegates. He then did his best, strategically, but inaccurately, to argue that the delegates and alternate delegates were all long-standing members of NoPoli, and therefore not a true representative cross-section of the governed.

Finally sticking to this morning's announced agenda, Esposito actually spoke for some time without further interruption. Brooks was impressed. Esposito had methodically and effectively ticked off every vulnerability in the NoPoli convention that he would have raised had he been in Esposito's shoes. As for the Justices, Brooks couldn't tell whether they agreed with Esposito or had lost interest.

Near the end, Hirschfeld lobbed Esposito a few softball questions designed to allow him a chance to emphasize the homogeneity of the NoPoli delegates and alternate delegates and to suggest that they did not fairly represent the American public. It struck Brooks that Hirschfeld wanted to monopolize the remainder of Esposito's time so that none of the Justices with a different point of view would have much opportunity to cut in.

At the completion of Esposito's designated time, Trotter interrupted the unofficial Hirschfeld and Esposito team to thank Esposito for his remarks and to state that they would take a ten-minute recess before hearing from NoPoli.

* * *

Webber watched his father-in-law going at it with Esposito, the lawyer he understood to be representing Congress. He was pleased that his father-in-law was doing everything possible to shoot down the amendment and save Cassie. His views were quite different than those he generally espoused at family events.

Webber hadn't noticed anyone during the past hour paying any inordinate amount of attention to Hirschfeld. When he spoke, people watched him. When he was quiet, they didn't, at least as near as he could tell. But it was like looking for a needle in a haystack. He hoped he'd have more luck as the day progressed. Enough to endure the wrath Jill would visit on him for being MIA on the home front.

* * *

Brooks and Klein had originally decided that Brooks would take both of the Thursday sessions. However, Hirschfeld had beaten Klein up pretty badly on Tuesday. Brooks knew she was down. He wanted her to know that *his* confidence in her had not been shaken. So last night he had asked her to first chair the Thursday morning session.

It was now NoPoli's turn to speak about the convention. Klein and Steve Kessler had run the convention. No one knew it better than Klein did. She approached the lectern, carrying only one thin notepad. Good sign, Brooks thought. No crutches. Less was more.

And so it was. The Justices let Klein speak with almost no dislocation. Ultimately, Stone, Lukesh, Nettleman, and Hirschfeld each put her through her paces, attempting to demonstrate that NoPoli was an elitist organization that did not reflect a broad spectrum of the country.

Brooks had assumed all along that Stone and Nettleman would each be against the amendment. Hirschfeld was a surprise on Tuesday, but no longer. Klein was armed and ready. She methodically walked the Justices through the manner in which each state chapter of NoPoli had independently selected delegates who reflected a balanced composition of their respective state citizenry, free from any centralized NoPoli influence or control. In this way, Klein argued, the 70,000 NoPoli delegates and alternate delegates from across all fifty states of the union represented a true national microcosm of Americana.

It would now be up to Brooks to pull it all together that afternoon. Hirschfeld had been turned into an outright adversary. It would effectively be Esposito and Hirschfeld together against Brooks. Not particularly fair odds, two to one. But then Brooks figured Hirschfeld and his granddaughter hadn't felt they'd been dealt a fair hand either.

CHAPTER 66
Thursday, May 8, 11:00 am

DURING THE TEN-minute recess between the two halves of the morning session, Thomas's mind returned to the Courtroom presence of Reyes and his goons. In the worst possible way, he wanted to believe this was just some kind of security detail, perhaps alerted to some possible terrorist threat attributable to the high-profile nature of the Supreme Court and this case. But Reyes had nothing to do with security. And the last thing he would do would be to place himself in any possible harm's way. Once again, Reyes's presence could only mean one thing: he had sorted out what had brought Thomas back to D.C. Still, he wondered why that would bring out Reyes and his support team. Sure, Thomas understood that he had lost his stripes, and was no longer affirmatively a member of their team, included in their plans. That was precisely why he was here to make amends, to earn back his stripes. *But are they actually against me having another chance to show that I do deserve a seat at the table?*

* * *

Poppy was still on her mind when Cassie woke up. Something the man said had bothered her. He told he got her diabetic supplies from her grandfather. But her grandfather didn't have any of her diabetic supplies and would have had to get them from her mom and dad. Kids were usually kidnapped to get something from their parents. The man should have been speaking to her parents, not her grandfather. Why then wouldn't he have gone directly to the source, her parents, to get her insulin and supplies?

CHAPTER 67
Thursday, May 8, 11:55 am

JOEY HAD FOLLOWED Mark Webber to the Courthouse parking lot, then into the queue to enter the Courtroom for the morning session. By the time Joey got to the front of the line, security had stopped letting any more people in.

He flashed his NBN-TV credentials. That did the trick; they let him through.

It took a while, but he finally spotted Webber sitting in the last row of the gallery. Webber seemed less interested in the proceedings than in another spectator only a few seats away from him. Every now and then, Webber scanned the gallery. He appeared to be looking for someone, but his attention always returned to the nearby spectator. Maybe, Joey thought, it was because the subject of Webber's interest was well-known White House Chief of Staff, Manny Reyes.

Reyes was also restless, gazing around the Courtroom, as if he too were looking for someone. Joey wondered whether they possibly could both be searching for the same person.

At the noon recess, Reyes joined a wooden looking guy standing at the back of the Courtroom. They exchanged a few words and then walked out together. And there was Webber, right on their heels.

Joey tried to follow, but the exit was crowded; he lost them. When Joey got outside, Webber and Reyes were nowhere to be found.

* * *

Nishimura felt her cell phone vibrate. Seeing it was Joey, she anxiously picked up.

"I'm here at the Courthouse."

"You're supposed to be watching Webber," she whispered, looking around to be sure no one was listening to her.

"Followed him here this morning. He just left. Guess who *he* was following?"

"Joey—get to the point."

"Manny Reyes."

Nishimura hesitated, unable to process what that might mean. "Where are they now?"

"I lost them in the crowd."

"Jesus. Keep looking."

"For Webber or Reyes?"

Again in a whisper so no one nearby might overhear, but with no room for doubt, she said "Webber!"

"Got it."

"Find him, damn it, and make sure you don't lose him again. Try to figure out what the hell's going on."

* * *

Webber followed Reyes and the other man out of the Courthouse. Catching up to them at the curb, he realized this might be his only chance: "Mr. Reyes?"

The other man quickly stepped in to shelter Reyes, pushing Webber back, almost knocking him off his feet.

Webber recovered. "Who the hell do you think you are? You can't do that."

The man flashed a gold shield. "Actually, I can. Back up and tell me who *you* are."

"My name's Mark Webber. I'd like to speak to Mr. Reyes for a moment."

"It's all right, agent. Something I can do for you, Mr. Webber?"

Webber's felt his juices reaching full boil. "You bet there is."

CHAPTER 68
Thursday, May 8, 12:05 pm

JOEY CAUGHT sight of Webber and Reyes standing at the curb, accompanied by some gorilla wearing a Bluetooth in his ear, and giving Webber a bad time. He continued slowly past them, as close as he could get without drawing attention to himself. He couldn't hear what they were saying.

Trying to look like a typical tourist, he pulled out his phone and began taking pictures of the surrounding landmarks. And the three men.

The swing Justice's son-in-law meeting with the White House chief-of-staff; he had to let Nishimura know. *Must be a story in this somewhere. And just maybe a thank you party for me.*

* * *

Thomas watched the three men from a safe distance. *Jesus H. Christ. That's the girl's father, Webber. The fuck's he doing here? Talking to Reyes no less.*

Thomas wasn't close enough to hear what they were saying above the din, but he couldn't move any closer, and risk being spotted. Thomas could tell Webber was agitated. The two by four with the ear piece was making a scene, drawing a lot of attention. *Manny never did crave the limelight. Looks like he wants to crawl into a hole and disappear.* Reyes said something to the goon and he backed off.

* * *

Reyes looked right into Webber's eyes. "What is it I can do for you, Mr. Webber?"

Webber was flummoxed. He had to say something. He wanted to ask Reyes what he knew about Cassie, but it suddenly dawned on him that he might be putting Cassie in even greater jeopardy than she already was.

Reyes looked at Webber harshly. So did the FBI agent.

"Excuse me, Mr. Webber, I'm really in a hurry. Is there something you want to say to me?"

If the name "Webber" meant anything to Reyes, he sure wasn't letting on. "Mr. Reyes, you're the White House Chief of Staff. I was intrigued. I guess. About, well, what interest the White House has in this case."

Reyes studied Webber's face, as though looking for a place to insert a knife. "I'm sorry, Mr. Webber. White House policy doesn't permit me to comment on pending litigation." A chilling smile appeared on Reyes's face. "You have yourself a nice day."

With that Reyes and the FBI agent walked off, leaving Webber standing there, feeling a bit like a deflated balloon.

* * *

Just like that, it was over. Thomas *hated* surprises. And this one had the smell of disaster written all over it. He hurried to where he'd parked the van, scrambled inside, grabbed one of his phones, slipped in a new SIM card, and punched in the number.

CHAPTER 69
Thursday, May 8, 12:15 pm

As MUCH AS he hadn't allowed it to show, Reyes was spooked by his confrontation with that sputtering goof ball. Webber. Mark Webber. The name meant absolutely nothing to him.

He decided to skip the afternoon Court hearing and return to the White House. The FBI would have to handle the vigil for Thomas without him.

* * *

Hirschfeld sat alone in his office, sipping a cup of soup brought to him by his assistant. He was going round and round in his head, thinking about Brooks's bizarre suggestion that morning.

Could an escrow strategy actually work? Or would suggesting something so outrageous push Cassie's captors to an even worse extreme, to prove once again that they were the ones in control?

His cell phone rang. He glanced at the incoming number. It was unfamiliar. He quickly answered. "Hello?"

"Don't hello me, old man. The fuck you doing with Reyes?"

"Reyes? Reyes who?"

"Smart. Go ahead, play games. See where that gets your little girl."

"Manuel Reyes? White House Chief of Staff?"

"Give the man a kewpie doll."

"I'm not doing anything with him. I swear. I barely know the man. What are you talking about?"

"Look, old man. I don't want to hurt the kid if I don't have to. I'm just in this to get you to perform. Anything happens to the girl, it's on *you*. No one else. Not only was Reyes in Court this morning, but he had a bunch of ear-pieces stationed all around the perimeter of the Courtroom. Then, out of nowhere, your *son-in-law* approaches him outside the Courthouse a few minutes ago. They talked to one another! Now you better damn well talk to *me* and tell me what's going on."

Hirschfeld panicked. Brooks? Maybe Brooks had secretly reached out to the President. But why? "Please, listen to me," he said. "You need to believe me. I have no idea what's going on. None. I've not been in touch with Manuel Reyes or the President or anyone else. Just *you*." His throat tightened up at the lie. He closed his eyes, grimaced. "I've not contacted *anyone*. I can't imagine that Cassie's father would have done anything that foolish either. But I'll find out for you."

The silence was excruciating.

"Better not be lying to me. Maybe I need to send you a little piece of your girl in a nicely gift-wrapped box. Watch for it." The line went dead.

* * *

Thomas's anger moved toward redline. Way too many loose ends between the girl's grandfather, her father, Reyes, and the FBI heavies stationed around the Courtroom. He had no idea who was working with whom. Or why. Or who exactly—if anyone—was on the lookout for him.

It was too risky to return to the Courtroom. He'd watch the afternoon session from the sports bar. He'd still be able to text the old man if necessary. But his view of the proceedings would now be at the mercy of the TV cameras. And their visual priorities didn't coincide with his.

CHAPTER 70
Thursday, May 8, 12:30 pm

LOTELLO HAD MADE the first attempt at eight that morning. His call was intercepted by an automated recording that said the office opened at nine. He didn't leave a message. He called back at 9:15, this time reaching a live person who said that Mr. Lance would be tied up for most of the day. When Lotello explained that the matter was extremely urgent, she asked him to please hold. She returned to the line two minutes later, advising that she could fit him in for a few minutes between meetings at 12:30. Lotello thanked her, said he'd be there.

The offices were located in a new industrial park twenty minutes outside of D.C., intended to resemble the more prestigious inner-city high-rise office buildings, but at lower rents. He entered the contemporary modest reception area at 12:20. When the receptionist asked him for some identification, he chose to share only his civilian driver's license, not his Metro D.C. credentials. She inspected the name and photo. He seemed to pass. He was shown into a large, well-appointed conference room with a high-tech look and feel—ergonomically angled computer devices built into the conference table opposite each chair and several wall-mounted large screen monitors.

He was invited to help himself to water, coffee, or tea and was informed that Mr. Lance would join him shortly. Intimidated by all the technology, Lotello reviewed his low-tech notepad while he waited.

He had reached out to several contacts for a short list of "escrow agent" candidates. When the name J.R. Lance appeared on three different lists, Lotello looked into his bio, and decided he might have found the right man.

Lance had joined the army out of high school, and had served several tours in both Iraq and Afghanistan. He was highly regarded by his superiors, and ended up in an almost invisible elite black ops unit reportedly comprised of highly skilled and trained members, discreet, selfless, committed to the country, and used to carry out extremely covert missions.

Lance ultimately retired, honorably, from the military and immediately transitioned into the security business. His company handled such things as installing and maintaining computer security systems, finding hackers and turning them over to the authorities, providing human security systems—body-guards—and recovering stolen 'assets'—the kind that breathed as well as the kind that didn't. He enjoyed a singular and unblemished reputation for excelling at his engagements, almost always below the radar and without fanfare.

At 12:30 sharp, Lance entered the conference room. He was as physically imposing as his background suggested. Lotello stood and they shook hands.

"J.R. Lance. Nice to meet you, Detective. Was there some reason you didn't mention your occupation to my receptionist?"

"Only because I thought it might end our meeting before it started. I didn't want to chance that, possibly make you nervous."

"Why would you think that? My services are usually pretty low profile and sometimes a bit on the edge, but I have lawyers to be sure they're always above board and legal. I frequently work with the authorities.

"And whether or not we end up working together, no one will ever learn what we discuss today. At least not from me. So, how can I be of assistance? What brings you to see me?"

Lotello knew Lance was between meetings and wasn't sure how much time they'd have. He got right down to it, laying out all of the background, including how he and Brooks had come to be involved, and the escrow arrangement they wanted to explore with him.

"The two of you believe you are free to pursue this in private, unofficially, rather than formally turning it over to authorities more traditionally charged with such matters?"

"Frankly, that's been the subject of considerable debate between us. Let's say he's given me a crash course in the relevant legal and ethical considerations;

I've cautiously come around to his way of looking at the matter. At least for the moment, I'm satisfied that we are not legally or morally obliged to report any of this to the authorities. Do you feel differently?"

"Let me answer you this way: this is not the first time I've been asked to do something like this. Nor is it the first time I've agreed to do so. But I've also said no, more often than I've said yes."

"How do you decide?"

"It's not just how I feel, but also how my lawyers feel. They concentrate primarily on the legalities, making sure I remain within those boundaries. Done the right way, things that some might intuitively think unlawful, really aren't. In contrast, I concentrate on the ethics—*my* ethics. On both scores, it usually comes down to making sure that there is a clear understanding and agreement among all of the parties involved. Where's the girl's family on all of this? Are they on board?"

"That's a work in progress. They are fully aware that we are exploring this alternative on their behalf, but not with whom. They haven't committed as yet, and won't until they know more."

"Fair enough. Let's talk then about my ethics. Taking possession of the girl and turning her over to her family in the event the 28th Amendment is invalidated is easy. The harder question, of course, is my returning her to her kidnappers in the event the 28th Amendment is upheld."

"I agree. So, how do you feel about that?"

"I'm driven by several competing interests. One is the girl's welfare. I'm sure you'd love me to tell you that I'd never return her to the kidnappers no matter what, but it's not that simple. I must—and will—strictly adhere to the terms of the negotiated agreement, no matter how harsh they might be. In this day and age of increasing extreme tactics, I, and a few others like me, are trying to build a cottage industry, so to speak, of helping to resolve cases like this. In order to succeed—not only for Cassie and her family today, but for all those similarly situated in the future—it's essential that I remain neutral and non-judgmental, and that my integrity remains inviolate. If the hijackers can't rely on me to honor my word, then, by definition, I will be useless to present—and future—victims. If Cassie's kidnappers don't firmly believe that about me, then I can't realistically be of any possible help to her, and there's no reason for me to become involved."

"So you're saying those who wish to save Cassie need to focus on the language of the escrow agreement, not on trying to influence or co-opt you."

"That's precisely what I'm saying. Yes."

"But isn't that calculated to fail?"

"Why do you say that?"

"Because if you or we tilt the language for our benefit, the kidnappers will never agree to it. We won't be able to reach an agreement."

"First of all, I won't tilt the language in anyone's favor. My lawyers simply make sure the arrangement is lawful and that I know what my rights and responsibilities are. Who the agreement favors or doesn't favor is strictly up to the parties. If *you're* patently obvious, of course you're right. However, keep in mind that the assailants and victims don't necessarily look at written agreements in the same way, or from the same perspective."

"That last point. You lost me. Can you run that by me again?"

"Sorry, sometimes I forget that it's easier for me because I've been through these situations before—several times. They're all unique, but they do have some common threads. I don't mean to talk down to you, but how about if I share a few basic observations?"

"Sure, that's why I'm here."

"Okay. Kidnapping for political ends is arguably extreme, but it's nothing new—and perhaps on the rise. The Vikings were adept at it. It was prevalent with fringe guerrilla groups in the Sixties and Seventies, not just Patty Hearst but others as well, including a number of American businessmen kidnapped in Argentina. One Exxon executive was held 144 days before the company finally coughed up $14 million to secure his release. More recently, the baton has been passed to Mexico, where much of my experience has been.

In your case, we know what the kidnappers want, but we don't know who they are, how they think, or how they operate. From my experience, however, they'll put much less stock in the language of a written document than your side."

"Why do you say that?"

"Because they have to remain invisible. For them, the agreement is not something they will ever be able to take to court to enforce, or to use as a basis to obtain an award of damages from a court if you breach your obligations to them under the agreement."

"Well, then, how can we ever expect to get them to settle on language?"

"I didn't say the agreement won't be important to them, just that they'll look at it differently than you will. For them, it's simply a barometer to decide whether they feel they can trust me to honor it, especially since your side would be the one recommending me.

"The family's focus will be both on me and on the contract language. The kidnappers's focus will mostly be on me. They'll buy off on the agreement, but likely only after someone on their behalf first meets with and fully vets me, and concludes that I can be trusted to honor the terms of the agreement on behalf of *each* of the parties."

"Language that serves Cassie's purposes, but without causing the kidnappers to be concerned that you won't also honor their objectives, isn't that a pretty fine line?"

"It is. And just as important to me as it is to you. The last thing I want is to have the girl's captors think I haven't honored my commitment to them. I can take care of myself. But I have staff. I can't be everywhere at once. Not only do we need them to conclude they can trust me, I also want to be sure they won't think I've abused that trust."

Lance glanced at his watch and stood, signaling the end of the meeting.

"I've gotta run. My receptionist will show you out. Give her all of your contact information, and two dollars. My lawyers will prepare a first draft of the escrow agreement and I will email the draft to you first thing in the morning. The email will include contact information on how to reach me 24/7. You and Judge Brooks will need to correct any factual errors in the document and fill in any blanks or other gaps. You can also propose any revisions you want, but keep in mind the 'fine line' we've just discussed. Once we're in accord, you'll have to figure out how to get the document to the kidnappers to review. And give them a chance to have a representative meet with me on their behalf—a meeting that may provide an opportunity for me to find a way to bring the parties somewhat closer together."

"Sounds right, but two dollars? You couldn't be saying your fees are two dollars are you?"

"My charges are spelled out in the agreement. They're a lot more than two dollars, but they're generally the least difficult thing for us to agree on. The two dollars is a lawyer thing, one dollar from your side and one dollar from the other side. You're advancing the other side's for them. Your wife's a lawyer. She or Judge Brooks can explain it to you better than I can. It has something to do with establishing my agency on behalf of each party. That I'm not acting as a volunteer, what the law calls an officious intermeddler, which could increase my legal exposure."

Lotello stood as well. They shook hands once again. Lance turned and exited through the same door he'd used twenty minutes earlier. As if on cue, the receptionist appeared and escorted Lotello back to the lobby. Before leaving, he gave her his contact information and two one dollar bills. It had been worth the price of admission.

He had come there to interview Lance, but had the feeling that it was Lance who had interviewed him. And offered him quite a bit of insight along the way. He was anxious to review all of this with Brooks, but the final session in *Congress v. NoPoli* was about to get underway. He'd have to wait his turn.

CHAPTER 71
Thursday, May 8, 12:50 pm

BACK IN THE COURTROOM, Joey waited for things to get underway. He'd located Webber in the gallery, a new seat several rows closer to the front, and was dialed in on him.

He also noticed the big guy, the one who'd held Webber at arm's length in the encounter with Reyes. He was back inside now as well, standing at the rear near the entrance, examining the crowd. He wondered who they were looking for. It wasn't Webber. The agent's eyes glossed right past Webber. It wasn't Reyes, either, because he didn't seem to have returned for the afternoon session. It was someone else. But who? And why?

He'd tried calling Nishimura but her phone rolled over to voicemail. Unsure how often she checked her messages, he sent her a text as well—before having to check his phone with Courtroom security. There was nothing more for him to do now but to keep an eye on Webber.

* * *

Nishimura, Elliott, and Kessler had just finished another short special to introduce the afternoon proceedings. She heard her phone humming inside her purse several times, and figured it was Joey with an update, but had to let his calls go to voicemail. Fortunately, he'd also texted, and when the cameras cut away for a close-up on Elliott as he summarized the morning's debate over NoPoli's constitutional convention, she'd taken the opportunity to open her phone and glance at his message.

Webber mtg w Manny Reyes outside ct. Can't hear conv. Chk your VM.

Nishimura found herself staring at the words. Was she reading them right? Was Hirschfeld's son-in-law in touch with the White House?

A voice in her earpiece brought her back: "Anne! Camera One! Now!"

She looked up and beamed her customary smile and re-entered the conversation, even though the confluence of the words swirling around her seemed a thousand miles away. More than ever, she felt convinced that she was on to something of Pulitzer Prize magnitude. Washington's power centers were colliding in unimaginable ways. But she was going to get to the bottom of it, reveal all, and become one of those power centers herself.

CHAPTER 72
Thursday, May 8, 1:00 pm

BROOKS LOOKED on as Chief Justice Trotter welcomed everyone to the fourth and final session and invited Esposito to begin his presentation. Brooks knew it would all come down to this session. And whatever developed concerning Hirschfeld's granddaughter.

Esposito spread out several notepads on the speaker's podium in front of him and looked up at the Justices. "If it please the Court," he began. "NoPoli asks this Court to believe that Article V limits only the way in which the *government* can amend the Constitution. While the *governed* are free to amend the Constitution however and whenever they wish. Isn't that mighty convenient?"

Esposito's opening hardly surprised Brooks. It was an old but sophomoric ploy. When you're worried about an opponent's position, restate his argument in an exaggerated and more vulnerable way—create a straw man—then attack the fabrication. It worked better in politics than in courtrooms, especially this one, but Brooks couldn't leave it to chance. He began scribbling notes as Esposito continued.

"The Congress of the United States sees it differently," he said. "First of all, ladies and gentlemen, NoPoli's contention is simply not what Article V provides. In plain, straightforward English, Article V—"

"You lost me there, counsel," Taser said. "Article V may be brief. I'll give you that. But plain and straightforward? You're kidding? Right? Just saying. Carry on."

"Yes, Your Honor. Article V sets forth two, and only two, ways to amend the Constitution. It does not distinguish between who proposes the amendment. It does not contain one word about that. Not one court decision in the history of the United States has ever drawn such a distinction. Ever."

"Excuse me, Mr. Esposito," Gaviota interrupted. "Didn't Ms. Klein already argue, and rather effectively I might add, that this Court does not require a prior published precedent in order to advance a supposedly new point? As she eloquently put it, if that was necessary, the law would be rather static. And, how would the point have been made the first time?

"*Point* taken, Justice Gaviota." Esposito smiled. "Nevertheless, wouldn't you think that if the framers of our Constitution had intended such a novel thought, they would have said so—spelled it out—right there in Article V? However, they didn't. Not. One. Word."

Brooks smiled at Esposito's exaggerated attempt at dramatic effect, then glanced up at the Justices. None of them seem to share his amusement. Nor did any of them counter Esposito's argument.

Seemingly encouraged by the silence, Esposito moved on. "Without more, such observation requires this Court to invalidate the 28th Amendment. But there is more. Much more. It's true that our constitutional framers engaged in some limited colloquy about a theoretical broader power of the governed to amend the Constitution. However, in addition to the fact that they decided, after such discourse, not to incorporate a single word to that effect in Article V—"

"Is it not possible, Mr. Esposito," Lukesh asked, "that the drafters of the Constitution considered this so fundamental as not to require that it be spelled out?"

"Respectfully, not in my opinion, Justice Lukesh. But it is clear that any notion of amending power on the part of the governed was expressly and consistently alluded to in terms of requiring a *majority* determination of the governed. In sharp contrast, the 28th Amendment was ratified—using that word ever so generously—by only 50,000 members of NoPoli, a rather modest number in comparison to more than 300 million Americans. In fact, that represents less than two one-hundredths of one percent of the population. If my math is correct, that's a little bit short of a majority."

Trotter leaned forward. "Just a minute, counsel. Are all of those 300 million Americans of voting age, and registered to vote?"

"I should, but don't, have that number at hand, Chief Justice Trotter. Still, there is no denying that NoPoli's 50,000 delegates comes up a far cry short of a majority of the number of Americans registered to vote. And the lack of any semblance of a *representative* majority is worse. This modest 50,000 vote was open only to those elitist card carrying members of NoPoli. I'm reminded of sadder times in our history when you had to be a white male to vote."

Well done, Brooks thought. Play the race card. But the elitist card? You'll regret that one, Raul. Actually, you'll regret the race card too.

"For any or all of the above reasons," Esposito concluded, "Congress respectively contends that this document which NoPoli contends is the 28th Amendment to the U.S. Constitution is an insult, not only to all of America's public representatives, but to all Americans who were not entitled to vote on this matter and who believe in our Constitution as it was enacted more than two hundred years ago. Thank you for your attention."

Esposito started gathering his papers. A voice from the bench stopped him.

"I'd like to ask you a question, Mr. Esposito, if I may."

Esposito glanced up and respectfully smiled. "Of course, Justice Nettleman."

"Do you think the views of the plaintiff here—Congress—deserve any more weight than the views of any other plaintiff would?"

"Thank you for asking, Justice Nettleman. I do. After all, Congress is one of the three branches of our federal government."

"Yes, I understand that, but is that relevant when they are not legislating, but merely bringing a lawsuit as any other plaintiff might? If a member of Congress slipped on a banana peel and brought suit for damages, would that Congressional plaintiff deserve any more favorable consideration than a private citizen bringing such a lawsuit?"

"Perhaps not in that instance, Your Honor. But this isn't a lawsuit brought by one member of Congress in his or her private capacity. It's brought by the entirety of Congress in its constitutional capacity."

"Interesting. Thank you, Mr. Esposito."

"Thank *you*, Justice Nettleman. My thanks as well to all of the Justices for hearing me out."

Brooks glanced up at Hirschfeld, who seemed lost within himself. Stone-faced. He'd not said a word during Esposito's presentation. Brooks wondered if his friend weren't lying back there in the weeds, setting a trap for him. Forcing Brooks to go first so Hirschfeld could gain the last word. Especially if Brooks blundered. Brooks recalled the premise of his remarks to Arnold that very morning: *He who goes first loses.* He grimaced at what there was to lose: The young girl? The 28th Amendment?

Trotter returned Brooks to the present. "We'll be in recess for ten minutes, after which we'll hear from Judge Brooks on behalf of NoPoli."

CHAPTER 73
Thursday, May 8, 1:45 pm

NISHIMURA TURNED to her two talking heads. "Chris. Steve. It's not hard to understand why Esposito has the track record he does. I was so impressed. How do the two of you see his performance?"

"Esposito held up well," Elliott said. "That will be a hard act for Brooks to follow. But it sometimes comes down to who has to go first and who gets to go last."

Nishimura turned to Kessler. "What about you, Steve? *Your* turn to go last. For now."

Kessler offered his customary smile, but Nishimura couldn't help but notice the apparent concern in his eyes. "Well, Anne, I don't have much experience when it comes to grading oral argument in the U.S. Supreme Court, but I think Esposito did do a nice job."

"*Nice?*"

"Well, he is engaging. I'll give you that."

"So is Charles Manson. But do you think Esposito made a positive impression on the Justices, convinced them of Congress's position, that enactment of the 28th Amendment was unconstitutional?"

Kessler took a moment to respond. Buying time, Nishimura thought.

"I agree with Chris. Esposito's performance was very . . . Goliath-like. We'll just have to wait and see what the Justices think. My money's still on . . . David.

* * *

Hirschfeld thought Esposito had acquitted himself quite well. He was relieved he didn't have to come to his rescue. *This way, Cyrus has to go first—at least as between he and I.*

* * *

Cassie was trying to be as diligent as she could to manage her fear—to lower her stress and her blood sugar. She was trying so hard to make the most of a difficult situation. It wasn't easy. Her fear lingered like an all-pervasive cloud hanging over her head.

To calm her nerves, she had reorganized the location of some of the furniture in her prison cell to create a mini circuit training course, sprinkling in some stretching, push-up, and core and glute stations in between the circuit power walking. She preferred the variety of mixing in this circuit training with just sprinting laps in a straight line back and forth from one end of the room to the other. At least it gave her something else to think about.

As she stretched to cool down from her latest workout, her mind wandered to what she and Madison had missed in the Supreme Court on Tuesday. Well, what *she* had missed. Madison no doubt had gone with her dad anyway. Now that Cassie was older and smarter, her poppy had been discussing the case with her, getting her ready for the big field trip. Not being there to see her grandfather in action after their preparation together only made her feel worse than she already did.

And then . . . it hit her.

* * *

Thomas nursed his beer and thought about what he'd just watched. So far, so good. Maybe Esposito had turned a vote or two on his own. That would make life a lot easier for the old man. With his own flipped vote in the bag, that'd seal the deal.

His mind drifted to the girl. He slipped a twenty beneath his glass and signaled to the bartender that he was stepping outside for a moment. Out on the sidewalk, he launched his video app. She must have heard the camera because she immediately looked right into the lens. She got up off the bed, walked closer, and spoke into the hidden microphone.

"I know what you're trying to do. You think you're going to use me to get my poppy to do something you want in Court. That's why you got my insulin from him and not my parents. You've been talking to my poppy. You can't do that. It's not right. You're terrible. Worse than terrible. I bet even your *mom* can't stand you."

Thomas could hardly believe what that little bitch was saying to him. *How dare she question Mother's relationship with me? Mother always loved me. Even if she didn't always show it. Same with Father. There was no question about their love—or respect—for me. Who does she think she is, talking to me like that?*

"Here's what I think of you and your camera, creep." She reached down, tugged off her shoe, and threw it straight at the camera.

There was a loud clank, a blur of static, and then both the video and audio went dead.

Thomas was pissed, completely out of control, throwing all caution to the wind. *Fuck it. I don't care who might be looking for me. I'm going back in that Courtroom and watch the exchange between Brooks and Hirschfeld in person. End of discussion.*

CHAPTER 74
Thursday, May 8, 2:00 pm

"BREAK A LEG, Judge," Klein whispered as Brooks rose.

He smiled in response and walked unpretentiously to the podium. He carried not a single note or sheet of paper. Ignoring the cameras in his face, and the anticipatory buzz emanating from the gallery behind him, he took one deep breath and acknowledged the nine Justices.

"Honorable Justices, thank you for your attention and for allowing me to assume the burden of carrying NoPoli's—if not the people's—message to you today concerning both the importance and the integrity of the 28th Amendment to the U.S. Constitution."

He ventured a glance at Hirschfeld, but received only a steely glare in response.

"First, I would like to thank my esteemed colleague, Mr. Esposito, for assuming NoPoli unable to state its position on its own, and kindly volunteering to assist it in that regard. Seldom today do we experience such chivalry extended by one's opposition. No doubt solely through innocent inadvertence did Mr. Esposito not quite correctly paraphrase NoPoli's position, gracious and well-intended as I know he was."

Chuckles arose here and there in the gallery. *Careful, this isn't the time to play to the cheap seats.*

"Mr. Esposito attributed to NoPoli the ill-defined position that the governed are free to amend the Constitution *quote* however and whenever they wish. I didn't bring any notes with me to the lectern, but I do believe nonetheless that those were his exact words. NoPoli has *never* taken such a position. If the Court will permit, I will endeavor to recite and present NoPoli's *actual* three-part thesis, the very same that is set forth in its papers on file with the Court. And previously served on my esteemed colleague."

The chuckles had turned to murmurs. *I've beaten that dead horse. Time to move on.*

"*One*, Article V sets forth two means by which the Constitution may be amended. Article V is barely a few sentences long, as Justice Taser correctly noted." Brooks caught her smile out of the corner of his eye. "Nowhere does Article V state that its alternative two procedures are exclusive.

"If the framers of our Constitution had meant Article V to be exclusive, I can only presume they would have said so. The written historical data is clear—if not simple and straightforward: our framers informally and formally debated Article V for six long months before agreeing on its language.

"It would have taken them just a few seconds to add a short sentence to Article V stating that it provided the only two ways by which the Constitution could be amended, either by the government or the governed. *If* indeed that had been their intention."

Except for the creaking of seats and the whirring clicks of cameras, the gallery had fallen silent again.

"*Two*, the same record, documented in the Library of Congress, the very same Congress that initiated this lawsuit, makes perfectly clear that a *majority* of the governed—we the people—can *amend* the Constitution with the same fundamental authority by which they originally *adopted* it. This is not a huge leap. It is the governed who created it. If they could make it, then they could also fix it. Amend it. Respectfully, that logic is not complicated."

"Excuse me, Judge Brooks."

"Of course, Justice Stone."

"My apologies for cutting in before you get to your third point, but I'm troubled by something you just said, and I don't want to lose the moment."

"Certainly, Your Honor."

"You say that if the governed could make the Constitution, which no one questions, then it follows that they could also change it, amend it. Do I understand you correctly?"

"You do."

"Well, how do you know that when they made it they didn't intend a sense of permanence, and reliability, that even *they* couldn't alter? In other words, how do you know they didn't waive their right to amend the Constitution? Are you not engaging in rank speculation?"

"Hmm…" Brooks could feel all eyes in the Courtroom on him. *Perfect. He who goes first loses.* After another few seconds of theatrical pause: "I think not."

Justice Stone sat back in his chair, looking puzzled, perhaps even a little irritated. "Sorry. Are you now acknowledging that we don't in fact know that the governed can amend? The opposite of what you said just a moment ago?"

"Not at all, Justice Stone. My apologies if I confused you. What I intended to say was that I didn't think I was engaging in rank speculation. I firmly believe the governed *never* waived their fundamental right of amendment."

"And you know that how?"

"As you, of course, know, Your Honor, our present Constitution is the *second* constitution in the history of our great country. It was adopted in 1787 and ratified in 1788. Our first Constitution, labeled the Articles of Confederation, was adopted in 1777. It lasted less than eleven years, at which time the *governed* decided to amend it by restating it in its entirety, with some notable changes, in the form of our present Constitution. Given that famous—or infamous, depending on your point of view—precedent, I submit that the governed would have spoken up loud and clear had they meant to waive any *further* right on their part to amend the governing documents *of we the people—the governed.*"

"Touché, Judge Brooks." Justice Stone's air of puzzlement lifted. He now wore an appreciative smile. "I believe you were about to share with us the third leg in NoPoli's thesis when I rudely interrupted you."

"I was, thank you, Justice Stone. And my third point. Yes. Um, let me think." Brooks feigned uncertainty, and drew the laughter he was after.

"Ah, yes. *Three,* NoPoli is not a hypocrite. Just as our framers did not say Article V was the only way the *governed* can amend, it is true that they also did not say Article V was the only way that the *government* can amend.

"However, the question of whether the government can amend outside Article V is not before this Court today. If and when such a question is raised, no doubt this Court will, in its wisdom, answer that question. After, hopefully, first taking into account this humble student's observation that the government is supposed to work *for* the governed—not the other way around—and that our framers had that notion firmly in mind when they drafted Article V."

Brooks, readying for his finale, clasped his hands behind his back and straightened his shoulders. Hirschfeld still refused to look at him. "This brings us to the remaining two questions: What definition of majority would our framers have had in mind when they enacted our Constitution? And, with apologies to Justice Stone, would they have meant for that definition to have been set 'in stone' for all time?"

He waited out the resulting laughter. "When our Constitution was enacted we were a relatively small nation by today's standards—a relatively small populace situated in a relatively small geography. Arguably, the idea of a true majority, one vote per one citizen assembled in one venue for a one-time vote, was manageable. I hasten to repeat, arguably."

He turned a bit toward the gallery and extended his arm, as though to include the spectators in his next remarks. "Today, we are spread far and wide. There are three hundred million of us, if I may borrow Mr. Esposito's calculus. A true majority today is no longer manageable. If our framers meant a true majority for all time no matter the circumstances, then they would have been guilty of providing for the certain demise of the very right of the governed to chart our course. As clearly they were advocating."

He returned face-front and gripped the lectern. "However, one of the primary cornerstones of our Constitution is *elasticity*. Our Constitution is meant to be sufficiently flexible to serve over time as circumstances logically warrant."

"That's hardly a settled question," said Chief Justice Trotter.

Brooks had anticipated such an interruption at this juncture. "For purposes of the issues now before this Honorable Court, I believe it is settled. As I will endeavor to demonstrate if I might first be permitted to conclude my remarks?"

Trotter waved for Brooks to proceed.

Brooks continued. "We must remember: We are a republic, not a democracy. Majority means fair representation, not one for one. So, we use an electoral college to elect our Presidents. And we have but 435 members of our House of Representatives and 100 members of our Senate to run Congress—the plaintiff in this lawsuit. They don't like that 50,000 delegates adopted and ratified the 28th Amendment to the Constitution. But they are quite content for 535 individuals to file suit to strike it down."

Finally, Hirschfeld circled and moved in. "That's all well and good, Judge Brooks, but aren't you just crafting all of this out of whole cloth?"

Brooks wondered how long Hirschfeld would be able to contain himself. He was visibly agitated. Given his circumstances, how could he not be? This was the moment Brooks had dreaded. "Not at all, Justice Hirschfeld."

"How are you so sure of all this?"

"It's right there in the history books."

"What are you talking about?"

"The vote to adopt our Constitution."

"What about it?"

"It was by a vote of 30 to 27. That was the vote of the *delegates* to the Constitutional Convention of 1787."

"Yes, but how were those delegates selected? Weren't they selected by a majority of the voting population?"

"No sir. They were selected by the legislative bodies of the states that then comprised the union."

"Correct, by a majority of we the people of the United States."

"No sir. By a majority of each state. We the people of the United States never elected those delegates. Just like they don't elect the President today. The fact is that the term 'majority' as we have used it throughout American history, is quite different than the common meaning of that term.

"Under our Constitution, each state receives two seats in the U.S. Senate. So, New York, which has 33 times the population of its neighbor, Vermont, receives only the same representation in the Senate as Vermont. Yet the notion of 'majority' still predominates our sense of representation. And if a majority of the governed were not okay with this approach, they'd do something about it."

Hirschfeld shifted in his seat, his expression darkening.

"Haven't you just disproved your very argument? The governed have very little to say in how they're governed. And yet they soldier on."

"Only to the extent, and for so long as, they choose to delegate to their representatives. But from the very formation of this extraordinary republic, they have preserved their right at all times to intervene when not satisfied with how their representatives are performing."

"That's anarchy," Hirschfeld barked. "You're talking revolution, not the rule of law."

"If our country did not allow for some degree of what you speak of as revolution," Brooks countered, "our country would not be here today. We'd still be an appendage of Great Britain."

He glanced at his watch. Time was short.

"Justice Hirschfeld, do you doubt for a minute that a majority of our governed are disenchanted with our Congress today, and support the 28th Amendment?"

"That isn't the point."

"Ah, but it is. NoPoli took great pains to come up with 50,000 delegates from all around the country genuinely representing a fair cross-section of our country. NoPoli didn't need to hunt those delegates down. They freely volunteered. The only requirement NoPoli imposed was eligibility to vote in federal elections. And each state chapter of NoPoli selected its delegates— and this is the key point—in the very same way that, once upon a time, we selected our delegates to replace the Articles of Confederation and adopt the Constitution we enjoy today."

Hirschfeld wasn't budging. "There's a crucial difference, Judge Brooks. Citizens of each of the states voted for their representatives who in turn voted for their constitutional delegates. That did not happen here. Citizens of each of the states did not have the opportunity to vote for the NoPoli delegates."

"I must respectfully disagree with you, Justice Hirschfeld. Every citizen in every state was just as free to join NoPoli and vote for the NoPoli delegates from their state as they are free to register to vote in their state."

"But did they know that?"

"Respectfully, Justice Hirschfeld, the impending NoPoli convention did not take place on the dark side of the moon. There were press releases, flyers sent out by snail mail, email, Twitter, Facebook, and virtually every other social media platform you can think of. There were television and radio advertisements, interviews, editorials in local and national newspapers. The ability to participate in the adoption and ratification of the 28th Amendment was publicized every bit as much as any other aspect of our electoral process."

"That evidence is entirely anecdotal," Hirschfeld said.

"I beg to differ, Your Honor. The supporting details are in our briefing papers.

"I see my allotted time is almost up. Please allow me to sum up. If the government is to serve the governed, and not the other way around, and if this Court is not to lose its compass and intrude on we the people—as our elected representatives have certainly been doing—then the 28th Amendment, long the *missing amendment* to our Constitution, must be allowed to stand. Judgment in this case should be entered for NoPoli. We the people thank you."

Brooks heard a smattering of applause as he turned away from the lectern and headed for his seat in the well. Chief Justice Trotter banged his gavel to quiet the crowd, then said. "Thank you, Judge Brooks. We are adjourned until the scheduled announcement and reading of our decision or decisions on Monday."

It seemed everyone in the Courtroom rose at once. Except Hirschfeld. Brooks watched his old friend, as he had done on Tuesday, visibly hold up the universal "call me" signal to his cheek and ear.

CHAPTER 75
Thursday, May 8, 3:30 pm

THOMAS RETRIEVED the van and headed back to the cabin. He tried to use the video app to check in on the girl, but she and her shoe had apparently fixed that for good. He admired her gumption, yes, but that didn't matter. He could not let her insulting remarks go unchallenged. *She doesn't know about my relationship with Mother. Or Father. How could she? Especially since Mother is no longer able to tell anyone about that.*

He was also troubled by the number of people in Court today who seemed to be looking for someone. He pondered whether that someone could be him, whether someone had outed him. *The old man? Reyes? Someone else?*

His mind returned to the girl. He had to keep his guard up. *Don't let her shake you.* As much as Thomas desperately wanted to be in Court Monday to personally witness the outcome of his efforts, that could prove dangerous if Reyes and his FBI gofers were there again, possibly looking around for him. That would require more thought.

He hadn't missed Hirschfeld's signal to phone him. He thought it best to let Grandpa stew overnight, to remind him again just who was in control. The call he *had* to make today was to Reyes.

* * *

Brooks answered the incoming call from Lotello. "Detective," he sighed, "does *everything* have to take so long?"

"He wasn't able to see me until 12:30. By the time I finished there, you were already back in Court. I had to wait until you were out.

"And?"

"I was impressed. He's done this kind of work before. He's sharp, knows what he's doing. He'll take the job if everyone agrees on the terms."

"Who's everyone?"

"He and his lawyers, Cassie's family and the kidnappers."

"Did he offer any thoughts about getting them on board?"

"He said it would all come down to their vetting him, assessing his integrity. He's sure they'll insist on some 'come to Jesus' meeting with him before they decide. I think he'll be able to handle that if these people are rational."

Brooks heard the satisfaction in Lotello's voice. And a residual bit of nerves as well. "Let's back up. Please take me through your full conversation with Lance. From start to finish. Don't leave anything out. Put me in the room with the two of you."

"Okay." Lotello paused.

Brooks could hear Lotello flipping through the pages of his trusty notepad. He didn't say a word until Lotello finished. "That's about it," Lotello said.

"Interesting man," Brooks said. "His lawyers email us a draft agreement in the morning. We work through any changes we want with them. When we're agreed, Hirschfeld gets the papers to the kidnappers for their reaction. Once we're hopefully all in accord, they deliver the girl to Lance. How soon do you anticipate we can get Cassie away from them and into his hands?"

"Hard to say yet. It depends on how long it takes to get signed copies of the agreement exchanged. Even then, my guess is that they'll want to hang onto Cassie until the last minute."

Brooks exhaled. "Probably so. I'll speak to Hirschfeld tonight."

"How will he reach them," Lotello asked, "now that Court's dark until Monday?"

"Not sure," Brooks answered. "Hirschfeld signaled them to call him at the end of the Court session this afternoon. I assume they saw the signal too. I don't know if or when they'll respond."

"By the way, Judge, Lance said you would explain to me the two dollars he required me to leave with his receptionist, one dollar for each side."

236

Brooks thought about that for a moment. "Required no doubt by his lawyers, to protect Lance from being characterized as an 'officious intermeddler.' One who voluntarily comes to the aid of another actually has a greater liability if something goes wrong than if he was hired to help. You said you paid the two dollars, right?"

"Madison did."

"As in your daughter, Madison? You didn't mention she was there with you. Explain, please."

"Sorry. No, of course Madison was not there. But she's pretty much sorted things out on her own. First, Cassie didn't show for their long-planned Court outing together. Now, Cassie's not answering any of Madison's calls or texts. Nor is Cassie's mom. Cassie and Madison are best friends. Madison knows Cassie wouldn't just ignore her. Madison wants to help. I understand, but Madison's been driving me nuts. I'm not about to involve her, but I thought I'd subtract the two dollars from her allowance, let her think she's helping."

"And what if things don't turn out so well?"

"I won't consummate the subtraction unless and until we first get Cassie back safe and sound."

"With everything going on, you have to worry about this too?"

"Not a problem. With a pre-teen daughter and a wife who's a lawyer, I've learned to multi-task."

"You're sure you can?"

"Didn't say I was good at it."

"Better you than me. I have my hands full with just a wife. And a dog and a cat.

"Good work, Detective, but it's just a start. We're going to be very busy the next few days. Hopefully."

"Your Honor. What if we're not able to persuade Hirschfeld and his family to go this route? Or if Hirschfeld's not able to persuade Cassie's captors to do so?"

"At the moment, I don't have a clue. Keep your fingers crossed that we don't have to answer that question. Email the agreement to me in the morning as soon as you receive it. I'll be in touch right after I speak with Hirschfeld."

* * *

Nishimura knew that Reyes had a reputation for generally cooperating with the media. And for chasing the pretty ladies. She didn't know him well, but she'd wangled a meeting with him a couple of times on prior stories. It was hard getting the first meeting, but when she didn't shy away from his thin-ly-veiled innuendos, the second one came easier. Along with his private cell number.

She left a message as soon as Court adjourned. She didn't say what it concerned, only that it was urgent. If she didn't hear back by the end of the day, she'd try again in the morning. This time she'd raise the ante, mention that her calls concerned his interest in *Congress v. NoPoli*.

If she were correct, he'd return the second call, if not the first. If he didn't, she'd have no choice but to then play her Webber card. She reminded Joey to get used to living out of his car for the next several days. And sticking to Webber like glue.

CHAPTER 76
Thursday, May 8, 3:50 pm

So far, Reyes had nothing to show for his suspicions concerning Thomas. Neither he nor the FBI had spotted him in the Courtroom. If he were ever there. But, of course, it had been years since he had seen Thomas. And he remembered Thomas's special ops skill when it came to disguises.

Reyes had also been disturbed by the incident with that oddball Webber outside the Courthouse. The man had instantly morphed from aggressive to flustered. It was strange enough that Reyes had asked the FBI to do some background on Webber. When they reported back that Webber was the son-in-law of Supreme Court Associate Justice Arnold Hirschfeld, Reyes had become even more uncomfortable.

First, a vague message from someone almost certain to have been Thomas. Now, out of nowhere, he had been approached by the son-in-law of a Supreme Court Justice. He wanted to turn the FBI loose, find out if Hirschfeld's family were going through anything out of the ordinary, but he decided that might be unwise. The FBI was already wondering about his interest in Thomas.

And now this nondescript call from that looker over at NBN-TV. His instincts told him to put her off. At least for now. Meanwhile, he had to think about bringing this up to POTUS again.

He decided to sleep on it for the night. If he could sleep.

* * *

Hirschfeld was scrambling to figure out his next move.

Whatever had prompted the call from the hijackers asking him about the White House Chief of Staff? He hardly knew the man.

He also had to work around the schedule Trotter had set for the Justices through Sunday: A roundtable discussion Friday morning to poll the Justices to see where they each stood, at least preliminarily; with a follow-up meeting Saturday morning to see if anything had changed. Majority, dissenting and possible concurring opinions had to be assigned, written and shared. What normally was allowed around three months had to be completed in this instance in three days.

Obviously, Hirschfeld would have to attend each of these sessions, impinging on everything else he had going on. Had the kidnappers spotted his signal for another call? Would they respond? How quickly? What exactly would he say? As yet, he had no idea. And right now his family was waiting for him at Jill's home. He didn't know what to say to them either.

* * *

Webber was upset when he left the Courthouse. He needed to clear his head. He started walking.

He'd been gone all day. How was he going to explain his absence to Jill? And what about the mess of things he'd made with Reyes? He'd really screwed that up, giving Reyes his name. He was petrified that would come back to haunt him. And, worse still, perhaps Cassie too. He didn't want to mention the Reyes episode to his family. He decided he might have to do so, but only if it turned out that Reyes was somehow involved in Cassie's kidnapping.

He looked at his watch. He couldn't believe it. He'd been lost in thought for almost an hour. It hadn't helped. He really needed to get home. As he drove through the commuter traffic, he considered checking in with Adams, but ruled that out for the time being as well. Adams would have contacted him if he had any news. Maybe Arnold would know something more.

CHAPTER 77
Thursday, May 8, 5:30 pm

CASSIE HAD HEARD the man arrive upstairs almost an hour ago. It struck her as strange that he hadn't come down to check up on her yet. Since she'd pulverized his camera only a couple of hours earlier, she had fully expected him to come charging into the basement all bent out of shape. She couldn't understand what was keeping him, and what he might have in mind to do to her to get even. She had spent the last couple of hours developing a strategy to hold him at bay. She hoped it would work because she wasn't sure she could endure another onslaught.

* * *

Thomas was restless. Too many loose ends. Hirschfeld and Esposito had each done all they could, but Brooks was good. He didn't like that asshole during the *Norman* trial. He liked him even less now. He should've taken Brooks out of the picture then. Better late than never, before Brooks could make trouble for him again.

He knew what bothered him the most though was the girl. In the beginning, he had planned to dispose of her the minute her usefulness was over. It was no longer quite that simple. Of course, he still had to get rid of her. But this was starting to wear on him. *She* was starting to wear on him. His feelings were becoming muddled. He kept thinking about her relationship with her grandfather. *Listen to this shit. Quit stalling. Get down there. Now.*

* * *

"Hey brat. What did you think you were doing? Smashing my camera like that. That's gonna cost you."

"Says who? What're you gonna do? Dock my allowance? Take away my bread and water?"

"How 'bout I toss your insulin?"

"Don't think so, Frankenstein face."

"Yeah? Why not?"

"Because without a healthy me, you lose. Your plan crashes and burns. I'm your only ticket. You know it. I know it."

"What're you talking about? You don't know squat."

"I do too. I know plenty. You kidnapped me just before the start of my poppy's Supreme Court case. You must have wanted him to do something for you. But that's crazy. He'd never do anything for you. He wouldn't even talk to you.

"Unless maybe you first kidnapped me, and told him you'd kill me if he didn't do what you wanted. But Poppy'd make you promise not to touch me, and to let me go if he agreed to do what you wanted.

"So you have to keep me safe. When you found out I needed more insulin to live, you went to Poppy, not my mom and dad. But my parents are the ones who have my supplies, not him. Why would you go to my poppy? Answer: Because you were already talking with him about what you wanted him to do and you had to show him you were doing everything you could to keep me safe.

"So I know plenty. See? You can't dare hurt me. Even when you get mad at me."

Christ! How'd this little bitch work all this out? I couldn't have done that at her age. According to Mother and Father, I could never do anything right.

Thomas was furious. He swiftly closed the distance between them. Before she could react, he reached around and grabbed her by the back of her neck, pulling her face right up into his. "Don't think you're so smart, brat. There's a whole lot I can do short of killing you. Without your grandfather being any the wiser. Why don't I give you a little example of just what I mean? Right here and now."

He slowly tightened his grip on her neck. He expected her to cry out. She didn't. *The brat is one tough cookie.* With a final shove that caused her to stumble and lose her balance, he turned and walked out, locking the basement door, as always.

* * *

Cassie was glad the camera didn't work anymore. If it did, in spite of all of her pretending to the contrary, he would've seen just how terrified she really was.

CHAPTER 78
Thursday, May 8, 6:00 pm

IT WAS around six when Webber finally arrived home and entered the family room. Linda and Jill were huddled close together on the sofa, Linda's arm around Jill's shoulder. Jill wore the same robe she had on when Webber had left that morning. Dark circles shadowed her swollen eyes. Hirschfeld was slumped in an adjacent chair. His breathing was labored, his eyes were closed. Webber couldn't tell if he were asleep or just deep in thought. Webber took a seat opposite them.

Jill was the first to speak. "Where've you been all day?"

"At the Courthouse," Webber said, "watching the proceedings. Hoping I might spot someone looking sideways at your dad. I didn't."

"You should have called. Mom and I have been out of our minds."

"I'm sorry. I should have, but I couldn't. They don't allow phones in the Courtroom. The place was packed. If I'd stepped out to call, someone would have been given my seat. I wouldn't have been able to get back in."

Webber changed the subject. "By the way, your dad was terrific, arguing to defeat the amendment at every turn. I can only imagine how hard that must have been on him given his true beliefs. Not to mention having to behave as if nothing out of the ordinary were going on."

"Jill and I kept watching the phone," Linda said, "waiting for it to ring. Not knowing whether the silence was a good thing or a bad thing."

Hirschfeld stirred. He didn't appear to be handling this conversation very well. He looked drained. Webber wondered how much longer he could keep this up. "I received another call from Cassie's kidnappers today. It—"

The words flew out of Jill's mouth. "Jesus, Dad, when were you going to tell us?"

"I was waiting for Mark to get here. I wanted to tell everyone at the same time.

"White House Chief of Staff Manny Reyes was in Court today. The kidnapper on the phone was extremely anxious. Rattled. He accused me of breaking our 'agreement' to say nothing to anyone, instead bringing Reyes into the picture. Along with a bunch of federal agents who were also there.

"I swore I've not had anything to do with them. That's the truth. I haven't. But I don't know if he believed me. He hung up on me."

Webber was cringing inside. He was sure everyone in the room was looking at him.

"Dad," couldn't the White House just be interested in the case? Why would he blame us?"

"I have no idea. Or why the kidnappers would be interested in Reyes.

"But this leads me to something else we need to discuss. When I first heard about it, I thought it was rubbish. After the latest call from these thugs, I think it may be worth considering."

"Arnold," Linda said, "you're speaking in riddles. *What* may be worth considering?"

"Everyone hear me out, please. Let me finish before you react."

Hirschfeld recounted his early morning secret meeting with Brooks, and the escrow concept Brooks raised. "I was totally opposed. But then as—"

Webber cut him off, "What are you talking about? Isn't Brooks lead counsel for NoPoli? How could you possibly be meeting with him in the middle of your case? Doesn't that violate all kinds of rules?"

"Technically, yes. But—"

"No buts. You can't—"

"Knock it off, Mark," Hirschfeld snapped. "You want to talk about rules, or about getting your daughter safely back home?"

Webber bristled. What he wanted to say was: "Who the hell do you think you are, old man, talking to me like that? You're in my home now. Not your fancy Courtroom." What he actually said was . . . nothing.

"I asked you all not to interrupt until I finished. As for you, Mark, you need to quit worrying about the small stuff and concentrate on what's important. Do you really think I need a lecture from you on the rules of Court?"

Webber remained silent. For the moment.

The scowl on Hirschfeld's face hinted that Webber's silence might not be enough.

"You know, Mark, I was originally going to wait to speak to you in private about this, but since you feel so entitled to criticize me, when were you planning to tell us about your little escapade with Reyes outside the Courthouse this afternoon? Is there perhaps something *you* did to bring Reyes into the Courtroom today, prompting the kidnapper's call to me during the noon recess?"

All eyes instantly redirected to Webber. He swallowed hard. "That was the only contact I've ever had with Reyes. I wanted to know why he was there, but I chickened out and just asked him what he thought about the case. Our conversation lasted only a few seconds.

"Until you told us about your call with the kidnappers, I didn't think there was any reason to mention this. But I did tell Reyes my name when the agent with him insisted I identify myself. Your call must have come within a few minutes after I met Reyes. My behavior was lame, I know that now. You have every reason to call me out on this."

"Aren't you still omitting something, Mark? What prompted you to approach Reyes in the first place?"

Webber looked pained. *Shit. Caught again. No choice but to come clean now.* He described his earlier confidential outreach to Larry Adams, and that Adams had somehow electronically intercepted a suspicious call from Reyes to the FBI.

"And you questioned me about not following the rules? I take it you've heard about unlawful wiretapping."

So rules don't matter only if he's the one breaking them. Webber still held his tongue.

Hirschfeld shook his head. "Look, I don't give a damn about any rules at this point. But we need to be straight with one another. What else did this Adams fellow tell you?"

"Just that Reyes arranged for the FBI to come with him to Court this morning. Adams thought that the call might have something to do with Cassie. I Googled Reyes, looked at some photos of him. I decided to go to Court and confront him. After I introduced myself, it suddenly dawned on me that this could prove dangerous to Cassie. And so I backed off."

Hirschfeld wasn't finished. "But not until you gave him your name, right?"

"Yes. But that's all. I never said anything about Cassie or what I first wanted to discuss with him."

"Okay. I guess we've cleared the air. No point dwelling any further on what we can't change. But from here on we need to stay a lot more coordinated. No more individual heroics. Agreed?"

No one answered.

Hirschfeld then explained his long-term relationship with Brooks, dating back to when they were law school classmates, and his high regard for him. He added how Brooks guessed what was going on, offered to help, and suggested using an escrow arrangement to save Cassie.

Webber couldn't believe his ears. "Arnold, I don't care what you think of Brooks, or his suggested underground arrangement in human traffic. Even if we might hypothetically agree to it, what makes you think Cassie's captors would? Why would they ever trust some former Delta Force military outsider?

"Their possession of Cassie is the only leverage they have. If I were them and you made that proposal to me, I'd cut off one of Cassie's fingers and send it to us in a box. To remind us who's calling the shots."

Webber stood up, as if to emphasize the importance of what he was about to say. "I'm Cassie's father. Not you, Arnold. I've had enough of this. We should have gone to the FBI in the beginning. That's exactly what I intend to do now."

"NOOOO!!!"

Jill's hysterical shriek took Webber by surprise, if not his in-laws as well. Webber couldn't tell whether the wail was planned or spontaneous, but it didn't matter. Either way, Jill now had everyone's undivided attention.

"You may be her father, Mark, but I'm her mother. After going behind our backs today, and maybe making things worse than they already were, you've now forfeited your right to decide anything. I say we have to give Dad and Judge Brooks a chance to quietly find a solution directly with the kidnappers. At least for one more day."

They reviewed the details of Brooks's proposal one more time. And the odds that they saw Hirschfeld's latest signal in Court. And would call.

As if on cue, the cell phone sitting on the table in front of Hirschfeld's rang.

CHAPTER 79
Thursday, May 8, 6:20 pm

LOTELLO HARDLY HAD a foot in the door when Madison accosted him. Leah was only a couple of steps behind Madison.

"You're home! What does that mean? What's going on? Dad, tell me!"

"Nothing to tell yet, sweetheart. When I have something for you, I will."

Madison's eyes pierced right through him. "Not fair, Dad. You're doing it again." She spun around and stormed off. Seconds later, he heard her bedroom door slam.

Lotello turned to Leah. "Hmm, but how do you think she really feels? What more does she expect me to say to her right now? There are things going on that I just can't share with her."

"Then you have to pay the price, putting up with her 'tweener' emotions. I get it. She's still just your baby. But she's old enough to know what Cassie could be going through, and to be worried sick. When you hold her at bay, she doesn't know if that means the news is bad, or you just don't trust her."

"She's just eleven-years-old. What the hell are you talking about, Leah?"

"Frank?"

"Yes."

"I'm not just eleven years old. Were you planning on telling me what's going on?"

"Of course."

When he came to the possible role of J.R. Lance, she just stared at him. He asked her what she thought.

"That's a lot to process. Do you really think it can work?"

"You're the lawyer. You tell me."

"This is not about law, Frank. I have no idea. I want to know what do *you* think?"

"I don't know. But time's running out and we don't seem to have any other options."

* * *

"Hello?"

"Arnold, it's me, Cyrus. I saw you signal them at the end of the hearing. Have they called?"

"No. I don't even know if they noticed."

"I noticed. They noticed. They'll call. After they sweat you. Anything else to report?"

Hirschfeld told Brooks about the earlier call from the kidnappers concerning Reyes.

"Reyes? Did you speak with Reyes?"

"No. Why would I?"

"Don't know. They asked. I'm asking."

Brooks walked Hirschfeld through his conversation with Lotello about the possible use of Lance as an escrow intermediary. He focused on the big picture, omitting unnecessary details.

"This morning I thought your escrow idea was crazy. Not anymore. The call this afternoon from them about Reyes made me realize how things are. They are completely unbalanced. At least the one I've spoken with. I can't possibly rely on them. Or their word. I can't go first. I won't. I'm scared to death, but I'm convinced we'll never see Cassie again if I deliver the result they want without getting her back first. And I can't see them agreeing to go first. So how do we put this escrow business in place?"

"Lance told Lotello he would email the papers to him early in the morning. Lotello will forward them to you and me. Under the circumstances, someone besides you needs to look through the papers. By default, that seems to be me. Another conflict, but who's counting? Where will you be in the morning?"

"Wait a minute. Who is Lance?"

"He's the potential escrow agent."

"Oh yeah, right. No way Lotello can email that to me. I'll be at the Courthouse in conference with the other Justices from eight until about ten. Courthouse security filters would intercept any such email."

"I'll ask Lotello to drive a copy of the escrow papers to you at the Courthouse while I'm studying them. I'll call him before he reaches you to tell him they're okay, or what revisions I think we need. He'll insert any revisions I want in hand on your copy. How does he get the papers to you where you'll be?"

"He won't be able to get to me. Nor can I be seen with the husband of one of the lawyers in the case. Tell him to go to Courthouse security and say he has an envelope for me. Lotello should make sure it's sealed and has my name on it. My assistant will make sure security is expecting the package and will immediately bring it to me. I'll sign whatever you okay."

"The question is these people. I can make the 'whoever goes first' speech and point out that with the escrow no one has to go first. What I don't know is if or when they'll call, or how they'll react."

"We'll know when we know. There's one more thing we need to discuss."

Hirschfeld let out a long sigh. "I don't know how much more I can process, Cyrus."

"Convincing them the escrow is best for everyone is just the first step. There's still the question of selecting the escrow agent. We're good with Lance. He's solid. But it remains to be seen whether the hostage-takers will accept our candidate."

Brooks walked Hirschfeld through Lance's background.

"I think I get how to pitch Lance to them. If they call. Obviously, they'll insist on checking him out on their own.

"By the way, I told Linda and Cassie's parents about our conversation this morning. Our family will only give this until noon tomorrow. If they don't agree by then, we're going to the FBI. We're unanimous on this. We just can't wait any longer."

Brooks thought about that. It wasn't for him to second-guess the family. All he could do is help them carry out *their* wishes. "I understand."

"Thank you, Cyrus. Sorry for being so hostile this morning."

"No apologies necessary. I probably would have been worse. One last thing. If you and your family decide to go to the FBI, make sure you call me first. *Before* you do."

"Why?"

"Just some additional information that will be helpful for you to have if your family does decide to go to the FBI. We don't need to talk about it now. Just don't forget to call me. *First.*"

Brooks hung up before Hirschfeld could press further.

CHAPTER 80
Thursday, May 8, 6:30 pm

BROOKS KNEW Eloise had heard his side of the Hirschfeld conversation. When he wasn't as confident as he put on to others, it helped him to talk things through with her. Precisely why he'd placed the call to Hirschfeld with her in earshot. Which he also knew would not be lost on her.

Said Eloise as soon as Brooks hung up: "Cyrus, are you sure about all this?"

"Interesting that you ask. Do you have a couple of minutes?"

They spent the next hour talking. Initially resistant, Eloise was nevertheless a quick study. Albeit reluctantly, it didn't take her long to join. "I find the thought of 'depositing' this poor girl in a conceptual vault as if she were a Rembrandt or the Hope Diamond to be offensive. But I don't see any alternative.

"Who is this proposed middleman, Lance, how did you find him, why would he agree to do this, and why would these people accept anyone proposed by the girl's family?"

"All good questions, especially the last one. Let's take them one at a time. His name is J.R. Lance." Brooks highlighted Lance's pedigree.

"What I find disturbing about your presentation of Mr. Lance's qualifications is how comfortably you seem to have crossed over some unmarked line of civility. You've expanded your vocabulary to include words and concepts I would have thought foreign to you—black ops, covert missions, the permanent elimination of opponents, human beings referred to as assets."

Seldom at a loss for words, the only comeback Brooks could offer for Eloise's disappointment was a frank dose of reality. Not himself persuaded, he ignored her observation and turned to her second question.

"Detective Lotello is the one who located Mr. Lance. He reached out to several associates for a list of prospects. When several sources independently mentioned Lance, Lotello examined the man's bio. Lotello was pretty sure he'd found our man. I more or less deferred to his opinion because, as you observe, he's more experienced than I in matters of this nature."

Brooks waited for Eloise to offer some barbed comment about how infrequently he 'more or less' deferred to anyone. If it occurred to her to do so, she chose to refrain.

"And how interested is this Mr. Lance in taking on the assignment?"

"Hard to say, exactly. Lance is apparently not a man of many words. But according to Lotello he seems highly principled and committed to helping resolve imponderables such as ours. After Lotello explained the situation, Lance asked a few questions, listened to Lotello's answers, and then said he'd do it. Within lawful boundaries set by his lawyers. Lotello has the impression Lance might stretch those boundaries a little."

"I can see how Lance would appeal to you. Maybe to the kidnappers too. But again, how will you overcome their likely paranoia causing them to reject anyone put up by our side?"

Our side? That Eloise had transitioned from disappointment to ownership of the concept was not lost on Brooks. He found it reassuring in the face of his own insecurities about the approach. "Well that is the $64,000 question, isn't it?"

"I would think Cassie's life is worth a lot more than $64,000, Cyrus."

"Come, come. That's a cheap shot. You know I was talking about the challenge of the issue, not the value of the girl's life."

"Sorry. You're right. This time. Don't let it go to your head. Just my natural reluctance, I guess, to accept anything akin to human trafficking."

"Apology accepted. You are right, however, about the negotiating instinct to distrust whatever the other side proposes. However, the best results in any negotiation are when the parties find a genuine common ground on which they can build."

"What common ground? I can't imagine any ground less common than what we have here."

"I think not. At least, I hope not." Brooks wondered if Eloise were becoming a bit defensive. He loved trying ideas out on her, but this was the risk of disagreeing with her.

"I'm waiting, Cyrus. When are you planning to divulge your analysis to me? Are you becoming a bit defensive?"

Jesus, the woman's been hanging around me too long. "Not at all, dear. We have this incredible stalemate. Both sides share that. In common. Unless we get creative, there will likely be no more than one winning side, and maybe none. And neither side has any assurance that it will be the side that prevails. Therefore, each side should rationally be motivated to maximize the chances of both sides coming away with a win.

"This is why I think the hijackers will come around to our suggestion. It increases the chances of both sides winning."

"Cyrus, we've already agreed on that much, but you still haven't told me why you think they'll accept Lance. Rather than insisting you accept some intermediary they come up with?"

"The reasoning is exactly the same as buying into the escrow concept. For this win-win procedure to work, we need a mutually agreeable handler. Someone has to come up with a credible candidate the other side is willing to trust, and accept. I think Lance is someone with whom they will identify."

"Again, I ask you . . . why?"

"Look at the result they want on the 28th Amendment. They are pro-government. Everything in Lance's background cries out that he's pro-government.

"Also, I think they consider themselves very righteous. Their *means* may not be righteous, but you know the old argument that the end justifies the means. Everything in Lance's background reeks of honor and trust. Righteousness. My hope is that their instinct to distrust anyone we propose will be overcome by their affinity to respect and identify with Lance.

"We have no guarantee, but we also have no other bright ideas, and we're quickly running out of time. They are, too. At the end of the day, a common lack of time may be what brings us together. Still another thing each side has in common."

"Still? What is 'still' is the fact that you're still making quite a leap of faith. So, what haven't you told me, Cyrus Brooks? You know I know you all too well. You always have a trump card you hold back. Quit beating around the bush. I heard you tell Hirschfeld that if his family decides to go to the FBI, it would be important that he call you first. What are you holding back?"

Brooks grinned. "Aren't you the observant one. I do have an additional reason for pressing this approach, and for believing it will appeal to the kidnappers. You remember when Detective Lotello was shot while the jury was out deliberating in the *Norman* trial?"

"Cyrus, do you think I could *ever* forget that? How it almost destroyed both you and Frank? Your remaining scars from that episode are greater than his. He's moved past it. You haven't. I don't believe you ever will."

Brooks pretended his wife's remarks had not struck a chord. "A little less theatrics, dear. Please. More to the point, do you remember *who* shot Lotello?"

"I do. That obnoxious CIA man with the strange name. Thomas Thomas. Pretty hard to forget him too, unfortunately."

"Right. And you remember how we couldn't prove it, but always thought Thomas was acting under instructions from the President to manipulate the direction of the *Norman* trial. And that his handler was none other than White House Chief of Staff Manny Reyes?"

"Yes. But what have Thomas and Reyes to do with Cassie?"

"Out of the blue, Reyes showed up at the Supreme Court hearings this morning and spent several hours there."

"Why do you find it unusual that the White House would take an interest in the fate of the 28th Amendment?"

"There's more. Reyes had a bunch of government agents stationed all around the perimeter of the Courtroom. Maybe outside as well."

"Doesn't surprise me. Don't White House chiefs of staff always have secret service agents to protect them?"

"That's just it. None of these agents were hovering around Reyes. They were deployed throughout the Courtroom. As if they were looking for someone, not safeguarding Reyes. Reyes appeared more interested in who those agents were looking for than in the Courtroom proceedings."

"I don't follow."

Brooks loved nothing more than a stimulating exchange, especially when he thought he had the upper hand. "At the noon recess, one of the assailants called Hirschfeld and accused him of teaming with Reyes to take them down. According to Hirschfeld, the guy on the phone was irate, screaming threats, beside himself with rage."

"And you make exactly what of that?"

"I think the kidnappers may be just one person. Thomas."

"My God, Cyrus, how'd you ever come up with that? Didn't Frank say he believed Thomas left the country after the shootout and was in hiding?"

"He did. But what more would bring him back than to think he was again needed by 'his' President? Thomas could see this as his ticket back into the fraternity. The chance to make amends by bringing down the anti-government 28th Amendment to the U.S. Constitution."

"That's some imagination, even for you, Mr. Brooks. But if you are right, why would Reyes have been in Court today looking for Thomas? For that matter, why would Thomas have been there? Why wouldn't Reyes just watch the proceedings on the live television coverage from the comfort of his White House office?"

"If Reyes was Thomas's former handler during the *Norman* trial, who would be more worried about Thomas now than Reyes? Especially if he suspects—or knows—that Thomas is back, possibly delusional and out of control? Wouldn't he want to personally be at the Courthouse to see if he could spot him, arrange to have him quietly taken down?

"And," Brooks continued, "if Thomas saw Reyes with those agents in the Courtroom today, and thinks they're after him, have 'abandoned' him, and are looking to take him out before he can embarrass the administration, then his dreams of patching things up might now be dashed. And he might be feeling more than a little incensed. And isolated. Everyone looking for him. Foes and supposed friends alike.

"If delusional, and not merely disillusioned, he might be even more desperate than he originally was."

257

"If you're right, then Hirschfeld's granddaughter is in the hands of a ticking time bomb, on the verge of exploding at any moment, and doing only God knows what with the poor girl, Cyrus."

Brooks nodded. "Yes. But it also means our kidnapper, hoping to salvage his psychopathic plan, and longing for fraternal reunion, might be prone to accept as the escrow go-between another member, or at least another former member, of his black ops fraternity."

"But returning to my last question, why did you implore Hirschfeld to call you first if his family decides to go to the FBI?"

"Because the FBI is part of the executive branch of the government, and the President of the United States is the head of the executive branch. If Hirschfeld's family reaches out to the FBI, that would likely come to Reyes's attention as White House Chief of Staff. What if I'm wrong and Reyes is actually still handling Thomas, in this case using Thomas to help defeat the anti-government 28th Amendment?

"Going to the FBI in that event would tip the family's hand to Reyes and Thomas and would be tantamount to signing Cassie's death warrant. I couldn't bring myself to load Hirschfeld up with that additional complication on top of everything else he's already dealing with. But I also can't let him be blindsided by a possible fox in the hen house if he and his family do decide to go to the FBI."

PART FIVE

More Stuff
And The Decision

CHAPTER 81
Friday, May 9, 7:30 am

BROOKS DID some of his best thinking while marching back and forth in his home office. Actually, it was more of a rectangle than back and forth, hugging the perimeter of the flat weave kilim rug on the hardwood floor. The rug was worn thin along his path of choice. Often single purpose of mind, his subconscious coupled with the feel of the rug to keep him from occasionally missing a turn and veering off into one of his office walls.

Hands clasped behind his back, head fixated on the tips of his walking shoes, he'd been at it for around twenty minutes when the cell phone sounded amid the electronic devices and organized stacks of documents on his "partner" desk. Not wanting to appear too anxious, Brooks waited until the third ring to answer.

Short winded, he wasted no words: "Got the papers?"

"Geez, Your Honor, are you okay?"

"Fine. Exercising. What about the papers?"

"Right here," Lotello said. "One single-spaced page. Pretty straightforward. Some legalese, but mostly plain English. Just emailed it to you. Check your inbox."

"Hold on."

Brooks punched the speaker button on the cell phone and set it down next to the computer keyboard. He launched the email application, found the email, and opened the attachment. "Got it," he said. Give me a couple minutes."

"No problem," Lotello answered.

He read through the document on his computer screen. Then read it a second time. He looked up at his office ceiling, and reflected on what it said. And didn't say. He was fine with what it said. He typed in one additional sentence.

He confirmed that the font, and the tone and attitude, of the additional sentence were the same as the remainder of the document. Lance and his lawyers would, of course, immediately spot the insert, but they wouldn't object. He was less certain about the kidnappers. He wanted to make sure they wouldn't detect the presence of a second author when Hirschfeld furnished Lance's agreement to them.

He moved through it one more time:

Confidential Escrow Agreement

1. Creation: After first consulting their respective attorneys on matters of legality and morality, this Agreement was entered into on the date (Agreement Date) it was initialed and exchanged by J.R. Lance (Agent) and the other two parties who also initialed it (Anonymous Party and Other Party).

2. Performance: Within 24 hours after the Agreement Date, Anonymous Party shall deliver (Delivery Date) the acknowledged subject of this Agreement (Asset) to Agent. If Agent determines that Asset is not in reasonably good condition, Agent shall immediately release the Asset to Other Party and this Agreement shall then be void. So long as the contemplated triggering event occurs within 72 hours following the Delivery Date (Deadline), Agent shall immediately release the Asset to Other Party. If not, Agent shall immediately return the Asset to Anonymous Party at the Washington, D.C. return location Anonymous Party designates to Agent prior to the Deadline. Should Anonymous Party not do so, Agent shall immediately release the Asset to Other Party.

3. Fees/Expenses: Other Party agrees to reimburse Agent for any expense he may incur as a result of entering into this Agreement and/or performing any related services. Upon completion of such performance, Other Party shall pay Agent a fee of $25,002. Should

Anonymous Party or Other Party reveal this Agreement, or any of its terms to any third party, he shall be required to pay Agent an additional fee of $1,000,000.

4. Miscellaneous: This Agreement has been initialed and exchanged in duplicate counterparts and shall be governed and interpreted under Washington, D.C. law. Without recourse, Agent shall be entitled to subcontract the performance of any service to sub-agents in accordance with applicable law. Should any term of this Agreement be found illegal or unenforceable, this Agreement shall nevertheless remain in effect without such term, giving the fullest meaning possible to the original intent of the parties. Anonymous Party and Other Party shall promptly take any further action directed by Agent to further the purposes of this Agreement.

When he finished: "Still there, Detective?"

"Where would I go?"

"This is a very unusual agreement. Hardly taken from some handbook. The lawyers who custom drafted this for Lance knew what they were doing."

"Do you need to make any changes?"

"The agreement was fine as Lance's lawyers prepared it. I've taken the liberty, however, of inserting one additional sentence."

"Should I run the insert by Lance before taking it to Hirschfeld?"

"No. The language won't bother Lance. Or his lawyers. I've just emailed the revised document back to you."

Brooks went over Hirschfeld's delivery instructions from the night before with Lotello. "You should be able to print what I've returned to you 'as is' and take it to Hirschfeld."

"Shouldn't you first explain to me what you've added?"

"When we have more time. It'll keep for now. You need to get cracking so Hirschfeld can hopefully arrange to get the document to the hijackers as quickly as possible."

"Alright. I'll call if I run into any snags."

"Please call either way. I'll update you as soon as I hear from Hirschfeld."

* * *

Lotello appreciated that Leah had assumed his usual job of getting the kids to school. Just as well, he thought. Madison was still refusing to speak to him.

Thanks to the typically lighter Friday traffic, he made good time. Courthouse security was expecting him. He waited while they called Hirschfeld's office and announced his presence. Hirschfeld's assistant came out and took the sealed envelope. She confirmed that Hirschfeld had instructed her to interrupt the Justices's conference and bring him the envelope.

Lotello texted Brooks as he walked back to his car:

H has agr.

Brooks immediately replied:

Thx. Stand by.

CHAPTER 82
Friday, May 9, 8:15 am

REYES PICKED up a second message from Nishimura:

Calling about Congress v. NoPoli. We need to talk this morning.

She didn't know it, but this time she had his undivided attention. He closed his office door and dialed her number. She picked up on the first ring.

"Anne Nishimura."

"Hey, Annie, Manny Reyes." His tone betrayed a smile his face refused to divulge. "Two calls in two days. How do I rate all your affection?"

"Noticed you in Court yesterday. What's your sudden interest in our judiciary?"

Reyes fiddled with the vintage Montblanc Meisterstück pen the President had given him. "I always try to stay on top of the important news. The 28th Amendment qualifies. As you know, our Attorney General and our Solicitor General are our chief representatives in the Supreme Court, but they fall under my watch."

"Maybe we can do a piece on that for the nightly news. Our tax dollars hard at work."

"Now you *are* stroking me. Or so I wish. Are you going to tell me what this is really about? Or do we need more foreplay?"

"The name Webber mean anything to you?"

The oddball who confronted me yesterday—how would she know about that?

"The people who make the outdoor grills?"

"Very clever. No, add one more 'b' and give it another try."

Reyes took a moment, as though thinking. "Nope. Sorry. Doesn't ring a bell. Should it?"

"He's Justice Hirschfeld's son-in-law."

He stopped twirling the Montblanc. "Okay. And—?"

"Are you saying you're unaware of that?"

"Look, Annie, I've got half a dozen meetings lined up back to back this morning. Much as I love hearing your sultry voice, and would enjoy spending some quality one-on-one time with you when things are a little quieter, for now, can we just cut to the chase?"

"Alright, Manny. I have it from reliable sources that Hirschfeld has some kind of problem and that it might have something to do with the *NoPoli* case. Care to comment?"

"I love saying 'No comment,' even when I have a comment I could provide. Makes me seem more important than I really am. But in this instance, it's not a stretch. I've got nothing for you. No idea what you're talking about."

"Well, you can't blame a girl for trying. Guess you don't get lucky today, Manny. Remember where you heard this first. Please give me a call if you stumble across anything."

"Always cherish happy endings and getting lucky, Annie. You'll be the first to hear."

As soon as he hung up, Reyes placed another call. "Supreme Court Justice Hirschfeld. Something's going on with his family. With him or his wife. Kids. Grandkids. Haven't a clue, but need to know. Two hours tops. Don't let me down."

CHAPTER 83
Friday, May 9, 9:00 am

THE MEETING of the nine Justices was just ending. It had taken a little more than one hour to go around the table. Congress's standing was not in issue. The vote that Congress has standing was seven in favor, two against. Hirschfeld was one of the seven voting for standing. This assured that Congress was entitled to sue and be heard and that the Justices would now have to decide whether the 28th Amendment was valid.

Even with Hirschfeld in the nay column, the vote to uphold the 28th Amendment remained five to four—five to uphold and four to invalidate. Hirschfeld had to move one of the five uphold votes over to the invalidate column. But they each appeared firm. He wasn't going to pick up a vote arguing the law or the social merits of the case. He would have to take someone into his confidence, and plead for their sympathy. Just thinking about it made him ill.

He removed the escrow agreement from the sealed envelope his secretary had given him. What he read sickened him almost as much as the thought of having to approach one of his colleagues. At least he had already decided who he was going to ask.

He read through the document once more. He couldn't imagine treating another human being so coldly, especially his own granddaughter. As if she were an inert piece of property.

Just then his private cell phone rang. A wave of dread swept over him.

"Saw your signal, old man. Make it fast."

"I can't make it fast. We need to talk. Within the next thirty minutes."

"Or what?" After a moment: "You know the drill. Outside. Where you made the insulin drop. Wait for me. I'll call when I see you."

* * *

Webber glanced up and down the street before ducking into the Alexandria café where Larry Adams sat waiting. The man had chosen a dark corner table far in the back. No one in earshot. Webber drew back a chair and sat.

Adams smiled gamely. Webber watched him make one last nervous check of the room, presumably to be sure no one was trying to listen in. "Sorry to drag you out like this, Mark, but things have taken a turn. We needed to meet in person."

Webber felt the blood drain from his face. "What—?"

"My contact intercepted another Reyes call. Reyes seems to be getting warmer. He gave some subordinate two hours to find out what's amiss in the Hirschfeld domain. Do you know something I don't?"

Webber sank deeper in his chair. His foolish approach to Reyes the day before came to mind. He couldn't bring himself to share this with Adams. "I don't, but it sounds like we're running out of time. If something doesn't break by midday, we're going to take our chances with the FBI."

"Probably best. I'm wearing out my welcome, but I'll call if I learn anything more."

"Thanks, Larry. I really appreciate what you've been doing."

"No worries. Wish I could do more."

* * *

Nishimura was frustrated. She felt she was onto something, but Reyes was stiff-arming her. He knew more than he was letting on, but she had to come up with something for him first. In her business, you had to give to get.

She called Joey. "We need to make another run at the Webber family. How soon can you pick me up?"

"See you in fifteen."

CHAPTER 84
Friday, May 9, 9:45 am

THE FOURTH DAY. Nothing for her to do but exercise, read, sleep—it had grown routine. Boring. Infuriating. She wished the man would give her a bucket of balls and a fairway wood or a nine iron, and take her outside for a few minutes, and let her empty the bucket. Probably afraid she'd clobber him. She wondered if he were as antsy as she was.

She missed her family, her friends, even feeding Whitney. *What are they all doing and thinking right now? This has to be hard on them, too, worrying about me.*

Her blood sugars were higher this morning. She told herself to stay positive, stay brave. That was much easier for her to say than to do.

* * *

Hirschfeld gazed in every direction from his position near the park drop point, looking for any sign of the man. Nothing he could detect in any direction. His phone rang.

"What's so urgent, Gramps? Your little girl has her insulin, a roof over her head, three squares a day, all the comforts of home. The case is over. All you have to do now is deliver. What's the frigging problem?"

Hirschfeld's patience was growing thin. "Enough with the tough-guy routine, huh? It's really getting old."

"Gee. Sorry. Didn't know you were the sensitive type."

"The bottom line is I can deliver the results, but I don't trust you. What assurance do I have that you'll let Cassie go once I deliver?"

"You don't have any assurance. You don't have any choice either. I make the rules. You follow them."

"No. Not anymore. I'm done with that."

The line went dead. The bastard hung up on him. Hirschfeld thought he was beginning to understand. It wasn't just that this man, and whomever he was working with, were trying to intimidate him, maintain control. They were changing telephones every few minutes so they couldn't be traced. They were worried someone was monitoring their calls. They didn't trust Hirschfeld any more than he trusted them.

Sure enough, the phone rang again. "The hell you mean you're done?"

"Just what I said. If I give you what you want, how do I know you'll let Cassie go?"

"You don't."

"If you think your bluster is having a positive effect on me, it's not. And as scared to death as I am, I'm done giving into my fright. It doesn't accomplish a damn thing. Not for me, not for Cassie. And not for you either, wise guy. Painful as it is, Israel has the right approach to deal with terrorist extortion."

"So, what do you and the Zionists suggest, keeping in mind, schlepper, that Israel is not always as tough as it pretends to be?"

"You have to show some trust in me. Let Cassie go first if you expect the results you want."

"Oh, yeah, right! That's a helluva chuckle. Fat chance of that, gramps. You don't trust me, but I'm supposed to trust you?"

"Why not? I'm a Supreme Court Justice. What are you? A common criminal."

"Now, now. Sticks and stones. Bully for you, old man, but your status doesn't mean shit to me."

"Exactly. Then you need to wake up. You don't trust me, an honorable, respected, law-abiding citizen, but you expect me to trust you? A bully and a thug. Why would I do that?"

"I told you. The difference is you don't have any choice. I do."

"I don't think so. As desperate as I am—and, yes, I am desperate—I think you are too. Just as much as me. For you to kidnap and repeatedly threaten to kill an innocent young girl, you must be pretty desperate too. And without any other viable options either. If I'm wrong, then," he choked trying to get the words out, "Cassie's probably going to die no matter what. So, I've decided you can just rot in hell before I'm going to give you what you want without knowing my little girl's safe, and coming home."

Once again, the line went dead. Right on schedule. It was about changing phones, not just for dramatic effect.

And then he was back again. "How about I let you hear the girl scream as I—"

This time, Hirschfeld was the one who hung up. No choice. The die was cast. He had to see it through.

His heart pounded, waiting, sweat breaking out all over his body, the fear so intense he felt like he was going to pass out. *Steady. Steady. Hang in there.*

The phone rang again. He answered.

"*You* don't hang up on *me*."

Hirschfeld did *exactly* that. Again.

He felt no sense of triumph in any of this. His fear segued into unfathomable grief. *Cassie, baby, I am so sorry . . .*

The phone rang once more. Hirschfeld looked at the God awful thing, thrumming in his hand, wanting to throw it as far away as he could. Instead, he answered.

"Stop being so melodramatic. I asked you, what's your proposal? Other than letting the girl go first. Believe me, that's *never* gonna happen."

It's time, Hirschfeld thought. "Our problem is that neither of us trusts the other. And neither of us is willing to go first. We need a way to break this deadlock. I have a thought, if you're willing to listen."

Silence. Then: "I'm listening."

"This is going to take a few minutes. I'm not trying to trace your calls, but do you want to hang up and call me back?"

It took five more calls for Hirschfeld to finally lay it all out. He wondered how many phones they had. At least they were still talking to him.

"I need to think about this. Check out your escrow agent, this Lance fellow. See if I think I can trust *him*. I'll get back to you."

"Don't hang up."

"What do you want? We're talking. I'm telling you . . . maybe. You press me too hard and you'll blow any chance you have."

"I'm not pressing. Take some time, just not a lot. Cassie's parents don't like this. My wife doesn't either. They don't want to do this. I've persuaded them to let me try, but they've given me an ultimatum. If we don't reach an agreement by noon today, my son-in-law is going to the FBI. He won't wait another minute. And his wife and mother-in-law are behind him. If that happens, you *can* trust me that the 28th Amendment will be upheld. You will not get what you want—whether or not you're willing to release Cassie."

In the brief silence that followed, Hirschfeld looked around him at the park, the busy street, the maddening, humiliating normalcy of it all.

"And you can trust me, old man, if anyone goes to the FBI, no one will ever see the girl again."

Hirschfeld was shuddering head to foot. And doing his best not to let it make its way into his voice.

"Here's what I'm going to do. I have this escrow agreement. In an unmarked envelope. It's only one page. I'm going to leave the envelope in the trash receptacle just like I did with Cassie's insulin. As soon as we hang up. Then I'll walk away. No one's watching. I know Cassie's life depends on the truth of that. You'll be safe to retrieve the envelope, look over the document, and make your decision. Call me back before noon. I can't emphasize that timing enough. Alright?"

No answer. The line went dead again. This time a full, five agonizing minutes before the man called back.

* * *

"Are you crazy? A fucking written agreement?"

"It's the only way. The agent won't get involved without one. His lawyers say he needs to be able to prove that he's acting as an agent at the request of each of us and not on his own. He won't participate without his lawyers's okay and they won't give it without a written agreement. The agreement actually favors *you*."

"Yeah? How's that?"

"It says the arrangement is confidential. The middleman doesn't want any of this seeing the light of day. It provides a $1 million penalty for him if either you or I divulge our deal.

"I can't imagine you talking to anyone, or paying the $1 million penalty even if you do. But I'm not judgment proof. I have assets. And I'm not anonymous like you are. This tells you that if I talk about any of this—even after we have Cassie back—Lance will make me pay him that penalty for exposing him to public notoriety he doesn't want. This is critically important to him. He tells me a good part of his business success requires him to assure his clients that he operates under the radar."

"That's a lot of money. Why won't he leak the story and make it look like you were the source so he can come after you for the money?"

"He doesn't really care about money here. When you read the agreement, you'll see he's doing the deal for a very modest fee. Just $1 a piece up front from each of us to make the deal legal. And then $25,000 on the back end, which is on me alone to pay, not you.

"If he cared about the money, he has to know I would pay all I could for him to break this stalemate, and get my Cassie back. This $1 million penalty is not about the money, it's to maintain his low profile. He knows that once I have Cassie back safe and sound I'm not about to wipe myself out financially."

"I don't know, old man. You might be willing to do that to get back at me."

"Really? Think about it. Aside from ruining my reputation, what could I possibly accomplish? You and your accomplices will be long gone. I don't even know who you are. The only one I'd hurt would be myself. This penalty is his assurance—and yours—that I won't bolt after we have Cassie back, go public with what happened and cause the Supreme Court to reverse its decision invalidating the amendment. With this penalty exposure on top of destroying my name, I couldn't dare afford to do that."

"A million dollars doesn't mean that much to you."

"You're missing the point. If I betray this agreement, I not only face financial ruin but also complete humiliation and destruction of the reputation I've worked my whole life to build.

"I'm telling you this deal—and this agreement—is good for both of us, a true win-win, or as close to that as either of us can hope for. We each get what we want. Read the agreement and decide for yourself."

Silence. Then: "Lance's lawyers? How many people are already in on this? I warned you not to tell *anyone*."

"I told you, I don't want anyone knowing what I'm doing either. They're bound to confidentiality by the attorney-client privilege."

"Maybe you trust lawyers, grandpa, but—"

"I'm doing the best I can here to get *both* of us what we want. This was the only way I could get us to where we finally are. This is our only chance. *Our* only chance."

Hirschfeld didn't bother to mention that Brooks also knew what was going on, and maybe Lotello too.

"How do I know I won't be grabbed the minute I go to the trash to get the papers?"

Hirschfeld knew what he had to tell this man. Feed his ego. "Again, think about it. What good does that do me? You won't break and start talking the second you're in custody. I know Cassie dies if you're captured. As much as I'd like to see you go down, hard, I'm more than willing to see you walk—so long as we get Cassie back."

More silence. This one seemed to drag out for an eternity.

"Alright. we'll pick up the envelope. Check out this guy Lance, I'll talk it over with my people, try to get back to you before noon. If I can. It's gonna be tight."

Hirschfeld was encouraged. It was now or never.

"There's one more thing."

"Jesus Christ! You're getting pretty damn greedy, Gramps."

"Cassie has to sign the document too. Right below our signatures. I have to see her do it, and I have to talk to her when she does."

"Unbelievable." An acrid laugh. "You know that's not going to happen."

"I'm not saying it has to be live. Just do that FaceTime thing with our phones."

"No tricks?"

"No tricks. I swear it. On Cassie's life."

"You got that right, old man."

The line went dead. Once again. Hirschfeld sat there, shaking. Trying not to let it show in case they were watching him at this very minute. He got up from the bench, dropped the envelope in the trash, and hurriedly walked away. Like the trash can was a pox on his life.

CHAPTER 85
Friday, May 9, 10:05 am

REYES PICKED up the phone and looked at his watch. He wasn't sure why he actually still wore one—with cellphones everywhere, what was the need? Force of habit probably. Plus, it was elegant, a Girard-Perregaux. A perfect companion to his Meisterstück pen.

"Right on time," he said. "What'd you find out?"

"Nothing for sure, but here's what I do have. I checked on Hirschfeld a couple of hours ago. He was closeted with the other Justices in the Courthouse. Next, I checked on the Webber home. The parents were there. Hirschfeld's wife, too. But not the Webbers's daughter. Hirschfeld's granddaughter. So—"

"It's a school day. She'd be at school."

"Give me a chance. That's precisely the point. I checked out the school. The girl's not there, either."

"How do you know that?"

"Let's keep your deniability plausible. Just accept the fact that she's not there."

Reyes paused. "Anything else?"

"That's all. You didn't give me much time. You want me to do anything more?"

"No. We're good." Reyes already knew more than made him comfortable. "This is all offline. Never happened. Right?"

"Right."

"Thanks." Reyes put down the phone and just sat there, thinking. On impulse, he downloaded the TV coverage from the first day of the *Congress v. NoPoli* Supreme Court hearings. The day he wasn't in the Courtroom. He fast forwarded through the coverage, slowing to regular speed whenever Hirschfeld spoke. He listened to Hirschfeld's words. He couldn't believe it. He walked out of his office and down the hall.

* * *

Reyes asked for a couple of minutes. She tapped something out on her console and waited. After a minute, she told him to go on in.

Tuttle looked up from the computer screen on his Oval Office desk as Reyes approached.

"Mr. President," Reyes said. "A moment?" Just a formality because he was already told to go in.

Tuttle took a second to register Reyes's expression. He removed his reading glasses and sat back. He didn't say anything, just stared with a blank look that said he was listening.

"You remember that old loose end I mentioned the other day? The one I said might have resurfaced?"

"The one you were supposed to have taken care of a long time ago?"

"Unfortunately, I think my hunch was right. I'm pretty sure he's back."

An uncomfortable silence settled in between them. Tuttle glanced away.

"Have you seen him?"

"No, Mr. President, but—"

"Have you spoken to him?"

"I haven't, but—"

The President stopped him with a raised hand. "The only thing I want to hear about this problem is that you've fixed it. Once and for all. Let me know when it's done. Soon."

He put his glasses back on and redirected his focus on his computer screen. The meeting was over.

Reyes returned to his office. He wasn't sure what to do next. He had no idea where Thomas might be, or how to reach him. He didn't even know what he looked like today. No one had spotted him in the Courtroom yesterday. How would they find him if he had altered his looks beyond recognition?

Reyes revisited Tuttle's demeanor during the meeting. The only thing scarier than one of the President's tirades was when he was calm.

CHAPTER 86
Friday, May 9, 10:48 am

NISHIMURA ASCENDED the porch steps to the Webbers's front door. This time she left Joey and the camera in the van parked at the curb. Having him right behind her had backfired the last time. She would take a softer approach this time.

She rang the bell. After only a moment, Webber answered. So far, so good, she thought. At least she didn't have to start all over with someone else.

"Again? Lady, what don't you understand about *no?*"

"The name's Anne Nishimura, not 'Lady.' I'm sorry to bother you, Mr. Webber. I know what's going on."

If Webber's looks could kill, she'd already be dead. "What is it you think is going on? You don't know anything about us."

"I'm a journalist, Mr. Webber. It's my job to uncover the news. And report it."

"So? What do we have to do with that? Interviewing the family of a Supreme Court Justice is hardly newsworthy. Especially in D.C."

"Let's stop pretending. I'm not here to do some kind of puff piece. I'm here to cover what's happened to your daughter."

He stepped back a little in the doorway. "Our daughter? What are you talking about?"

"Someone has kidnapped your daughter. I believe she's being used to control your father-in-law's upcoming vote in the *Congress v. NoPoli* case."

Webber feigned the best wide-eyed look he could. "That's some imagination you have, Ms. Nishimura. Where'd you concoct a story like that?"

"I didn't get where I am by making things up."

"That's not only preposterous, but it's downright offensive. You ought to be careful before you make unsubstantiated allegations like that, especially derogatory statements impugning Justice Hirschfeld's integrity. I think you're in way over your head, Ms. Nishimura."

"Your concern is touching, but I know what I'm doing." Actually, she couldn't prove anything at this point, but she'd learned to trust her instincts. "Did you hear your father-in-law's remarks in Court on Tuesday? I'm sure you know what I'm talking about—his comments about hostages and extortion.

"I was right there, Mr. Webber. I heard every word he said—and I know he wasn't talking to the lawyers arguing the case. I've gone over the tapes several times. If I introduce them in an investigative piece—"

She didn't finish the sentence. She didn't have to. She saw the look of resignation on Webber's face. He stood aside and motioned her inside. He followed and closed the door.

CHAPTER 87
Friday, May 9, 11:03 am

THOMAS HAD TOLD Hirschfeld he had to review the document with the others. There were no others, of course, but the old man didn't know that. He retrieved the envelope with the document from the drop, returned to his van, and read. It wasn't long, or complicated. He'd seen a lot of strange documents over the years, but nothing quite this strange. He read it once more. If there were any tricks, he didn't see what they were. But, then again, he wasn't a lawyer. And time was short.

That didn't mean he liked it. He didn't. Not one bit. He would be giving up his chief advantage: Control. No more upper hand. But what did that matter if they weren't going to go first anyway? He was inclined to believe they were serious. Scared to death. But serious.

He forced himself to be objective. What would he do if the tables were turned? He wouldn't trust a bunch of kidnappers to honor their word and return the girl after they had extracted what they wanted—especially when she might be able to identify them. Under those circumstances, he'd expect them to kill the girl and vanish. Exactly as he planned to do.

I have to prevail. I have to.

He could see only two options: Preserve his theoretical control, and run the risk that the girl's family would go the FBI, in which case he would lose everything he had worked so hard to rebuild. Gone.

Or give up some of that control—and ego—and maximize the chances of achieving his ultimate goal.

He was no dummy. He knew this might be a setup to recover the girl and never make good on their promise. But to do this, they would need the cooperation of this guy Lance. The intermediary. He wished he had more time to study the agreement, find a lawyer to carefully go over it with him, but, hell, he'd never been impressed with agreements. Especially not in D.C.

And if the old man were not bullshitting him, there wasn't enough time to do that *and* vet the escrow agent. What mattered in his experience were the people behind the agreement. In his mind, it all came down to Lance. Whether *he* could be trusted. No document could tell him that. And it wasn't like someone would ever be able to find and sue Thomas over the document. Did it really matter what it said?

He combed through Google. There was actually quite a bit of information on Lance. He skimmed the last of the material on his cell as he drove. The man appeared to be for real. In fact, his background was not that different from Thomas's. They could even have crossed paths once upon a time. Lance might rationalize reneging, but the odds were good that he would honor the arrangement for the sake of his reputation. Just as he would if he were in Lance's shoes. Even the shadow world in which they both operated had its code of honor. Honor and trust were everything to Thomas.

Ten minutes later, he tapped in the number on his cell.

"Lancer Solutions."

"Anonymous Party here."

"Yes?"

"Face to face. Your office. Fifteen minutes. Send anyone else there out for an early one-hour lunch. One more thing: I have to text a different number with a different code every five minutes you and I are together. I miss one text, my partners kill the girl dead on the spot. Understood?"

"Understood." The line went dead.

Thomas was pleased. Having to share his space without warning and meet in person with no one else present didn't seem to rattle Lance. Impressive.

* * *

Thomas was five minutes early.

"Anonymous Party, I presume. Cute mask, nice touch," Lance scoffed.

"Thanks. Under the circumstances, I'm a little shy. And careful. Especially considering all your security cameras. But for the cameras, I like your offices."

"Not to worry, I don't shoot any of my clients. As in record. Unless, of course, they give me reason to."

As Thomas sent his first text to no one: "Good. I don't shoot my representatives either. Unless of course they give *me* reason to."

"Good to get that out of the way. So, Anonymous Party, what would you like to know? And help yourself to one of the drinks in the frig over there. Didn't have time to slip anything in them. Besides, I wouldn't want to interfere with your texting schedule."

"Thanks, I'm good. Tell me a little about yourself. The stuff *not* available on Google."

Took Lance only a few minutes. He stuck to the executive summary. Thomas sent his next text before Lance finished.

"Not a lot of detail, Lance."

"You're not the only one here a little shy. I tend to get that way when talking to guys wearing Frankenstein masks. Might have been a little more relaxed if you'd chosen Bambi."

"Touché. How'd you get into your line of work?"

"A pretty easy transition from the work I was doing in the military. I also recognized a growing hole in the marketplace I thought I could fill."

Another text. "So, is business good?"

"No complaints. And I don't have to advertise. Word of mouth gets around when you do good work, and when there isn't much competition. And a lot of what I do is for repeat clients. I give volume discounts by the way. In case you might have more need for my services."

"Work ever become dangerous?"

"Nothing I can't handle. At least so far. I'm pretty careful."

"How'd you come by this particular gig?"

"The other party just reached out to me. A new client."

"Any misgivings about taking on this role?"

"I'm not judgmental if that's what you mean. I like the job because there's a valuable service I can provide."

"Any questions you have for me, Lance?"

"Not really. I trust you understand my agreement. Sorry about that. Lawyers. They tell me I need to have it down in writing."

"Seems straight forward enough." Thomas stood. Lance did too. "Gotta run. I'll be in touch. In case you get any ideas, my next text'll be due just after I'm safely in my car and back on the highway."

* * *

No, it wasn't perfect. And it wasn't the way he had planned it. He wondered whether he would ever come to regret it. But he dialed the number.

Hirschfeld picked up almost instantly. "Yes?"

"I'll do it. Only because I kind of admire the brat. No need for it to turn out badly for her *if* you're able to deliver on your end of the bargain. I noticed that Lance and you signed the document as 'Escrow Agent' and 'Other Party.' And that I'm to countersign it as 'Anonymous Party.' In case the document ever sees the light of day. Isn't that clever. I'll leave it for you to pick up at our usual spot, and let you know the time to be there."

"You're forgetting something."

"What?"

"I told you. Cassie also has to sign the document. And I have to watch her signing it on FaceTime."

"You're really pushing your luck. Why is this necessary?"

"Because I need to speak with Cassie to know that she's okay. And to let her know that what's about to happen is a good thing, that she doesn't need to be frightened. I want her to hear that directly from me, not you. She won't know she can believe you. I have a lot to accomplish with my colleagues tomorrow, to get the result you and I both want. I won't do that until I know that Cassie has already been moved to the escrow agent without being scared to death about what that might mean."

A momentary silence. Thomas smiled to himself, imagining that Hirschfeld wondered if he had hung up.

"But why does the girl need to sign the document? There's no signature line for her."

"Because I want her to feel empowered. I want her to know that she's a part of this, not just a pawn in your and my machinations. I want to start the process of rebuilding any self-esteem you've cost her."

"If you think that kid's lost any self-esteem, you don't know your granddaughter."

"I know her as well as anyone on this earth."

"Seems to me you're being a bit theatrical. Doesn't really matter to me, but I want to think about it anyway, just to be sure. If I'm willing to do it, I'll FaceTime you in the morning with the girl so you can tell her what's happening, and watch her sign the document. Then tell you when you can pick it up."

"Wait a minute. Why not today? The document you have is already signed by the agent and me. Why can't we do the FaceTime, get your and Cassie's signature on the document, and have you move Cassie to the agent today?"

"First of all, we have to work out the logistics. How and where we do the transfer. I have to figure that out. Cassie has to go straight from me to the agent. There can't be any opportunity for her to escape, or for anyone to take me out. The agreement gives me 24 hours to make the delivery. I intend to use them. Are we clear?" Hirschfeld had pressed all Thomas was going to allow. And made a lot of progress. He'd have to be patient for one more night.

"Yes," Hirschfeld said.

"I'll also be watching and listening in on your progress with the other Justices. If that hits a dead end, I may rethink all this. Keep your phone charged, old man. I'll be in touch."

He hung up. Actually, he had no way to watch or listen to anything. He had tried to set that up when he was hiding his cell phones in the Courtroom. It wasn't possible. But Hirschfeld had no way of knowing that. He wanted every edge he could get, even if only imaginary. And he had work to do before he would be ready to connect with the agent in the morning about the transfer details.

CHAPTER 88
Friday, May 9, 11:05 am

WEBBER INTRODUCED Nishimura to his wife and his mother-in-law and everyone took a seat around the dining room table. She expected Webber to set the stage for the others, but he left her totally twisting in the wind, to fend for herself. He wasn't going to make this easy on her. She had barely begun speaking when Mrs. Hirschfeld interrupted her.

"Pardon me, Ms. Nishimura. We don't need any background. Just tell us what is it you want?"

Don't let her gray hair fool you. This lady has ice water coursing through her veins.

"It's simple. There's a blockbuster story here. The country's entitled to hear it. I want to be the one to tell it."

Webber said nothing. His wife was also quiet.

Mrs. Hirschfeld said, simply, "Why?"

"Because I'm the one who's pieced this story together."

"No, Ms. Nishimura. Why is the country entitled to hear this story?"

"This is bigger than the Lindberg kidnapping. It will become a part of history. A Supreme Court Justice torn apart, forced to choose between his public oath and his granddaughter. The decision your husband makes will have consequences far beyond this room. It'll affect the whole nation, the entire world. People will want to know what he chose, and why." *I want to be in all those history books, too. The one who broke the story. This is going to be my legacy.*

"That's quite an imagination you have, Ms. Nishimura. Putting aside your rank speculation, what I find most intriguing is the fact that you would place your contemptible ambition over the life of an innocent 11-year-old girl—my granddaughter—and the distinguished career of a lifetime public servant—my husband. If memory serves, the Lindbergh story broke only when the body of that unfortunate little boy had already been found. My granddaughter and husband are still very much alive. But you can't wait to pick the carcass clean."

Nishimura took a second to reflect on how best to word what she wanted to say next. "I appreciate what you're saying, Mrs. Hirschfeld. And how you feel. I promise you, I want nothing to do with endangering anyone, or ruining anyone's reputation. I know who the victims are here. But that includes the American people, who will be irreparably harmed if criminals can highjack the Supreme Court to their own ends."

"Well, that's an interesting perspective, Ms. Nishimura. We've apparently found something upon which we *can* agree: Priorities. I don't understand yours, but do please allow me to tell you something about mine."

"Of course."

"You have two choices. You can remove yourself from our home this very second, and do whatever you please. Tell the world whatever make-believe story you think you've stumbled across. However, if you embarrass or otherwise harm either my granddaughter or my husband, I assure you I will make it *my* priority for as long as I live and as long as anyone will listen to me to let the world know how loathsome and uncaring you are. I will do my very best to make sure history, which you claim to cherish so greatly, properly defines you."

"Mrs. Hirschfeld, the press is constitutionally protected because the truth is important, not just to a few, but to everyone. Go ahead and think of me however you want, but you and I both know I'm not making up anything here."

"On the other hand," Mrs. Hirschfeld said, as though Nishimura hadn't even bothered to speak, "you can subordinate your selfish interests and your lofty concern for the people, the right of free speech, and so on and so forth, to the privacy and welfare of my innocent granddaughter and husband. In that case—as soon as your imagined saga plays out—or doesn't—we will give you an exclusive, and publicly commend you for your professional restraint and good taste. That's what I think you call that, right, an exclusive?"

Nishimura could barely suppress her admiration. She glanced toward Webber and his wife to see if their solidarity might be wavering, a weakness she might exploit, but they just glowered back at her.

"An exclusive," she said. "I can hold you to that?"

"I believe I've said all that needs to be said. I'm not a person who needs to repeat myself." Mrs. Hirschfeld rose from her chair. "We'll be watching you, Ms. Nishimura, and your coverage of the news. With great interest, I assure you. Mark, please show Ms. Nishimura out."

CHAPTER 89
Friday, May 9, 11:15 am

BROOKS SAW Hirschfeld's name in the dialog box. "Good news, I hope?"

"They've agreed to sign the document."

"They?"

"I've been referring to the kidnappers in the plural all along because—well because it just seemed like this was too much for one person to pull off by himself. But I've never seen any of them. And I've only spoken with one man. He said he would be signing as Anonymous Party, just the way the document provides."

"Lance is a pretty smart fellow," Brooks said. "Or his lawyers are. The escrow agreement was always for his protection, to establish his agency, and his authority. He has no need for the person or people to use their real names. Which obviously they wouldn't do anyway."

"The man I've been speaking with will let me know when and where I can pick up the document with his signature. I'll make a copy of the fully executed document and put it in my safe deposit box, although I'm honestly not sure to what end. It just seems like the thing to do. I hope it'll never see the light of day. I'll deliver the original to Mr. Lance."

"When is Cassie to be transferred to Lance?"

"Hopefully sometime tomorrow. I was trying for today, but that was wishful thinking."

"I would have preferred that too," Brooks said. "Obviously, we all would."

"All except for 'Anonymous Party.' I'm on the way home to tell my family. I called you first because if I had called them first, I'd never have gotten off the phone to let you know. And to thank you."

"Nothing to thank me for, Arnold. Besides, while I don't want to rain on anyone's parade, we're not out of the woods yet. First, the kidnappers have to make the transfer. That's going to be extremely delicate. We're dependent on Lance to help pull that off. Fortunately, he has the credentials."

"And then there's also the small matter of the Supreme Court decision."

"I've hardly forgotten that, Cyrus. Trust me I haven't."

CHAPTER 90
Friday, May 9, 11:40 am

HIRSCHFELD PULLED into the Webber driveway. His family intercepted him at the front door. But when his wife, Linda, saw how pale and spent he must have looked to her, she herded everyone into the family room and insisted that he sit and take a moment to compose himself.

"While there are still some details to be worked out," Hirschfeld began, "we seem to have a deal. I tried to arrange for Cassie to be transferred to the middleman today, but the agreement provides for 24 hours, to allow time to work out the transfer details, and the kidnappers refused to deliver her any sooner. Hopefully, it will be done by mid-afternoon tomorrow."

"That's well and good," Jill said, "but what about the Nishimura woman. Could she ruin everything?"

Hirschfeld stared back in exhausted puzzlement. He lacked the capacity for any more surprises, or complications. "Nishimura? The TV broadcaster? What's she got to do with any of this?"

"She came here earlier today, Arnold," Linda said. "She claims she knows what's happening. And that history demands she tell the world."

Hirschfeld was crushed. "That can't happen. It could—"

"Relax," Webber said. "Linda took command. You would have been incredibly proud. She made Nishimura an offer she couldn't refuse."

As Webber explained, Hirschfeld regarded his wife with redoubled pride. And gratitude. She offered him only a troubled smile in return.

"Well, it sounds like you all made the best you could of a tough situation. If Linda slowed Nishimura down long enough for Cassie to be transferred to the agent tomorrow before she acts, we're probably okay. If not . . . He didn't finish the sentence.

"I'd love to pay Nishimura a visit myself, but to what end I'm not sure. My presence might only spur her on. And it would violate the terms of our agreement with the kidnappers. No way to know how the escrow agent would react if that came out. We can't run that risk."

"Even if Cassie is safely transferred to the middleman," Webber said, "there's still the question of what the Supreme Court will decide. Any better feel on that?"

"Still five to four, counting me in the four. I have to flip one other Justice. I don't yet know how I'm going to do that, but somehow I will."

CHAPTER 91
Friday, May 9, 1:45 pm

REYES WAS SITTING at his desk when his secretary walked in with an odd expression on her face.

"There's a man on the phone who wants to talk to you. He says he's an old golf buddy of yours, but wouldn't give me his name. He said you'd know. Ordinarily, I would've just routed the call to security, but something told me to let you know first."

"You did well. Stall him for a minute. Tell him I was down the hall but will be right with him. Have security put a trace on the call."

* * *

Thomas held. Reyes came on the line after a couple minutes.

Stalling as long as he thinks he can without making me suspicious? Tracing the call? I'm hardly going to give him enough time.

"Hey, Tommy, thought that was you who left the voicemail the other day. The last time we played I said we'd do it again soon. You shouldn't have become such a stranger. How the hell are you? What brings you to town now?"

How the fuck does he know I'm in town? I never said where I was in the voicemail.

"Fine, Manny. Thanks. Here to take care of some unfinished business. Quick turnaround. Probably have to take a raincheck on the golf this time, but I'll be back. I remember our round together at Congressional fondly.

Love to play it again. And to catch up. Next time for sure."

"That would be great, Tommy. Anytime. Just—"

"Hey, Manny. In my voicemail, I said I wouldn't let you and the President down this time. And I won't. Why were you and those earpieces over at the Courthouse yesterday? Were you looking for me? Why would you do that, Manny?"

"Whoa, Tommy. Why would you think anything like that? You and I, we're on the same team. The FBI was there on unrelated security matters. I was there to observe and report on the case to the President, *our* boss, POTUS. Just chatted it up a bit with the security boys while I was there."

Bullshit! Chief of Staff doesn't handle assignments like that. White House Counsel does. No good son of a bitch is definitely playing me. So disappointing. "Gotta go, Manny. My guys are calling me into a meeting. Just wanted to check in, say a quick hello. You take care. I'll be in touch. Count on it."

* * *

Moments later, Reyes was on the phone to security. "Did you locate him?"

"Depends on what you mean. We were able to complete a number of pings before he hung up, not enough to identify an exact location, but enough to put him within a couple of square miles. And we caught a break. He was calling from a fairly uninhabited forest area outside of Maryland. Our satellite cameras captured a total of only 57 vehicles in the area at the time."

"What the hell good is that?"

"We now have 57 plates. We can track the records of those vehicles within an hour or so. It's already happening as we speak."

"What if he wasn't calling from a vehicle?"

"He was. The location of each ping we completed during the call was traveling too fast to be anything other than a call taking place from within a moving vehicle."

"All right. So he was in one of those 57 vehicles. You'll check each of the 57 vehicle owners as soon as you get their information?"

"Yes, but I need as much help as you can provide."

"What help?"

"First off, do you know what kind of vehicle the target is driving? That would help us narrow down the field."

"No idea. What else?"

"Male. Female. Young. Old. Black. White. Hispanic. Asian. We don't need to spend time chasing down a 23-year-old Asian if you know our target is a 50-year-old Caucasian. We can access the tapes of the call. I can listen to those, but what can you tell me right now?"

"Stay away from the tapes! They're classified. So's his real name. It wouldn't do you any good anyway because he won't have registered a vehicle under his real name or to a real address. And I have no idea what name he's using today anyway. Plus, he's probably driving a leased or stolen vehicle registered to someone else."

"Mr. Reyes, no disrespect, but you're making it—"

"The guy is a former covert CIA operative, previously on loan to the White House for highly classified national security purposes. He's very sharp, and very careful. And very dangerous. White. In his late 40s. About six feet tall. Maybe a little taller. Used to weigh around 170 to 180, but it's been a few years since I've seen him. He could look totally different today. Man's completely off the grid. And unbalanced. He won't come in voluntarily."

"Okay. That means there's no point checking public records. What we should be able to do, though, by process of elimination, is to reduce the field, hopefully to a single vehicle, two or three at the most."

"So what? Say you're able to wheedle the 57 cars down to one or two that we can't rule out. What then?"

"If he's staying in the two-to-three-mile radius and hasn't gone to ground, moved somewhere else, then we man the satellites over the same area until we spot the vehicle on the move again. We'll then swoop in on it. If he's still in the area, we'll get him for sure. Just a matter of time."

"And if he's relocated outside the area?"

"Then we got nothing. Back to square one."

"How long until you can eliminate the uninvolved vehicle owners?"

"How long do I have?"

"Two hours. Three tops."

"Then I need at least twenty agents."

"Take 'em. Just keep this under the radar. No one knows anything they don't need to know. Got that?"

"Got it. I'll be back to you as soon as I have something."

CHAPTER 92
Friday, May 9, 2:10 pm

BROOKS OPENED THE DOOR. He was right on time. Even a few minutes early, no less. With a couple of subtle prompts, he knew Lotello grasped how important punctuality was to their relationship.

"Kudos, Judge, for coming up with this. And making it happen."

"Nonsense, Detective. Occam's razor and Hirschfeld deserve the credit. I just delivered the mail."

"When is the drop supposed to go down?"

Brooks wiggled into a jacket. "The drop, as you so eloquently put it, is not until tomorrow, but there are a few things we need to talk about. Let's take a walk. It's a nice day and I need to stretch my legs."

Brooks guided Lotello to a path that led through some nearby woods.

"First, we can't breathe a word about this, not before Cassie gets home—*if* she gets home—and maybe not even then. That's the agreement. As agents of Hirschfeld, we have to honor his confidentiality commitment. How do you feel about your daughter knowing anything about this?"

"Aren't you the perceptive one? As usual, she's been all over me for information. No way I'm comfortable sharing what's going on with her. She's a kid. It's not a matter of wondering whether she'd talk out of school. Or in school for that matter."

"Pun intended?"

"For me, Judge, the problem is I don't think an 11-year-old should be exposed to these kinds of things."

"Including Cassie," Brooks responded. "Well, Detective, don't expect Madison not to learn all about this from Cassie, *if* we're able to get Cassie home."

"Whatever Cassie tells Madison is out of my control. I can't worry about that. Actually, I can, and no doubt will, but I can't prevent it."

"Even assuming Cassie is safely transferred to Lance, I don't know exactly what that gets us," Brooks said. "We still have at least two problems."

"Only two?"

"Of course, our first priority is to get this little girl safely back to her family. But Ms. Klein and I still have an obligation to NoPoli, and to we the people, to achieve a result that is inconsistent with Cassie's ultimate release by Lance. And, while Hirschfeld and I haven't discussed it, and can't, I believe Hirschfeld wants the same result, a 28th Amendment that is upheld by the Supreme Court."

"That sounds like one problem, Your Honor, maybe with two integrated parts. What's the second problem?"

"The second problem overlaps with the first. You're the one who met with Lance. What do you think Lance does if he's in possession of Cassie and the Supreme Court upholds the amendment?"

"Tough question," Lotello said. "I can't imagine that Lance would want to return Cassie to her kidnappers. But, as I reported to you, his word is everything to him and I don't believe he'll compromise his duties as set out in the escrow agreement. He's committed to returning Cassie to the kidnappers if the amendment is upheld. I believe he'll honor his word to them."

"So do I. It's a matter of precedent," Brooks said. "If the agreement is not honored on the rationale that the snatching is so abhorrent that it justifies breaking it, and if that gets out, how many future hostages will die because a deal like this one can't be brokered for lack of reliability? Even if it saves Cassie and allows an untainted result in the Supreme Court. Do you not feel the conflict between this Cassie and future Cassies, so to speak?"

"Not necessarily," Lotello responded. "Doesn't that depend on whether what goes down here becomes common knowledge?"

"Perhaps. But 'common knowledge' is elusive, hard to avoid. Hirschfeld has to decide how to vote, or maybe even to abstain because of his own conflict. He also has to decide how to beseech some or all of his fellow Justices to vote or abstain. That's a slippery slope down the hill of common knowledge. And whether that will actually matter may turn on how Lance would truly perform under the agreement if the amendment is upheld.

"How do you and I cope," Brooks continued, "if the Supreme Court instead upholds the amendment, and Lance returns Cassie to the kidnappers?" How do we live with the fact that your wife's and my performance in the Courtroom may be the very reason the Supreme Court votes to uphold the amendment, and send this young girl to her death? It would be of little solace to me that our performance was in discharge of our sacred duty to our client, and is that which we believe to be best for our country. I don't know if I could carry the girl's demise on my conscience.

"And you, Detective? And Ms. Klein? And even Madison, for that matter, once she figures it all out, which, sooner or later, she will? How will your family reconcile your respective actions and inactions if Cassie doesn't make it through this?"

"Other than to say that we did our best to implement what the family decided and what we thought was right, I have no answer, Judge. We've done our best. I don't see any other options."

Brooks didn't answer. But he did stop walking. So did Lotello. Brooks bent over and touched his toes. Pretty close anyway. He leaned left and then right. Then he lifted his arms chest high and twisted to each side, first left, then right.

"Damned sciatica." He repeated the maneuvers once more. "Okay. I'm good."

They picked up the pace again.

* * *

"On a slightly different subject, Detective." Brooks paused to make sure he had Lotello's attention.

"Your Honor?"

"Did you know that the White House Chief of Staff was in the Courtroom yesterday?"

"And how would I have known that?"

"Don't know. You're the detective."

"Don't recall you mentioning it. Were you aware?"

"I wasn't. He was apparently sitting behind me, in the gallery. I was focused on the Justices up on the bench in front of me."

"So how'd you find out?"

"Thought you'd never ask. Hirschfeld told me he received a call from the kidnappers accusing him of turning Reyes onto them."

Now it was Lotello who came to an abrupt halt. "Did he?"

"Did he what? Receive a call from them or turn Reyes onto them?"

Lotello smiled at Brooks. "Yes."

"Very smooth, Detective. Good to know you haven't lost your repartee. Did Justice Hirschfeld turn Reyes onto the kidnappers? Not according to Hirschfeld."

"Then how would Reyes have any knowledge about the kidnapping? And why would he have been in Court yesterday?"

Brooks could almost see the wheels turning in Lotello's head. Or at least in his eyes.

"No. You're not telling me—"

"Oh, you are so sharp, Detective. I just can't slip anything past you."

"Tommy Thomas? And Reyes? Again?"

"Maybe so. Or maybe this time Thomas is just a loose cannon acting without a handler."

"Jesus. The description Hernandez gave me of the van's buyer isn't far off from how I remember Thomas. It didn't occur to me at the time because there was no reason for me to make that connection. Doesn't this make things more . . . I just don't have the words."

Brooks's mind drifted back to the death of Bernie Abrams on the eve of the *Norman* trial. *First, Leah Klein's mentor and one of my own best friends. Now, Hirschfeld's granddaughter. Where does it end?* "That's putting it mildly. Or, more accurately, not putting it. This is becoming *very* personal, Detective. At least for me. If not, I suspect, for you as well."

"So much for any hope against hope that the assailants might just be bluffing about killing Cassie." Lotello didn't say anything further.

"So," Brooks added, "did you think I didn't hear your question a moment ago about what other options we have? I think you may now be ready for my answer."

CHAPTER 93
Friday, May 9, 3:00 pm

NISHIMURA WAS STILL REELING, trying to decide what to do. Hirschfeld's wife really threw her a curve. Breaking this story was a virtual lock on a Pulitzer Prize. Unless perhaps her story was found to have contributed to a youngster's death. Either way, was she really prepared to live with that prospect on her conscience? She had a little more time to think all of this through. She would give herself until tomorrow to decide.

CHAPTER 94
Friday, May 9, 5:30 pm

THOMAS WAS DISILLUSIONED. He didn't know with absolute certainty that Reyes and POTUS were lying to him, but he sure didn't have the feeling they were in his corner, had his back, appreciated all he was doing. For the country. For them. Hadn't he always loyally carried out his President's wishes?

His thoughts turned to the girl and her grandfather. What loyalty they displayed toward one another. Their relationship was . . . admirable. That was it. Their relationship was admirable.

First, Mother and Father. Now, Reyes and POTUS. Is it something about me? Could there be something wrong with me?

* * *

Reyes took the call. "What'd ya find out?"

"He was driving an older White Nissan van when he spoke to you. If he hasn't ditched it or moved on, we'll get him. Just a matter of time."

"Good work. Don't let up. Stay on it. Around the clock. We may not have much time. Let me know the minute you have something. No matter what time it is."

Reyes was about to hang up when it occurred to him. Like his own boss, he didn't always remember. "Thanks."

* * *

Cassie heard him come down the steps, unlock the door, and enter her room. It bothered her that she was now thinking of this hole as 'hers.' That was the last thing she wanted. She stood, but didn't back away.

"Hey, brat, had some pizza and spaghetti left over from my dinner last night. Thought by now you might be more receptive, maybe a little tired of the palatial stuff I originally stocked for you."

Wow, what's got into him? All of a sudden he's like my best friend. She thought she should probably play along. "Sure, why not? The food in the palace here is becoming a little dull. And now I have enough insulin to cover the carbs in your Italian delight."

"I brought some plastic utensils. Nothing strong enough to inflict any wounds."

"Uh, sorry about that. You understand. You would have done the same if the tables had been turned. This junk actually tastes pretty good, Frank."

"Frank? Name's not Frank. I didn't tell you my name."

"Short for Frankenstein."

"Oh yeah, right. Very funny. Say, how long do you hit your tee shots on average?"

"Between 210 and 230. Sometimes 250. Do you play?"

"Now and then. I like Congressional. When I'm in town. My tee shots are usually about 200, maybe 220."

"Well, what do you expect? You're not a pro like me."

"Pretty cocky, brat. I think I could give you a game."

"Anytime, Frank. So, where do you play when you're not in town?"

She knew she had gone too far the minute the words were out of her mouth. She should have quit while she was ahead, knowing from his slip that he wasn't local. He tightened up the minute she snooped. He instantly turned quiet and sullen. She watched him pack up the scraps and boxes. He walked out of the room, and locked the door. *Guess he's no longer my best friend. That didn't last very long.*

CHAPTER 95
Saturday, May 10, 7:30 am

"LANCER SOLUTIONS."

"Anonymous Party."

"You're up early. More questions? Any decisions?"

"Depends."

"On?"

"Yesterday, we talked about delivery, but only philosophically, the need to assure no gaps in possession and control of the asset. I need to go over some details with you.

"Shoot. Figuratively speaking, of course."

"Sunday would be best for me. Will that work for you?"

"I work 24/7. Sunday's fine."

"If we're on, you'll receive a call from me or one of my associates at this same number at approximately ten o'clock—"

"Is that oh-ten-hundred or oh-twenty-two hundred? The latter might be cutting it a bit tight in terms of the follow-up work. Other Party has to conclude things by early Monday."

"Oh-ten-hundred. Morning. I'll provide you with an address for pickup. You'll need to move very quickly because the goods are highly perishable and will need to be secured and promptly remediated. We'll be evaluating your performance under a zero tolerance policy."

"Understood. No problem. That's always the case with our clients. Will you need a receipt?"

"Not necessary. We'll know."

"Very good, A.P. I'm sure you'll be very pleased with our services. If O.P. performs as well, we will not need to speak again. Thank you for allowing Lancer Solutions to be of service."

CHAPTER 96
Saturday, May 10, 8:30 am

HIRSCHFELD WATCHED Trotter lead the discussion around the table. One by one, the Justices expressed their views, many of them forcefully. The arguments were occasionally heated, but never discourteous. They debated, but they didn't shout. If there was not affection, they at least maintained a genuine respect for one another. With an exception or two.

No one was budging. The issue on standing to bring the lawsuit was still seven to two in favor. With Hirschfeld voting to invalidate the amendment, the vote was still five to four in favor of upholding. Hirschfeld was outwardly composed. Forced to oppose what he deeply espoused, he was suffering internally. He imagined the other Justices recognized how curious his stance was, but undoubtedly were at a loss to explain it. None, however, chose to press him.

Trotter assigned the drafting duties. He would write the majority opinion upholding standing and the amendment. He asked Nettleman to write the dissenting minority opinion favoring invalidation.

Ordinarily, the opposing opinions would be circulated to all of the Justices who would then be given several months to offer their editorial input before the opinions would be finalized and announced. Because of the short turnaround here, Trotter scheduled a second meeting for Sunday morning to collectively edit and finalize the two opinions.

* * *

Nishimura had to decide. NBN-TV had scheduled two thirty minute live specials Monday morning, the first just before and the second immediately after the Supreme Court Justices took the bench to announce and read their majority and minority decisions. The first would recap the Tuesday and Thursday arguments and describe the announcement procedure. The second was to discuss the decision and its likely consequences for the country.

If Nishimura chose to reveal the story without waiting for the promised Hirschfeld family exclusive, she'd have to decide between the first and second specials. History might not be kind to her if she were perceived as possibly impacting the outcome of the judicial process by going first. Or the fate of Cassie Webber.

If she waited until the second special, she would reduce the prospects of any blowback in reporting the story. Waiting for the promised exclusive would definitely be more professional, but entailed risks of its own. What if the family reneged after the decisions were announced? What if someone else beat her to the punch in the meanwhile? What if NBN-TV executives decided to give the plum to someone higher up in the network? She could control her destiny now, but not after the existing programming was concluded.

But something kept nagging at her. Was there something she was overlooking?

* * *

Hirschfeld could not put it off any longer. He'd thought about approaching Lance, to see if he would be willing to release Cassie to her family once she was delivered to him. He concluded that was pointless. If the amendment were upheld and Lance did not return Cassie to her kidnappers, Lance's reputation and business interests would surely suffer, as well perhaps as his own physical well-being.

He hesitated one last moment. And then knocked on the door to his colleague's private chambers.

"Enter," Gaviota said with his customary zest. Seeing Hirschfeld, he added, "Hola, amigo. Como estás?"

"Bien. E tu?"

"Bien, gracias. But why do you not look so good, amigo?"

"Jose, tengo una problema. There's no way to sugar coat it. I need to ask you for a favor. A huge one. I wouldn't ask if I had any choice."

"Well, one does not have to be a rocket scientist to know something is terribly wrong given that you are voting opposite me on this matter. Very strange for sure. Siéntete, por favor. Dígame tu problema."

Hirschfeld told him as succinctly as he could. Gaviota's expression registered a range of emotions, from outraged to wary to stunned, but his eyes retained a sad embrace for his colleague and friend.

"This I didn't imagine. Who would?" He shook his head. "You've come to me, I assume, because you believe I can help somehow. I'm not sure how, but . . ."

Hirschfeld told him—and watched the blood drain from his face.

"Arnold. I would do anything I could for you. You know that. I love Cassie as if she were my own flesh and blood. But this . . ."

Hirschfeld waited, letting the silence make his point.

"Arnold, I don't know. How would we do this?"

"At the last minute, you would simply change your vote. Five to uphold would become five to invalidate. Trotter's opinion would become the minority and Nettleman's would become the majority. Once Cassie was released and was safely home, I would come forward, thank you for your selfless compassion and understanding, and resign from the Court. The decision could be set aside on grounds of undue influence, and revoted. The disgrace would be mine alone."

"The disgrace would not be yours alone. It would be mine as well. I would also have to resign from the Court. But that's not the issue, mi hermano. I would gladly do that, for Cassie and for you. The issue, however, is the possible indelible stain on the integrity and sanctity of the Court. Who would be next? What would they try next? To bend the Court's will."

"I need to think about this. Very carefully. I'll give you my answer tomorrow when we meet to go over the draft opinions. If my answer is no, I will never speak to anyone of this meeting."

"I understand." Hirschfeld offered a grave smile. "Thank you, Jose."

He walked out of Gaviota's office and closed the door behind him. There was nothing left for him to do now but head back to the kids' home to wait for the FaceTime call he desperately prayed would be coming. If the kidnappers agreed to his insistence on that.

CHAPTER 97
Saturday, May 10, 10:20 am

AFTER SPEAKING to Lance about the details of the girl's delivery, Thomas's next call was to Hirschfeld. He had been procrastinating, but it was time. He couldn't put it off any longer. "Showtime, Gramps, you ready to FaceTime?"

"Now? I'm on the turnpike. Give me a minute to pull off the road and stop my car."

Thomas decided to keep Hirschfeld thinking that he was being monitored. "I know where you are, old man. That's why I called now. We'll call you back in five minutes. Only 48 hours to go until Monday morning. Drive carefully. Your granddaughter needs you around to vote to invalidate the amendment."

* * *

Hirschfeld had pulled his car off the turnpike and found a spot to park. He was waiting for the call. Five minutes stretched into ten. Finally, his phone rang.

He answered using the FaceTime app, just the way Cassie had once taught him to do. "Hello?"

"Poppy! It's me, Cassie. Can you see me? I can see you. Are you okay?"

"I'm fine, baby. I can see you perfectly. How are you?"

"Homesick, a little tired, but I'm okay, Poppy."

She didn't look so good to Hirschfeld. Not at all. She looked nervous, anxious. He could tell how she really was, no matter what she said. He wondered if the man knew too, or even cared.

Thomas cut in. "Okay, enough small talk. I'm putting the document and a pen in front of the girl. Make your speech. Fast. I'm still hurting from the last time the brat had something sharp in her hand."

"What did you just say?" Hirschfeld asked the man.

"Forget it, Gramps, stick to the business at hand."

With this maniac, Hirschfeld had no way of knowing how much time he had. And he didn't want to get into an argument with him in front of Cassie. He suppressed his curiosity about the man's remark, at least for now, and spoke directly to his granddaughter: "Listen to me, baby. Do you see the document there?"

"Yes. I just read it. I think I understand it. Well, sort of. Am I outta here now, Poppy?"

He could sense her fear and confusion. He wanted to kill the man. Literally. But he had to focus. "Soon, baby. I wanted you to see the document and know what's going on. You need to sign the document below the other signatures. It's Saturday morning now. This afternoon, you'll be going to a safe place. I—"

"Tomorrow, Gramps," Thomas interjected. "I've worked it out with Lance, but it can't happen until tomorrow."

"Who's Lance?"

"None of your business, brat."

"I wasn't asking you, Frankenstein."

"Frankenstein?" said Hirschfeld, who could only hear but not see the man.

"Yeah, Poppy, he wears a Frankenstein mask so I can't see his real face."

That's a good thing Hirschfeld thought to himself. "It's okay, baby, tomorrow's fine. Just one more day. I wanted you to hear it from me. That moving you like this is a good thing. You don't have to worry about it. I don't want you to be scared. By Monday, you'll be free and home, with your mom and dad." Hirschfeld watched Cassie sign the document. "I just saw you sign it. That's great. Now, give it back to—"

"The creep. It's alright for me to call him that. He calls me brat. It's okay. I don't mind. I did stab him pretty good. Deeper than I meant to."

"You did what?"

"I told you, Pops, forget about it."

Cassie handed the document back to the man.

"And the pen too, girl," Thomas said. After a moment, during which Hirschfeld watched him put pen to paper himself: "Okay. I've now signed the document too. Are we done?"

"I guess so. Are you sure you're okay, Cassie?"

"I'm fine, Poppy. Honest. Tell Mom and Dad and Nanny not to worry. Madison also. I know she's upset, too. And don't forget to rub Whitney's tummy for me. By the way, is this man Lance a creep too?"

"No, baby, Lance is not a creep. He's a good man. He's helping us to bring you home. We all love you, honey. See you soon."

"Enough already," Thomas said.

Hirschfeld watched Thomas grab the phone away from Cassie.

"Listen up, Grandpa," Thomas continued, "you need to retrieve the signed document at the usual pickup spot in exactly one hour. Remember, I'm watching you. No funny stuff. Not any sooner and not any later. The girl's counting on you."

"I—"

Hirschfeld watched his phone turn dark. He realized Thomas had terminated the call.

* * *

Hirschfeld wondered how the kidnappers always knew where he was. He figured one of them must be tailing him. And they must have bugs planted in the Court. And on his phone or maybe in his car too. He called the house anyway. He didn't see how it would hurt if they heard. Linda picked up.

"I just talked with our little girl on FaceTime." Hirschfeld didn't want to alarm Linda, but he also craved someone he could talk to. "She's fine."

"Thank God! Just a minute." She shouted to the others in the room with her, "It's Poppy. He just talked to Cassie on FaceTime. She's fine."

Back to Hirschfeld: "How did she look? Are they feeding her?"

"She sounded strong, looked great." It just slipped out: "Well, maybe a little anxious."

"Of course, she's anxious. Who wouldn't be anxious in her position?" To Jill and Mark: "She sounded strong, looked great. Maybe a little anxious. What would you expect?"

"By the way," Hirschfeld added, there was some kind of . . . incident. Cassie stabbed one of the kidnappers."

"She did what? She stabbed someone?"

Hirschfeld was trying to talk, but Linda was already repeating what he had just said to the others. "Cassie stabbed one of her kidnappers!"

Through the phone, Hirschfeld heard his daughter in the background: "What did you say? When? What happened? Is Cassie okay? How could she stab someone? With what?"

"I don't know any of the details," Hirschfeld responded, "but whatever it was it seems to be under control and in the past. It doesn't seem to be an issue now. We'll learn more after we get Cassie back home."

That seemed to bring Linda back to the present. "When does she get to—"

"I was trying for this afternoon," Hirschfeld said, "but they wouldn't agree. The transfer logistics won't be in place before tomorrow. We'll just have to be patient for another day."

Linda went quiet for a moment. Then: "Are *you* alright? Are you on the way here now?"

"Not yet. I have to pick up the signed agreement at the drop spot and take it to the escrow agent. I'll be there as soon as I can."

Hirschfeld knew the unexpected additional one-day delay in transferring Cassie must have let the air out of the family's balloon somewhat. And unfortunately raised the stakes concerning Nishimura, and how long she would sit on her story.

Like he'd said, they'd just have to be patient a little while longer. They'd made a lot of progress. He believed—hoped—they'd soon make it across the finish line. Just in case the kidnappers were listening, he had said nothing about Cassie's request to call Madison. She'd just have to wait like everyone else. *Just another day. Right?*

CHAPTER 98
Saturday, May 10, 11:00 am

REYES CALLED HIS FIELD AGENT. "ANYTHING?"

"Not a thing. Either he's holed up, changed vehicles, or moved on. We've got agents spread all over the place. We've just about exhausted the motor pool."

"Keep me in the loop." This time he didn't bother to say thank you. He was getting testy.

CHAPTER 99
Saturday, May 10, 11:30 am

HIRSCHFELD RETRIEVED the fully executed document and returned to his car. He dialed the number.

"Lancer Solutions."

"Mr. Lance?"

"Who's calling?"

"This is Justice Hirschfeld, Mr. Lance. I—"

"Lancer's fine."

"Yes, okay, well I have the fully executed escrow document. Where can I drop it off to you?"

"Where are you headed after that?"

"To our kids' home."

"You don't need to get it to me. I'll send someone there to pick it up."

"Okay. Their address—"

"I have it. He'll be there in a couple of hours. You'll be there until he arrives?"

"Yes. When will my granddaughter be moved to you?"

"Tomorrow. A.P. is being very skittish. Not surprising."

"A.P.?"

"Anonymous Party. The kidnappers. By the way, Mr. Justice?"

"Yes?"

"I know it's a difficult time. Try to relax. Focus on what you need to take care of on your end. Leave your granddaughter to me. That's my job. I'll call you when the transfer to me is completed."

"Okay. I guess. Thank you so much. We're counting on you. I don't know what else to say."

"Nothing else you need to say. For everyone's sake, just get the amendment invalidated."

CHAPTER 100
Saturday, May 10, 3:00 pm

THOMAS WONDERED whether he actually suffered from OCD or was just very careful, but his call with Reyes had put him on edge. Was Reyes genuinely interested in him? Or just trying to keep him on the phone long enough to nail down his location?

When he got back to the cabin, he parked the van further into the forest and covered it with brush and leaves. Satellites everywhere taking pictures. He couldn't be too cautious. So far so good, but when he made the run in the morning to transfer the girl, the van would be out in the open and he could be spotted. If they were, in fact, looking for him. He thought about stealing another set of wheels, but that could lead to a police report, and even more attention.

If that weren't bad enough, he had to work through all of the transfer details. OCD or not, meticulous planning was key. To everything.

The sooner he could destroy the van, the better. Once he transferred the girl, there would be no reason for him to return to the cabin. He would stay in town Sunday night and then catch his flight out of Dulles Monday following the final Court proceedings. They might have made the van, but they would have no idea what he looked like or under what alias he was traveling.

In the morning, he'd move the girl to the van. Then he'd pack up and move everything other than the furniture into the van and fully sanitize the cabin, upstairs and down.

He had originally planned to rent a car in town on Monday afternoon, and follow his ex-accomplice Haddad in the van to where he intended to dispose of it. Along with everything he had packed into it, including Haddad and the girl. With the premature disposition of Haddad, the logistics had become somewhat more complicated.

Now he'd have to order a taxi to pick him up somewhere after he dumped the van. He'd choose a nearby pickup point within an easy walk, but that also might arouse suspicion. The taxi driver might wonder how he'd gotten there on foot. He'd work it out. Maybe say he and his girlfriend had a fight and she drove off and left him behind. Lucky that his cell was in his pocket and not in the car.

He thought through the drop mechanics he would use to deliver the girl, and also worked out what he'd do if someone started to chase the van on the way. The greatest exposure would be the first few miles on the highway as he exited the forest. If any satellites had picked up the van while he spoke with Reyes yesterday, that's where it would have occurred. And where there would be virtually no witnesses to any pursuit. They would have a much tougher time trying to locate him in heavier traffic as he approached D.C. Again, it was all just a matter of careful planning, and timing it correctly.

There was nothing to do now but wait. He was restless. His lung was mending. He would've liked to go for a run, but his instincts told him to lie low. He was feeling lonely, isolated. Sometimes that was a good thing. Sometimes it wasn't. At least the girl had shared the leftover pizza and spaghetti with him last night. That was nice. Until she started snooping.

* * *

Cassie finished exercising and tested her sugars. Her numbers were okay, still a little on the high side. As they'd been throughout the entire week. She'd taken a little extra insulin the night before to cover the carb intensive pizza and spaghetti she'd shared with the man as part of her plan to win him over. She thought it might be working because, more and more, he was making excuses for being around her. He didn't do that at first. But she had made a mistake asking him where he usually played golf.

She kept thinking about FaceTiming with Poppy. She couldn't wait to get home. She'd have tons to talk about. Maybe she'd write a book about all of this during summer break.

She also thought about what tomorrow would be like. When the creep took her from the cabin to wherever this Lance person would be waiting for her. She definitely wanted to get out of here, but she was nervous about being with another strange person in another strange place. Why couldn't she just go straight home? But she didn't have anything to worry about. Did she? Hadn't Poppy said that everything would be fine, that she'd soon be home with her family?

CHAPTER 101
Saturday, May 10, 3:20 pm

NISHIMURA FINISHED WRITING the copy for her breaking news piece. She'd read it out loud over and over in front of the mirror to make sure she had it memorized and that it was the right length. She'd go over it again in the morning. She only had to focus on the opening remarks. No need to prepare beyond that. Once she exposed the story, all hell would break loose. She'd then be the person of the moment, and could wing it from there.

She'd been waiting for this for a long time. All of the years of preparation would finally bear fruit. She was eager. The weather was inviting. She decided to go for a run.

* * *

Brooks returned home to find Eloise putting away the groceries.

"Please, dear, if you wouldn't mind, there's a couple of heavier packages still out by the car."

"Of course. I just need to check my email first."

"There's some stuff that'll melt if you leave it. Your email can wait."

"Melt? What if I wasn't here now?"

She didn't answer. Brooks brought the remaining packages in and went to check his email. Her voice reached out to him from the kitchen: "What've you been up to?"

"Didn't I mention I had a meeting with Steve Kessler at the NoPoli offices? Maybe I forgot. Just some stuff we needed to go over concerning the final Court proceedings Monday morning."

That was more or less accurate. He would fill her in later.

* * *

Trotter and Nettleman had exchanged email copies of their respective draft opinions. They were just ironing out some details between the two that needed to mesh more seamlessly.

"These two opinions are as different as night and day," Trotter said.

"And civil," Nettleman added.

"See you tomorrow morning to share them with the others and make any last minute necessary revisions. No one ever said writing by committee was easy."

"Revisions? Do you think anyone's going to want to make any changes?"

CHAPTER 102
Saturday, May 10, 3:35 pm

HIRSCHFELD WAS STRETCHED out on the sofa in the Webber family room. Eyes closed. Trying to get some sleep, which was proving impossible.

All he could think about was what Cassie would be going through during the transfer in the morning, while he and the other Justices were reviewing and tweaking the majority and minority opinions. In spite of the surprising degree of bravado she had exhibited during their FaceTime, he figured the move would be quite hard on her.

Even without his mind straying to Cassie, his heart was not into refining the dissenting opinion he would be joining in the attempt to invalidate the amendment. It would prove to be a hollow gesture if Gaviota didn't come through. Gaviota. He kept going over their discussion. He wanted to pick up the phone and call him, but there was nothing more he could say. He had to leave it alone. Give the man his space. But without Gaviota's help, Cassie's transfer would all be for naught. She would end up right back in the hands of her kidnappers.

And then?

He hadn't discussed this with his family yet, but his present thinking—assuming that Gaviota turned him down tomorrow—was to go to the FBI immediately *after* Lance called him to verify that the transfer had been completed. Even if Lance felt obliged to return Cassie to the kidnappers to protect his reputation, he couldn't imagine that he'd countermand directions from the FBI to stand down. The problem was that he didn't know where Lance would be holding Cassie, although he did have his telephone number. That would have to do.

"Hon," Linda whispered, "are you sleeping?"

Hirschfeld opened his eyes. "Tried. Can't."

"The kids would like to talk. I'll get them."

Everyone was gathered around him in the study. Not a smile or a hopeful expression among them.

Webber said, "Dad, hopefully Cassie will at least momentarily be separated from her kidnappers in the morning, but where do we stand on the vote? If you haven't secured a second vote, aren't we just delaying the inevitable?"

Hirschfeld sighed and rubbed his temples. "Yes. Right now the vote to invalidate is only four strong, including me. I need one more vote. I've reached out in confidence to one of the others. He's considering switching to give us the necessary fifth vote."

"What do you think the chances are?"

"Honestly, I really don't know. Maybe 50/50, but that's just a guess."

"Which Justice is it?"

"Are you kidding? I can't tell you that. I'm not going to violate his confidence. Besides, you don't have any reason to know who he is."

"If he refuses, what then?"

Hirschfeld walked them through his plan. No one said anything.

CHAPTER 103
Saturday, May 10, 7:00 pm

LOTELLO HAD BROUGHT in Japanese because no one felt like cooking or going out. And because Madison loved sushi. Lotello and Leah were quietly cleaning up, neither one of them saying much. The food had briefly coaxed Madison out of her room, but she went right back. Normally a pretty good kid who pitched in, she hadn't offered to help with the cleanup detail, part of what she was supposed to do for her allowance. Lotello decided to cut her some slack.

Leah finally broke the silence. "I think we're going to win the battle, but lose the war."

"Pardon?"

"I think we have at least five votes to uphold. NoPoli wins, and I should be thrilled, a win in my first Supreme Court case. But I'm not. We win, Cassie loses."

"We have a better chance with Cassie moved tomorrow than if she remains in the hands of the kidnappers."

"Not if the Court upholds and the intermediary sticks to the terms of the arrangement."

"Well, you're the lawyer."

"What does *that* mean?"

"Sorry." He held up his hands in surrender. "I didn't mean anything. I'm as much at a loss about how to feel as you are. I don't know what more I can say, what more we can do, I—"

"Well, you better say something to Madison. She's scared to death, and furious with you. Can you blame her?"

Lotello pushed his chair back from the dining room table and stood. "I'll try talking to her."

He walked down the hallway to Madison's room and knocked gently on the closed door.

Five seconds passed with no response. He knocked again, a bit more firmly. Still nothing. Leaning close to the door, he called out, "Madison, may I come in, please?"

Another minor eternity. Then, finally: "Do I have a choice?"

"You do."

"I guess you can come in."

Well, that was a start. He opened the door and walked in. "Are you talking to me yet?"

"That depends."

"On what?"

"On whether you're talking to me."

"I always talk to you."

"I mean the real stuff."

"I always tell you what I can."

"Yeah, I know. Your favorite loophole."

"Well, would you want me to tell you something I knew if I had promised to keep it a secret?"

"If I really needed to know? Absolutely."

"What if you told me a secret only if I promised not to repeat it? Wouldn't you expect me to keep your secret? No matter what?"

"That's not the same, Dad."

"Why isn't it?"

She didn't answer. That was progress. He bent down and gave her a kiss on the forehead. She didn't protest. That was more progress. He smiled and beat a hasty retreat. Before she thought of an answer.

CHAPTER 104
Sunday, May 11, 7:00 am

CASSIE ROSE EARLY, as usual. She tested her sugars, ate, checked and double-checked to make sure that her knapsack was fully packed, including her insulin and diabetes kit, plus a couple of bottles of water. She felt ready, anxious to be getting out of there. She could hear the man moving about upstairs. She sat down to wait.

* * *

Thomas had everything upstairs packed and in the van. The rooms were sanitized to his satisfaction. Things with the girl were now going to get a bit unpleasant. He put on his mask, went down to the basement, and unlocked the door.

"Morning, brat. Or should I call you baby?"

"I'm not a baby."

"Well, I don't know about that. Your grandfather kept calling you baby."

"Not. He called me *his* baby. That's because he loves me. You wouldn't understand that. Like I've said, who would love anyone like you? Maybe if somebody loved you, you wouldn't be the way you are."

He changed the subject. "Moving day, brat." He reached into his pocket and took out the handcuffs. "Give me one of your hands."

She backed away. Ready to fight. "No way! Why do you have to do *that*?"

"Have to keep you tied down out of sight in the back of the van while I'm driving. You want to get going or just stay here?"

Reluctantly, she held out her left hand. He snapped the cuffs in place. "C'mere, girl."

She tried to back away, but he was holding the free cuff. "No way. Why?"

"Need to lock you to the pipe in the corner while I clean the basement."

"You don't have to clean it. I kept it very clean. You can see for yourself."

"I'm talking about fingerprints and footprints. I need to make sure no one ever knows you were here."

"Why?"

"Listen, brat, stop giving me a hard time or this is going to get unpleasant." She reluctantly gave in.

He cuffed her to the wall and sanitized the room. As he had already done upstairs. The goal was not to hide the fact that someone had been in the room, but *who* had been in there. That meant obliterating the ability to identify fingerprints and DNA as opposed to their existence. CSI to the contrary, all that took was a bucket of hydrogen peroxide and some elbow grease.

He took all of her stuff out to the van and put it in the back.

When she heard him open the outside door, she quickly put her fingerprints all over the wall as far as she could stretch. She also stepped up and down on the floor to mark her shoes. She was standing still when he returned. He took out the vial and syringe and came toward her.

"No!" she screamed. "Why?"

"You just showed why. That loud mouth of yours. Have to keep you quiet. Can't have you screaming while I'm driving. Thought you weren't a baby. Are you afraid of a little needle?"

"I'm not afraid of needles. I live with needles every day. But I don't want to be put to sleep. I can't manage my blood sugars. Do you really have to do that? I promise not to make any noise. I'll lie down in the back of the van and be quiet. You'll already have me locked up with the handcuffs. Isn't that good enough? *Please!*"

He looked at her through the mask's eyeholes for a long time. His posture softened.

"Not one sound. Not one word unless I tell you to speak. You get out of line *one* time and you'll be out like a light. Deal?"

"Yes. Deal."

"Okay. I'm going to undo the cuff and carry you upstairs and out to the van. Ready?"

"I don't need you to carry me."

"Footprints. Remember?"

"Oh, right. Okay."

He got her into the van and cuffed her to the side railing. "Remember, not a peep."

The cabin was completely isolated. No one would hear if she screamed, but if she did the deal was off. He'd put her out in a flash.

He went back to the basement, and wiped down the walls and floor where she had been cuffed. *Did she think I wouldn't expect her to contaminate everything within her reach while I was upstairs?*

He returned to the van. She had kept their agreement. Not a sound. He wouldn't sedate her. He stuck to his agreements too. *Stuck. Apt choice of words.*

* * *

He locked up the cabin for the last time and walked about one hundred meters past the van, beyond where she'd be able to hear him speaking softly into his cell phone, but where he could easily hear her if she started making any noise. Still not a sound.

He called Lancer and arranged the time and location for the drop. He chose a time that would allow him to get there two hours ahead of time and make sure no one was watching. "Like we discussed yesterday, you need to be right on time. I'll be watching. Understood?"

"Understood."

He hung up, took one last look at the cabin, walked back to the van, retracing his steps and used some branches to rub out his footprints, climbed in, and drove off. This really was supposed to have been a two-man job. But he'd manage.

He looked at his watch. The drop was set for 11 o'clock. He would be there in about thirty minutes, right around nine.

CHAPTER 105
Sunday, May 11, 8:35 am

REYES ANSWERED HIS CELL. "Tell me something good."

"We got him."

He fought back a smile. "Clarify."

"Satellite picked up and is tracking the van. We can close in any time you say."

"How far away are you?"

"We have one resource within two minutes of the target. Three tops. It would be preferable if we could bring a few more resources to the party, improve our odds, but their coordinates are further away. We've been canvassing a much bigger grid than where he now turns out to be. It would take a good fifteen minutes for additional resources to close and engage."

"Traffic?"

"Virtually none."

"Can you tell where he's headed?"

"On the highway headed toward D.C."

"Where the traffic will soon become much heavier?"

"Correct."

"We took Osama bin Laden and his security out with not many more assets."

"Not quite. And they never saw it coming. This guy's going to see us approaching."

Reyes reflected for a moment. "Do it! Take him out. Now! Before he gets any closer to D.C., before there are witnesses."

"Repeat."

"You heard me. This is authorized at the highest level. This man is an extreme national threat. Very dangerous. Eliminate and sanitize. Now! Confirm when accomplished."

"Understood."

CHAPTER 106
Sunday, May 11, 8:38 am

THOMAS SAW the black SUV with special plates and flashing lights closing on him. Fast. *So much for any chance that what Reyes and POTUS were interested in was my best welfare.* He only saw one vehicle. They must have thought that was all they needed to take him out. And would also involve fewer witnesses.

He was ready. So were the special wheels and original run flat tires he had installed on the van for just these occasions. They would be disappointed if they tried to shoot out the tires.

If they came after him, he had expected it would be here. The narrow artery was one lane in each direction. Cut through a steep mountain pass, elevations climbing to his immediate right, a several hundred foot embankment to his left, across the one oncoming lane.

He guessed they weren't planning on taking any prisoners. Didn't matter. He had no intention of stopping, or being taken alive. He would slow down a bit. At the right moment. They'd have to overtake and pass him on his left. Exactly where he'd mapped it out.

He floored the gas pedal, as if he were going to try to outrun them. The van lurched forward. They sped up in kind. He eased his foot back off the accelerator and they rammed into the rear end of his van. They motioned him to pull over and stop. *Yeah. Right.*

He accelerated once again, but not full out. This time they rammed the back of the van more violently. The girl began screaming from behind him. Loud.

"Hey, brat, pipe down. Remember our deal. I need to concentrate. You're not helping."

He pulled away from them in a burst. They gave chase. *Now!* Before they had a chance to ram him again, he eased his foot completely off the pedal. As if he were tossing in the towel. They took the bait and attempted to pass him on the left. As they pulled alongside him, they flashed their guns and signaled him to pull over and stop.

He glanced at the girl in his rearview mirror. She was huddled in place thanks to the handcuff holding her to the rail. Not as good as a seatbelt. But close. It would have to do. She couldn't see what was happening outside, but the look on her face was one of sheer terror.

"Hold on, brat, it's gonna get a tad rough. Here we go."

"No!"

He saw the men in the SUV still waving him over to the side of the road, what little side there was. He slowed a little more, stared back at them, took a deep breath, and jammed his steering wheel hard left, simultaneously pumping his foot down on the gas pedal. Without warning, the van collided with the SUV. He knew the other vehicle seriously outweighed his, but the element of surprise gave him a brief advantage. He saw the frozen looks of astonishment on their faces and the muzzles of their blazing guns as the SUV veered to the left, sailing right out over the embankment.

Before the van could follow, Thomas gently coaxed the steering wheel back to the right, managing precariously to keep the van on the highway. He was pretty sure there'd be no survivors in the SUV to call in what had happened, to ask for backup, but he quickly stopped and ran across the road to make sure. He was just in time to see the SUV explode into flames at the bottom of the ravine. There would definitely be no survivors.

Except for the shots they had managed to get off before the SUV went over the precipice, his plan had been flawless. Almost exactly as he had designed it. His high-tech tires were somewhat torn up, but still holding air. They had been well worth the investment. In contrast, he hadn't held up quite as well; one of those shots had caught him in his left shoulder.

He didn't know how badly he was hurt or how much time he had. Others would soon be on the way when they couldn't raise their departed comrades. He opened the rear of the van to check on the girl.

She stared straight into his eyes. "You're not wearing your mask. And you're full of blood."

"I'll survive. And now you know how good looking I really am. We gotta move. Fast. It's gonna be bumpy again. Can't help it."

Slamming the back door, he jumped in front and took off. At full throttle. He kept it that way until he reached the outskirts of D.C. He didn't see anyone following him, but he now had to slow down. There was more traffic. He couldn't afford to draw attention, get pulled over by any Highway Patrol.

He made it to the drop slightly ahead of his timetable. The bleeding from his shoulder had slowed to a trickle, but he was feeling weaker. He circled the area several times. He didn't see anyone. He parked, then came around to the rear of the van and opened the door.

She just looked at him. "You really don't look so good," she said.

He ignored the comment. "Odd how things turn out, brat. Six days ago I knew you'd be dead by now. I didn't expect to care. Just part of the job. Sorry. Now, I hate for it to have to end this way."

Before she could protest, he plunged the syringe into her handcuffed arm. For the last time.

CHAPTER 107
Sunday, May 11, 8:43 am

REYES WAS FRANTIC. He called the number back several times. No answer. He called a backup, providing a sanitized version of what little he knew.

"Not the first time, sir. Won't be the last. We'll take care of it. Sit tight."

Right. Sit tight. What else can I do? Thomas had been his worst nightmare for almost five years.

Or was it POTUS?

* * *

While he'd managed to fully stop the bleeding with some compression bandages he had in the van, Thomas knew he could still lose consciousness at any moment. He had his false CIA identification on him. He might be able to cry national security and talk his way past his shoulder wound. But certainly not the girl's body.

He stuffed it into the wheeled golf travel bag he'd purchased after his former associate had become unavailable. Big enough to hold two sets of golf bags, it also nicely accommodated one full sized human. Thank God for the wheels. He couldn't have done what he had to do without them.

He looked around. He still didn't see any onlookers. With considerable effort, he rolled the travel bag toward the bushes. It was close to a hundred yards off. Every ten yards or so, he had to stop, catch his breath. He was hyperventilating. Probably going into shock. He finally reached the bushes. Dropping to his knees, he clawed at the ground with his hands until he was at least able to fashion a shallow grave. He pushed the bag into the depression and covered it with nearby loose brush. It wasn't perfect, but would have to do.

He had originally planned to remain in sight. To make sure no one else discovered the mound before Lance arrived. The mound would hopefully suffice until then.

The physical exertion had caused his shoulder to start bleeding again. He didn't want to pass out and be found next to the girl's body. Not by Lance. Not by anyone else. Worse, if he didn't get to where he could remove the bullet and clean and close the wound, he might bleed out. Lose consciousness for good.

He crawled out of the bushes, smudged out his tracks behind him, and stumbled back to the van. He turned and glanced one last moment at the quiet mound. Before he drove off.

CHAPTER 108
Sunday, May 11, 11:00 am

ALMOST TWO HOURS LATER, the man almost tripped over the undisturbed mound. He moved the brush aside, unsure what to expect. He saw the large bag and unzipped it. He couldn't believe his eyes. He opened the large-sized envelope that accompanied the body and spilled out its contents. He read the note. And grabbed the syringe and injected the girl's shoulder.

Nothing. He waited. She didn't move. *Had he fucked this up?* Ten minutes went by. Then twenty. Nothing. He sat there. Not sure what more to do. Maybe call 911? Finally, a slight gasp. Then a moan. She tried to sit up.

"Take it easy. Give it some time."

She looked at him and started to weep. Uncontrollably.

"Cassie, you're okay. It's all over. You're safe now. I've got you. I won't let you go."

He held her body close, as tightly as he dared. He softly stroked the back of her neck, tried to reassure her. He picked her up in his arms and carried her to his car. He wanted to bring the travel bag too, but had to leave it back there under the bushes. He had covered it back up. *Not like we're gonna find any fingerprints on it. Other than mine.*

He fastened her seatbelt. Her sobbing gradually lessened. She looked at him. As if confused; afraid to get her hopes up.

He smiled at her gently. "I need to make a call. To let your family know I have you."

He speed-dialed as they drove off. "I've got her."

"Yes! Well done, Detective," Brooks said. "How is she?"

"A bit shaky and weak, as you would expect. But she seems okay. At least outwardly. You'll call her family? We'll be there in about forty minutes. Please also call Leah for me. And make sure she tells Madison."

"No one else," Brooks said. "Not yet. We have some damage control to tend to first. Maybe a few offensive maneuvers as well. Nice job, Detective."

"I may have done some of the heavy lifting—literally—but this was you all the way, Judge."

* * *

Lotello thought he overheard Brooks mutter something like "Pshaw" just before the call ended. *'Pshaw?' Who talks like that?*

CHAPTER 109
Sunday, May 11, 12:15 pm

THE FRONT DOOR of the Webber home flew open as Lotello pulled into the driveway. He'd hardly stopped before Cassie leaped from the car and into her mom's arms. He reached behind him and grabbed her backpack, climbed out of his car, and, after her mom begrudgingly released her, watched the girl hug each member of her family, first her dad, then her grandfather, and, finally, her grandmother. Even Whitney, the family pup, was in a frenzy. Cassie bent down and swooped him up. "I missed you too, Whit," she said as she cuddled him in her arms and relished every lick of her face.

It finally occurred to someone that perhaps they should move the party inside before they became a neighborhood spectacle. Webber retrieved the backpack from Lotello. "Thank you so much for bringing Cassie back to us. Please come inside."

"You go ahead. My wife Leah called to say she and Madison were on the way, but Leah wanted to give you guys a few minutes first. I'll wait out here until they arrive. Don't worry about me. Go ahead and enjoy some private reunion time with your daughter."

* * *

Lotello glanced around and spotted what he was looking for, and parked across the street, two doors down. As he cautiously approached the dark, non-descript vehicle, the driver lowered the window. He remained inside the car.

"Good afternoon," the man said to Lotello.

"That it is. Nice to see you."

"You know, you're supposed to be turning the girl over to me. It's so hard to get good help these days."

They shared a laugh, but then quickly dispensed with the levity.

"I have a handful of associates parked throughout the neighborhood," Lance said. "No one followed you. Kidnappers haven't called me. Too soon for them to wonder why I haven't yet acknowledged receipt of the 'asset.' My men and I will stick around until we're sure it's safe. At least for a couple of days. We won't let any strangers near the house."

"Thanks."

"Not necessary. I have just as much reason as the family to avoid any possible unwanted or unnecessary attention. Including my presence here right now."

The car window closed.

As Lotello turned back toward the Webber home, Leah and Madison pulled up and parked at the sidewalk. Madison jumped out of the car and dashed to him. "Thanks for this, Dad. You have to fill me in—whatever you can—but that can come later." Without waiting for him to reply, she raced off and disappeared into the house.

Leah came up and gave him a quiet kiss. "How is she?"

"Hard to know. You'd think she was just returning from a week at summer camp. Unbelievable. No doubt she's running on adrenaline and the letdown will come. But for now, she's great. We'll have to see what tomorrow brings."

They walked into the house. Lotello and Leah joined the family as they watched the emotional hug fest between the two girls, tears flooding both of their faces in orchestrated unison. Several times, they let go of one another, only to grab on again a moment later. Finally, obviously wanting some space of their own, the two of them unobtrusively made their way down the hallway towards Cassie's room.

Lotello heard Cassie say to Madison, "I'm okay. I think. So much to tell you."

"I want to hear *everything*," Madison responded.

Lotello whispered something to Leah and quietly took his leave. If anyone noticed, they didn't comment. Brooks was waiting. They had things to discuss.

CHAPTER 110
Sunday, May 11, 1:00 pm

THOMAS WAS HOLED up in the Georgetown safe house. He knew they'd be checking all of the hotels for him. He'd arranged this contingency several months ago, and was confident they'd never find the place.

He'd cleaned the wound. Examining it in the mirror, it wasn't as bad as he first thought. Stitching it up was another matter. Even with painkillers, that had not been any fun. But he got through it.

Tomorrow was going to be a big day. Would Hirschfeld come through—for all of them? If not, would Thomas retrieve the girl? He was no longer as sure about that as he had been. He wanted to watch the results from the Courtroom, but that was now out of the question. Far too dangerous. And he was still too wobbly. Television would have to do, even if there would be no intimacy. If all went well, he would be able to leave town right after the announcement of the decision. No longer via Dulles—that was for sure—but he had arranged contingencies for that too.

He picked up his cell and called the number. "Lancer Solutions."

"A.P. here. Status?"

"Asset received. In working order."

"Tomorrow's a big day."

"It is."

Thomas ended the call. There was nothing more for them to discuss. Now.

CHAPTER 111
Sunday, May 11, 2:00 pm

BROOKS AND LOTELLO walked to the nearby park and sat at one of the few empty tables. It was a nice day; lots of people were enjoying themselves. Barbeques. Chess matches. Horseshoes. Shuffleboard. Even a pickup basketball game.

They talked through everything that would still need to happen. It would happen only once. But they went through it twice.

PART SIX

The Announcement

CHAPTER 112
Monday, May 12, 7:15 am

In spite of the strong meds Thomas had taken, his shoulder was on fire. Everything he had done the night before to attend to the van instead of resting had taken its toll. What choice did he have? Rest would have to wait.

The vehicle was now sitting at the bottom of the Potomac, in who knew how many pieces. It had been a grueling exercise.

First, in order to remove any means of tying either him or the girl to the vehicle, he had meticulously acid washed the van, both inside and out. In light of the dismantling process that followed, this had probably been unnecessary, but he preferred not to gamble. And it was always possible that he could have been interrupted before he got the van into the water.

Next, he had placed the charges throughout the van in their watertight containers and driven to the location he'd selected months earlier. He positioned the van near the water's edge, put it in gear, released the brake, and jumped out. He watched it enter the water and slowly sink below the surface. He removed his latex gloves, filled them with pebbles which were lying alongside the river, and dropped them in the water as well. He wondered what else was hidden along the river's bottom.

He climbed back up to the road, and used his phone to detonate the charges. The water muffled the noise somewhat, but it was still loud. He watched the water roil before taking off down the road to where he had called a taxi to take him to his nondescript economy rental car. He would only need it for a day or two before he would abandon it.

He had placed another call to Lance this morning. It rolled over to voicemail: "Lancer Solutions. We can't take your call right now. Leave a message, please. We'll get back to you. Have a safe secure day."

This was the first time, Thomas noted, that Lance had failed to pick up one of his calls. He couldn't leave a number, and didn't leave a message either.

Because of his shoulder, he wouldn't be able to attend the final Court session. Which meant he also couldn't retrieve the cell phones he had housed under the Courtroom seats. It wasn't a matter of fingerprints. He had used only one of the phones; the others were fingerprint free when he'd originally planted them. He had also wiped down the one phone he'd used before reattaching it underneath the seat.

He enjoyed the thought of keeping them in the dark as to where he'd been when he texted Hirschfeld. That source of amusement would now be lost. Sooner or later, the phones would be found. Not that it would do them any good. Still, it was a loose end. And he hated loose ends. Even harmless ones.

CHAPTER 113
Monday, May 12, 7:30 am

In spite of Cassie's safe return, and the fact that he was now free to withdraw his painful request of Gaviota and to vote his conscience, Hirschfeld had still spent a restless night. His mind had kept returning to the unfortunate Fortas-Wolfson scandal back in the '70s, which had led highly respected Supreme Court Justice Abe Fortas to resign from the Court.

Hirschfeld didn't see any choice. He would first meet with Gaviota. Better than nothing. He would never be able to erase his original request, but at least he could apologize to him once more.

He would next meet with Trotter to retroactively recuse himself from *Congress v. NoPoli*. And resign from the Court. Now that Cassie was safe, he would explain everything to Trotter, and how he had stained the integrity of the Court. He had no assurance that Trotter would hold their meeting in confidence, a cross he would have to bear.

Just then, his cell was flooded with simultaneous telephone and text alerts. He sighed.

The text was from Jill, the call from Brooks. Another violation of the no one-sided attorney communication rule? That would hardly matter now. Lost in family celebration the night before, Hirschfeld had overlooked calling Brooks to thank him for designing Cassie's safe return. His daughter's text would have to wait a moment.

* * *

"Good morning, Cyrus. Sorry for not calling you last night. Still struggling with these damn rules. But not for much longer. My family and I are *so* indebted to you. Words fail me."

"Words aren't always necessary, Arnold. They aren't here. At the risk of stretching our rules once more, I do have something I'd like to discuss with you."

Not waiting to find out why Brooks was calling, Hirschfeld shared with Brooks what he intended to say to Trotter that morning.

"Arnold, your wounds are still raw, and will be for some time. I would like to suggest to you another way of looking at all of this. I know you think the integrity of the Court requires you to come clean and resign. I get that. However, I submit to you that the Court's integrity would be better served by you *not* doing that."

"How do you figure?"

"What purpose does it serve to emphasize to the world the human frailties of the Court, and to encourage others to employ similar tactics? And deny our country the outstanding scholarship you bring to the Court? In exchange for what? Allowing President Tuttle to nominate your successor? It's beyond the scope of this call, but trust me Tuttle is the last person who should be permitted to orchestrate the selection of your successor."

"Cyrus, I'm no fan of Tuttle. I accept your veiled comments about him. However, there's no way I can ignore what I've done. Besides, there's no getting around the words I uttered on the record. That TV journalist, Nishimura, is already on it like a bloodhound, and others will certainly follow."

"Why don't you leave Nishimura to me? As for others who might follow the trail, I have a thought or two about that as well."

* * *

Hirschfeld opened Jill's text.

Surprise, Poppy! Had to borrow Mom's phone. Don't have a new one yet. Really exciting news. You remember my friend Madison. You met her yesterday at our house. We are coming to the Court this morning to watch you—to make up for not coming on Tuesday. Can you take us on the tour you promised? See you soon. Love you! Cassie

"No, no, no, no, no!" The word kept reverberating over and over somewhere between Hirschfeld's head and his soul.

Too much to handle by text. He picked up the phone and called.

"Hi, Poppy."

"Hi, baby. I thought you'd still be sleeping after everything you've been through, and all the excitement yesterday."

"No way. Too much to do. Anyway, don't forget I slept through much of what went on yesterday. Courtesy of the creep."

"Very funny. Seriously, but aren't you the least bit tired? Don't you think you should take it easy for a couple days?"

"Mom and Dad said the same thing. I wanted to go hit balls this morning before coming to Court. I haven't swung a club or hit a ball in almost a week. I miss it. I know coming to Court means skipping a little more school, but I studied all week in that dingy basement. I figure I'm way ahead right now."

"I don't know, baby, they say after an ordeal like yours—"

"I negotiated a deal with Mom and Dad. You would have been proud of me. They wanted to take me to the doctor this morning and then make me go home and rest. I said if they would bring Madison and me to Court this morning, I would skip golf one more day and they could take me to the doctor this afternoon. Then, yeah, I said I would rest. For a day, two at the most. I really want to see you in Court in this case. Remember, I'm now connected to this case forever."

Hirschfeld found himself equivocating—disbelief, joy, relief, pride. "It sounds like you worked out a good deal, sweetheart, but I'm still not sure it's wise for you to come to Court today. We can always do that another time."

"Why, Poppy? Don't you want me to see you finish the case?"

"Of course I do, but there will be other cases." *Well, maybe not.* "I just don't think it's such a good idea for you to come to Court with that man still out there running around."

"Him? I don't think so, Poppy. I know it sounds weird, but I don't think he'd hurt me any longer. Besides, if we have to keep worrying about him, then how can I practice my golf? Or go to the mall with my friends? Or go anywhere else? I think he's probably the one frightened now, with everyone trying to catch him."

Hirschfeld smiled. She just never ceases to amaze.

"Poppy? Are you still there?"

"I am, baby. I have to go get ready. I'll see you and Madison later. I hope the two of you will both have lunch with me afterward in the Courthouse cafeteria. Perhaps Madison's parents would like to join us. I have something I have to do at the Courthouse afterward, but maybe Madison's dad can give you a ride home when we finish our tour and lunch."

"Great! Thanks, Poppy. Sounds like a plan. Love you."

"I love you too, baby."

CHAPTER 114
Monday, May 12, 7:40 am

JILL WAS GETTING DRESSED to take Cassie and Madison to the Courthouse. They would stop and get her mom on the way. Three generations of Hirschfeld women, that would be nice, but this was all still against Jill's better judgment. She didn't want any of them going anywhere near that place.

Jill had wanted to take Cassie for a complete medical examination this morning, and then bring her straight home, but Cassie was having no part of that. And everyone was siding with Cassie. Even Jill's own mom. *How could they?*

At least Madison's father had seemed to side with her. Sort of. When he called to say at what time he would drop Madison off to ride with Cassie, he said he was also going to the Courthouse to watch the decision and would be happy to caravan behind them and escort them into the Courtroom.

The doctor was scheduled to give Cassie a complete checkup that afternoon, but if Cassie thought she was resuming her golf activities tomorrow, she'd have another thought coming. *Certainly the doctor will side with me on this.*

* * *

Out of the corner of her eye, Jill saw Mark staring at her.

"What?"

"Nothing, really. I was just wondering what you were thinking."

"I was wondering if our life will ever be the same. And when? I don't see how it can."

"It will, and soon, because that's the way things work. They have to. We just can't live in fear. Besides, do you really think something like this is going to happen again?"

"It seems to me it could—as long as Dad continues to be a Supreme Court Justice."

"So, what do *you* suggest? Do you want your dad to resign, or retire?"

"Why not? He doesn't need it. The money or the stress. Either that, or the government should have to expand the Secret Service and provide us with bodyguards."

"Provide *who* with bodyguards? There are nine Justices. That's a lot of family members. Would you include brothers and sisters? Nephews and nieces? What about the next-door neighbors? Friends? Everyone whose safety and welfare any of the nine Justices cares about? Where would you draw the line?"

"I don't know And I really don't care. I just want *our* family to be safe. Let someone else worry about all of your fancy questions."

"That's the problem. No one wants to be bothered having to answer the questions. They want others to do it for them. But to their satisfaction, of course. It would be a terrible precedent for your dad to resign or retire out of fear. And the government isn't going to provide and pay for all of these bodyguards. Nor do most families have the resources to do so on their own. Life has to go on. We have to responsibly play the odds."

"Yes, but because of Dad, we're high profile. For us, playing the odds responsibly doesn't work. Why can't the government provide us with protection? Look at the billions they spend on security at all of the airports across the country."

"Exactly. At the airports. And at courthouses. But not on the way to and from."

"Unless you're a political leader. They all have their drivers and security people. All paid for by our tax dollars."

"So, you want Cassie to live in a cocoon? No golf? No freedom? No privacy? Possibly no friends? How long do you want her chauffeured around? A year? Two years? Until she goes off to college? Do you really expect her to put up with that?"

Jill didn't answer. It just hurt too much. She didn't know what more to say. *What is he doing? Why doesn't he understand? Take my side for once. Stop talking. Just hold me.*

CHAPTER 115
Monday, May 12, 8:00 am

HIRSCHFELD KNOCKED, receiving the usual welcoming response. He entered Gaviota's chambers and closed the imposing door. A sign of authority. But Hirschfeld no longer felt his own authority.

Gaviota stood and came around from behind his desk. The awkwardness hanging in the air between these two old friends was obvious. Gaviota skipped his customary bilingual niceties and got right to it, without giving Hirschfeld any opportunity to speak first. "Arnold—"

"No, Jose, I have to go first, please. Cassie's back, safe and well." He quickly summarized what had transpired.

Gaviota looked like the weight of the world had been lifted off his back. "Arnold, Dios mio. What a relief. I can't tell you how happy this makes me."

"I also want to tell you," Hirschfeld said, "that I had made the decision *before* we learned of Cassie's good fortune to withdraw my request of you. I was not thinking clearly when I asked you what I did. I don't expect you to believe me, but—"

"Arnold. No mas. Por favor. Stop. I *do* believe you. Completely. It's not necessary for you to explain yourself. Our conversation never happened."

"Oh, but it did, Jose. I won't ever tell anyone because I don't want *you* to be compromised, but I'm going from here to prepare my resignation and take it to Trotter."

"Pero por qué, Arnold. But why? It's not necessary."

"Thank you, Jose, but I think it is. This morning, I have two reasons. One, I don't want to bring any more danger to my family. And two, for what I was prepared to do, I've dishonored the Court—as I have dishonored you."

"Please, stop talking about how I've been—"

Hirschfeld silenced him with a raised hand. "Earlier this morning, Cassie telephoned to tell me her mom is bringing her here this morning to watch the decision in our case. She seemed so excited. In stark contrast, I cringed, arguing that it would be too dangerous for her to be here today. She told me that was no reason for her not to come. Imagine that, Jose. A child grasping the correct perspective quicker than her grandfather. It's really time for me to leave."

"You're blessed to have such a youngster in your life. And to have her back safely."

"Of course, a thousand times. But that doesn't change my other reason, the shame I have brought to the Court."

"Arnold, I think you are perhaps being too hasty. None of your colleagues would think ill of you given the circumstances. I recognize that only you can make this decision. I will of course respect whatever you decide, but please don't rush yourself. You don't have to decide today. And I don't think you should."

The two of them were still standing. Gaviota closed the distance between them and embraced his colleague. Hirschfeld struggled to accept Gaviota's heartfelt gesture. He gently broke away, turned, and walked out of Gaviota's chambers, closing the door behind him.

* * *

Hirschfeld sat and watched Trotter read his resignation. Looking up at him, Trotter took the letter and ran it through the shredder sitting at the side of his desk.

"Sorry, Arnold, while I understand your reasoning, your decision is not acceptable. And I won't accept it. Certainly not today. Nor will I permit you to recuse yourself from this case."

Trotter glanced at his watch. "I am, however, going to take the liberty of quickly making a few minor changes in the majority decision upholding the 28th Amendment before we have to take the bench in ninety short minutes. Thank goodness my clerk will help because it would take me that much time by myself just to open the two files on my computer."

He punctuated his statement with a self-deprecating smile. "I see no need to alter the seven to two vote in favor of standing. Your vote on that was not changed because of the events. However, I am going to change your vote on the amendment from invalidating to upholding. Your vote on that obviously was impacted.

I am also going to revise the opinion to identify its author as you rather than me. A modest expression to those who would unduly influence this Court that they will never succeed. My apologies for the fact that history will forever attribute to you my inferior writing skills. There's obviously no time to let you improve upon it with any of your personal touches. You'll have to live with that ignominy."

Hirschfeld started to protest. Trotter cut him off. "We're out of time. You're just going to have to trust me on this, scary as I know that is. I guess that's why they call me *Mr.* Chief." Trotter grinned sheepishly, as though to acknowledge his clumsy attempt at humor. "The best I could muster on such short notice. For the good of this noble institution, Arnold, we will get through this. On my watch, my way."

CHAPTER 116
Monday, May 12, 9:25 am

KESSLER DIDN'T WANT to give her any time to wangle, but he had waited as long as he dared. Their thirty-minute special leading up to the Court's ten o'clock announcement of its decision would begin shortly.

"Anne, I know we're short on time, but we need to talk. It'll only take a minute."

"Make it quick, Steve, I'm kind of busy here."

"There's a rumor floating around that you intend to break a highly inflammatory story about Hirschfeld and his family today. I—"

"Who told you that?"

"Like you, Anne, I can't reveal my sources, but I do know you visited the Webber home, and how out of line you were. And what I will tell you is that if you so much as *think* about dropping your so-called bomb on the air, I will interrupt you on the spot and tell the TV audience that you are mistaken and acting out of some kind of inflated and narcissistic self-aggrandizement."

"What are you talking about? How dare you talk to me this way? You'd never have the guts to challenge me on national television. I'd eat you alive."

"Anne, for your sake, I really hope you won't choose to put me to the test. You have more experience in front of a camera than I do, but I'll muddle through. Keep in mind that I have nothing to lose. I'm retired and financially secure. Can you say the same? Are you ready to gamble your career, and your livelihood? Journalists used to be able to get away with whatever they wanted.

Not anymore. Things are changing. As you know better than I, television broadcasters are being fired overnight for far less than what you have in mind."

Nishimura didn't say another word.

* * *

Nishimura scowled silently at Kessler. She was incensed. *That ungrateful son-of-a-bitch! I prop him up all week long, make him a national figure and this is the way he thanks me?* She'd have to hold back during the first piece. But just as soon as the first piece was finished, she'd go straight to the show's producer and report that Kessler had made a pass at her and touched her inappropriately following the special. The producer understood those things. She'd back Nishimura and have security immediately remove him from the set—before he would have a chance to interfere with the final broadcast.

Thanks to Kessler, she now realized she couldn't wait any longer to break her story. She would have to do it in the final coverage immediately following the Supreme Court decision. Kessler would win the first battle, but she'd show him who'd win the war.

CHAPTER 117
Monday, May 12, 9:50 am

THOMAS HADN'T SLEPT VERY WELL. His shoulder had ached throughout the night. He was also anxious for the decision that this morning would bring.

He had been up early, and had managed to eat something. He was feeling slightly better. He used his cell to double check and confirm his travel arrangements. It was still a matter of being on top of all the details, taking nothing for granted.

It was close to ten o'clock. He pulled a beer out of the refrigerator, sat down on the chair opposite the TV, put his feet up on the ottoman, and took a swig. He used the remote to turn on the TV, set the channel, and start the DVR recorder. He'd have some time before leaving and would no doubt want to watch it all a couple extra times.

He'd done his job. If the old man did his too, Thomas was about to enjoy the greatest victory of his life. Once and for all, he would finally be . . . home.

* * *

At ten sharp, the television cameras panned the Courtroom. First, the nine Justices, then moving away from the Justices to the lawyers standing behind their tables, Esposito and his gofers at one end, Brooks and Klein at the other end. Then onto the first few rows of the gallery, the select Congressional leaders behind Esposito, Lotello and his kids behind Brooks and Klein. And . . .

Wait a minute. Wait a damn, fucking minute! The brat. The fuck's she doing there?

In a matter of seconds, Thomas's cautious optimism had bowed. He was up on his feet, standing eye to eye with the TV, still gripping the beer bottle in his right hand. Watching intently. Waiting impatiently.

Hirschfeld mounted the dais in the midst of his eight other colleagues at ten o'clock sharp. As usual, the Court Marshall promptly read the opening invocation. Hirschfeld never tired hearing it. He looked right at Cassie and winked. When he saw the proud look on her face, he knew he had made the right call. Or that someone had.

Chief Justice Trotter readied himself to announce the decision to all in attendance and to those watching in front of their television sets.

"Ladies and Gentlemen, on the first question of whether Congress had standing to bring the lawsuit known as *Congress v. NoPoli*, the vote reached by this Court is seven to two in favor of standing. Accordingly," Trotter continued, "Congress was entitled to sue and the Justices were thus compelled also to decide the fate of the 28th Amendment to the Constitution of the United States."

Trotter paused, no doubt due to his sense of theater, Hirschfeld thought. The Courtroom was perfectly silent.

Trotter resumed: "On the second question, then, whether the 28th Amendment of the Constitution was legitimately enacted and ratified by The National Organization for Political Integrity, otherwise known as NoPoli, at its convention last year: by a vote of nine to zero, the 28th Amendment is ..." Trotter conveniently cleared the frog in his throat, milking the moment for all it was worth. "Upheld. The—"

The gallery erupted. After his own initial shock, Hirschfeld couldn't help but quietly take pleasure in the somber mood among the Congressional leaders sitting alongside Esposito at his table. His eyes skated across to Brooks and Klein. She was unable to hide her astonishment. In marked contrast, there was no telling on Brooks's face or perfectly still frame what was going on inside his exterior.

The Court Marshall continued to bang his gavel until the raucous hubbub finally subsided.

"As I was saying," Trotter resumed, "the unanimous opinion of the Court will now be read by its author. As Chief Justice, I have counter-signed the final opinion and hand it to my colleague for the customary reading. If you will, please, Justice Hirschfeld."

Hirschfeld glanced at Brooks before beginning. Nothing. Cold, stone sober. He looked again at Cassie. She was brimming, and quietly fist bumping with her friend Madison.

He read the opinion aloud. For the most part, it was unchanged from what had previously been circulated among and edited by the Justices. And, for the most part, Hirschfeld read in a steady, even monotone. However, when his eyes came to the particular footnote, presented in an unusual, but not unheard of, personalized style, he paused before then continuing:

"The author understands that considerable speculation has occurred regarding the meaning of certain remarks made by him on the record during argument. To clarify, the remarks were intended merely to empha-size the intention of the fathers of our Constitution that the *government* never be allowed to extort or hold hostage the *governed* in conducting the business and affairs of these United States."

When Hirschfeld completed the traditional reading, Trotter thanked all in attendance and those watching on television for their attention, and stated that the matter of *Congress v. NoPoli* was now concluded, and adjourned.

* * *

He listened to the decision, the numbers. *Nine to zero to uphold. Impossible! How?* No answers. Just all the shouting and screaming. It was everywhere. In the Courtroom. On the television. Right there in his safe house, as the thunder churned up from somewhere deep inside his very being. He involuntarily slammed the beer bottle against the television screen. Glass exploded all over him, and the room.

He was beside himself in a tangle of rage and frustration. He had no idea what he had just witnessed. And he couldn't even back up and watch it again because he had destroyed the DVR monitor in his fury.

What he did know was abject failure. Again. He was not back home. He had . . . no home.

Lance must have been behind this. How could he have been so wrong about him? If it were his doing—if he'd reneged on the agreement—he'd get even with him. Somehow. Some way.

When he finally was able to calm down, gather himself, a little, he opened the screenshot he'd made of the escrow agreement and saved in his smartphone. He read through the document to see if he'd missed something. It looked just like he remembered it. *That bastard cheated me, took advantage of my trust in him because of our similar backgrounds.* And then, suddenly, the image flashed across his mind. He went back and read it once more. *No. NOOOO!*

CHAPTER 118
Monday, May 12, 11:10 am

NISHIMURA HURRIED to the adjacent production room. They only had a moment before she had to return for the second special. She had milked the sexual abuse card for all she could. It hadn't gotten her what she wanted. What she had expected.

"Oh, Annie, I am sooo sorry. There's just no way we can pull him at the last minute like this. But I'll arrange two security officers off to the side of the set right away. He won't dare bother you again while they're there. And they'll haul his ass off the set just as soon as we finish."

Nishimura hadn't answered. She had just shrugged her shoulders in obvious disappointment, turned, and walked back to the set. *I don't think the bastard's bluffing. No way I can take a chance.* She had to play it straight for now and count on breaking her 'exclusive' later in the week. Hopefully.

* * *

Kessler thought the television post-mortem of the unanimous opinion was somewhat anti-climactic. The country wanted to party, not dissect. Still, Nishimura gave it her best shot, and he and Elliott, of course, did her bidding. When the producer confirmed that it was a wrap and thanked them all for their great work, Nishimura stood and stormed off without a word.

Elliott looked at Kessler. "Wow, what got into her?"

"Beats me," Kessler responded.

"Well, whatever, I enjoyed working with you, Steve. Maybe we can do it again sometime."

"I enjoyed it too, Chris, but this was a one-off for me. I think my broadcasting career is over." He spotted the two security officers standing off to the side. But they made no move as he and Elliott walked off the set without incident.

CHAPTER 119
Monday, May 12, 11:20 am

HIRSCHFELD GAVE special souvenir badges to Cassie and Madison and escorted them through all of the nooks and crannies of the Courtroom and its back offices and corridors. He took them up on the dais and let them select chairs and gaze out into the Courtroom. Madison chose Trotter's center seat, Cassie her Poppy's.

He then introduced them to all of the Justices who had not yet left for lunch. While Madison practiced her Spanish with Gaviota, Trotter told Cassie that he had heard a lot of wonderful things about her. She smiled politely, and thanked him. Hirschfeld just raised his eyebrows in feigned surprise and ushered the girls on through the balance of their tour.

They had lunch in the Courthouse cafeteria. As they finished dessert, Cassie said: "It's okay to cheat once in a while, Poppy. The key is not to do it too often."

The irony of an occasional cheat for a greater good, if only a little satisfaction, was not lost on Hirschfeld. He had set out to save Cassie, but somehow it seemed like she might have saved him.

CHAPTER 120
Monday, May 12, 3:30 pm

CASSIE'S DOCTOR had spent about an hour with her, mostly just talking. She understood what the doctor was after. Cassie was okay with that because she knew the doctor was just doing her job and Cassie was the only one who could answer the question. Cassie assured her that nothing like that had happened. She hoped that she could now go home and just think about the next day's golf and school.

* * *

"Considering what she's been through," the doctor said to Jill, "her resilience is remarkable. No temperature, so no infection. Blood pressure and pulse fine. Lungs perfectly clear. Her blood sugar's just a little elevated, nothing to be concerned about under the circumstances. I've drawn blood and collected urine and will run the customary lab panels. I won't have those results for a few days. I'll call if there's anything out of the ordinary, but from what I'm seeing I'm not expecting any problems. I collected the samples to test because it's the prudent thing to do. I have patients who don't recover from the flu this quickly. I can only attribute it to the incredible shape Cassie was in preceding this ordeal."

"Thank you, doctor. So far, so good, then. I guess. Thank God. But don't we have to have her examined by a psychiatrist too?"

"We can if you want. But why would you want to?"

"Well, what about PTSD? That kind of stuff."

"PTSD is a convenient label, frequently used and frequently misused. It generally refers to an emotional breakdown induced by extreme or prolonged fear. But you can't generalize it. Different people react differently to the same circumstances.

"All I can say is that Cassie's emotional strength is no less extraordinary than her physical well-being. Look. From what I can see, and from what Cassie tells me, she was slapped around and grabbed a couple of times, and definitely has some bruises and black and blue marks to show for it, but that stuff will be gone in no time at all. She was not battered in any ongoing sense of the word, and she was not molested. Not physically anyway."

Sitting across her desk from Jill, Cassie's doctor watched Jill twisting her hands in her lap. She imagined that Jill was having a difficult time processing what she was being told.

"I don't understand," Jill said. "Even if she is okay, what about emotional scars?"

"Well, based again on what Cassie tells me, her captor did subject her to quite an ordeal, but so far she seems to have come through it fairly well. In military combat, some soldiers fall completely to pieces while others perform at heroic levels without blemish.

"Personally," the doctor continued, "I find it insulting to compare the stress Cassie experiences in her golf tournaments to what she has endured in the past week, but who's to say that her competitive experience hasn't somehow helped prepare her to get through the past week? That she has also learned to cope with and manage her diabetes so well has no doubt also been a positive for her.

Cassie's doctor wasn't through. "Cassie is a young lady with a great deal of well-earned self-esteem and confidence. You should not underestimate the value of that and you should not ascribe to her what you would project an experience like this to do to others her age. Cassie is simply not like other youngsters her age. It may also be in her DNA, so to speak. And yours too. *That last point was for Jill. I really hope she's not going to smother Cassie.*

"Moreover, she seems to have a good grasp of what was visited on her. And why. I think this helps her a lot. She knows this wasn't anything she did wrong, or caused. And she doesn't seem worried that it's going to happen to her again."

The doctor could see that Jill still wasn't convinced. "What are we supposed to do going forward?"

"If she were my kid, I'd let her get back to her normal routine just as quickly as she wants. Don't push her, but do *not* hold her back. Watch for any classic symptoms, nightmares, moodiness, and those kinds of things. If you see any of that, we'll immediately put her under the care of a psychiatrist, but let's not create any self-fulfilling prophecies by treating her like she's a fragile, broken rag doll. I see no reason to subject her to any therapy right now. PTSD-like symptoms often do show up further down the road. Stay vigilant, but don't drive yourself—or Cassie—nuts. And for God's sake don't treat her like something's wrong with her."

CHAPTER 121
Monday, May 12, 5:30 pm

CASSIE HAD BEEN on her computer video phone with Madison for about half an hour. She was all caught up on what schoolwork she had missed. Madison wasn't convinced, but Cassie assured her that she had done more on her own in her self-monitored basement home study program than what Madison said they had covered at school while Cassie was out.

She wondered if any of the kids in school had missed her.

"Well, aren't we obsessing about our self-importance? Sorry to tell you, but near as I can tell no one knew you were gone. Not even that special guy you seem to dwell on."

"Do not! Oh well. Besides, we have to keep all of this stuff I went through a level nine top secret. My parents have said 'not a word to anyone.' Ever. It's not for me. It's for my poppy."

"Tell me about it! My dad has been all over me about this. One word about any of it and I will be grounded until I graduate from college. At least we can talk about it with each other."

Cassie laughed. "I know. I'm glad we're able to talk about it normally, like two grown-ups. So far, I can't really talk with my parents about it. They just get too upset. They can't seem to handle it, especially Mom. Maybe after a while."

"What about the creep?" Madison asked. "Do you really think he's gone? Are you worried he'll come after you? Dad says lots of people are looking for him. I don't know if that's really true since this is all so hush-hush. I think he might have just said that to make me not obsess."

"I don't know if he's gone. He was shot, and he was bleeding a lot. But if he's still alive I don't think he'll hang around. And I honestly don't think he wants anything more to do with me. I was a major pain for him, a lot more trouble than I think he expected. Besides, there's no way now for him to get what he was after. The Supreme Court has already decided the case against what he wanted."

"But won't he blame you and try to get even?"

"I don't think so. He knows I wasn't the one who caused his problems. Except maybe for the hole in his chest."

"That was *so* buck. Tell me about it again."

And so Cassie did, for about the hundredth time.

"Yuck!"

"I know."

"What about your perks?"

"Well, I have to wait one more day before I can get back into my golf and training. And I probably won't be allowed to walk by myself between the driving range and school until I'm at least twenty."

"That sucks! It's like being grounded for something that wasn't your fault."

"Tell me about it. But, hey, I get it. I can deal with it. I guess. My parents have been through a lot. I have to cut them some slack. For a little while. We'll get past it." They both laughed at that.

"Besides, um, don't tell anyone," Cassie said, "but I don't think I'd really like going anywhere on my own right now."

CHAPTER 122
Monday, May 12, 7:00 pm

THOMAS SLEPT ALL AFTERNOON. He tried to put the recent events out of his mind, at least for the time being. Even the rage and frustration. He needed to focus on other matters. With a clear head.

However, once again, he found himself trying to sort it all out. He couldn't help it.

He took out a pad of paper and jotted down a list of names. Possible enemies. And possible targets. Then he copied the list over on a second page, this time in alphabetical order. He didn't want to play favorites—at least not until he'd made up his mind.

Brooks, Cyrus.

Hirschfeld, Arnold

Klein, Leah.

Lance, J.R.

Lotello, Frank.

Reyes, Manuel.

Tuttle, Roger.

Webber, Cassie.

The first name he crossed off the list was the girl's. None of this was her fault. He had no gripe with her. Truth be told, he liked her. She stood up for herself. She was honest with him. She had shared his pizza with him. And he had a date to play golf with her. Sometime. Somewhere. Maybe after she became a famous pro.

The next name he crossed off the list was the old man. Unlike the girl, he was at least partially to blame. And had lied to him. Played him like a fiddle. But could he really blame him? Would he have acted any differently in his place? The old man was fighting for his granddaughter. He was a soldier. A good one. No, he had no real quarrel with the old man. Besides, the girl would never forgive him if he hurt her "Poppy."

Figuratively, he crossed one more off the list. Well, not completely. He just moved the name to the bottom of the page. Lance. Thomas couldn't help but feel that Lance had taken advantage of him. Of their fraternity. Even if the man were genuine, true to his beliefs. But had Lance actually lied to him? The language was right there in the contract. Time had been short. Still, Thomas had no one to fault other than himself for not reading the escrow agreement more carefully. Had Lance actually deceived him, though? He wouldn't know for sure until he developed the facts he didn't yet have. *Yet.*

So, Lance went to the bottom of the list. First things first. But Thomas decided to keep Lance in his cross-hairs. At least for the time being.

Five names remained at the top of the page, divided into two groups. Two priorities. In the lower priority were Brooks, Klein, and Lotello. He didn't know if any of them actually had anything to do with the girl's release. But if one did they all did. And his instincts told him they did. They'd been his nemesis dating back to the *Norman* case. For them, it was not if. It was when.

This brought him to the final two. He should say the first two. Reyes and Tuttle. When troops turned on their own, that was the worst. The very worst. Treason. They had abandoned him. Worse. They had turned on him.

He tore up the pages. But not until he first entered what he had written there on his laptop. He saved that file. He would look at it again. He would not forget.

CHAPTER 123
Tuesday, May 13, 1:15 am

TUTTLE WAS SURPRISED to receive a call on his private line at this hour. He glanced at his telephone console. All it said was "Night Security Officer."

He punched the speaker button. "Yes?"

"Mr. President?"

"We're you expecting someone else? Awfully late isn't it? Something bad happening somewhere in the world that can't wait until the morning?"

"Yes, sir. Right here in Washington. Very bad, I'm afraid. Thought you'd want to know right away, sir."

"Too late to rethink that now, Officer. What is it?"

"Two hours ago, sir, the White House switchboard received what was thought to be a crank call. At this time of day, standard protocol was to report the call to Mr. Reyes."

"To my chief of staff? This goes to him personally?"

"Well not directly to Mr. Reyes, sir. To his after-hours security detail."

"And?"

"We couldn't raise him on his phone. So we entered Mr. Reyes's condo unit. He was nowhere to be found. We—"

"Hold on. *Who* was nowhere to be found? Mr. Reyes?"

"No, sir. The after-hours security detail was nowhere to be found. Sorry for not being clearer."

"Okay. Carry on."

"We found him. Lying on the floor. He was dead, sir. With—"

"Wait a minute. You're doing it again, Officer. Found *who* dead? The after-hours security detail?"

"No, sir. I'm sorry. I get flustered when, you know, when I'm speaking with the President of the United States and all. I realize I have to be clearer, sir. I won't fail you again, sir. Anyway, we found Mr. Reyes, sir. With what appears to be a self-inflicted gunshot wound. From the looks of things, he put his weapon to the roof of his mouth, and fired."

"Good God. You telling me—"

"Yes, sir. It's quite a grizzly scene here, Mr. President."

"Wait. Wouldn't his after-hours security detail have heard the shot?"

"Missing, sir. The after-hours security detail, that is. He's missing. Difficult to explain, isn't it? Perhaps he left his station to find help, sir."

Tuttle couldn't make sense of what he was hearing. The more the man talked, the stranger it all sounded. The stranger the man sounded. Tuttle was losing his patience. "Was there a note?"

"Yes, sir, there was. And a rather odd one at that."

"Read it to me."

"It's short. All it says is 'I'm sorry. I've failed you again. But treason is the worst kind of disloyalty. It cannot go unpunished.'"

"That's it?"

"That's it, Mr. President. Do those words perhaps mean anything to you, sir? Do you have any possible idea to whom the word 'you' might be referring, Mr. President?"

Tuttle paused. "No idea. This is all extremely distressing. What happens now?"

"I'm just the evening security detail, Mr. President. I've alerted the Secret Service dispatch. They'll take it from here, sir."

"Thank you." Something about all this didn't feel right to Tuttle. "By the way, please give me your name."

"My name? You want to know my name, sir?"

"Yes, Officer. Isn't that what I just said?"

"You did, sir. Thomas, sir. My name is Thomas. Good night, Mr. President. Sleep well. And again, sir, my apologies for failing you. Again. Sir."

Tuttle recoiled. "Thomas? What—"

The line went dead. Tuttle dropped the receiver, as if it was covered in something infectious. Deadly infectious. He hurried over to the window, pulled the drape aside and looked down into the garden. He didn't think he saw anything out there. Among the shadows. But it was dark. He couldn't be sure. He swiftly stepped away from the window, releasing the drape. Watching to make sure it fully closed.

CHAPTER 124
Wednesday, May 14, 8:00 am

NISHIMURA FINISHED READING the routine interview she'd given concerning her experience televising *Congress v. NoPoli*. It was a far cry from what she'd expected to be reporting.

The problem was that her exclusive had evaporated overnight. Technically, the family had never admitted anything to her. Or to anyone else. Cassie Webber was in Court for the reading of the final ruling, in which Hirschfeld himself explained away his odd remarks in Court earlier in the week.

Kidnapping? Extortion? By whom? Cassie had merely been at home with the flu for a few days. That was the party line. And they all were sticking to it. The girl was already back in school, practicing her golf again two times a day. Hardly sounded like much of a kidnapping. NBN executives refused to let Nishimura tell her supposedly extraordinary story without corroboration she couldn't produce.

Timing was everything. Kessler had stopped her dead in her tracks. When Cassie was nowhere to be found. When Nishimura actually had a story. Momentarily. She remained irate with Kessler, who somehow knew just when to shut her down. For just long enough.

Hirschfeld. The Webbers. Klein's husband Lotello, right there at the Webber home. Klein and her partner Brooks, the two of them NoPoli board members. Along with Kessler.

Lotello at the Webber home was the only tangible thing she had. A cop possibly working the kidnapping, but whose wife also happened to be

NoPoli's co-counsel. It smelled. The problem was that Lotello's daughter was Cassie's best friend. Supposedly just bringing Cassie her missing schoolwork for his daughter.

Nishimura was furious. She knew she had a story. She just couldn't quite piece it together. They really had closed ranks on her.

She opened the streaming News service site on her laptop and read with interest the White House press release that Chief of Staff Manny Reyes had suffered a fatal heart attack and died in his sleep Monday evening. The coroner stated that death was instant and peaceful. President Tuttle said the nation had lost a fine public servant and he had lost a good friend.

Awfully coincidental. Wonder if there's possibly a story behind this story?

CHAPTER 125
Wednesday, May 14, 3:00 pm

BROOKS WAS IN HIS SWEATSUIT, out for what he—but probably no one else—would characterize as an afternoon "power" walk. He tried to get one in every day, at least when all the stars were properly aligned and nothing else got in the way. On average, he managed to make three a week. Sometimes four.

He didn't think the name for the clothing—sweatsuit—made much sense. At least, not for him. He never managed to work up much of a sweat on his so-called power walks, but Eloise told him they were good for him nonetheless. He assumed she was referring to the power walks. Not the sweatsuits.

Lotello had called after lunch and said he had some loose ends he wanted to go over and hoped he could stop by. Brooks told him to bring his walking shoes. Maybe even some workout clothes. And not to slow him down.

"Your meeting, Detective. One lap through the neighborhood. What's up?"

Lotello fell in line, to Brooks's immediate right. "A few unsettled matters. I was hoping to get some closure. I guess I should say 'we' because a few of these actually come from Madison."

He took out his small sized notepad and skimmed several of the pages.

Brooks glanced over at him without breaking stride. *Oy, so much he had to make notes?* To Lotello: "So much you had to make notes?"

Lotello didn't answer the question. Instead: "What do you think about Manny Reyes's heart attack? A little pat? Newspaper reports say he was in good health. No prior heart issues and no heart disease in his family."

"My my. Aren't we sounding a little paranoid?"

"Well, according to Cassie, someone had fired gunshots at her kidnapper as he was driving her to the drop on Sunday. He was hit."

Brooks wasn't yet sweating, but his breathing was becoming labored. Between breaths, he uttered, "And your point?"

"You'll recall that Cassie's description of the kidnapper pretty well matched Thomas. Also fits the description in a missing person's report filed with the police about a Supreme Court nightshift janitor who hasn't shown up for work since last week, and whose contact information was falsified. Hirschfeld received multiple texts from one or more kidnappers apparently observing Hirschfeld from right there in the Courtroom. Where the public is not allowed to bring cell phones past Courthouse security. The janitor angle might explain that. Aren't you curious about any of this?"

"Relentlessly," Brooks said. "Unable to sleep wondering about it all." Pausing to take a couple more breaths, "But what does this have to do with Reyes's death?"

"It's not hard to imagine that Reyes—and Tuttle—would have been anxious to rid themselves of Thomas dating back to the aftermath of the *Norman* trial. And the shootout involving Thomas and yours truly. Reyes was at the Courthouse last Thursday. Maybe he was on the prowl for Thomas. Maybe Thomas saw him. And struck back. Do we really know the cause of Reyes's death?"

Brooks winced at the reminder of the shootout in which Lotello had been seriously wounded. Another couple of breaths. *In through the nose, out through the mouth.* "Circumstantial. But fun to speculate." He started to pick up the pace, but then thought better of it. He quickly managed to squeeze out a few more words. "And to imagine how Tuttle might be feeling right now if the cause of Reyes's death were not as reported." A couple more breaths. "Anything more there in your notepad?"

"Nishimura seems to have completely dropped her big story. Would you know anything about that?"

Brooks stopped, bent over and put his hands on his quads. A couple more gasps of air. "Did have a little conversation with Kessler about her. No idea what he might have done. You'll have to ask him. Sure hope he didn't do anything untoward. First Amendment free speech and all that."

Without warning, Brooks was off again. Lotello followed.

"I have known you to cut an occasional corner or two, Your Honor."

"C'est moi? Surely you jest. Give me three examples."

"How about your substitution of me in place of Lance to take delivery of Cassie on Sunday? Not altogether cricket."

Brooks seemed to be getting his second wind. "Pray tell why not? Authorized right there in the signed contract. Figuring out how to use that provision—and convincing Lance to allow you to sub in so the girl would see a face she recognized on delivery—was hardly cutting corners. Lance didn't ask us to say you'd bring her to him. We didn't represent you would. He's no dummy. Maybe he didn't want to ask. Plausible deniability."

"I was his sub-agent. Wasn't he still responsible as the primary agent to return Cassie when the Supreme Court upheld the 28th Amendment?"

"No. Read the 'without recourse' language in the document. It says he has the right to assign subcontractors to carry out his duties *and* that he would not be responsible for their performance, or failure to perform."

Brooks barely managed to finish that last sentence. Too many words. All lawyers should have to rehearse their Courtroom arguments on power walks.

"But what if Thomas now comes after Lance?"

"Lance told me he'd deal with that. Said his staff agreed."

"By the way, why do you think Thomas didn't demand that the provision be removed? Don't you think he would've spotted the language on which you and Lance relied?"

"Apparently, he didn't review the agreement that carefully—or at all. He would have benefitted by having a good lawyer, but I would love to have seen that conversation: 'Hi, I'm in the middle of a kidnapping. We're going to have a contract covering the ransom arrangements. Can you help me review and revise the contract language, please? You know, to make sure our kidnap scheme is successful.'"

"Guess you're right about that. But hard to think he wouldn't have reviewed the document pretty carefully on his own."

"Hirschfeld told Thomas his family was going to the FBI in just a few hours. When the chips were down, Thomas wasn't a very good poker player. Who knows, after spending some time with the girl, perhaps he really didn't have the stomach to harm her after all. Whatever, the reason, he chose to spend what little time he had vetting Lance's integrity rather than the contract language." *In through the nose, out through the mouth. Lower the shoulders. Engage the core. Squeeze the glutes.* "I might have done the same. How important was the language to Thomas anyway? Not exactly like he could come out of the shadows to assert a contract claim."

Just then, Brooks emitted something in between a cough and a wheeze.

"You okay, Judge?"

"Fine. What else?"

"Okay. If you're sure you're alright. Some 'what ifs.' What if Thomas had refused to go along with the arrangement, or at least the sub-contractor assignment provision?"

More deep breaths. "We'd have been back to square one. Without the assignment provision, we could have gotten the FBI to order Lance to stand down and release Cassie. Better chance with Lance than with Thomas."

"And if there was no escrow at all?"

"The family would have had to go to the FBI. Fortunately, that didn't happen. Okay, then, Detective, we're almost back to my place—after *two* laps, no less. Can't keep this up forever. Anything else?"

"How about your improper calls with Hirschfeld? Weren't you cutting corners there?"

"Some say rules are made to be broken. I prefer to say there are exceptions to every rule. Recall the doctrine of justifiable homicide from the *Norman* case. Where justification exists, even murder is permitted. If a burglar brandishes a knife and threatens a property owner's family, the property owner is free to shoot and kill the burglar. Do you really think the authorities would find fault with an improper communication between judge and lawyer with a child's life hanging in the balance?

"Wasn't expecting all this, Detective," Brooks managed to slip in between gasps. "Anything more in that notepad of yours? Starting to wilt here. One more shot for you to show I cut corners. Sometimes."

"What about that nine to zero vote of the Justices to uphold the amendment? Did you have anything to do with that? Wouldn't that amount to an unethical cutting of corners, unduly influencing or attempting to influence an independent judicial process?"

"For sake of argument, let's say I did have a conversation with a certain Chief Justice. Wasn't it my duty as an 'officer of the court' to do that? To let Trotter know about a fraud being perpetrated on the Court."

"Even if such a hypothetical conversation was against the rules?"

"Exceptions, Detective, exceptions. I would've felt more obliged—hypothetically—to protect the independence of the judicial branch of our government. Trotter could have included Esposito in any such imagined conversation if he thought it necessary. That was on our Chief Justice, not me. I am but a humble servant of the Court, struggling to do what I can."

"Where did that footnote in the opinion about what Hirschfeld supposedly meant when he used the words in Court about extortion and hostages come from? Did you have a hand in that?"

"Same answer. Just as far as Trotter *may* have permitted. I said 'may.'"

Open palms facing out, Lotello raised his hands in front of his face as if to deflect a blow.

"Okay, I surrender, Your Honor. Just two more questions, and I'll let you go inside and hit the showers. How far do you really think you can go with this officer of the court business?"

Brooks stopped just outside his door. Hands on his quads again. Breathing deeply. "Pretty far, actually. Thomas was waging war on the judicial system of our country. To me, that was intolerable. Unacceptable. I believe it would've been fair for me to advocate—as we have been *hypothesizing* that I did—a cover-up of Hirschfeld's understandable compromises and the closing of ranks by all nine Justices to send a loud and clear message to all who might think to unduly influence our courts."

"Would you have been as quick to do that if you thought the nine to zero result actually would have changed the result the Court was otherwise going to reach?"

"That didn't seem to be the case, but I would have done it even then because the Court, knowing the real result, could always have set aside its decision after the girl was rescued."

"Last question. What if no deal was reached and you believed the Court were going to uphold the 28th Amendment?"

"Again hypothetically, I would have gone to the Chief Justice and asked him to solicit his colleagues to invalidate the 28th Amendment in order to save the girl, and then set aside the decision and take the real vote after she was safe."

"Do you think they would have done that?"

"Don't know. I would like to think so, but let's hope we never have to find out the answer to a question like that. However, I do think the nine to zero vote suggests the answer to your question—and perhaps suggests to those who believe they can manipulate the Court that they may have a tougher time of that than expected."

Looking at the time on his phone, this was the longest power walk Brooks could ever recall—*two* laps through the neighborhood no less—yet it seemed like nothing. And he had also learned two things from the experience. First, a good distraction, such as Lotello had provided, is invaluable. Better than his headsets and music. He wasn't even panting any longer. Second, he had gained a new appreciation for his delightfully damp sweatsuit.

CHAPTER 126
Wednesday, May 14, 5:00 pm

LOTELLO USUALLY GAVE Madison her weekly allowance on Sundays, but they had been pretty busy this past weekend. He had just handed it to her. She counted it out as she always did. Not that it was ever the wrong amount. It was just the principle of the matter.

She finished counting. And frowned. "Dad?"

"Yeah? What's that look, princess? Something wrong?"

"Haven't you given me two dollars less than you're supposed to?"

"Oh yeah. Right. Didn't I already mention that to you?"

"I don't think so. Dad?"

"Well, when the kidnappers had Cassie, you kept giving me a bad time for not letting you be more involved in what was going on?"

"So?"

"And you remember how I told you after we got Cassie home that we had worked that out through an escrow company?"

"I remember. Spooky."

"Well, the escrow company charged two fees for their services. The opening fee, paid when we first hired them was two dollars. That was paid by me when I was at the escrow company's office. The final fee, paid at the end, after Cassie was returned, was a bit more. That was paid by Cassie's family.

"Since I knew how much you wanted to help Cassie, I thought you might want to pay the first fee, the initial two dollars, that cemented the deal and made possible Cassie's release. So, I paid the two dollars for you, as a loan, interest-free, and just now subtracted it from your allowance to pay myself back. I guess I forgot to mention it."

She looked at her dad, gave him a big hug, and yelled. "Dad, that was *so* cool!"

She let go and looked at him with a puzzled expression.

"What?"

"Cassie and I don't have any secrets, Dad. But somehow I don't think I should tell her about this. I want to share this with her *so* much, but it feels like it would be the wrong thing to do. Like I was bragging or like I was telling her she owed me. What do you think?"

"I think that's a pretty thoughtful analysis, princess."

"Yeah, I understand. Besides, it's not necessary. Cassie and I are already best friends forever. Dad?"

"Yes."

"Do you think I can tell Leah?"

"I think that might be okay."

CHAPTER 127
Wednesday, May 14, 6:30 pm

"HI POPPY, how was your day?"

"Great, baby. What about yours?"

"All good. I had my first golf workouts this morning and this afternoon. I crushed it. Coach said I looked like I never missed a day. Said he couldn't tell I had the flu at all. Of course, I didn't tell him I didn't."

"I believe we can let that just be our family's little secret."

"And Madison and her parents. And the doctor because she had to give me an exam."

"Right. And just those others."

"Hey, guess what, Poppy?"

"Tell me."

"I get to play in a regional juniors's tournament this Saturday. Dad's going to caddy for me. Mom's coming, too. And Madison. Can you and Nanny come?"

"We wouldn't miss it, baby."

"Great! Love you, Poppy. Talk to you tomorrow."

EPILOGUE
One Month Later

CASSIE SPOTTED the strange email in her inbox. Strange because she didn't recognize the sender's handle, or even the domain name. She figured it was probably just spam. But when she saw "Brat" in the preview window, she held her breath and opened it.

Dear Brat,

Hope you're well.

I'm back home. If one can really think of my whereabouts as home. At least it's safe. I'm safe. Even though I know they're looking for me. My wounds, physical and emotional, are slowly healing.

And I've had time to think. About those who are and are not my real friends. In that regard, I do have some unfinished business to take care of. And I will.

You and your family have nothing (more?) to fear from me. I want you to know I don't blame you or them for what happened. You and they had every right to do what you did. If the tables were turned, I would have done everything I could too.

I'll be watching (from a good distance?) to see how you are faring on the fairways.

Be safe.

Your (not so?) secret admirer,
Frank(enstein)

P.S. Think we might ever be able to get in that round of golf together?

ACKNOWLEDGMENTS

WRITERS DO THEIR thing in what can only be described as a "lonely space," especially in the case of those who are relatively new to it.

Fortunately, there are some exceptions. I'd like to thank a few of them, whose support means more to me than I can possibly express (writer that I nevertheless strive to be).

In no particular order, and with apologies to any I may inadvertently overlook:

The writers—Sandra Brannan, Lee Child, Anthony Franze, Andrew Gross, K.J. Howe, Jon Land, John Lescroart—the ones who already know how to do it. Read their books if you haven't already done so, and you'll see for yourself. Writing is an incredibly busy profession. For those who generously and graciously took the time out from their demanding schedules to read my manuscript and favor me with their praise and encouragement, and their fraternity, what could make a newbie feel more grateful, and welcome? Not much.

The editors—formally Jean Jenkins, David Corbett, and Benee Knauer, but others informally as well, including in particular Andrea Marsden—who beat me up, over and over. And who put up with me when I resisted. But who through it all somehow made me a better writer. And this work a better story. (Hey, clipped sentences really are okay.)

The professionals— Eileen Lonergan (website developer extraordinaire), Lynne Constantine (public relations and marketing guru, in addition to building her own career as an outstanding author), Amy Collins (best ever book distribution channels manager on the back of a motorcycle), Jaye Rochon aka Immortal Jaye (whenever you need book trailers and other videos), Gwyn Snider (to make sure your book looks as good as it should), everyone at Gander House publishers (they know who they are), Meryl Moss and her best ever book cover design team at Meryl Moss Media, aka Jeffrey Michelson and John Lotte, M. J. Rose of Author Buzz who graciously shared her time and marketing expertise, and Sue Ganz of Sue Ganz photography (who can turn a very poor photographic subject into at least a better one)—have all helped me to get my message out there and to make sure this book actually looks like a book, inside and out, and that you'd know this story exists, and how and where to find it, and why you just might want to read it, and to assure that my website really is worth visiting.

And, finally, but not really finally at all, the members of my family who have provided me with their very own special kind of sustenance. The Wife, Barbie—I call her the Goose, tit for tat—who has egged me on when I needed eggs, and who has done the stuff no one else wanted to do, including me. The Brother, Gregg, who is always supportive. And The Son, Mark, who never ceases to amaze his mom and dad, who can do anything he chooses to do. And do it well. Who found all the holes in *The Amendment Killer* that were still there.

AUTHOR NOTE

THANK YOU FOR reading *The Amendment Killer*. I hope you enjoyed it. If you did, I think you'll also enjoy learning how it all came about in *The Puppet Master*, the prequel to *The Amendment Killer*, on sale to the public wherever fine books are sold in Fall 2018. A hopefully titillating sample of the beginning of *The Puppet Master* for your reading pleasure appears at the end of this work. If you are not among my growing reader community who have already done so, please sign up for my newsletter at www.ronaldsbarak.com to learn everything exciting about . . . me (well, at least my writing), including further details about when and where *The Puppet Master* can be purchased. Hey, what's another occasional email in your Inbox?

If you did enjoy *The Amendment Killer*, I will be eternally grateful if you will spread the word however you can, including posting a brief online review of *The Amendment Killer*. It's easy. Honest. Even fun. Simple instruction on how and where to do that may be found at www.ronaldsbarak.com/how-to-leave-an-online-review. Besides growing my fan base, it will impress my family and friends, who wonder why I do all this.

Thanks for connecting, and for your support.

ABOUT THE AUTHOR

RON BARAK, Olympic athlete, law school honors graduate, experi-enced courtroom lawyer, and himself a diabetic, is uniquely qualified to write this suspenseful novel which will appeal to all political and legal thriller aficionados. Ron and his wife, Barbie, and the four legged members of their family, reside in Pacific Palisades, California.

To connect with Ron, visit
www.ronaldsbarak.com
www.facebook.com/ronaldsbarak
www.twitter.com/@RonBarakAuthor

To book Ron to speak, please contact info@ganderhouse.com.

THE PUPPET MASTER
Available Fall 2018

Herein lies a mighty fine . . . sample of the beginning of *The Puppet Master*, the prequel to *The Amendment Killer*, on sale to the public wherever fine books are sold in Fall 2018. When and where *The Puppet Master* can be purchased will appear in my occasional newsletter, to which you can subscribe at www.ronaldsbarak.com.

This sample is actually part of the Advanced Reader Copy of *The Puppet Master* and is subject to revision before the final version of the novel is released. To be sure, the sample is made available to generate interest and buzz. However, I have a second reason: I like to encourage feedback and suggestions from readers. The first five readers who email suggestions to ron@ronaldsbarak.com that I actually incorporate in the final version of *The Puppet Master* will receive any or all of the following thanks and expressions of appreciation as desired:

- The right to name a non-recurring Brooks Lotello thriller series character appearing in *The Puppet Master*, whether yourself, your next door neighbor, your best friend, or—of course, subject to privacy rights—your worst enemy.

- An acknowledgment of appreciation in the Acknowledgment pages of *The Puppet Master*.

- An autographed free copy of the final version of *The Puppet Master*.

PROLOGUE
Undated

HE DIDN'T THINK HE was a bad person. But he acknowledged how that could be open to debate. How others might disagree. Maybe it all comes down to the definition of "bad."

The window shades were drawn. What scant light there was came from a single lamp sitting on the desk.

It was quiet. Just the two of them. In the one room. He wondered how the prowler had missed him, sitting right there at the desk? His desk. *It is my desk, damn it. In my room. Looking at my computer. Right there. The words I had chosen to read right there on my computer. How could this trespasser be so fucking brazen? So damn impudent?*

A lesson needed to be taught. For sure. And he would be the teacher. Starting right now.

Without warning, the man stood and charged the intruder. Startled, certainly now aware of the man's presence, if he hadn't been before, his adversary seemed surprised now and hurriedly sought to withdraw. Realizing there was no avenue of escape, the interloper turned and confronted the man. *Mano a mano.*

They stared at each other. This was not going to take long. It was not going to be a happy ending. Not for the villain it wasn't. The man edged forward, backing his foe into the corner. Now perched on one leg, the other elevated, ala the black belt expert that he was. Poised like a rattle snake ready to strike.

Trapped, sensing the misfortune about to find its mark, the invader made one last desperate attempt to dart away, beyond the man's reach. But it was too late. The blow squarely found its target. A second assault would not be necessary.

These insufferable parasites just don't get it. Understand there's a price to be paid. A lesson to be learned. Right from wrong. I will be the one to teach them. Someone has to do it. Now. And as often as required.

The man bent down, grasped the smashed cockroach between his thumb and finger, and deposited it in the wastebasket. His wastebasket.

No. Everyone might not agree. But he didn't think he was a bad person. Not at all.

* * *

There were 117 active trial court judges comprising the Washington, D.C., Superior Court infrastructure. Their primary task was to *impartially* assure a fair and balanced system of justice, the kind of justice that was supposed to be at the heart of every civilized society.

In the criminal courtroom, "fair" generally meant the avoidance of surprises. And "balanced" meant equal respect for the interests of all concerned, the accused, the victim, and the public. Without "impartiality," the ability to distinguish between accused and victim often proved unclear. As did maintaining the civilized character of our society.

Judge Cyrus Brooks always thought of himself as among the best of them. Those 117 active D.C. trial court judges charged with dispensing a fair and balanced judiciary. Lately, however, he was beginning to wonder whether he was still up to the task.

If a man was arrested for robbing a convenience store, it was clear who the accused was, who the victim was, and that what the public craved was upholding peace and order. Simple and straightforward. Easy for any disciplined and competent judge to impartially manage his courtroom to achieve the "correct" outcome. Right?

But what if the accused had been down on his luck? Destitute? Try as he had, not able to find a job. What if all he had been doing when caught was stealing a loaf of bread and a carton of milk to feed his kids? After he had already exhausted his food stamps for the month? He wasn't carrying a weapon when he had entered the convenience store, but the store proprietor was. And hadn't hesitated to use it.

Once upon a time, if you were unhappy about things, you wrote your congressman. If he ignored you, then you didn't vote for him the next time around. You voted for the other guy. Maybe, you even campaigned for the other guy.

But what if the problem you were unhappy about *was* your congressman? What if you thought he wasn't doing his job? Worse. What if you thought he was on the take? Corrupt? And what if the other guy was just as bad? Then what?

Brooks knew you couldn't just take matters into your own hands. Go out and shoot someone just because you were unhappy. Let alone shoot a *bunch* of people. People you didn't even know.

Or could you?

More and more, there were those today who seemed quite willing to do precisely that. To kill complete strangers just . . . because.

That was the crux of what had been troubling Brooks of late. What if one of those killers was arrested, and assigned for trial to his courtroom? Could he still—today—assure the accused, the families of the victim—or victims—and the people of Washington, D.C., that he remained able to impartially administer a fair and balanced trial? Could he genuinely suppress his personal views in the face of everything going on in our society today? Easy to frame the questions, right? But not so easy to answer them.

Once upon a time, Brooks had no trouble doing precisely that, remaining impartial and objective at all costs and under all circumstances, subordinating his own personal views when inside his courtroom. No matter what. Of late, however, he was finding it more and more difficult to achieve that vital impartiality.

Brooks wondered if his recent doubts and concerns meant it was time for him to step down. To retire. To pass the baton to someone else.

But he waited too long.

BOOK ONE

THE CRIMINALS

FEBRUARY 5–8

CHAPTER 1
Thursday, February 5, 7:20 p.m.

U.S. SENATOR JANE WELLS had been wondering whether tonight might be the night.

Her last two companions had been disappointing, downright boring, in *every* respect. Almost as boring as her political constituents, and having to pretend that she actually cared about them.

Being single again definitely had its benefits. No longer back home in dull, sedate Kansas—first the wife and then the widow of former U.S. Senator Arthur Wells—but things were still pretty boring. Maybe she had just found it more exciting sampling the other merchandise when still married. She hoped tonight would prove more fulfilling.

Wells glanced in the mirror opposite her desk, making sure everything was in order. *Not too bad for a fifty-year-old strawberry blonde in a bottle. Well, admittedly with a little help from Dr. Nip N' Tuck.* Looks had never been her problem. Or maybe that *was* her problem. Tall and curvaceous, she still managed to fill out her power suit in all the right places. Wells closed her briefcase and walked from her oversized private office into the also spacious and well-appointed reception area. She carried herself in a way that was not easy for anyone to miss.

"Night, Jimmy," Wells said to her Chief of Staff, boyishly good-looking James Ayres. When her husband had died suddenly, most Kansas locals had expected Ayres, her husband's Chief of Staff, to be tapped to fill her husband's remaining term. But the Kansas Governor had concluded that picking the distraught, martyred widow made more political sense. For him. It was rumored that it made more personal sense for him as well. Disappointed, Ayres nevertheless agreed to stay on as her Chief of Staff.

Wells considered Ayres's sandy brown locks and piercing hazel eyes— kind of a younger, chiseled version of Robert Redford—imagining for more than just a second what a frolic in the hay with Ayres might be like. *Probably a lot more virile than my somewhat more successful, but also older, recent partners. Hard not to visualize that hard body of Ayres gliding back and forth across mine. Certainly one way to get better acquainted with the staff!* She'd had no luck with her not so subtle outreaches to date, but she still kept that image tucked away in the recesses of her mind. For further consideration.

Wells's mind drifted unintentionally from Ayres to her parents, how disappointed they would be if they knew her real interest—like that of most of the other members of the Senate Wall Street Oversight Committee —was not to manage Wall Street, but to be rewarded by Wall Street for *not* really managing it at all. She also couldn't help but wonder how her parents would feel if they also knew about her fast and loose lifestyle. Actually, she didn't really wonder at all. She knew precisely how they'd feel. She didn't feel much better about herself.

"Goodnight, Senator," Ayres replied, bringing Wells back into the moment. He summoned the elevator for her. "Robert's here to drive you home. He'll pick you up again in the morning at nine o'clock and get you to the WSOC hearings on time." Wells nodded absent-mindedly and stepped into the elevator.

* * *

AYRES STOOD THERE, STARING at the closing elevator door. He had agreed to stay on as Chief of Staff to the *new* Senator Wells following her selection. He just couldn't fathom how a low-life empty suit like Wells had been chosen over him to succeed the *real* Senator Wells. He quietly shook his head in dismay, turned away from the elevator bank, and walked back into his office.

* * *

AS ALWAYS, GOOD OLD dependable Robert Grant was right there, waiting for Wells as the elevator deposited her into the underground parking garage. "Evening, Senator. How are you tonight?"

"Okay, Robert, bit of a long day. You?"

"Fine, Senator. Thanks for asking. Let's get you home, then."

That was pretty much how it was with Grant every night, just a warm and fuzzy ride home, someone harmless with whom to make small talk. Wells had occasionally confided in Grant about her dates, but he just listened; didn't judge.

Riding home, Wells thought about tomorrow's hearings, to consider whether possible Wall Street malfeasance had contributed to the country's economic collapse. She knew the hearings were not going to be any fun. With increasing pressure and hostility from both the media and various public interest groups, it was becoming more difficult to keep up appearances without actually *doing* much of anything. Lately, she felt as if it were she—rather than Wall Street—who was under the microscope and being scrutinized.

The job was taking a greater toll on Wells every day. *What do people expect of me? Why are they so damn naïve?* Life was a lot easier when she was just a Midwestern farmer's daughter looking to find herself a rich husband and settle down. Maybe that simple life was not so bad after all. *Maybe I should return to that after my term is up.*

Wells' mind returned to the present. She had a premonition that someone was watching her. She glanced back over her shoulder but saw nothing out of the ordinary. Just a lot of cars on the road. Nothing unusual about that on the crowded D.C. roadways.

Wells tried to convince herself that she was just being silly, imagining that someone was following her. But she couldn't help herself. Her anxiety wasn't a matter of logic. It was what it was. Her heart was beating faster, and her breathing was becoming more labored. She'd take an Ativan when she got home. That always did the trip.

A few minutes later, Grant pulled his car into the rotunda outside the townhouse project where Wells lived. "Here we are, Senator. Let me walk you to your townhouse."

Somewhat calmer, Wells resisted giving into her anxiety any further. She was far more worried about the awkwardness that would ensue if Grant saw her guest for the evening, possibly already waiting at her front door. "No need, Robert," she said as she slid out of the limo. "I'm good, thanks. See you in the morning."

* * *

GRANT WATCHED WELLS WALK off through the outside lobby entrance to the townhouse project. He shrugged, and peeked at his watch. *Still time to make it home before the Lakers–Wizards game comes on.*

* * *

HE WATCHED WELLS ENTER the lobby, punch her identification code in the interior lobby security door, pass through the released door and start down the attractively landscaped path toward her individual townhouse unit. He wasted no time.

Being a former engineer had its advantages. One tap on the device in his hand and an alert on the lobby security console built into the security desk sounded. The security guard glanced at the console, and swiftly headed outside to find whatever it was that had set off the alarm.

The man smiled at the security guard's anticipated reaction. Two more taps on the device and the network of surveillance cameras immobilized and the interior lobby security door lock was deactivated. The man rapidly passed through the disabled door and briskly moved down the path he knew led toward Wells's townhouse.

He watched Wells enter her townhouse and close the door behind her. He carefully surveyed the surrounding environs as he inconspicuously approached her unit. He didn't see anyone.

Outside the entrance to her unit, the man paused and removed a pair of latex surgical gloves from his shoulder bag and snapped them onto his hands. He tried the door. Locked. No surprise there. He hurriedly withdrew a tiny instrument from his pant pocket and inserted it in the door lock. In a few seconds he had the door unlocked.

He tried again to see if he could open the door. Still no luck. It opened a little, but was held fast by a chain lock. The man was becoming agitated. Every second he remained outside the unit increased the likelihood of someone coming along the path and bearing witness to his presence.

He had to get inside the unit. Now.

He grasped the gun and attached suppressor from inside his shoulder bag, removed the safety catch, inhaled, and let fly a desperate kick at the door. He wasn't sure which would give way first, the chain lock, the door itself, or perhaps neither. But he had no choice. He had to try. He had to break this impasse. If not his foot as well. He couldn't risk standing around outside the unit any longer.

* * *

Fortunately, the chain lock proved less sturdy than the door. And his foot. He was inside the unit. And had closed the undamaged door.

Hearing the noise, Wells rushed into the entryway of her townhouse when she heard the loud noise of the man's foot meeting the door. She looked right at him. She appeared momentarily confused. "What the hell? I thought . . ."

Before Wells could finish her exclamation, two bullets only partially muffled by the suppressor attached to the man's gun screamed through her chest. Cutting off any chance for *her* to scream. She involuntarily reached for her chest, where the blood was already spreading, but it was too late. She collapsed to the floor.

He checked for a pulse. There wasn't any. No reason to fire any more shots.

He lifted the body, carried it into the bedroom, and spread it out on the bed, face up, stripped it naked, and scattered the articles of clothing on the floor. He then opened his shoulder bag, removed a tube of Crazy Glue and a Monopoly make believe $100 bill. He applied an ample amount of Crazy Glue to the entire back side of the Monopoly bill and pressed it firmly against the forehead of the dead body. *Let the shrinks figure out the meaning of that signature marker.*

Despite the brief delay in gaining access to the unit, the man was quite pleased with the scene—his constructed body art as it were—and how smoothly things had generally gone. He allowed himself a moment to gloat over how well he had executed this first step in his plans. *Just the first step. More to follow. Soon. Very soon. Until they learn. Until I teach them. I will prevail. I must prevail.*

He quietly left the townhouse unit—intentionally choosing not to lock the door on the way out—and discreetly made his way back nearby the glass security door separating the townhouse grounds from the lobby. He paused the stopwatch feature of the smart phone clipped to his pants. Less than eleven minutes had transpired since he had first passed through the security door.

The security guard was back at his desk in the lobby. The man clicked the device in his hand. He watched the security guard momentarily stare at his console in apparent disbelief, utter something the man couldn't quite make out, and leave his post unattended for the second time in less than fifteen minutes, no doubt in search of whatever was setting off the repeated false fire alarms.

The man waited another minute for good measure. He then entered and walked through the lobby and back out into the world desperately in need of his services. He clicked on his device once more to reset the security feature on the interior lobby door. He didn't reset the surveillance cameras. There was no reason to leave a roadmap as to when the cameras had not been working. That would not be an issue with the security door lock.

Once again, the man reflected on how well things had gone.

* * *

AND HE WOULD HAVE been right, if not for the pair of eyes that had peered out at him from the nearby shadows as he had exited Wells's townhouse.

CHAPTER 2
Friday, February 6, 5:30 a.m.

FRANK LOTELLO WAS ALREADY awake when the alarm went off. He had not been sleeping well since that day, almost six months ago, when he lost his wife, Beth, to the carelessness of a drunk driver. Beth was his love, his best friend. She was the person Lotello had always discussed his cases with, *every* one of them, large or small, simple or complicated.

On extended bereavement leave, the department shrink they made him see said to be patient. Give it time, he said. The ache would lessen, he said. *Hey, I know I need to get past this. I do. But the thing is, I'm not sure I want to. Without you, Beth, I don't know who I am. What I am. I can't touch you—hold you, hug you—anymore. I can't feel you—hear you—anymore. It's even becoming harder for me to remember what you look like. I'm so afraid the ache is all I have left of you. If I let go of the ache, I'm afraid you'll disappear completely. Then what?*

Lotello's bereavement leave was now officially over, but he had not yet been assigned any new work through his on-call rotation. He wondered how much longer they would continue coddling him. Without saying as much, his homicide department was unofficially cutting him as much slack—and additional time—as they could.

He had spent years working his way up to homicide. Watching the needle on the scale and the inches on the tape measure climb as he put in the time. At least he still had an enviable full head of hair.

He loved homicide. Almost as much as he loved Beth. He hated the thought of possibly having to give it up. But—as a single father of two young kids, eleven-year-old Charlie and nine-year-old Maddie, who had just lost their mother—he wondered if he could balance the 24/7 on demand protocols of a large urban city homicide department with the always on demand requirements of single parenthood.

Of course, his first priority would have to be the kids.

People were always telling Lotello that his kids looked just like they had been lifted out of Mark Twain's novels, Charlie, the spitting image of brown-eyed, red-haired Tom Sawyer, and Maddie, the perfect clone of blue-eyed, blond, freckle-faced Becky Thatcher. But whenever Lotello looked at them, all *he* saw was Beth.

It was just the three of them now. It was up to him. Lotello was painfully aware his priorities needed to change. *I have to get past this all-consuming funk, feeling sorry for myself. Thinking about myself. I need to concentrate on Charlie and Maddie, not on myself.*

Nevertheless, he had told the department he wanted to give remaining in homicide a try. He explained that he had suitable primary and secondary parenting backup from his housekeeper and the next-door neighbor. The housekeeper was primary. The next-door neighbor was secondary. Both the housekeeper and the neighbor loved Charlie and Maddie and would do anything for them. They could be trusted. Completely.

Even with these arrangements theoretically in place, Lotello wondered if he was truly ready for a "big leagues" *real* case.

ALMOST AS IF ON cue, the telephone rang. "Lotello."

"Hey, Frank, it's me, Jeremy."

Jeremy Barnet was Lotello's younger homicide partner. "No shit, J. Who else would be calling at 5:30 in the morning? While the kids were still asleep. What's up?"

"You know Jane Wells? *Senator* Jane Wells?"

"Sure, make it a point to have lunch with *Jane* at least once every other week. How many senators do *you* know?"

"Funny. Don't really need your sarcasm right now. It's just as early for me. Do you know *who* Wells is?"

"I see her on the news now and then. *So?*"

"Dead, murdered in her townhouse. We drew next on the wheel. The case is ours. I'm on the way to her townhouse now. Just texted you the address. How soon can you get there?"

"Not supposed to text and drive, J. To early for the housekeeper. Gotta get the kids up and out and over to the neighbor's. Make sure she'll get the kids to school. I'll call when I'm on the way."

"Drive'll take you about 30 minutes at this hour. See ya there."

Lotello's question about how much longer they were going to shelter him had been answered. In spades. It was not lost on Lotello—or his pride—that the first case back he'd caught was this high profile. No way that was on his young partner. "Wait up, J. When did all this supposedly happen?"

"I'm not sure. I got the call a few minutes ago. I was anxious to reach you and get going."

"What's the rush? Where'd you think I'd be at this hour? Find out who called this in, and when. I'll meet you at Wells's place as fast as I can."

Barnet hung up. Lotello knew Barnet was not happy with his answer; that he probably was tearing out to Wells's townhouse on a Code 3 emergency response, lights and siren, and wanted assurance that Lotello would be doing likewise. *Barnet is such a fuss budget. Not necessary. Maybe a Code 3 for the patrol cars, but not for homicide. Not like it's going to bring Wells back to life.*

Lotello dragged himself out of bed, pulled the covers up over the pillows, threw on some sweats, and bent down to stroke Beau, the youngest member of their family, a German shepherd rescue pup, one of Beth's many thoughtful acts. Lotello went out front, grabbed the newspaper, glanced at the headlines while waiting for Beau to piddle, and then went back inside and into the kitchen. He opened the refrigerator and took a few sips from the carton of orange juice as he quickly skimmed the remainder of the newspaper to see if there was anything about Wells. If there was, he didn't see it. He did notice that the Lakers had pummeled the Wizards the night before.

Lotello put some food and water down for Beau, who needed little coaxing. He also put out some dry cereal, milk, and fruit for the kids, and confirmed their lunch pails were in the refrigerator ready to go from last night.

He knew he had to get out to Wells's townhouse. But he needed to take a couple minutes on the treadmill in his combination home office and exercise room to get the kinks out and to get his juices flowing. It was going to be a long day. He spent two minutes in the shower—one of his favorite thinking spots—and drying off. He thought it odd that someone reported the Wells body around 4 or 5 in the morning. *What do you think, Beth? If Wells had already been missing for any period of time, wouldn't that have made the morning newspapers? You know I read the papers every morning. There were no such reports. If the murder happened last night or early this morning, who—other than the killer—would have known about the body, and called it in so early this morning? This means the killer probably made the call. Why would he do that, especially at that hour?*

Beth didn't answer.

NO MORE STALLING, THEY had to get going, but he needed to ease in the next-door neighbor. Just this first time.

"Dad," said Maddie, as he gently woke her, "what are you doing? It's still *way* too early."

"Morning, Pussycat," Lotello said, kissing both of her sleepy eyes. "It's not *still* way too early. Breakfast's out and your lunches are in the 'fridge. I've already fed Beau. You and Charlie need to get up, brush your teeth, get dressed, eat breakfast, and take Beau with you next door to stay with Mrs. Schwartz 'til Elena gets here. Mrs. Schwartz will get you and Charlie to school. C'mon, get a move on it! And remind Charlie that Elena'll pick you up after school. I gotta go. See you tonight, Princess. Love you."

"Love you too, Dad," Maddie parroted back.

Beth had been right about Beau. It was good for Charlie and Maddie to have some responsibility, and a friend who would watch out for them. Maddie seemed to be adjusting to Beth's death okay, at least as near as Lotello could tell, but Lotello wasn't so sure about Charlie, who was a lot quieter than he used to be, and a lot more moody. He needed to keep a closer watch on both of them, especially Charlie.

AS LOTELLO DROVE OFF in the "family-safe" Volvo, he inconsistently snuck an unsafe peek at his text messages to see exactly where Wells lived—

where she used to live. *Not supposed to text and drive, but, hey, I'm just reading. And I may have broken protocol by about seven minutes. So I'll break a few speeding rules and make up half of that on the way. Not gonna matter.*

CHAPTER 3
Friday, February 6, 7:35 a.m.

HE SAT THERE IN the dark, all alone. Things weren't like they used to be. He had lost *so* much, but he was going to get even. They would be sorry.

So far, so good, it had all gone much easier than he had imagined. The first call was a little dicey, but he was off the phone in a flash, well before the cops could have thought to trace it. If he had called 911 instead, the call would have been recorded, if not traced, before he could have hung up.

The timing of the second call, to the reporter, also went pretty easy. The story would soon make the media outlets and begin drawing attention. He wondered what she would say to explain how she got her information.

He knew the next murder would also be easy, but they would then start becoming more difficult to pull off. He didn't care. *I have to shake things up, bring about some real change.*

He liked the dark. It was quiet, peaceful. No one bothered him. Not anymore. It allowed him to think, and to plan.

CHAPTER 4
Friday, February 6, 8:47 a.m.

GRANT ARRIVED AND PARKED in the rotunda of the Townhouse complex at 8:45 a.m., fifteen minutes before Wells was to meet him there at nine o'clock. When she still hadn't shown at 9:10 a.m., he tried to raise her on her cell phone. There was no answer.

He entered the lobby and told the security guard sitting at the desk what was going on. Or more precisely what was not. The two of them hurried to Wells's unit. The front door was closed, but looked as if it had suffered some recent assault. Grant grimaced and absently pulled at his throat. The guard knocked on the door. Nothing. He knocked again. Louder this time. Still nothing.

Grant called out, "Senator?" No response.

The security guard tried the door. It wasn't locked. He opened it and entered. Grant was right behind him. Grant called out again. Nothing. It was only two seconds later until the guard entered the bedroom, Grant right on his heels. Beads of sweat appearing on his brow.

They both gasped at the same instant. And at the same sight. Wells lying face up on the bed, naked, looking very still, although certainly not peaceful. And then there was the fake $100 bill stuck to her forehead.

Grant unsuccessfully attempted to swallow a cry of despair: "Senator. Oh my God." He reached for his cell phone, dialed James Ayres, Wells's Chief of Staff, and frantically described to him what he was looking at. The guard, professionally a bit more stoic, but just barely, used his cell phone to call 911. Ayres said he would be there as quickly as traffic would allow. 911 said both a patrol car and ambulance were already on the way.

Grant walked toward the body. The guard grabbed him. "What are you doing?"

"I want to cover her up. She's entitled to that."

"I don't think we should touch anything until the police and the ambulance arrive. They're on the way. It should just be a few minutes. We need to let them take charge of things."

Grant didn't agree, but he deferred, sat down on a lone ottoman against the wall, put his head in his hands, and softly said, "No, no, no. No."

Neither man said another word until the authorities entered the townhouse.

* * *

WHEN LOTELLO ARRIVED, THE multi-residential townhouse complex in which Wells's townhouse unit was located looked more like Grand Central Station than the upscale multi-residential community that it was. People seemed to be coming and going everywhere. But Lotello knew that was not quite so.

He first walked from outside the complex to the center of the crime scene, Wells's townhouse unit. He then reversed his course and slowly walked back to the rotunda outside the interior lobby, taking it all in. He then retraced his steps back to the Senator's unit.

In keeping with standard custom and practice, the first patrol car to arrive at a possible crime scene would have first gone inside to verify that no persons were lurking or hiding in wait. Only then would they have "yellow tape" secured the immediate crime scene perimeter to assure no unauthorized entry.

Given the layout of the overall complex, one of the two patrol officers would have remained at the unit to enforce its integrity while the other patrol officer would have established second and third yellow tape perimeters—one around the grounds just inside the interior lobby and the other around the grounds just outside the interior lobby. Because of the secure perimeter of the complex itself, this was perhaps somewhat of an overkill, but this also was a U.S. senator. Lotello knew that crime scene protocol would have been be strictly enforced.

While the several perimeters were still being secured, ambulance personnel would have arrived, and been permitted to enter the unit to confirm that the body was dead. They would then have departed. Additional patrol cars would have been assigned to prevent the breach of any of the yellow tape perimeters—inward bound or outward bound.

One of the first patrol officers to arrive at the scene would also have reported in to dispatch, which would in turn have notified the medical examiner, crime lab officials, the homicide department, and the district attorney's office. Lotello and Barnett were next up on the wheel and homicide department seniors had obviously decided that Lotello's bereavement was now in fact over.

LOTELLO SILENTLY CAUGHT BARNET'S eye, but his arrival didn't seem to offer Barnet any solace. "Damn, Frank, what took you so frigging long? Place's a madhouse. This case is gonna be nothin' but trouble."

"Lighten up, J. Wells isn't going anywhere. What do you have so far?"

"Already *two* people here from Wells' office. First one's her limo driver, a Robert Grant. Here to drive Wells to some senate committee hearing this morning. Along with the security guard, they found the body when Wells was a no show."

"Who put the call into 911?

"Grant and the security guard. Grant also called Wells's Chief of Staff, a James Ayres. Grant's quiet. Not much of a problem. Ayres is an absolute piece of work, a real *prima donna*. Acts like *he's* in charge."

"Where are they now?

"One of the patrol officer's babysitting Grant and the security guard in the lobby entrance to the complex. Ayres wanted access to the Senator's townhouse, ostensibly to see the body. Went ballistic when he was told he would not be allowed to enter the crime scene. He's been threatening to call in everyone he *supposedly* knows—from the FBI Director to the U.S. Attorney General, even the President—if he's not afforded the respect to which he thinks he's entitled."

"I trust all that got him was an assignment of his very own patrol officer—outside the outer perimeter."

"Exactly."

LOTELLO CHECKED OUT the body and looked around the townhouse. *Nice digs. Nothing surprising about that. Nothing out of the ordinary about the body, except for the chest wounds and that phony hundred-dollar bill glued to Wells's forehead.*

Barnet followed after Lotello. He started in again. Lotello understood Barnet's apprehension. This was obviously going to be a high-profile case, lots of attention, lots of pressure. He didn't want to add to Jeremy's anxiety. "J . . ." Lotello paused for effect. "Calm down. I'll take the security guard and Grant. And then the high and mighty Mr. Ayres. You should stay with the lab guys and photographers. Don't let anyone *else* in. Let's not compromise the crime scene any more than it already has been."

* * *

LOTELLO WALKED INTO THE free-standing lobby area. He saw two men sitting together off in one corner of the room, both in uniform, one dressed like some kind of a security guard, the other dressed like a limousine driver. He approached the two men. "Would you two be Mr. Robert Grant and Officer Thornton Smythe?" Granted nodded yes but didn't speak. Officer Smythe said his name was pronounced the same as Smith, but added that most folks call him Smitty.

Opening his wallet, Lotello handed each of the two men one of his cards. "Detective Frank Lotello, Metropolitan D.C. Police, Homicide. Sorry to be meeting under these circumstances. Mr. Grant would you please sit tight, give me a few minutes to briefly talk to Smitty?"

"Sure, I guess. Is this going to take long? I'm not feeling too well."

"Just a few minutes. I'll be back as quickly as I can."

* * *

LOTELLO LED OFFICER SMYTHE over to the desk at the other end of the lobby. He wanted to separate Smythe and Grant.

414

"How long have you been in charge of security at this complex, Smitty?" Lotello knew Smythe was not in charge, but it never hurt to gratuitously elevate a witness's status. Make them feel important.

"Oh, I'm not in charge of anything, Detective, just one of the security staff. This is my second year on the job."

"How many security folks are there?"

There's eleven of us, not counting Joel Kirst, who's kind of the security boss around here. I don't know who Joel reports to. We provide onsite security 24/7. Always two of us on duty, one here for unit owners, tenants, and guests and another one slightly down the road for employees and trades. That's also where trucks come in and out."

"So, how are people allowed to come and go?"

"Identification cards are issued to owners and tenants and project employees. Guests and other workers are admitted by the security guard on duty only if an owner, tenant, or employee calls in their names in advance. They have to show a matching photo ID as well."

"Sounds like you guys run a pretty tight ship."

"We try to."

"What about all this fancy equipment?"

"Not really all that much. We have a video surveillance system that covers the entire complex. We also have a fire alarm system. And then of course we have electronic control of the secured admissions at each entrance. Exits are not controlled, although they are picked up by the surveillance cameras."

"Did you know Senator Wells?"

"Just a little. To say hello, chit-chat for a moment here and there. She was always polite. That was about it."

"So, I'm going to need to go into all of this security business in some detail, but I think we should do that down at the station, but probably not today." Lotello knew that Smythe would have to come when they were ready for him, but there was no reason not to appear as accommodating as possible. "When's your day off?"

"Probably best if you talk to Joel about that." Smitty wrote down Joel's telephone number and email address on a card and handed it to Lotello. "My day off floats; it would be hard for me to know what day to schedule with you.

Besides I don't know much about the technical side of our equipment. I can use it, but I don't really understand it very well."

I'll talk to Joel, Smitty. But please keep my card, hold yourself available, and give me a call if you think of anything more to tell me in the interim."

"Okay."

"By the way, let me ask you one question on the equipment side for now. Did you happen to have any technical difficulties last night?

"Funny you should ask. For the last week or so, we've had several false positives with our fire alarm system, maybe once every couple of days. But last night we had two false positives in about fifteen minutes."

"Back up a second, Smitty. What do you do when a fire alarms goes off?"

"I have to run out and check to see if there's a fire that actually set off the system."

"How long does that take you?"

"About ten minutes."

"And it happened twice last night?"

"Yep. I was back less than five minutes after verifying a false positive and resetting the system when we had a second false positive. First time that happened twice in a row like that."

"And when that happens, you're away from your desk here?"

"Yes, like I said, for at least five or ten minutes."

"And while you're away, an intruder could just walk through the security door here?"

"No, not really, because it still requires a permanent or temporary identity card passcode."

"If someone somehow bypassed your passcode system, would we have anyway to know?"

"We should still be able to spot the person on our surveillance cameras, including the ones directed at the entrances."

"Smitty, I have to go visit with Mr. Grant for a few minutes. He's been waiting patiently while you and I talked. Could you check your surveillance system for last night to see if it was working properly? And, if it was, whether there were any people wandering around on the grounds last night who were not unit owners or tenants or other guests or workers you recognize?"

"Sure, it'll take me a few minutes."

"That's perfect. It'll give me time to talk with Mr. Grant. When I'm done I'll come back over here to see what you've found."

* * *

LOTELLO WALKED BACK ACROSS the lobby where Grant seemed to be a bit anxious. "Sorry Mr. Grant, that took a little longer than I expected. I'll be quick. What brought you out here so early this morning?"

"I'm Senator Wells' driver. I was here this morning to pick her up, like I always do when she's in town."

"What time did you arrive?"

"Around 8:45, maybe a few minutes earlier."

"How long have you been driving the Senator?"

"About four months."

"And before that?"

"I drove for a local limo service."

"For how long?"

"About eight years or so."

"How did you become the Senator's driver?"

"I got a call one day from our dispatcher to pick her up. I gave her a ride. She asked me if I could drive her again the next day. I did. After that, she said she'd lost her prior driver and wondered if I would be interested in driving for her on a regular basis. It sounded good to me, I said sure, and that was that."

"What will you do now?"

"I'm not sure, I'll probably go home. I don't mind telling you that I'm more than a little upset."

"No, no, not today. I mean now that you won't be driving the Senator any longer."

"Oh, sorry. Don't really know. Probably go back to driving for a limo service."

"What was the name of the limo service you worked for before?"

"Tri-Star Limousine Service."

"Can you go back there?"

"Don't know why not."

"By the way, did you drive the Senator home last night?"

"Yes, around 7:45."

"Do you know what plans she had for the evening?"

"Nope. She didn't mention any to me."

Lotello sensed some discomfort on Grant's part with that last question. His denial seemed a little too quick. "Would you have driven her last night if she was going out for the evening?"

"Sometimes, but I didn't last night."

Again, Lotello thought Grant was holding back, but it could just be the shock of Wells' unexpected and grisly death. In the meanwhile, he caught Smythe's return to his desk out of the corner of his eye.

"Okay, Mr. Grant. I may have some follow-up questions for you, but that's it for now. Do you have a number where I can reach you?"

Grant gave Lotello his cell phone number. "Can I go now?"

Lotello made a mental note not to forget Grant's visible agitation when Lotello had asked about Wells's plans last night. If Wells had any strange goings on, there was a good chance that Grant would know about some of them. "Sure. See you."

* * *

LOTELLO WALKED BACK OVER to Smythe. "Any luck, Smitty?"

"Yes and no. The first false positive fire alarm last night was at 7:50. Our camera system went down as well last night at 7:51."

"When did it come back up?"

"It didn't. It's still down."

Lotello thought about that. "How about the passcode lock on the interior lobby security door? Anything unusual with it last night?"

"I thought you might ask. So I checked. It was turned off at 7:52 last night."

"Who has the ability to turn the passcode system off?' Besides me, no one that I know could have done that last night."

"And is it still off?"

"Nope. It was turned back on at 8:10."

"And let me guess: You don't know of anyone who could have done that last night other than you and you didn't do it."

"Exactly."

"Okay, Smitty, you've really been helpful. If you think of anything further, please do call me. In the meanwhile, please let Joel know I'll be in touch with him."

"Will do, on both scores."

* * *

LOTELLO WALKED OUT THROUGH the lobby to the rotunda, looking for Ayres. Before Lotello could figure out who was who, a man in an obviously expensive dark pinstripe business suit came bustling up to him. "Are you in charge here?"

Opening his wallet, Lotello responded, "Detective Frank Lotello, Metropolitan DC Police. Can I help you, Mr. . . . ?"

"Ayres, James Ayres, Senator Wells's Chief of Staff. What happened here?"

"Sorry for your loss, Mr. Ayres, but I understand you've been here longer this morning than I have. Not much information I can share with you yet. Are you usually at the Senator's townhouse this time of day?"

Ayres seemed taken aback, exactly the effect Lotello had intended. "No, of course not." Pausing, he added, "The Senator's driver arrived to pick her up earlier this morning. She didn't show. He and the security guard went to her unit and found her body. He called me and I came as quickly as I could. Isn't there something you can tell me?"

"Aside from the fact that Senator Wells is dead, no, I'm afraid not. Why don't *you* tell *me* where the Senator was supposed to be this morning? And where she was supposed to be last night?"

"She left her office last night a little after seven. Her driver brought her home. Then went home himself. No idea what plans she had for the evening. She was supposed to be at the WSOC hearings this morning. That's the Senate Wall Street Oversight Committee."

"Her driver? That's Robert Grant?"

"Right."

"How long did Grant work for the Senator? How well do you know him?"

"About three months. I met him when he started working for her. Seems like a nice enough guy. He cleared the government security check okay."

"How is it you know Grant went home last night after he dropped the Senator off?"

Ayres thought about that for a moment. "Guess I don't. I just assumed it."

"Assumptions aren't very helpful, Mr. Ayres, especially ones you keep to yourself. Do you know anyone who might have wanted Senator Wells out of the way?"

"No, but she is on the Senate WSOC. They deal with lots of contentious and inflammatory issues concerning the economy. No shortage of kooks out there, but I don't recall any out-of-the-ordinary threats against her."

"Okay, Mr. Ayres. Thanks. You can be on your way. I'll speak to Mr. Grant. We may release a statement later this morning. I'll be in touch."

Lotello watched Ayres turn around and leave. Ayres didn't seem to like being told what to do.

* * *

LOTELLO WALKED BACK TO the townhouse and found Barnet. "Finish up here as we discussed. I'll see you back at the station."

* * *

LOTELLO WALKED OUTSIDE THE townhouse complex, stretched, looked around the exterior of the complex once more, and headed back to his car. He was surprised to see one of the local beat reporters, Rachel Santana, already at the scene. Santana wasn't a bad looker, Lotello thought, if you liked the flamboyant, ostentatious, over the top look, heels too high, skirt too short, top too tight, too much make up. "Hey, Rachel, what brings you out here so early?"

"Missing your pretty face, Frank. You know, when the boys and I have nothing better to do, we just start following you around. Figure sooner or later something interesting will pop."

"Yeah, *right*. Suppose it wouldn't do me any good to ask you for a more serious answer?"

"Probably not. Any chance you might have something for me?"

"Probably not."

"C'mon, Frank, give me *something*. I will tell you I got an anonymous voicemail message earlier this morning saying Wells was caught without her panties one too many times, that it would be worth my while to stop by her place. Couldn't pass that up. So what gives, Frank?"

"Nothing yet. Hey, Rachel?"

"Yeah?"

"You still have that voicemail message?"

"Not sure, Frank. Guess I could check."

"I can get a search warrant for it. Anonymous calls aren't protected."

"No point, Frank. You know how I am with technology. All thumbs. Voicemail's probably long gone."

"Never learn, do you, Rachel? See you around."

"Right, Frank."

Frank drove off, mired in thought. *Okay, that's two mysterious telephone calls this morning, one to the station and one to Santana. Who's making all these damn calls? And why?*

CHAPTER 5
Friday, February 6, 10:00 a.m.

FIRST CAME ANGER. THEN anger turned to rage. Then rage led to confusion. He was becoming more and more confused. It was all becoming more and more confusing. He had not always been this way. Things had not always been this way. *But I will prevail. I must prevail.*

* * *

THERE SHE SAT, ONE week earlier, frightened, miserable, and all alone, in the lobby of the psychiatric ward of that local Washington, D.C., hospital. Paige Rogers Norman wondered how all of this could have happened so quickly, in the blink of an eye one might say.

Blink once. There was Paige, with husband Cliff and their young son Ryan. It was early 2008. They were on top of the world, happily married for twelve years, the owners of a highly successful local electronics business they had toiled together for more than a decade to build. Paige was now retired from the business and in charge of all family matters, including Ryan and their beautiful Georgetown home. Originally an engineer, Cliff now ran the business and was in the midst of merger negotiations to sell their company to a large national electronics chain. They were both looking forward to more family time together, and hopefully an addition or two to the Norman family.

Blink again. It was still 2008, but a few months later. The economy had come crashing down around them. Paige first thought the economy was just a problem for others, not for the Normans. But then their business began suffering too. Company accounts began drying up. Cliff was forced to lay off employees that were like family to him, and to Paige as well. If that was not enough, the merger fell through and their business failed altogether. The low teaser rate on their home mortgage expired, and the value of their home fell below the amount of their mortgage, making a sale all but impossible. The bank foreclosed on their home. They were now living in a tiny one-bedroom apartment, depleting what little savings remained while Cliff looked for a job to sustain their family—His success had proved unsuccessful. There were no jobs to be had.

When it seemed like nothing more could go wrong for them, something else *did* go wrong. Terribly wrong. Ryan had become ill. They had found a tumor. It was malignant. Ryan's only chance was a prohibitively expensive new course of treatment. The Normans had a healthcare policy, one of the few remnants left over from their failed company, but the insurer wouldn't cover the procedure because they said it was "experimental."

Cliff had no family to help. Paige had only her parents, retired in Flagstaff, Arizona, barely making ends meet. Frantic, Cliff went to New York and tried to meet with senior executives of the insurance company, but they were in the midst of a weeklong corporate "retreat" at some fancy island golf and polo resort. And unavailable. His messages went unreturned.

Conventional treatment had proved inadequate. Ryan died barely two months later.

Blink once more. Cliff had all but died with Ryan. The Normans were hardly functioning, or even speaking. Paige would watch Cliff go off in the morning without a word, not returning until late at night, again completely silent and withdrawn.

Still grieving the loss of Ryan, Paige worried more and more about Cliff. He wasn't eating. He wasn't sleeping. He had nothing to say, except on rare occasion when he barely muttered to himself. Paige begged Cliff to let her take him for medical help. He just quietly stared back at her.

Then, one night, Cliff didn't come home. Not that night. Not the next day. Not *any* time thereafter. Paige went to the authorities. They said there was nothing they could do, which was exactly what they did. Nothing.

Weeks went by. Nothing changed. Paige finally decided there was nothing more she could do. Heartbroken, she gave the authorities a forwarding address and reluctantly went to live with her parents in Arizona.

One more blink. Ten days ago, DC authorities contacted Paige. Cliff had finally turned up, on the steps of the Capitol Building. He was physically and emotionally disheveled, ranting at the top of his lungs. "It's all your fault. You did it. You killed Ryan. Now I'm going to get you."

The police were quickly summoned. Cliff was committed to a local psychiatric facility. The authorities contacted Paige. She returned overnight to D.C., all to no avail. Cliff was completely unresponsive, to the doctors and to Paige. After expiration of the short mandatory confinement procedures under D.C. law, the hospital was forced to release Cliff. He vanished all over again.

* * *

On the same day Cliff was released, a short story appeared in one of the back pages of *The Washington Post* under the headline:

LOCAL MAN TRAGICALLY LOSES FAMILY, IS ARRESTED

Anger turned to rage. Rage turned to confusion. He read the words again. *It's all your fault. You did it. You killed Ryan. Now I'm going to get you. Am I crazy? Who knows? But I will prevail. I must prevail.*

CPSIA information can be obtained
at www.ICGtesting.com
Printed in the USA
FSHW011554170420
69291FS